the summer cottage

Books by Viola Shipman

VIOLA SHIPMAN

the summer cottage

GRAYDON
HOUSE

GRAYDON
HOUSE

Recycling programs
for this product may
not exist in your area.

ISBN-13: 978-1-525-83152-2

The Summer Cottage

GraydonHouseBooks.com
BookClubbish.com

Printed in U.S.A.

To my grandparents, who taught me that the tiniest of cottages could feel like mansions if they were filled with love.

And to Gary, who taught me to break all the rules.

"What makes our summer cottage so special? The fact that we don't need anything else in this world but inner tubes, fishing poles, books and each other."

—My grandma, on the log cabin
—*Creaky Cabin on Sugar Creek*—
where I spent every childhood summer,
from Memorial Day to Labor Day

PROLOGUE

The Rules of Cozy Cottage

July 2006

"There it is!" I said, rolling down the car window and sticking my head out.

Even though I was a grown woman—a married mom now in her thirties—there was nothing like seeing my family's summer cottage again. I smiled as Cozy Cottage came into view. It looked as though it had been lifted from a storybook: an old, shingled cottage sitting on a bluff overlooking Lake Michigan, an American flag flapping in the breeze. The cool wind coming off the lake whistled, the grass on the dunes swayed, the leaves rustled in the aspen trees and the needles of the tall pines surrounding the cottage quivered.

My heart raced, and all the years fell away. I instantly felt as excited as the little girl who knew she'd be spending her entire summer here. I waved at my parents.

"We're here!" I called. "We're here!"

I could hear them whooping and hollering from the screened porch. Their happy voices echoed back, enveloping the car.

"Welcome, campers, to Cozy Cottage!"

Our SUV pulled to a stop at the end of the long, gravel drive leading to the summer cottage. My seven-year-old son, Evan, bounded out of the SUV before it had even come to a complete stop.

"Grandma! Grampa!" he squealed, leaving his car door open and sprinting up the labyrinth of warped, wooden steps to the porch. My mom and dad were rocking on a barn-red glider, but they leaped off it, faces beaming, waving little American flags, "Yankee Doodle" blaring from a vintage stereo. They pulled Evan into their arms and rained his head with kisses.

I laughed and turned to my husband, Nate, who was rolling his eyes.

"Please," I said softly. "Don't."

"We're not campers," he admonished in the professorial tone he used to intimidate college freshmen. "It's so juvenile, Adeleine."

"You know they've done it forever," I said, reaching over to pat his arm. "Let's just have fun. It's summer. It's July Fourth vacation. It's our only time away from all the stress of life."

Nate didn't agree or nod, but instead walked around to the trunk to retrieve suitcases.

I hated when he didn't respond to my comments—which had been more frequent of late—but now wasn't the time to tell him this. We hadn't seen my folks since Christmas, and I just wanted our visit to be pleasant.

"Adie Lou," my mom and dad cooed at the same time as I headed toward them. They pulled me into their arms and hugged me tightly. "Our Yankee Doodle Dandy is home!"

"I love you, too," I said. And I meant it. My parents were more than a little corny, but I loved them more than anything.

Nate caught up, lugging a big suitcase and an oversize cooler up the steps.

"Jonathan," Nate said formally to my father, extending his hand, before turning to my mother. "Josephine."

Everything Nate did was formal. It was one of the first things that attracted me to him in college. He opened doors, and wore sweaters with leather patches on the elbows. He took me to the theater and read books to me. He told me I could be and do anything, and treated me as an equal. He was unlike any beer-guzzling fraternity boy my sorority sisters typically dated. And his seriousness and manners gave him an air of authority that made me feel safe, things that now just felt distant and cold.

"Nathaniel," my dad said just as seriously, before busting into a laugh. "Smile, Nate! This is Cozy Cottage. Not Cranky Cottage."

"Yeah, Dad!" Evan added, before turning to his grandparents and jumping excitedly. "Are we ready?"

Nate smiled, but it came across as more of a smirk.

"Ready for what?" my dad teased, deciding to ignore Nate's response and focus on Evan instead.

"Ready to recite the rules!" Evan said, his eyes as blue and wide as the expanse of Lake Michigan behind him.

"It's the only time I've seen you pay attention to rules," I teased him.

My dad tucked his flag into his shirt pocket, reached into the woven Nantucket basket hanging from the front door and then turned as if he were a magician, his hands behind his back.

Evan giggled.

"Ta-da!" my dad said, producing five sparklers. He handed one to each of us, forcing the last one into Nate's hand. He then pulled a long fireplace lighter from the basket and lit them. Evan giggled even harder at the shimmering sparks.

"Remember, we have to recite all the rules before our sparklers go out," my dad said, his voice warbling with excitement. "Go!"

"First rule of the summer cottage?" my mom asked quickly as she held her sparkler high, looking a bit like the Statue of Liberty.

"Leave your troubles at the door!" Evan and I yelled together.

"The second rule of the summer cottage?" my dad asked.

"Soak up the sun!" we said, big smiles on our faces.

"Rule number three?" my mom chimed in.

"Nap often!"

"Four?"

"Wake up smiling!"

"Five?"

"Build a bonfire!"

We recited every rule as quickly as we could—go rock hunting, dinner is a family activity, ice cream is required, be grateful for each day, go jump in the lake, build a sandcastle, boat rides are a shore thing, everyone must be present for sunset—until we got to the last one.

"And what's the final rule, Nate?" my dad said pointedly, turning to my rigid husband, who'd yet to say a word.

"I don't remember," he said. "I want to get this stuff in the fridge before it spoils."

He opened the door, dragging the cooler and suitcase inside with a loud grunt and then shut the door. Evan's face drooped as his sparkler sputtered.

"We didn't do it in time," he said, his voice sagging.

"*We* did," my mom said, emphasizing the first word for effect. "Great job, Evan. Want to go for a swim?"

"Yeah!" he yelled, his mood changing. He grabbed his grandma's hand and pulled her through the front door.

Sorry, I mouthed to my dad.

He winked. "Some people don't get the beauty of a summer cottage," he said softly, putting his arm around my shoulder. "But the magical campers do, don't they, Adie Lou?" He gave me a kiss on the cheek. "I'll go grab some stuff from your car," he said, heading down the steps.

For a moment I was alone on the front porch. Lake Michigan was as flat as glass, and the blue water was indistinguishable from the horizon. It all just ran together, and the beauty of it made me catch my breath.

Sailboats dotted the water, boats and Jet Skis zipped by in the distance, and the golden shoreline arced gently as if it were yawning and stretching its sandy back.

Such a contrast from the traffic of Chicago, I thought. *Saugatuck, Michigan, is magical.*

I'd been coming here my whole life, just as my parents and my dad's parents had. There wasn't a moment in my life where Saugatuck and Cozy Cottage hadn't been a part of it.

How old are you? I wondered, looking at the cottage.

Its shingles were weathered and gray, and those on the roof were a tad mossy in spots. The windowpanes were wavy, and the paint on the trim was peeling. My dad always talked about how much "sweat equity" he put into the cottage, but Nate always said at some point it would cost a small fortune to fix it.

I looked up. A turret topped the house with a window I always believed kept a lookout on the lake like a magical eye. A narrow staircase—so tight you had to crawl up at the top—led to the turret, where there was a 360-degree view of the lake. I spent summers at our cottage reading, dreaming, believing that I could be anything I wanted.

I called the cottage "quaint" and "charming," but Nate referred to it as "old" and "decrepit."

The cottage creaked, and I smiled.

I loved the sounds our summer cottage made. It creaked in the winds that roared off the lake at night. The attic groaned in the heat, the wood floors moaned as we walked, the screens on the porch exhaled in the breeze. Hummingbirds whirred near the feeders my mom placed in the trees, moths thumped in the outdoor lights at night, bees buzzed in the towering gardens and overflowing window boxes, wild turkeys called to the thunder that boomed over the lake. The cottage actually seemed to sigh when it was filled with people.

I walked inside, and its distinctive smell—woody, watery, a bit moldy—greeted me. I took a step into the foyer.

Creak!

The cottage was a mix of shiplap, angled, beamed ceilings featuring endless coats of white paint, wide windows, paintings of the lake and gardens, vintage finds that were part shabby chic and part old cabin. Framed photos of my family going back generations lined coffee tables, walls and bookshelves. High-back chairs, a worn leather sofa draped with old camp blankets and a mammoth moose head hanging from a soaring lake-stone fireplace greeted visitors. My grampa—a Chicago grocer who used nearly all of his savings to buy the cottage so my grandma could get away from the store they never left—always called the moose that jutted from the fireplace Darryl, because he said its eyes looked as glassy as his best friend's after a few manhattans. When I was little, my grampa would tell me that the cottage was built around Darryl, and that his tail still popped out the back of the house. I spent hours searching for Darryl's tail end.

But the biggest focal point of the cottage was a hole in the wall with a frame around it. Visitors always wondered at first if my family was simply lazy housekeepers or terrible renovators who took pride in our mistakes until they got close enough to read the little plaque under the frame:

BULLET HOLE FROM AL CAPONE
AFTER DRUNKEN SHOOTOUT

Rumor had it Cozy Cottage had once been Al Capone's hideaway, a place where he ran liquor during Prohibition in collaboration with Detroit's Purple Gang. The noisy cottage—far away from Chicago and Detroit and difficult for police or other mobsters to sneak up on—was supposedly beloved by Capone.

I never knew if this was true or just another of my grampa's tall tales.

Creak!

Evan ran down the stairs dressed in his swimsuit, a towel draped around his neck like Superman's cape, screaming, *"Wheeee!"*

My mom followed, yelling, "Wait for me, camper!"

"Rule number ten!" I could hear Evan yell as he raced toward the lake, his voice echoing into the cottage. "Go jump in the lake!"

My mother slowed for just a second when she saw my face. "What's the first rule, Adie Lou?"

"Leave your troubles at the door," I said.

She nodded, winked and quickened her pace.

I smiled and the door slammed behind my mom.

July 2018

The slamming of a door jars me back to the present.

"The appraiser is finished," Nate calls into the cottage. "Inspection is complete, too."

I am standing in the living room of Cozy Cottage staring at Darryl, his eyes fixed on mine like I'm a traitor.

Nate strides past me, saying, "Boat guy just stopped by and thinks he might have a buyer for the *Adie Lou,* too. It's a good day."

Good day? I think.

He spins in the living room, follows my eyes and says, "That moose always unnerved me. Say your goodbyes. I'll leave you alone for a few minutes."

I can't move, or speak.

"Adeleine," he says, using the same, sly tone I suspect he used to make his grad student, Fuschia—*I mean what kind of name is that? It's even a terrible color!*—fall under his spell.

A car honks.

17

"She's not very patient, is she?" I ask. "You haven't trained her very well."

"Adeleine," he repeats. "Fuschia's doing us a favor."

"Us?" I ask, my eyes wide.

Against my better judgment, and even though the inspection was today, I agreed to let Nate come to the cottage to pick up some of his belongings as well as his beloved vintage Porsche convertible that my dad let him store in the garage. I guess I just wanted to rip the Band-Aid off in one fell swoop. I didn't expect Lolita to tag along.

I peek out the window.

"What time does prom start?" I ask.

"Just follow the course," Nate continues in his formal detached way. "Play by the rules, just like our attorneys have outlined, and we'll both get the new start we want. You'll get a fortune from this place, and we'll see a nice windfall from the sale of our home in Lake Forest. You're sitting on a gold mine *if* you sell now. This place has seen better days. It needs a new roof, new plumbing, new life…" He stops for emphasis. *"New owners."* Nate smiles and continues. "The Realtor will find some sucker who falls for its—what do you always call it?—'charm' before it falls apart."

I look at him, my mouth open.

Though my parents left Cozy Cottage to me, and Nate is entitled to none of its proceeds, I agreed to sell it because he convinced me that the rules were stacked against me.

On your salary, you will go broke maintaining the cottage and paying its taxes, Nate told me over and over. *And how often will you use it anymore? How often will Evan use it?*

"I need to smudge this place," I suddenly say out loud, as much to myself as him. "Get some better energy in here."

Nate laughs dismissively. "You and your sage, and crystals, and beads and essential oils. And what did you ever do with that yoga certification, which took so much time and cost so much money?" he asks. "The only thing that new age BS will do is make the cottage smell bad for potential buyers." He turns and looks at me, as if seeing me for the first time. "You're not the person I married, Adeleine."

Nate walks away, the floor creaking. The door slams behind him, and the cottage seems to exhale relief with his exit.

Play by the rules, I think. *But I've played by the rules the last thirty years, and where did that get me? I'm not the one who changed. You tried to change me. I'm the same woman you married.*

I turn, and that's when I notice that the Cottage Rules sign my parents had hand-painted on old barn wood so long ago is hanging askew, just like my life.

Who knew that so much could change in just over a decade?

My son is now in college, my parents are gone, and my husband and I are divorcing. Even my job—an ad executive creating cute slogans for corporations who poison the earth—is killing me. Everything my parents taught me seems to be fading away, just like the sparklers they used to hand out when we'd arrive.

I begin to walk out, but stop on the woven rug my grandmother made long ago, the colorful, circular one that has been in this same spot by the door for decades, collecting sand. I am unable to leave the sign askew.

I straighten the sign, running my hand over the letters.
Rules.

This summer cottage was a place whose only rules were to be happy.

I stop on the last rule of the cottage, the one Nate refused to recite so many years ago. My heart races as I read it, tears springing to my eyes, blurring the words.

SHAKE THE SAND FROM YOUR FEET,
BUT NEVER SHAKE THE MEMORIES
OF OUR SUMMER COTTAGE.
IT IS FAMILY.

PART ONE

Rule #1:
Leave Your Troubles at the Door

ONE

February 2019

"I can't do it."

"Yes, you can."

My attorney Trish, who not only happens to be one of the finest divorce lawyers in Chicago but also my best friend from college, stares at me, unblinking in disbelief.

"I can't."

"Sign. The papers. Adie. Lou."

She says this slowly, in a tone like the one my dad used when he caught me trying to sneak in the cottage past curfew.

"I can't," I repeat. They are the only words I can muster.

"You can," she says.

She continues to stare, her brown eyes that match the frames of her expensive tortoiseshell reading glasses still unblinking. Trish graduated top of our undergrad class and her law class at

Northwestern. Her gaze had broken some of the most ruthless divorce attorneys and husbands in Chicago.

She doesn't just stare, I finally realize. *She punctures your soul.*

"You're freaking me out," I finally say, after an uncomfortable pause. "You haven't blinked in a minute. You look like a snake."

"I am," Trish says. "That's why I'm a great lawyer." She stops. "Actually, *you're* freaking *me* out. What's going on, Adie Lou?"

She sits back in the banquette at RL, the posh Ralph Lauren restaurant on Michigan Avenue across from the flagship Polo store, folds her napkin in her lap and then folds her arms over her tailored jacket. The room is beautiful and bustling, and yet still hushed in that way that moneyed places always are. I look around the room. This is where Chicago's elite gathered. The preppy place where the ladies who lunch lunched (and had a glass or two of champagne), the place where businessmen threw back a whiskey to celebrate a deal, the place where tourists gathered to gawk at those ladies and businessmen...

I stop.

The place where attorneys bring clients to sign divorce papers, I add, *so they can't make a scene.*

I set the pen down and push the papers back into the middle of the table, clattering bread plates and utensils together.

"I can see we're going to need a drink," Trish says. "Now rather than later."

"It's noon."

"Then we're going to need a double." Trish motions at our waiter, who arrives without a sound, like a well-mannered ghost. "Two manhattans."

"Yes, ma'am."

"I'll be drunk by one," I say.

"Good," Trish laughs. "Then maybe you'll sign the papers." She stops. "What's going on? Square with me, Adie Lou. What's going on in that head of yours?"

Although the weather is brutally cold—typical for February

in Chicago—it is a bright, sunny day. I watch shoppers scurry past the frost-etched windows of the restaurant. Their cheeks are red, their eyes bright, they look happy, alive, excited to be part of the world.

I can feel my lips quiver and my eyes start to tear.

"Oh, honey," Trish says, reaching out to grab my hand.

"I'm sorry," I say, as the waiter drops off our drinks. He thinks I'm talking to him and gives me a sad smile.

"Here," Trish says, handing me my drink. She lifts hers into the air, and a huge smile comes over her face. She removes her glasses and begins to sing our old sorority drinking song.

"We drink our beers in mugs of blue and gray
"We drink to Zetas who are far away
"And seven days a week we have a blast
"And when the beer runs out we go to class
"And when our college days are never more
"We'll be alums and then we'll drink some more
"We are the girls who like to set 'em up and drink 'em up
"For Z-T-A!
"Hey! Hey!
"Z-T-A
"Alpha to Omega say
"oohm-darah, oohm-daray
"Eta Kappa Z-T-A!"

"Cheers!" she says to me, as everyone in RL stares. Trish turns to the patrons and lifts her glass. "Cheers!"

I laugh and take a sip of my manhattan. It feels good to do both.

"That's what I'm missing in my life," I say. "Remember those Zeta girls? The ones who thought they could conquer the world, do anything, be anything they wanted?"

Trish nods.

"You did," I say. "I didn't."

"Oh, Adie Lou," Trish says. "Listen. I hear you. I really do. But I have to be honest. I think it's the divorce talking. I've handled hundreds of divorces, and what you're feeling is natural. There's a sense of overwhelming loss, sadness and failure. More than that, many women often feel rudderless and bitter because they sacrificed their lives for their families, and then when the family is grown, their husbands have a midlife crisis and run off with someone half their age. Men used to just buy a damn convertible."

"He did that, too," I say.

Trish stifles a laugh. She stops, smiles and sighs. "But you have the greatest accomplishment I'll never have. A child. Evan is a gift to you and this world."

I match her sigh. "I know, I know," I say. "You're right."

"And let me be totally clear, Adie Lou," Trish continues. "You have the chance to start over."

I take a healthy sip of my manhattan. "That's what I want to do," I say. "And that's why I can't sign the papers."

Trish's raises her eyebrows about to speak, but I stop her. "Hear me out."

She leans back in the banquette holding her drink. "Okay."

I grab my bag off my chair and pull out a sheaf of papers. "I want you to look at something," I say. "I have a plan."

Trish's eyes widen, and she lifts her drink to her mouth. "Oh, God," she says. "A plan. With actual papers. Let me brace myself."

"What if," I ask, my voice rising in excitement, "I kept the summer cottage and turned it into a B and B?"

Trish chokes on her drink. "What?" she asks too loudly, people again turning to stare. "Have you lost it, Adie Lou? Or are you already drunk?"

"Neither," I say, squaring my shoulders.

"You have a great job making great money in a great city

with great friends," Trish says. "And you have a great offer on the cottage."

"I hate my job," I say. "I always have. You know that." I hesitate. "I don't want to be miserable any longer."

Trish cocks her head and softens. "I'm sorry," she says. "I didn't realize you were this unhappy."

"Just hear me out a little while longer," I say. "And try to blink."

Trish laughs. "Go on."

I spread the papers I've been holding on to for the right moment across the table. "What if I don't sell the cottage and turn it into a B and B," I start over. "I've been doing a lot of research."

"I hate to interrupt already," Trish says, "but there are a ton of B and Bs in Saugatuck. Isn't it called the B and B Capital of the Midwest?"

"Yes," I say. "But there are only two inns on the entire lakeshore. One is an older motel, and the other is tiny and for sale. Cozy Cottage has the potential to be eight bedrooms if I convert the attic and turn the old fish house out back into a honeymoon suite." I stop and shut my eyes. "And that turret… Wouldn't it be the most romantic place to serve wine at sunset?"

I look at Trish. "I've already talked to a contractor, too," I say, before adding, "Blink."

She does. Once. Very dramatically.

"And what if I kept the wooden boat?" I continue. "And use it for sunset cruises? I would be able to offer something the other inns don't have, something that would make me unique."

"The roses," Trish says, still staring at me. "You forgot about the roses."

"That's not fair," I reply, instantly remembering the first time Trish and I met.

We were eighteen, and we'd just finished sorority rush. It was late, and everyone was either passed out or still at the bars. I couldn't sleep from all the adrenaline, wondering if and from whom I might get a bid, and wandered into the common room to find Trish watching *Ice Castles*, one of my favorite movies of all time. Not only could we both recite nearly every line—including the big scene where everyone realizes figure skater Lexie is actually blind when she trips over the roses adoring fans had thrown onto the ice—but also immediately knew we'd be best friends forever.

From then on, Trish and I used that line when one of us was about to make a big mistake.

"I admire your enthusiasm, Adie Lou," Trish says, "but now hear me out."

She grabs the divorce papers I had pushed aside earlier and begins to shuffle through them. "Do you remember how many issues the inspection revealed in the cottage?" Trish asks, her voice immediately serious and in full attorney mode. "The roof needs to be replaced, the plumbing is ancient, you still have knob-and-tube wiring in some areas of the cottage, the stairs down to the beach are in need of repair, not to mention erosion that needs to be addressed, the windows are old, the house needs new insulation and shingles... Need I go on?" she asks. "Okay, I will."

Trish continues to rifle through the papers. "Your gas and electrical bills are astronomical even with no one living there, and need I remind you of the property taxes? Nearly $15,000 a year."

"But I'll be homesteading," I say, my voice still hopeful. "That should knock taxes down by a third."

"Oh, wow," Trish says sarcastically. "You're rich."

She continues, her voice a bit softer. "I'm not counting the upkeep on an old, wooden boat, much less the fact that—oh, yeah—you won't have steady income. How much does it cost to run a B and B? How long to make a profit? What about insurance and health codes and..."

"But Nate said he'd provide monthly support for me until Evan graduates from college," I say.

"*If* you agreed to sell the cottage and the boat," Trish interrupts.

"I know I might not be able to do the boat immediately," I say, my voice beginning to rise. "I know I can't afford everything all at once."

"That's an understatement," Trish says.

"Trish," I say, tempering my voice. "For the past twenty years I've raised a child in an emotionless marriage, I've endured a husband who regards me as critically as one of his philosophy books, I've excelled in a job I've despised, I've lost both my parents, I'm about to lose my family cottage…" I hesitate, trying to rein in my emotions. "I can't lose anything else."

"You realize what's at risk here, don't you?" Trish warns. "You're my friend, but right now I must advise you as your attorney first and foremost."

I nod. I know she cares about me and is just looking out for my well-being.

"You have a great offer—all cash, need I remind you—for the cottage. If you don't sell, you'll be losing a sizable chunk of change that would set you up for life. In addition, you'll be incurring a load of debt, you'll be leaving a city you love to start over in a resort town, you'll be starting a business that you have no experience in…" Trish stops. "You could lose it all, Adie Lou. Everything. Even the cottage in the end."

"I feel like I don't have anything to lose," I say. "And what if I don't? What if this is what I was meant to do? My grampa sacrificed everything to buy that cottage. My parents loved that cottage more than anything in this world. So did Evan and I. What does it mean if I just walk away from all of that so life is a little easier on me? My mom told me the worst thing to live with is regret." I stop. "That cottage is my history." I stop again. "I think it might be my future, too."

Trish nods and then smiles. "Okay, then should I remind you that you don't particularly like random strangers, and I haven't seen you make anything except reservations since I've known you."

"Hey!" I protest. "I cooked when Evan was young, but then Nate said he hated the 'smell of food' in our house. And he only really wanted to hang out with people he liked, intellectual elites who didn't understand the joy of eating a pint of Ben and Jerry's and watching *Sex and the City* reruns on a rainy afternoon." I stop to catch my breath, my anger rushing forth like the waves of Lake Michigan during a storm. "And I just don't like the people I work with or for..." I stop again and look at my friend.

"My God, Trish," I continue. "Look at me. I mean it! Look at me! Who am I anymore? I've gained twenty pounds. I wear sweater sets now. A man at an account meeting who's older than me called me 'ma'am' last month. I'm an online click away from purchasing a rose-colored sweatshirt with cardinals perched just-so on a snowy branch with matching sweatpants and giving up." I stop, and my lip quivers. "I need a new beginning. I've lost who I am. I'm trying to find that girl again. Help me."

Trish's face softens.

"And it's *my* summer cottage, not his. Nate always hated it. I don't know why I listened to him in the first place about selling it."

Trish looks at me for a long time, not blinking, and takes another healthy sip of her manhattan. "Give me a few minutes," she says. "Let me call his attorney." She stops. "He does owe you, and I'll make sure they know that."

As she walks away, I take a sip of my drink, and my head grows light. The world seems to fall away in sections right in front of my eyes—the walls of the restaurant first, followed by the tables, then the waiters and the diners, before the buildings outside slip into the ground, leaving me alone with only the sound of my heartbeat in my ears.

What am I doing? Trish is right. I could be making the biggest mistake of my life.

"Well," Trish says, walking back to the table startling me, "Nate doesn't want you making a big deal to the university, especially with his tenure review coming up and since Evan is a student there." Trish winks. "I might have made it seem as if you were going to storm into the chancellor's office or call the student newspaper if you didn't get your way." She continues. "And Illinois is a dual classification state. As I told you before, it separates marital property from separate property. Your parents left you the cottage. It's yours legally. It's separate property. It's not Nate's. So he has no rights to it."

She continues. "But the mortgage on your Chicago home *is* in both names. It's marital property. Illinois is an equitable distribution state, but equitable does not mean equal, or even half, but rather what the circuit court considers fair. The court divides the marital estate without regard to marital misconduct."

"Where are you going with this?" I ask nervously.

She smiles. "You have a deal. Nate will continue to give you two-plus years of support, only until Evan graduates. But he now wants two-thirds of the cash from the sale of the Lake Forest house."

I begin to protest, but Trish holds up a hand. "Hear me out. I can contest that, and chances are you'd likely get a fifty-fifty split of the home, if not more, but then they could contest the level of Nate's support, and I know how much that means to you moving forward. It extends your runway, gives you a little more time to get the plane off the ground." She continues. "And Evan goes to school free because Nate works there, so they have that in their back pocket to argue against the level of support."

I take a deep breath as Trish takes a seat.

Trish raises her glass. "Cheers!" she says. "I still think you're crazy, but I'm so proud of you, Adie Lou."

"Thank you," I say, the gravity of what just occurred hitting me with full force. "Cheers back," I add, taking too big of a drink.

"And I'm sorry," Trish says. When I look up, her eyes are filled with love. "For not asking how you were really feeling more often. For not being there for you. For not seeing that your marriage wasn't fine. For..." She hesitates. "Well, everything. You're taking a risk, and that is admirable. I envy and adore you, Adie Lou."

I reach across the table and take my friend's hand in mine, and give it a big squeeze.

"Thank you," I say.

"To no regrets," Trish says, before adding, "Promise me one thing?"

"Okay."

"Just watch out for the roses," she replies.

TWO

"Hi, Mom."

I am always taken aback when I hear my son's voice. I still expect him to sound like he did when he was a boy—high-pitched, singsongy, begging for me to hold him or help him—instead of the baritone that booms forth from his six-foot-two-inch, nineteen-year-old body.

"Lose my number?" I tease. I'm on my cell phone, sitting in my Volvo, which is packed with boxes from my office. *It's amazing how a career that can consume every minute of your life becomes insanely irrelevant the very moment you leave to follow your passion*, I think. "It's been a while."

"I'm sorry," he replies.

I move on cautiously because I don't want to worry Evan. "I have some news."

"I heard already," he says, cutting me off at the pass. "Dad told me."

Of course he did, I think, annoyed.

"Oh," I say, bracing myself. "What did he tell you?"

"You want the sanitized version?" he asks.

I laugh so Evan thinks his father's actions don't bother me, but it sounds hollow.

"Dad said you'd sort of, well, lost it, and that you were quitting your job, moving to Saugatuck and turning the cottage into a B and B."

"That's the sanitized version?" I ask.

"Yeah," he laughs. "Believe me."

"Well, I actually quit my job today," I say. "I'm sitting in my car trying not to freak out."

Evan laughs. There is a pause that worries me, but then he says quietly, "I'm proud of you, Mom."

This time, his words stop me cold, hit me so hard I feel as if I just might break down and cry. "Thank you," I say, my voice wobbly.

"I didn't want to lose Cozy Cottage either," he says. "It's part of our lives. It's who we are. I can't imagine my life without it. Dad never liked it, I know, but us…" Evan stops, and his deep voice cracks. I instantly remember watching a rerun of *The Brady Bunch* as a kid, an episode in which Peter Brady's voice cracks when he sings a solo. Evan continues. "Thank you for saving it," he says with emotion. "Some people don't get the beauty of a summer cottage, but the magical campers do, don't they, Mom?"

My heart leaps into my throat. Evan is repeating the words my dad always said to me when Nate refused to recite the rules.

"Oh, Evan," I say. "You remember."

"How could I forget?" he says, before suddenly asking, "But why, Mom? What prompted all this?"

How can I sum up a lifetime of wonder, love, loss, mistakes, heartaches, precious moments and wasted time to a nineteen-year-old? I think. How can I explain what happens to adults when they do what is expected, take the path of least resistance, playact through life?

"You know, Evan," I begin, "I feel like I need a new start. In my previous life, I would have fretted about quitting my job, and Nate would have grabbed a calculator to figure out lost income and what this would do to our retirement. But I've thought too long about health care plans and 401(k)s, and doing what everyone else wants and expects, and squeezing into a way of life that doesn't really fit who I want to be."

I stop and take a deep breath. "To be honest, I only have about four hundred months in my life's checking account if I live into my eighties, and that, for once, seems more important than what's in my retirement account. I want to do something meaningful and courageous, something that makes me deeply and achingly happy. For once, I want to hold my breath, close my eyes and jump."

For a long moment, Evan doesn't speak, and I think I have lost my reception or he's hung up, but then he says in a voice that sounds as if he is that little boy I used to hold in my arms, "Then jump, Mom. And I'll be there to catch you if you fall."

"Oh, Evan," I say, before covering the phone to muffle my sniffles.

"The fall can't hurt any worse than the one you just had, can it?" he asks. "You know, Mom, I get it. I really do. It's not easy to be on a campus where everyone knows Dean Clarke is your father, and that his new girlfriend isn't much older than his son." He stops. "I know I get free tuition, and that's huge, but sometimes I feel like I need a new start, too."

In the midst of my pain, I realize I've trivialized my son's, and forgotten that he is still more boy than adult. I believed he was sheltered at college, but he really is living at ground zero.

"Then jump," I say. "And I'll be there, too."

"Thanks, Mom," he says. "So, when are you headed up to the cottage? I'm assuming you want to get all the permits in hand and have all the renovations done before Memorial Day, so you can take advantage of high tourist season, right?"

My heart stops. Suddenly, it hits me that I've just quit my job and need to start a business and renovate the cottage in three months.

"You're insane," I think I'm saying to myself.

"You said it, Mom," Evan laughs, "not me." He hesitates. "A bunch of the guys were planning on driving to Florida for spring break next month, but now I think I should drive to Saugatuck and help you."

"Evan, no," I say. "You need a break from college and from all this stress we've put on you. I couldn't ask you to do that."

"You didn't ask, Mom," he says. "I want to."

I cover my cell again with a trembling hand. "Thank you," I say. "It will be a lot of work, and..."

Suddenly, music blares so loudly that my eardrum aches. A song I know—REM's "It's the End of the World as We Know It (And I Feel Fine)"—is playing.

"What's going on?" I ask.

"We have to start getting ready for our annual Around the World Party," he says. "Every room in the fraternity house is decorated as a different city or country, and a theme drink is served."

"Sounds fun," I reply. "Like margaritas in Mexico, or wine in Paris?"

"Well, maybe the first," he says. "Wine in Paris is a little fancy for fraternity guys. Josh and I are turning our dorm room into New York City and serving Long Island Iced Teas."

"Be careful," I say. "Those are strong."

"I *know*, Mom," he says. "That's the point."

"Well, I like the old-school music."

Evan laughs. "It's tradition," he says. "I love tradition."

My heart nearly explodes when Evan says this.

"The old-timers started the party in the '80s," he continues, "and that was the song that kicked it off. Can't change it."

"You know I'm an old-timer, right?" I ask. "I know that song. I danced to that song. Made out to that song while dancing..."

"La la la la la," Evan sings loudly, as he always does when he doesn't want to hear something I have to say.

"Well, I better let you go," I say over his singing. "Have fun."

"You, too, Mom," he says. "You deserve it."

"Remember to call me, okay?"

"Okay," Evan says. "I'll talk to you soon about coming up for spring break."

"Bye. I love you."

"Me, too," he replies, suddenly yelling, "Mom?" in the phone before I hang up.

"Yeah?"

"What's the first rule of the summer cottage?"

"Leave your troubles at the door," I say, smiling.

"Let's both remember that," he says. "Oh, and, Mom? Don't sit in the car and cry like you did when I started kindergarten, and grade school, and middle school and high school and college?" He is laughing.

"How did you know that?"

"Mom," he sighs, "the whole school knew."

"I get emotional sometimes. It's nothing to apologize for," I say. "And I promise. I won't. I'm getting stronger every day."

"I know you are," he says. "Bye, Mom."

"Bye, honey," I say.

I hit end on my cell, think of how proud I am of my son, glance in the mirror at my former life in the trunk of my car, and then lower my head onto the wheel of my Volvo and weep just like I did on Evan's first day of kindergarten.

THREE

As soon as I round the bend from Chicago to Michigan, I see a wall of clouds over Lake Michigan. Half of the sky is bright blue, the other half is steel gray, as if Mother Nature has hung a banner announcing, Nightmare Ahead!

Lake-effect snow. My hands immediately tighten around the wheel.

I see a Pure Michigan billboard, touting the beauty and landmarks of the state, and laugh.

Lake-effect snow is Pure Michigan, I think, my former ad exec coming out, *but I don't see any billboards touting that.*

Without warning, the world goes from clear skies to total blizzard. I slow the car, tighten my grip even more and turn on my headlights. Lake-effect snow is not just snow, it's as if the winter skies have opened up and are weeping centuries of frozen tears upon the earth. Within moments, the highway is covered and slick, and trucks and cars are moving at a snail's pace.

My heart is thumping like a jackhammer, and I immediately lament my life change.

How could I have forgotten that winter lasts longer than summer, fall and spring in Michigan? Combined! What have I done? My earnings season will be shorter than the one my parents had to grow tomatoes on the back deck.

I crank up the defroster and crack a window, realizing my near hyperventilation is fogging up the entire car. And then, from the depths of nowhere, I laugh, crazily, like a madwoman.

How long has it been since I've been this nervous, excited, uncertain? I wonder. It's a shock to the system. And it feels good.

I find REM's "It's the End of the World as We Know It (And I Feel Fine)" on Pandora and play it on repeat—singing at the top of my lungs, the lyrics taking on new meaning between the snow and my new adventure—and I don't realize I've made it to Saugatuck until I see the painter's palette, the sign that has marked the entrance to town forever as a welcome beacon, lighting the sky, the name of the town and each paint color twinkling.

Saugatuck is renown as an artist lover's haven—known as the Art Coast of Michigan—filled with galleries galore. I used to paint with my mom on the bluff overlooking the lake.

"Don't paint what you see," she used to tell me. "Paint what you feel."

"That's what I'm trying to do with my life now, Mom," I say to the sign.

As I ease my SUV down the snow-covered lane leading to town, gallery storefronts light the way, giant oils, pastels and watercolors of summer in Saugatuck—Lake Michigan at sunset, the grandeur of the dunes, gardens of purple foxglove, ice-blue hydrangeas and red rhododendrons as big as trees—offering the promise of what's to come.

What if I offered painting classes at my new inn? I think. *Or painting weekends in the fall? City people eat that up.*

I pass a historical marker on the way through town. Its history is embedded in my mind, as I used to work summers cranking the chain ferry, one of Saugatuck's biggest tour attractions. I speak as if I'm back on the chain ferry, reciting memorized lines in a robotic tone to tourists: *Saugatuck's setting has drawn urban-ites from Chicago and as far away as St. Louis since the early 1900s. A resort, tourist and cottage culture emerged in the 1880s and exploded in 1910 when a group of artists from the Art Institute of Chicago es-tablished the Summer School of Painting on the Ox-Bow Lagoon and when a huge dance hall, called the Big Pavilion, was built on the wa-terfront. The resulting influx of well-known artists and big-name Chi-cago architects resulted in a wave of buildings in the Arts and Crafts and Colonial Revival manner. Now, the galleries, the golden beaches and towering dunes, the wineries and U-Picks, and the unsalted majesty of Lake Michigan beckon tourists.*

I laugh. How can I remember old song lyrics and things like this from my youth, but can't remember to take out the trash?

Today, I smile at the quirky resort town, even more beauti-ful in the snow. Pine boughs are draped in white, and the old-fashioned streetlights make it feel as if Charles Dickens might pop his head out one of the storefronts. I find a parking space directly in front of my favorite coffee shop and hop out. The place is empty, save for a few locals and retirees who are sitting at tables sipping lattes or mugs of hot chocolate.

I order my favorite latte, a Caramel Silk—white chocolate and caramel blended with the shop's own roasted coffee—and as I wait, I see the owner wiping down tables.

"Dale?" I ask. "Adie Lou—" I stop and have to force out my married name as if I'm choking on it. "Clarke. Remember me? My parents owned Cozy Cottage?"

"Oh, yeah," he says, tossing the dish towel over his shoulder and extending his hand. "Good to see you. I was sorry to hear about your parents. Everyone loved them around here. What brings you up this way on a winter's day? Heard your place was for sale...or already sold?"

"Well," I start, "it was. And it almost did. But now I'm starting a business here. Turning the cottage into a B and B."

"Need another one of those like a hole in the head," cracks an old man in a stocking cap reading the newspaper.

"Don't mind Phil," Dale jokes. "Hasn't seen his shadow since the seventies. That's why he's so grumpy." Dale stares at me. He looks older than I remember, his hair now silver, his forehead lined, like a president you notice has aged significantly by the end of a first term. "That place needs a lot of work, doesn't it?"

I nod.

He grins, as if he knows a secret I don't. "Well, good luck," he says. "Coffee's on the house today."

"Thank you," I say. "But I already paid."

"Now, that's how you run a successful business," Phil laughs in the background. "He always offers when it's too late."

"Shut up, Phil," Dale laughs. He turns. "But he's right," he adds with a wink. "Seriously, next one on me."

"Liar," Phil says under his breath, before adding in an even more sarcastic tone, "Good luck with that B and B, Bob Newhart."

I look at Dale, and he nods, giving me the okay. "Shut up, Phil," I say as Dale laughs again and continues wiping down tables.

"Caramel Silk! Adie Lou!" a barista yells. I pick up my coffee, head back out into the snow and aim my car toward the cottage. As I turn onto Lakeshore Drive, the wind buffets my car, and the snow is no longer falling but flying horizontally. I feel as if the Wicked Witch from *The Wizard of Oz* might bike over my head at any minute.

Every summer cottage on the lane is dark. Not just dark, but empty. Hurricane shutters have been pulled over the windows, screened porches enveloped in plastic, and trees staked. There isn't a light on for miles.

I pull into the driveway of Cozy Cottage, my SUV struggling

for traction to get up the drive. I open my door and instead of my parents' voices, I imagine I hear the cottage groan in agony. I step out of the car, slip on the snow and have to grasp the car door to stop myself from falling. I grab my bag but leave my luggage in the car for now and move, one baby step at a time, up the steep stairs, my body at a severe angle like the snow to keep myself from being blown over.

I reach the front porch, my breath coming out in big puffs like steam from a locomotive. I look out at the lake. It is roaring and angry, so loud I can barely hear myself think.

I rarely came to Saugatuck in the winter, and never on days like this. Cozy Cottage was a summer retreat.

This, I think, *is like* The Shining. *But way, way worse.*

I turn to face the cottage, little tornadoes of snow lifting off the ground and hurtling into my face. I squint. The cottage's wood shingles are loose, and a few are now missing on the front. The paint is peeling, there is a crack in the stone foundation, and most of the shutters have come loose and are now banging against the house.

I manage to find the keys in my purse and unlock the front door. A mouse looks up at me as if I'm a stranger who has burst into its home. I scream. It screams. And then it scurries across the rug in front of me. I scream again, and the mouse stops, shocked, and stands on its hind legs scared out of its wits, before zipping toward the stairs.

I suddenly remember what Evan told me, and I retreat back out the door.

I open the Nantucket basket—still on the front door but now worn, the weave loose and unraveled—and I look inside.

No sparklers, I think, immediately sad remembering my parents. And then it hits me: I reach into my bag and pull out a big smudge wand of sage that I brought to cleanse the cottage and give it a new start. I move my hand around until I find a lighter. I turn my back to the wind, holding the sage close to my body and lighting it.

"Ready to recite the rules?" I ask myself over the roar of the wind and groans of the cottage. "What's the first rule of the summer cottage?"

I raise the sage over my head and yell to the cottage, "Leave your troubles at the door!" The house creaks as if in agreement. I repeat the rule, this time to myself. "Leave your troubles at the door, Adie Lou."

I yell again, this time into the winter wind. "To a new start! To a new life for me and you, Cozy Cottage! No regrets!"

I begin to open the door, but the wind gusts, nearly knocking me off my feet, and the burning sage goes dark. A shutter on the front of the cottage flaps wildly in the gale, making a sound similar to a hundred ducks taking flight from a pond.

And then, just like that, the shutter is airborne and flying directly toward my head. I move just in time, and it smashes into the ground, clacking down the dune and into the lake.

Before I run inside, now fearful for my safety, I see the sprawling, wooden trellis in the yard, the one on which my mom and grandma's knockout pink and red roses climbed for decades. The trellis is bare, trembling in the wind, shaking just as hard as I am, and I swear I can hear Trish say to me very clearly, "The roses, Adie Lou. The roses."

PART TWO

Rule #2:
Soak Up the Sun

FOUR

February

"What time is it?"
My voice echoes in the guest room.

The sun is shining directly into my eyes, and I sit straight up in bed, my heart racing. I glance over at the clock on the nightstand.

It blinks at me in red: *9:39 a.m.* I pull the blankets up around my body, feeling both cold and too warm. Worried about money, I refused to set the heat above fifty-eight degrees last night. My face is frozen, but my body feels flushed, nearly hot, and I realize I am embarrassed at having slept so long on my first day as an entrepreneur.

I glance again at the red numbers on the clock, and my body flushes in shame, as if I'm wearing a scarlet *A*.

For Apathetic, I start, before correcting myself. "No, capital *A* loser," I say out loud, the echo affirming my declaration.

I haven't slept this long in decades, I think. *Since I was teenager. In this very room.*

For some reason, I wasn't able to sleep in my parents' bedroom or the guest room Nate and I shared for so long. It didn't seem right. So I chose my childhood bedroom, the one Evan has slept in since he was a baby. I pull the covers around me even tighter and survey the room. Photos of Evan in the cottage and on the beach, from toddler to teen, growing up right in front of my eyes. Photos of me doing the same. The sun glints in my eyes, and I tilt my head and notice a common denominator in all the photos: sunshine. I smile and angle my head back into the light, closing my eyes and letting the sun warm me.

"Okay, Adie Lou," I say to myself. "Time to get moving."

I'm supposed to be meeting my contractor at 11, and I've barely prepared much less made coffee to be halfway coherent.

I step out of bed and the cold of the house slaps me. "Brrrr!" I yell. I try to recall all of the clothes I have left here—*all summery things*, I think—and then rifle through my suitcases. Nothing I hurriedly threw in seems warm enough.

Why did I pack as if I were going on a weekend getaway instead of forever?

I open a drawer in an old green-gray dresser—that's been painted probably a dozen different colors in my lifetime—and pull out a pair of Evan's thermal socks. I open another drawer and yank out a pair of his boyhood sweatpants, and then open the closet, stand on my tiptoes and stretch as far as I can—my knees popping—to pull one of Evan's old high school hoodies from a shelf with my fingertips. I turn on the bathroom light and look in the mirror. I lean in even closer, examining my face.

"Who am I?" I ask the mirror, my breath fogging it.

I feel rested yet exhausted. Excited but depressed. Happy and sad. Alone yet comforted.

"Essentially you're a complete mess," I say to my reflection.

I run a hand through my hair, which is flying around my head as if I just underwent electroshock therapy. I pull open the cabinet and find an ancient hair tie from a time when Evan grew his hair to his shoulders, and yank my own shoulder-length locks into it, which immediately gives me the look of one of those demented, too-old babysitters in every Lifetime movie.

I wash my face, grab my overnight bag and pull some moisturizer out of it. I smooth some on my face and neck. I reach back into it and pull out my essential oils, what Nate called my "voodoo potions."

There is something about my oils that calms me, centers me, seems to protect me.

The same feeling I get from being at this cottage, I realize.

I place three drops of lavender into my palms, rub them together, lift them to my nose and inhale, before rubbing them onto the back of my neck.

"That'll do for now," I say, feeling a bit readier for the day.

I pad down the stairs, and the house turns even colder. I walk over to the thermostat and begin to turn it up, but I can't get my finger to actually hit the arrow higher. I stop and instead pull the hoodie over my head.

"Morning, Darryl," I say to the moose as I head toward the kitchen.

The room is sunny and bright. I open the fridge and smile, remembering I'd at least been smart enough to bring a few provisions from the city: coffee, steel cut oats, snacks, a rotisserie chicken and some of my favorite frozen food from Trader Joe's. I start the coffee in my parents' ancient coffee maker and sigh as it begins to brew, filling the kitchen with the scent of roasted beans. The smell reminds me of them. I shut my eyes and smile. I can hear my father greet Darryl as I just did.

I open my eyes, grab a Saugatuck mug from the cabinet and pour myself a cup of coffee. I walk over to the patio door and look at the snow-covered deck—the snow now knee-deep in spots from drifting—and at the decaying fish house beyond. This is where—back in the day—they used to clean and store fish. Al Capone supposedly used it as a front for running liquor, and when he'd send out ice trucks filled with fresh Lake Michigan whitefish, most of the white packages were filled with booze.

I can tell it's warming a bit after the snowstorm, as the snow is drip, drip, dripping off the roof, leaving sunken spots in the snow around the cottage. A cardinal sits in my mom's favorite tree—a pine we planted decades ago that has now grown to be nearly twenty feet tall—and the simple beauty of the red in the white and green makes me catch my breath. The cardinal takes flight, and snow falls in dramatic heaves from the pine branches.

This is such a departure from my life just days ago: waking up at dawn, meetings in the city, working in a skyscraper... I stop.

Working for someone else.

For a moment, I feel as if I'm no longer a productive member of society, but I look at the fish house and can hear my grampa as clear as day, as if he's standing right beside me, his Old Spice overpowering the smell of the coffee.

"Owning your own business," I can hear Grampa Otto say in his German accent, "*that's* the American dream. It's up to you to make it happen every day. Dream big, *schatzi*."

I shake my head, pour another cup of coffee and hurry upstairs, toward the turret, the place I used to dream big as a girl.

My heart races—partly because of the climb and the caffeine, and partly because I haven't been up here in years—and as I reach the narrow, circular staircase that leads to the turret, I hold my cup above my head and bend over into a comma to reach the top.

Sunlight overwhelms me as I step into the round space, encircled by windows, making me feel as I have climbed to the top of one of the beautiful Michigan lighthouses that dot the coastline. It's even colder than I imagined up here, and I can see my breath in front of me. I take a seat on the cushioned bench my dad made to fit the space, sip my coffee and look out at the lake. It looks like it's frozen for miles. There are large boulders of ice on the snow-covered shore, and waves frozen in midair, big enough for people to walk into, creating mini-glaciers or...

I stop and actually laugh out loud at the ironic analogy I was about to make.

Don't say it, I think, but it's too late. *Ice castles.*

I narrow my eyes and focus my gaze, and I can pinpoint the line in the distance where the lake is no longer frozen. I move my eyes slowly toward the shore, and I can see the ice undulate, the lake ripple below it, life trapped underneath, just waiting for the spring thaw.

I shut my eyes and can see myself up here as a little girl, dressed as Wonder Woman, standing atop this bench, thinking all it took was a golden lasso and a firm belief in my own abilities to fly as high and as far as I wanted, to change the world. I remember thinking I could soar over the lake, just like one of the gulls that float on the current forever before diving headfirst into the water with a big splash to retrieve a fish.

Splish!

I open my eyes at the watery sound and look into my cup, the coffee moving in small waves as if I'd just skipped a rock across its surface.

Wait! I think to myself. *Did I do that?*

I shut my eyes again and picture myself as Wonder Woman soaring like a gull and then diving...

Splash!

I open my eyes, and my coffee is, indeed, moving. I feel like— *who was that psychic my grandparents said they always used to watch on* The Tonight Show?—Uri Geller! I shut my eyes again, bow my head and concentrate.

Splat!

This time, water hits the back of my head instead of my coffee, and I can feel a big, cold drop rolling down my back. I look up.

"Oh, shit," I say, as another drop falls into my open mouth.

There is a hole the size of, say, my open mouth in the top of the turret, and melting snow is now falling through it.

"Shit." I sputter and cough.

I look around and, thankfully, don't see any water damage, so the hole must be a recent development. I zip downstairs, find a pair of my mom's old snow boots in a closet and trudge through the snow until I can get a vantage point of the turret. I look up, down, all around, and there—in the yard by the cottage—I see it: a huge pine branch. It must have snapped off in the wind during last night's storm, fallen directly onto the turret and punctured a hole in the roof.

"Mornin'!"

I yelp.

"Sorry, Mrs. Clarke."

"It's Kruger," I say a bit too abruptly before turning to see Frank Van Til, the contractor whose grandfather and great-grandfather supposedly helped build Cozy Cottage. Frank lifts his arms innocently. "Sorry," he says. "I didn't know you'd taken your maiden name again."

I haven't officially. In fact, I don't know why I just blurted it out. But it just sounds right to me for some reason at this moment.

"No, I'm sorry," I say, extending my hand. "You just surprised me. I didn't hear you pull up. Lost in my own thoughts…and misery." I nod up at the turret and then down at the branch. "Hole in the roof. I've had enough surprises already today."

"I'll get that covered today while it's nice and sunny," Franks says softly.

Nice? I think. *Nice in Michigan is thirties and sunshine in February. I wouldn't be surprised to see kids playing basketball in shorts and tank tops later.*

"But let's take a look at your plans for the cottage first," Frank continues.

"Sure," I say, walking Frank inside and kicking off my boots. "What time is it?"

"Eleven," he says. "Isn't that the time we agreed on?"

I shake my head. "I overslept. By about three hours. My first day as an entrepreneur isn't going as well as I'd imagined," I say, forcing a smile. "Coffee?"

Frank nods, and I lead him into the kitchen, pour two cups of coffee and then spread out my drawings for the cottage renovations. Frank sets down the case he is holding and actually giggles, an odd sound to emanate from a burly, bearded Dutch man.

"What?" I ask. "Is there a problem?"

"I take it you're not working with an architect?" he asks.

"No," I say. "You asked for some drawings when we talked a while back, remember? I did some renderings."

Frank nods. "I see, I see. Well, these drawings are…" Frank stops, searching for the right words. "More like the ones my daughter used to draw."

"I admit my advertising experience is in copywriting and not design, but these aren't that bad," I say, leaning in to study them closely. "Are they?"

"They're…" Again, he stops. "Very sweet."

"Okay, Frank, I'm about to be offended here," I say.

"I'm sorry," he says, chuckling a little this time. "But they are sweet. Look," he says, pointing to a bedroom I've named Soak Up the Sun.

The room has its own bathroom and views of the lake, but it needs new windows and a design makeover. I want to add a pretty board and batten wall, and sunny yellow paint to the bedroom and its attached bath.

"I want each room to be based on one of my family's summer cottage rules," I say, taking a sip of coffee. "This room—Boat Rides Are a Shore Thing—will have a nautical theme and vintage photos of the *Adie Lou*, and the Rock Hunting Room will be beach-glass blue and feature all of the beautiful stones that my family has collected over the decades."

Frank turns to me and smiles. "It sounds beautiful, Mrs. Clarke... Kruger... Miss Kruger... Ms. Kruger."

I laugh. "I didn't mean to make you so nervous, Frank," I say.

"Let me get down to brass tacks here," he says. He pulls a pen and a stapled sheet of papers entitled Cozy Cottage RENO BID from the case on the floor. "I think this inn has the potential to be beautiful and unique," he says patiently. "And your willingness to save this cottage, preserve its history and honor your family is admirable. But..." He stops and begins to move his pen alongside the bulleted items on the sheet. "You not only need the turret roof repaired now, you likely need a new roof altogether. The shutters are shot. The house needs a lot of new shake shingles, and the whole cottage needs to be restained. There are some issues with the foundation we need to address, and I'll need plumbing and sewer out to check all the pipes and your existing tank. This cottage won't have ever seen the type of water and waste usage you'll get when running an inn. And the staircase to the beach needs to be reinforced, and you'll likely need to bring in some earth and piering to stop any further erosion on the dune leading to the beach." He stops and starts writing again. "And that's not including your renovation— Updating all the rooms, turning the attic into additional bedroom space and adding baths to each guest room, renovating the fish house into a honeymoon suite." He stops and surveys the kitchen. "And updating the kitchen since you'll be cooking for so many now."

He turns the page and tries to smile, although it looks like more of a wince.

"And now for the not-so-fun part," he says.

"That was the fun part?" I ask.

"I'll apply for all the permits, but there are a lot of specific rules you need to abide by to obtain a license," Frank says.

"I've read up on them and already applied for a license," I say, pulling out my phone. "The state license office has already become my go-to app, along with Tinder," I say, trying to make a joke.

"What's that?" Frank asks.

I think of explaining my joke but stop. "It's a heartwarming music station," I say. "The music is very...tender."

Frank cocks his head. "Sounds nice."

I pull up the state site on my phone and begin to paraphrase as I read the legalese. "So, according to law, if a Michigan B and B has eight or fewer rooms, a full breakfast can be served without a food service license as long as it is a packaged deal. Any more than that, and I'm going to have to jump through some hoops, it sounds like." I hand Frank my phone. "I need some backup this morning," I say with a laugh as he reads. When he looks at me, I ask, "So, I'm good, keeping the inn at eight, right?"

"Right," Frank says. "I'd suggest you need to make at least one room wheelchair accessible—the fish house would be easiest—and there are some requirements for fire regulations, including signage and reinforced doors to hold back fire and smoke." He stops. "I also think you need to create an owner's suite downstairs," he says. "You don't want to live on an upper floor with guests. You'll need a space of your own, big enough to accommodate a living area and bedroom. And you'll want a separate entrance to, well, avoid the guests when you want." He points to my renderings. "I'd suggest taking the downstairs bedrooms and make it a big living space for you, maybe add square footage onto the back of the cottage. The lot has more than enough room. It'll work." He stops again.

I look at Frank and then at the bid sheet. "I don't see any numbers attached," I say, not blinking.

Oh, my God, I think. *I've become Trish.*

Frank doesn't say a word. In fact, I can actually see him wince noticeably this time, like I do when I watch those Facebook videos of models tripping on the runway or people doing dumb things like diving into a frozen pond.

"Aaannnd…?" I ask.

"I think we're looking at about $250,000," he says.

"What?"

My heart stops, and I drop my coffee cup in shock. It falls to the tile floor and shatters.

"Are you okay?" Franks asks.

I look down and nod, and then remember the number he just quoted me. I shake my head no.

Frank grabs a roll of paper towels I have sitting on the counter, and begins to wipe up the coffee. "Broom?" he asks. I point to a closet.

I watch him clean up the mess, feeling as if he's sweeping up my hopes and dreams. I think of sitting in this kitchen, on this very counter, and my grandma reciting "Humpty Dumpty" to me when I would start to get too playful.

I begin to do quick math in my head, thinking of my savings, how much Nate will be paying me every month, the amounts I might be able to take from my IRA and retirement accounts without too much of a tax hit. My head grows light.

"I don't have that kind of cash readily available, Frank," I say. "Could I give you a quarter up front, and then go from there?"

Frank slides the remains of my broken cup into the trash with a big crash, sets down the pail and walks over to me.

"Of course," he says, his voice soft. "You know, my family has always loved this cottage. My great-grandfather helped build it, my grandfather and father loved your parents and grandparents. And Jonathan and Josephine were so kind to me. I feel like this cottage is a part of my family, too."

My eyes fill with tears. "It is," I say. "You know, my dad used to say that you had sawdust in your blood. A lot of that is from Cozy Cottage."

"I'll get started this afternoon," he says. "My crew will start on the roof and the outside of the cottage while we have a chance, and then we'll start on the fish house and interior. I promise we'll do our best to have this ready for Memorial Day weekend. Sound good?"

I nod.

Frank gathers his papers and his case, turns to leave but stops after a few steps.

"Kruger," he says, before turning to face me. "You know what that means, don't you?"

"I'm not sure what you're talking about," I say.

"Your maiden name," he says. "In German, Kruger literally means *innkeeper*."

My eyes widen.

"My grandfather loved family ancestry," he says. "He told me that a long time ago." Frank looks at me, and his bushy bearded face breaks into a smile, giving him the look of a gleeful cartoon character. "Maybe all of this is meant to be," he says. "Maybe everything in your family's history has led up to this moment."

Frank nods definitively and says, "See you soon, Ms. Kruger."

He turns and leaves, the house seeming to creak in agreement with every footstep he takes.

FIVE

"Welcome Wagon!"

I am just about to turn on the water to take a shower—at nearly 1:00 p.m., mind you—when I hear a chorus of warbly voices calling from downstairs.

"Mrs. Clarke? Welcome Wagon!"

I turn the water off, the sleeve of Evan's sweatshirt immediately soaked, and pad down the stairs where I discover four elderly women—each seemingly a decade older than the other—snooping around the cottage. Despite my creaks on the stairs, the women don't hear me. I watch them for a few seconds—picking up photos, touching the fabric, analyzing artwork, even running a finger over a table and inside a bookshelf to check for dust—and begin to wonder if I'm watching *The Golden Girls* meets HGTV.

I tiptoe until I'm a few feet behind the group now on their way into the kitchen, and say loudly, "Hello, ladies!"

The women jump as one.

"You startled us!" one of the women says in a clipped tone.

You're in my house, I think.

She turns and extends her hand. "Iris Dragoon."

The Dragoon Lady! I can immediately hear my mother say. *She breathes fire, Adie Lou!*

My first thought is—this woman is still alive?

I remember Iris Dragoon visiting my parents when I was a girl, always dropping by unannounced to fund-raise for the Preservation Committee, or Holiday Decorating Committee, or History Museum, or one of the endless committees on which she served. I thought she was ancient three decades ago, but it's as if she's been preserved, under glass, because I can't tell much of a difference in her appearance from years ago. To me, she's always looked as if she might be Joan Collins's mother: heavy, but impeccably applied evening makeup, complete with false lashes and a shockingly red lip. Today, she is sporting a pantsuit Joan herself might have worn to the Emmys in the 1980s: a be-jeweled jacket with giant shoulder pads and big, shiny buttons, a black turtleneck and shockingly tight black pants tucked into black boots with a gold buckle. But the topper—quite liter-ally—is that she is wearing two—*two!*—chestnut-colored wigs that give her the appearance of full hair in the front and lots of height in the back.

"On behalf of the Saugatuck Preservation Committee, wel-come!"

The Dragoon Lady doesn't really say this in a welcoming manner, but more as if she's holding court. Before I can say a word, she claps her hands. "Gladys!"

"Oh, yes, yes, sorry," a woman with blue hair says nervously, holding out a pretty basket wrapped in colorful foil.

I take the basket, the foil making a loud crunching sound, and set it on the kitchen counter. "That's so nice of you," I say, again hearing my mother's voice. *It's the same basket every year, Adie Lou. It just gets passed along, like fruitcake.*

"What brings you all here today?" I ask.

"Well," the Dragoon Lady begins, turning to her followers, two of whom I now notice have clipboards and pens at the ready. "The Preservation Committee was thrilled to learn that you've decided not to sell your family cottage."

"Thank you," I say, suddenly feeling a bit warmer toward her.

"As you know, preservation of Saugatuck's history and historical cottages is very important to us and our town," she says in a voice that sounds a bit robotic. "This cottage has such a unique history..."

"Such history, such history," her three committee members coo in unison.

"...from Mr. Capone to your family, who has kept the character of this cottage and fought to preserve its character."

I blush. "Thank you," I say again, wondering if my mother had been wrong about this woman.

"I...we...however, are concerned about your intentions for this cottage," she says, raising an eyebrow, her lashes tossing a shadow across her face. "The committee has learned about your plans to turn this into a..." She stops as though she's about to say a dirty word.

"Inn?" I offer. "B and B."

"Yes," she says with disgust. "We'd like to set up a meeting with our full committee to review your plans."

I stare at her, not blinking. Trish has taught me well. But it doesn't work on the Dragoon Lady.

"Which architect are you working with?" she asks. "We have two the committee approves of."

My head begins to spin. "I'm not working with an architect," I say. "I'm remodeling this myself."

My renderings are still sitting on the kitchen counter. The Dragoon Lady's eyes flutter toward them, and then scan every inch of my work.

"I see," she says, ice dripping from her ironic choice of words.

I can feel my face flush, and I immediately want to hide my work like a kid might hide a test on which she had received a bad grade.

"And I'm working directly with a local contractor who's done numerous projects on this cottage for years. In fact, his great-grandfather helped build the cottage."

"Frank," she says with a dismissive sigh. She turns to her committee, two of which are writing furiously. "The handy-man." She stops and acts as if she's thinking. She scratches her hair, and both wigs move atop her head. "So, what date would be convenient for you to meet? We meet every other week, either at the woman's club or at the country club."

My eyes are so large I feel as if they might bust free of their sockets and just roll across the floor. If they did, I'm sure two of the women would note it on their clipboards.

"I appreciate your stopping by," I start gingerly, "but this is my first full day here. My contractor and his crew are coming back in a bit, I have a million things to do and..."

The Dragoon Lady holds up a manicured finger, stopping me in midsentence. "Gladys?" She snaps her fingers, and Gladys produces a calendar. "Let's just pencil in a date, and we'll be on our way."

"Is this necessary?" I ask, my voice rising, my facade breaking. "I'm applying for all appropriate licenses. Frank is running everything by the city for approval. I'm meeting every necessary standard. I'm not changing the character of the home. I'm trying to improve it, share its history with others. This is not a rebuild of a historic home."

"Mrs. Clarke," the Dragoon Lady starts.

"It's Kruger," I say.

"Oh," she says, her voice filled with sadness. She turns to her committee. "A divorcée, ladies."

The women shake their heads.

"Excuse me?" I say. "Now you're just being rude. None of this falls under your committee's purview."

"There are a limited number of historic cottages on our lakeshore, Mrs. Clarke... Kruger...and the town cannot stand idly by and allow private residences to be turned into motels."

"Inns," I say. "And it's allowed by law."

"Strangers coming and going in this community of fine lakeshore cottages may be lawful, but it is not proper," she continues. "Making noise, screaming children on the beach, cars parked everywhere." She stops and looks around. "I know you need the money to keep this cottage, but your parents would be aghast."

"How dare you presume to know what my parents would think!" I say, my voice rising. "They loved me more than anything, and they would want me to do anything I could to keep this cottage in our family." I realize I sound like a child throwing a tantrum in Target, but I can't stop myself. "And my parents couldn't stand you! This cottage and this town mean everything to me, and I'll do whatever I need to do to keep it.

"Get out!" I thunder. "Get out of my house. And take your stupid welcome basket with you!"

I grab the basket and try to push it into the Dragoon Lady's hands, but she doesn't raise her arms. Instead, Gladys scurries forward to take it, while the other two women continue scribbling notes. I open the front door and motion dramatically with my arms for the women to leave. The Dragoon Lady stops on the front porch and turns. "We can make it very hard on you," she says with a sly smile. "Permits might be harder to come by... We'd hate to see your summer season delayed. It's so hard for a new business to stay afloat if it opens in October. Not to mention that bad word of mouth can ruin a new business, and we have very loud mouths, don't we, ladies?"

The women nod in unison.

"Get off my property!"

The Dragoon Lady takes a step and then stops again. "By the way, I just love your pants," she says with an evil laugh.

The women titter, and I slam the door, the house now empty but still filled with the smell of their perfume.

White Shoulders.

I immediately run over to the mirror in the front hall and turn around to look at my backside.

Evan, I think. *No! Why did I have to pick these of all days?*

I look again, undecided as to whether I should laugh or cry.

BEACH, PLEASE! is written across my rear end in bold lettering.

SIX

Ilift a bottle of Two Buck Chuck to my lips and take a healthy pull.

"Cheers!" I yell into the cold wind as I make my way down the stairs to the beach.

After the hole in the roof, the hefty price tag to repair the cottage and the Dragoon Lady, I have opted to get drunk instead of taking a shower. I have opted to follow the lead that has been displayed on my rear end all day long.

I unconsciously count the steps down to the beach like I've done since I was a girl.

51, 52, 53, 54…

My parents built a gradual staircase to the beach—with many landings—to make it easier to navigate, unlike many lakeshore cottages that feature steep staircases of hundreds of steps that make it seem as if you are scaling a castle to return home.

I take a seat at the bottom of the stairs and park my boots in the snow. My embarrassing sweatpants are now covered in a long, puffy winter coat. I am wearing earmuffs, mittens and boots, but the sun—shockingly strong for a February afternoon—warms my face before the wind sweeps over the frozen lake.

You are single, unemployed, poor and, most importantly, an idiot, I think. *Way to go, Adie Lou Kruger-Clark-Whatever-the-Hell-You're-Calling-Yourself-Anymore.*

The wind slaps my face again, and I don't like the feeling of sobering up whatsoever, so I lift the bottle of red wine from Trader Joe's to my lip and take another big gulp.

"I hate you, Nate!" I yell into the wind. "I hate you, Dragoon Lady! I hate you, Cozy Cottage!"

I stare out at the lake, its frozen appearance stunningly beautiful and incredibly menacing. The winter and summer versions of the lake are like twins who look nothing alike. Today, the shoreline is all jagged edges and hard lines, whites and grays, unlike its summery sister, she of soft shimmers and dreamy blurs, vibrant blues and greens. Chunks of ice—boulders really—dot the shoreline, and they are glazed and striated with sand, as if Mother Nature has been practicing her raku pottery techniques.

My back spasms, and I stand to stretch, slipping a bit on the icy shore causing me to throw out my arms for balance. Red wine from the bottle spews forth.

"No!" I cry, as if I've lost the last bit of oxygen in my scuba tank.

I look down, and—for a brief moment—seriously consider making a snow cone out of what has just escaped from the bottle, because I know I need every ounce of courage right now, but then I stop and watch the wine spread slowly through the slushy, sandy snow. It looks like blood, and it continues to spread in tiny lines as if I were drawing on an Etch A Sketch. I gasp when it stops moving: the image resembles a red rose.

I look up at the sun to clear my eyes and mind, and then back down, but the image is still there. When I cast my eyes toward the lake, the image fills my eyes—dancing sunspots—and the shoreline looks as if it's filled with roses.

In my wine-induced haze, I ask myself, *Am I seeing things clearly?*

I know I am walking too quickly on the slippery shore, but I need to see if this is real or a mirage. I move toward Lake Michigan, the roses beckoning me, and walk out onto the frozen lake. It doesn't scare me: I know how thick the ice is. My dad used to ice-fish out here, and my mind flits back to that happy time.

Suddenly, I hit a slick spot and go down, hard. My bottle of wine goes flying and it shatters on the ice, the wine exploding across the surface, leaving a grisly looking scene.

I can feel my back spasm again, and then my butt screams in pain—knowing there will be a large, unsightly bruise by tomorrow—and when I look up, the roses are gone. It's just me, buzzed, sitting alone atop a frozen lake.

I think of all the romantic movies I've watched in my lifetime. Right now, a man—a firefighter or, no, a lumberjack—would rush out of nowhere to help me up. We'd kiss, I'd fall in love and he'd rebuild the cottage while I drank green tea. *The Cinderella Complex*, Trish used to call it: American women have been fed a myth that men will save the damsel in distress, that marriage is a fantasy to which we all aspire.

But what happens when the big wedding is over? Trish asked me before I married Nate. I hated her for saying that. I thought she was just jealous. But she was being honest.

I press my hands down on the ice to stand, but then I stop: I can see the lake undulate underneath the ice, fish swimming under the frozen surface. I feel like I'm at the Shedd Aquarium in Chicago, watching sea life through clear glass. The sunshine and intense blue of the sky fill my view of this underwater world with prisms of light and color, and I rub my mitten over the surface to clear the frost.

"Maybe I'm just hibernating like you right now," I say to the fish swimming just below me. "Maybe I just have to learn to swim even if the world feels frozen."

I suddenly think of Elsa in *Frozen* and feel slightly more emboldened. I push myself up, and the sparkly world looks different now.

I turn and baby-step my way to the shore again, past the mini-glaciers of ice that have formed on the shoreline. My head clicks from *Frozen* to *Ice Castles*, and I say out loud, "What did Lexie do in the movie? What's the part I always forget? She got back up on her feet after she fell. She didn't quit. She rose above her obstacles."

A seagull stops directly in front of me and squawks. I decide it is in total agreement with me, and I shuffle back to the stairs, take a seat and pluck my cell from my coat pocket. I excitedly pull up Notes on my phone and begin to type, but with my mittens still on, I write *X&@2ghPB4*. I yank off my right mitten and start again.

What if I didn't just open a B and B? What if Cozy Cottage were more than an inn...a retreat center???...based on all the rules in my life and of the cottage that people have always downplayed or made fun of... What if women not only came here to relax but also to renew, restore, reinvent, rediscover themselves... I could host Women's Empowerment Weekends: yoga on the beach, entrepreneurship, believing in yourself postdivorce, starting over, the power of essential oils...even living by the rules of Cozy Cottage.

I stop, smile and yell back to the cottage, "I won't let anyone ruin us again with their negativity. Not Nate, not the Dragoon Lady, nobody. Even myself!"

I hear what I think is a howling squawk—a lonely cry—and turn to see if the seagull has followed me.

The shoreline is empty.

I look at my cell and smile. "Nothing can stop me," I say into the wind.

I begin my ascent up the stairs, when I hear the howl again, followed by the sound of car tires screeching away. I rush up the stairs—as best I can, slowed by my boots and dulled by a good dose of cheap wine, my heart thumping as loudly as a speaker at a concert—and when I reach the top, a filthy-looking dog is sitting on my landing, as though she's waiting patiently for me to return.

"Hi, baby," I say. "Are you okay?"

The dog does not acknowledge me. It simply lifts its head and howls a cry so sad and forlorn that I can feel my heart break. Beneath the dirt I think it's a yellow Lab, somewhere between a puppy and a grown dog, but it's hard to tell since it's so excruciatingly thin.

I take a seat on the top step and say softly, "C'mere, baby. Come see me." She doesn't budge. I pat the snow on the ground. "Come here. C'mon." The dog gives me an untrusting side-eye but—beyond that—doesn't acknowledge my presence, much like I used to do to Nate when he'd come home from "meetings" three hours after they had ended.

I inch my way over through the snow until I'm about a foot away. The Lab is filthy, covered in mud, and its nails are very long. Its rib cage heaves under its dirty coat. I inch a little bit closer, and I can see that the dog's dewclaw is so long it's growing into the paw.

"Who did this to you?" I ask, tears springing to my eyes.

I grab my cell to take a photo to send to a friend in Chicago, who heads a rescue organization. "Hi, baby," I say in a singsong voice. "Over here. Who's a good girl?"

The dog finally thumps its tail, sadly—once, twice—and then as if that effort has sapped all of its energy, it lays its head down and whimpers quietly.

"You're so pretty," I sing again. "Look! Look! Over here! I need a pretty picture of you." The Lab slowly lifts its head, and when the dog finally turns its full face toward me, I drop my cell. It is blind in its right eye.

I crawl over, no longer afraid, and pet the dog's back. It sighs the saddest sigh ever.

I then scratch her head and underneath her chin. I lift her pretty face up and stare into her eyes. The left is round, brown and perfect, stereotypically Lab-ish: gentle, innocent but inquisitive, the kind that melts people's hearts. The right, however, is just a blob, an orb, a gray mass that resembles a marble.

"You poor thing," I say, my tears plunking on top of the dog's head. "What happened to you?"

I pick up my cell, hold up the dog's head, snap a photo and send it to my friend, Julie, at the rescue shelter. The Lab begins to fall asleep as I hold her head. I now notice a deep indentation around the dog's neck, as if it's been kept on a tight leash outside for a very long time.

My phone trills, and I read the text from Julie:

Oh, Adie Lou! That poor dog! It's obv. been abused…probably a puppy mill…was blind at birth, or got injured…they couldn't sell it so dumped it to die in the winter…happens all the time, I'm sorry to say…does it have tags?

I stop reading and look. No tags.

If no tags, probably not chipped. But you can check by calling local shelters. Get it to the vet ASAP to check for worms, shots, etc. Malnourished. Needs water and food. But don't overfeed or it will bloat. Needs bath. Are you keeping it?

No! I think. *Of course not.*

If not, take it to a local no-kill.

No-kill, I think. I look at the dog. *Somebody already tried to kill it.*

Good luck! It came to the right person. Let me know if you decide to keep it. You can bring it here for free shots, etc.

No. I'm not keeping it. I have an inn. I have a new start. I can't take on more stress and financial burden. I can't have a blind dog running around my inn with guests.

The dog looks up at me and then—with all its remaining energy—scooches even closer to me, puts a paw on my leg and sighs.

I pick the dog up, carry it back to the cottage, set it in the yard. It looks around, sniffs, wobbles a bit in the snow and, finally, hikes its leg.

She is a he.

"Of course," I say to the dog. "Makes total sense."

I pick up the dog with a grunt, carry him directly to the bathtub—which, mind you, I've yet to use today—and partially fill it with warm water and lots of bubble bath. I grab a cup off the sink and a couple of towels out of a basket, and then pick up the dog. He begins to dog-paddle as I hold him over the water, and the scene makes me smile. I set the dog in the tub and slowly pour warm water over his body. I gasp. He's even thinner wet than I had imagined.

"You poor thing," I coo. "It's gonna be okay. It's gonna be okay now."

Dirt immediately fills the tub, and the water turns dark. As I wash the dog's ears and face, he sighs, and a look of utter contentment covers his face. Slowly, the Lab's true color emerges: he is golden, and his ears are the color of a daffodil.

I pull the dog from the bath and wrap him in a blanket, softly drying his face and the rest of his fur. I pick him up again with a grunt, carry him downstairs and into the kitchen, and begin to scrounge through the kitchen for any food I might have.

"Thank God," I say into the fridge, seeing the rotisserie chicken I'd picked up at Trader Joe's. I pull it from the fridge with my free hand and then walk to the cupboard where I find some white rice to microwave. I set the dog down on the floor, tear up some of the chicken and mix it with some rice in a big plastic bowl. The dog devours the food within seconds. I pour a big bowl of water and also place it on the floor, and the Lab begins to drink as if he's never had a drink in his life before. I think of what my friend had texted and pick up the bowl after a bit, afraid he might bloat.

He slowly begins to investigate the kitchen, walking around and sniffing every corner. And then I watch him pick up steam and scamper into the living room.

"Come here, you," I call. "Where are you going?"

As if pulled by a magnet, the dog beelines toward the old, hook rug by the door. He starts to paw at the rug, making a bed. He scratches and turns, butt in the air, tail suddenly wagging, and scratches and turns, until he suddenly drops like a rock. I walk over to him and smile. He looks up at me, thumps his tail weakly and again sighs. Within seconds, he is sound asleep on the rug.

I take a seat on the floor and watch the lost creature sleep.

I can't keep you, I think, my heart breaking. *I just can't.*

I assess my first day as an innkeeper: a cottage reno that will break my bank; nosy neighbors who want to kill my business; a hole in my roof; and, now, an abandoned, abused dog.

A misfit, just like me.

I pull my phone from the pocket of Evan's sweats I'm still wearing and pull up my Notes. So many good ideas. I stop.

So many good ideas that run smack-dab into the reality of life, I correct.

I stare at the dog.

"How ironic," I say out loud. "Just when I told myself I didn't need a man in my life."

The dog hears my voice, opens its eyes, sees me there and thumps its tail before closing its eyes once again.

Maybe, I think instead, smiling at the dog, *it's not me who needs saving.*

I look at my cell, at all of my scribbled ideas.

Maybe you're the one who needs saving. Maybe a lot of people need help if someone will just do it. I stop. "Maybe," I say to the cottage, "I'm the superhero, the Elsa, the Wonder Woman after all."

The dog again opens his eyes and barks gently.

"You agree, don't you?" I say, and his tail wags. I sit down on the rug next to him and pet his little head. "You've played by everyone else's rules, too, and they weren't very nice, were they? Maybe it's time we make our own rules."

I stop and stare at the handsome Lab.

"I can't call you 'dog' or 'he' or 'you' forever, can I?" I say to the sleeping dog. Then I catch myself and think, *Don't, Adie Lou. Don't name it. Don't get attached.*

The last of the afternoon's light is filtering through the windows and onto the dog's clean coat. It is as yellow and sunny as the day. The spot in which he has picked to lie is warm and bright. I look up, and the sun is illuminating the Cottage Rules sign hanging over where the dog is sleeping.

Rule #2 is spotlighted.

Soak Up the Sun!

I shake my head and laugh.

"Of course," I say, as if this whole thing has been predestined and the choice of names—just like Kruger—has been obvious the whole time. "Your name is Sonny."

PART THREE

Rule #3:
Nap Often

SEVEN

I awake with the uncomfortable feeling someone is staring at me. There is: Sonny. He is standing over me, looking down on me with the most intense gaze.

"No man has looked at me like that in a long time," I say to Sonny. "And you only have one eye."

He licks my face, his tail wagging so hard it makes the curtains on the nearby window flutter.

"All you went through," I say to him, "and somehow you're still able to forgive and embrace the day."

I give Sonny a kiss on the head and get out of bed, a shiver overtaking my body. I glance out the window and see light snow falling. The world is clean, covered in a new coat of white paint, and I listen to the house creak in the wind. Sonny barks, hops off the bed in a courageous leap and runs up to me, jumping on my legs.

"Hold on," I say, understanding already that's his signal to go potty. "Me first."

When I walk back into the bedroom, Sonny is hiding in the corner.

"What's wrong?" I ask. "Are you okay?"

He hides his face under his paws and shivers, and that's when I see a little wet mark on the rug. "It's okay," I say, immediately heading back into the bathroom for a washcloth and a towel. "Come here."

Sonny nervously walks toward me and flinches, and I can now see his past horrors reemerging. "No, sweetie," I sing. "It's okay. My fault. I should have taken you out first. We'll learn together, okay?"

Sonny thumps his tail hopefully, lifts his head and then barks. I clean up the mess and take him out, then come in, make coffee, his breakfast and call the vet.

I study my to-do list as I make my oatmeal: it's a mile long.

Workers

Pick paint

Website

Prep for meeting with the area Chamber of local business owners

Repair the Adie Lou

I stop on that item, as the irony is just too rich this morning.

"Sonny?" I call suddenly, wondering where he went. I set down the list and jog into the living room when I see him already curled up on the rug under the Cottage Rules sign taking a nap.

"Priorities," I say, again noticing the Cottage Rules sign hanging over Sonny.

Rule #3: *Nap Often*

"I wish," I say to Sonny. "Too much to do."

I head upstairs, Sonny on my heels, to shower and get ready—wanting to look presentable for my second day in my new world—dabbing on some essential oils to center me. I grab Sonny off the bed and head to the car. Our first stop is the vet's office.

Everyone—including my parents, who used to bring my childhood pets here—calls Dr. Peterson "Dr. Dolittle" because she is a doctor to all animals, large and small. She can give a shot to a cat, clean a dog's teeth and then deliver a foal or save a baby goat that's coming out breech.

Dr. Dolittle, an older woman whose skin looks perpetually windburned, sets Sonny on a table and gives him the once-over and then a lot of shots. "He's been through hell," she finally says, her face filled with sadness, "but he's going to be fine. With a lot of good care and love." She stops. "No chip. No tags. Bad breeder probably dumped him, thinking he'd die in the cold or some lakeshore homeowner would find him." She stops again. "Are you keeping him, or do you want us to call the shelter?"

I stare at her, and the emotion of the last day and of finding Sonny hits me full force. "I don't know," I say.

Dr. Dolittle lifts Sonny off the table as if he weighs nothing and then walks over, taking a seat beside me on the wooden bench in the exam room. "You have a lot on your plate," she says, her voice soft. "No need to feel guilty whatsoever. You did a wonderful thing. You saved this dog's life." She stops. "You're good stock, Adie Lou. Your parents would be proud."

Without warning, tears run down my face. "Thank you."

Again, without warning, Sonny jumps onto the bench and begins licking my face, clearing away my tears. And then, un-aware of his burgeoning size, he plops down in my lap and, within seconds, he's napping.

I stroke his head and then his back.

"I'll give you two a minute," Dr. Dolittle says. "I'm going to get you started with some good puppy food and some pills he'll need to take for a while. I'll check back in a sec."

She walks out but Sonny doesn't notice. He is snoozing, his chest rising and falling, before he begins to have a dream. His hind legs start twitching as if he's running, his heinie shakes and he begins to yip.

What are you dreaming about, little guy? I think. And then I start to cry again, thinking of him being abandoned, all alone. I've been through the exact same thing as Sonny: *tossed aside for being less than, unwanted for being not as pretty as someone else, trying to survive just because I want something better.*

I walk out of the exam room with Sonny in my arms, feeling strong, as if he weighs no more than a Chihuahua.

"I'm keeping him," I announce to everyone in the vet's office. "He's my soul mate."

The office explodes into applause, and Dr. Dolittle doesn't charge me for the visit.

EIGHT

Saugatuck Marina is nestled just off the bay. It's a full-service marina that offers deep-water boat slips, a pool, fully stocked store, green space for picnics, showers and stunning views. In essence, it's home to a lot of rich folks with big boats who take them to warmer climes during the winter.

My parents' beloved boat, the *Adie Lou*—the one I nearly sold—and I are not among them. My boat is in storage here. And it has been since my parents died.

"Keeping a boat in storage too long is like being in a coma," my father used to say. "Nothing will work the way it used to do."

My dad used to be the first one at Saugatuck Marina come spring. He'd watch the lake—when and how it thawed—and gauge its temperature by walking in up to his ankles. He'd observe the birds: when they began to build nests, when they began to peck the warming earth for worms. He seemed to know Lake Michigan—every nuance, the ways it would warm or grow cold—as if it were an old lover. And he knew the exact moment when it was safe to pull the *Adie Lou* from storage, put it into the slip here and take it for its first spin of the season. He'd pop champagne that first boat ride, even if it was still in the fifties, and exclaim, "What's Rule #12 of the summer cottage? Boat rides are a shore thing!"

The storage building is cavernous and cold, and it feels like I'm entering a mausoleum. Nate and I once traveled to Pompeii and Herculaneum, and this has that same haunting feeling. Things that were alive and vibrant now entombed. Boats are lined up, one after the other. Some are fully covered and encased, some sit open and empty, all ghost ships waiting for life.

"Hello?" I call, my voice echoing back.

Sonny barks. And then barks again, thinking his echo is another dog barking.

I head toward the back, where I find a door with a name plaque on it that reads: CAPTAIN. *I May Not Walk on Water, But I Can Land on It!*

There are blinds—bent and falling—over the window on the door. I angle my head to look through one of the slats, and there is a man sleeping on a cot.

I knock, and he jumps.

I can hear him clear his throat as he walks to the door. "Hello?" he asks, more like an inquisition than a question. The man does, indeed, look like a sea captain—silver, windblown hair, unkempt gray beard and lined face set atop a cowl neck sweater—an actor someone has hired from Central Casting to portray Ernest Hemingway.

"Hi, yes, sorry to bother you…"

"What makes you think you were bothering me?"

I think briefly about busting him, but decide against it. "I'm Adie Lou Kruger… Clarke… Adeleine Clarke," I say.

"Can't make up your mind today?" he asks.

I can feel my pulse race and the blood rise in my face. I inhale deeply and slowly, and the scent of the lavender I used earlier slows my heart rate.

"I have a boat in storage here, and I'd like someone to take a look at it," I explain. "It's a 1940 Chris-Craft that I'd like to get back in shipshape." I smile at my little joke.

"Good one," the man says. He begins to cough, violently, and then proceeds to cough up what sounds like a boatload of phlegm. He walks back into his office, grabs an empty bottle of beer and spits into it.

I nearly pass out.

"Pretty fancy boat," he says, a rivulet of spittle dangling from his mouth. "Husband must do all right."

My pulse instantly quickens.

"It's *my* boat," I say. "No husband."

He holds his hands up as if I were Capone himself. "Okay, lady," he says.

"It's not *lady*," I say. "It's Miss Kruger."

His face twitches, and I have a feeling he wants to curse me or call me a "women's libber" or "bra burner," but he heads toward a metal file cabinet in the back, and pulls open the third drawer. He rifles slowly through green file folders filled with manila envelopes, and I impatiently want to scream, "Don't you think it's time you updated your systems here?" but I keep my mouth shut, lean down to Sonny and stroke his ears to calm my nerves.

"Only Kruger we have in here is the ol' man Kruger and his wife," he says. "Jon and Jo."

"Those were my parents," I say.

His face breaks into a big smile. "They were some characters."

I can't help but smile, too. I like it when people refer to anyone—including my parents—as characters. To me, it means they have lived memorable lives.

"They were," I say.

He looks on the sheet of paper he is holding and then digs farther into the file. "Follow me."

"What's your name?" I say, realizing he hasn't told me.

"Cap'n Mac," he says, before grabbing his rather round stomach and breaking into a belly laugh. "Although my wife prefers to call me Cap'n Mac and Cheese." He stops. "Spot 42," he says, before checking the file again. "Been here awhile."

"I know," I say. "I think it's been in storage since my parents passed."

"Heard your dad died of cancer and your mom died of heartbreak."

His bluntness hits me like a hurricane. I pull Sonny closer and realize Cap'n Mac is just speaking the truth, like many locals do here. No time for BS.

"You heard right," I say, clenching my teeth as Cap'n Mac pulls back the tarp covering the boat to reveal its glorious, burnished back end: *Adie Lou* is spelled out in scrolling gold letters, *1940* in the far right corner of the wooden stern.

My heart catches in my throat. She's even more beautiful than I remembered.

"Hot damn," Cap'n Mac says, running his hand over the wood. "This is a piece of art."

I nod. It is. My mom used to joke my dad loved this boat more than her. He bought it from a dealer in Lake Tahoe and restored it back to its original glory: the original interior pigskin leather, the marbled steering wheel, the blue face gauges, the orange seams, the spotlight on the hull card. Every nut and bolt my dad used was vintage.

"I think it might need some work," I say. "I'm hesitant to pull it out until someone takes a thorough look at it." I stop. "I don't know what I'm able to afford right now."

Cap'n Mac nods. "I agree," he says. "Might cost a pretty penny."

I think of the cottage and the boat, and then of my savings, and I see an endless line of pretty pennies diving off a cliff and into the lake, like lemmings.

"Go see Scott Stevens," Cap'n Mac says. "He's the Chris-Craft master, the Yoda of wooden boats."

"I remember him," I say, thinking of the always tanned, silver-haired man, the only person my father trusted with his boat besides himself. "Thanks. Do you think he's in today?"

"He never stops working," Cap'n Mac says, reaching over to give Sonny a pet. "Unlike us, right, pooch? We need our naps."

NINE

Blue Star Highway is as cold and empty as the marina. All of the ice cream shops, bike rentals and art galleries are shuttered.

SEE YOU THIS SUMMER! the signs say.

The snow has picked up, and little tornadoes of white are whipping across the narrow road that connects west Michigan's resort communities. The bike trail, which is filled with activity May through October, is covered in drifts.

I am driving like Mr. Magoo, slower and more carefully even, my body hunched over the wheel, my eyes glazed on the road, the wipers whipping back and forth. It is suddenly dark as night, and my headlights are illuminating just a few feet in front of my car.

I barely see S.S. Boat Works through the snow. I slow the car, fishtailing slightly, and crawl into the parking lot. The building is an old boat storage facility, to which a small office has been attached to the front. It is old and weathered.

As much as Mr. Stevens must now be, I think.

I look over and Sonny is unconscious in the passenger seat, the heat blowing his ears to and fro.

"Nice time for a nap," I say to him.

I reach for him but decide not to disturb his sleep.

"You finally have a little peace," I whisper. "You must be exhausted."

I leave the car running with the heat on and lock it. I pull the hood on my coat over my head and rush through the snow. I enter to find an elderly woman asleep in her chair.

The woman looks a bit like Mrs. Claus. She is seated in an office chair, her head rolled to the side, her half-glasses barely on her nose, snoring.

The whole world is unconscious today, I think.

I don't know whether I should laugh, wake her up or just leave, but then she snores so loudly—making a sound similar to a trash truck—that she wakes herself up.

"Good morning," she says, not missing a beat. "Welcome to S.S. Boat Works. How may I help you?"

You're good, I think.

"Hi, I don't have an appointment, but I'm here to see Mr. Stevens. I don't know if he's in or not."

"He's in," she says. "He's always in, unless he's personally de-livering a boat."

He still drives? I think.

"Your name?" she asks.

"Adie Lou Clarke... Kruger... Adie Lou Kruger," I finally stammer, telling myself I'll stop doing that.

The woman picks up her phone and dials an extension. "There's a Ms. Culverson here to see you," the woman says, not even close to getting my name right, something that I can completely understand given my maniacal babbling. She looks up. "Mr. Stevens will be right out."

I pull down my hood, take off my coat and take a seat. I am

checking my cell when I see a pair of dusty jeans appear in front of me. I look up and drop my phone.

"Oh, my God," I say. "Scooter?"

"Adie Lou?"

I stand, and he hugs me tightly, so tightly my face smashes into his nubby sweater, which is dusted in wood chips and smells like pine. I inhale, and the dust fills my nose. I know what's coming next but can't stop the train: I sneeze, not once, or twice, but over and over again as I always do.

"Eight sneezes," he says, laughing. "You haven't changed."

"Do you mean me, or my allergies?"

He laughs again. "Both." He stops and just stares at me, until the silence makes me uncomfortable. "Do I have something on my nose from all that?" I ask, wiping the sleeve of my coat across my face.

"No," he says.

"What?" I ask. "Then what is it?"

"It's you," he says. "I can't believe you're standing in front of me."

I drop my arm. "Me either," I finally reply. "I thought that the Mr. Stevens I was told to see was…well, your dad."

"He passed away a while back," he says, his voice wistful. "Mom, too." He stops. "I heard about your parents. I'm real sorry, Adie Lou."

"Me, too, Scooter."

Growing up, everyone in Saugatuck except me called Scott Stevens "S.S. Golden Boy." The town idolized him: he was the golden-haired high school quarterback who led the team to its first ever state championship. His father was idolized, too: he made a fortune salvaging and repairing vintage boats, and then reselling them for a pretty penny, before *vintage*, *retro* and *HGTV* were buzzwords. Scott was the captain of his own ship, and he could do no wrong.

But I knew him before I knew all of that. To me, he was always Scooter, the little boy I met one summer riding a scooter on Lakeshore Drive. At the time, I had difficulty distinguishing his real name from his toy, and I forever referred to him by the nickname. We were fast friends, the city girl and the local boy, the tomboy who wanted to do everything her friend did.

Every high school summer I spent Memorial Day through Labor Day in Saugatuck, and Scooter and I worked part-time on the Saugatuck Chain Ferry, the only hand-cranked chain ferry left in the US. I was the first girl to work on the chain ferry, thanks to Scooter. No one questioned him in town, even when he'd drag down Water Street in his souped-up truck or wanted a girl to work one of the town's main attractions. We used to take turns cranking the pretty, white Victorian ferry—embellished with ornate woodwork—across the Kalamazoo River. It was a shoulder-aching, backbreaking two hundred cranks to move the ferry across the river from the town to the beach side, transporting passengers and their bikes. While one of us cranked, the other recited an oral history of the town and ferry to passengers.

Originally used to transport horses across the Kalamazoo River, this Victorian ferry is now a top tourist attraction...

The older Scooter and I got, the smarter, and by our second year working on the chain ferry, we began asking passengers if they wanted to give it a try.

I look at Scooter and say, "Think you're strong enough to crank this ferry across the river?"

He takes over, remembering our schtick. "I don't think your wife and kids think you can do it, sir. Want to prove them wrong?"

"They always fell for it, didn't they?" I laugh. "Saved our arms."

"Pride," he says. "Always gets in the way."

Scooter says this with incredible sadness, and then kneels to pick up my phone.

"Remember the time I came up for the Halloween parade, and we dressed as the chain ferry?" I laugh. "Sprites covered in chains."

"We were just kids," he says, his voice again wistful. "I still can't believe you're standing in front of me. What are you doing here?"

"Well," I start, bringing him up to date on the last few decades of my life. "And you?"

He smiles, and his eyes change colors, like a mood ring. Right now, in his gray sweater, his thick silver hair slicked to one side and matching silver stubble, his eyes are the same blue-gray color as a West Point uniform.

"I think you might need to sit for this," he says, interrupting my thoughts. "Want to come into my office?"

I nod, and then hesitate.

"Something wrong?" he asks.

I look back at my car, which is still running. "I sort of adopted a stray dog yesterday. I felt like I wasn't stressed enough." I laugh. "He's asleep in the car."

"That's so Adie Lou of you," he says with a smile.

Adie Lou of you. My heart again leaps.

"Want to get him?" he continues.

"I think he'll be okay for a few more minutes. Maybe we could ask your receptionist to watch the car?"

We turn, and she is asleep again, her neck like a Slinky. I stifle a laugh, and we tiptoe past her. We enter the hallway, and Scooter says, "She worked for my dad. I can't fire her."

"You can't even wake her to fire her," I say, and then burst into a fit of giggles.

Scooter laughs. The hallway is filled on one side with windows overlooking the former boat storage facility, now filled with wooden boats in various stages of restoration. Some are just skeletons, some are nearly finished. Wood and parts line the massive space, as big as an airplane hangar. Men are working slowly, meticulously on the boats, almost as if they're performing surgery.

"These are Chris-Crafts and Rivas, like George Clooney has," Scooter says, not an ounce of boastfulness in his voice. "They are works of art, like any painting you'd find in a museum." He points toward a corner. "We've even started working on vintage cars. That's a 1947 Ford Sportsman convertible. We're restoring and varnishing the original wood on the car."

He leads me to his office, a tiny space that holds just a desk with a laptop and phone, and two wooden chairs. I take a seat, my knees hitting the desk.

"And?" I ask, as Scooter sits. "What have you been up to?"

Scooter sighs, and his eyes seem to change color again, this time sadder, bluer—like a gas flame.

"You know I went to Western Michigan on a football scholarship, broke my arm in two places my sophomore year? Well, my backup went on to have a great year and become all-conference. I never played another down," he says softly. "I was so humiliated, I dropped out of college and couldn't return home. I felt like I'd let the town down. I felt like I let my dad down." He stops. "I felt like I let myself down.

"So I sort of just ran and I wandered around the world," he continues. "I worked as a deck hand and then a mate on some private yachts. I traveled along the east and west coasts, picking up jobs working on people's boats to earn enough money to keep moving."

"What were you running from?" I ask.

He looks at me, his eyes intense. "Rules," he says. "I did everything I was supposed to do. Followed all the rules in the playbook, on the field and off. And where did it get me?"

"Here," I say.

He smiles. "You're right, Adie Lou. You've always been such an optimist."

"Me? Really?"

Scooter nods. "What was that you used to say? 'A pessimist sees the difficulty in every opportunity. An optimist sees the opportunity in every difficulty.'"

"You remember that?" I say, my voice rising. "I forgot that." I stop. "I forgot who I was for a long time, too."

Scooter nods. "When my dad got sick, I came home. I was so angry at first, that he was sick, that everyone saw me as a failure. But then I remembered how much he sacrificed to make this place a success, to give me everything I ever wanted, and I felt a renewed sense of purpose. I didn't want to run from my history anymore, I wanted to embrace it."

My eyes grow big. "That's exactly how I feel," I say. "And I wanted to play by my own rules for once, too."

"So why are you here, Adie Lou," Scooter asks, "since you had no idea I was going to be here?"

"Remember the 1940 Chris-Craft my parents had?"

"How could I forget? The *Adie Lou*. What a beauty. Your parents got it after that trip to Capri, didn't they? Your dad found it in Tahoe?"

I nod. "It was my dad's pride and joy," I say. I'm impressed he remembers the story.

"Besides you," Scooter adds with a wink, causing me to smile. "That's why he named it after you."

"It's been in storage awhile, and I'm thinking of using it for sunset boat rides. Maybe serving some wine and cheese. But I think it needs some work." I hesitate. "And I think I might need a deal." I hesitate again. "Deal meaning I don't think I can afford to do it."

"Is that what you say to a small-business owner?" Scooter asks.

My face flushes. "No, it's what you say to an old friend."

"An old friend you didn't stay in touch with," he says, and my stomach drops.

"I'm sorry," I say. "I was in college, I met Nate, I got pregnant soon after... It was a blur."

"I know," he says. "I didn't mean it that way. It's just odd that two people who were in each other's lives for so long just fell away from one another." He stops and repeats what he said earlier. "We were just kids, though."

Scooter shakes his head and smiles.

"Let me do this," he says. "I'll shoot you an email after I look over my calendar. We'll set a time to see your boat, and I'll see what I can do." He stops and winks. "As an old friend."

He stands, and I follow suit. I notice there is a photo of him in his high school glory on a file cabinet behind him. He's being carried on the shoulders of his teammates, holding the state championship trophy, and the look on his face says that he is unbeatable, unstoppable, invincible.

That was before we grew up, I think. *Before we knew what the world had in store.*

We walk into the hall, and he gives me a big hug.

"It was great to see you, Adie Lou," he says.

"You, too."

I turn and begin to walk away.

"Oh, Adie Lou?" Scooter calls.

I turn around too quickly, my heart racing for some reason, wondering what he wants to say to me.

"Be careful not to wake up Gladys," he says. "She likes her naps."

TEN

A tarp is flapping on top of the turret when I arrive home. In the wind and snow, it looks like a ghost that got trapped in the midst of trying to enter the cottage to haunt it.

The front door flies open, and two men head outside carrying scrap lumber.

I'm guessing the ghost is trying to get the hell out of this cottage, I think.

Sonny starts barking, his head jerking between the roof and the construction crew, his one good eye racing from real people to perceived ghosts on the roof.

He's so excited that he lifts his leg and tinkles mostly on my snow boot. I groan and rush him inside, kicking off my boots and chunks of snow onto the braided rug by the front door. I am shrugging off my coat when Frank approaches.

"Who's this? Hi, buddy!" Frank says to Sonny. "Looks like you've had a tough go." He looks up at me. "Yours?"

I nod.

"Until now," Frank amends, his voice high and excited. "You hit the lotto!"

Frank plops on the floor and begins to play with Sonny, using his fingers to scamper around the Lab's legs. Sonny barks in excitement, and Frank laughs, the burly general contractor reduced to a giggling boy.

"I have good news and bad news," Frank finally says, looking up at me.

"Was this your way of softening the blow?" I ask. "Playing with the dog?"

"No," he says, grunting as he stands. He picks up Sonny and puts his face next to the dog's, panting alongside the Lab. "Does this help?"

"Good news first, please," I say, crossing my arms.

"Your septic is in good shape," Frank says. "Your parents got the mega-tank, which is lucky for you, so you don't need a second one. And they've kept it clean as a whistle, so to speak."

"Bad news?" I ask, my face already wincing.

"You know how you want to upgrade the kitchen with new appliances, including a big, gas stove? Well, we need to run a new gas line from outside."

"Okay...?"

"That means we have to demo the concrete pad on the patio as well as the kitchen floor and run a new pipe for the stove," Frank says. I groan, and Frank sets Sonny down, knowing he's not softening the blow any longer.

"How much?" I ask.

"Two to three thousand."

I fall back against the wall, hitting the Cottage Rules sign.

"But," Frank says, his voice rising, "what I suggest we do is add gas for your outdoor grill, so you don't have to worry about tanks anymore. You can grill for guests and just flip a switch. And your gas appliances will make cooking your breakfasts so much nicer." He stops. "I'm sorry."

"Me, too," I say, my voice and face sagging.

"We're going to clear out for the day," he says. "Snow's really starting to come down now. Roads are getting bad I bet?"

I nod.

"We'll be back early tomorrow to take a closer look at the fish house and—if the weather breaks—get your roof fixed." Frank stops, studying my face. "You look exhausted. Why don't you go take a nap?"

"I can't take a nap," I say. "It's still the middle of the day!"

"Do you mind?" Frank asks, walking over to the bookshelves in the living room.

My parents were voracious readers, and they made me one, as well. My mother loved fiction—from literary to commercial, even pulpy paperbacks—while my father adored nonfiction, especially historical or political biographies. The towering bookcases cover the entire wall around Darryl and the fireplace, my mom's books on the left, my father's on the right. My father always removed the dust jacket to the books he read. He would take the shiny jackets off, fold them and place them in a trunk he kept in the attic.

"This is the way a book is meant to look, Adie Lou," my father would tell me every time he started a new book, holding the hardcover as adoringly as he held Evan when he was a baby. "Unadorned, without all the commercial rigmarole. Nothing but the author's own words. In the old days, the cover would have been leather or linen." He would stop and turn the book over in his hands, before taking a seat next to the fireplace, Darryl reading over his shoulder. "Hard shell. Flexible, sturdy spine. An inside filled with stunning beauty and wisdom. Just like the best people, Adie Lou."

I stare at the high-back chair and can still see the impression of my father's body in it.

Frank scans the right side of the bookcase for a few seconds, before plucking a hardcover as if it were calling to him.

"Your dad loaned this to me a long time ago, when I was taking over the business from my dad," Frank says. "A biography of Winston Churchill. Your dad admired him greatly." Frank smiles and begins flipping through the biography, which I notice is underlined and highlighted, sticky notes jutting everywhere.

"Ah," Frank says. "Right here. Can I read you this?"

I nod, my back still pressed against the Cottage Rules sign.

"'Success is not final, failure is not fatal. It is the courage to continue that counts.'"

I smile. "That sounds just like my dad," I say.

Frank closes the book and runs his hand over the cover.

"My business was about to go under," Frank says softly. "Although I apprenticed under my dad and learned all of his skills, I wasn't as good of a salesman as he was. The old-timers who knew my dad weren't buying property, and the new guard were only hiring fancy builders and architects whose work had been featured in *Architectural Digest*."

I think of the Dragoon Lady and silently nod.

"Your dad was one of the first to hire me," he continues. "Worked on refurbishing that turret. Added on to that beautiful office and sitting area on this floor that will soon be your new owner's suite. Mr. Kruger gave me this and told me to read it. Said he'd know if I'd read it or not. Got to that passage I just read you, and beside it, your father had written, 'Don't ever quit, Frank!'"

He stops, and I swear I catch his jaw tremble under his bushy beard. "Helluva guy," he says in a near whisper that gives me goose bumps. He looks at me. "Don't ever give up, Adie Lou!"

Frank hands me the book with a definitive nod and heads into the kitchen. I cradle it sweetly, thinking of my father and then of Evan. As the workers clean up and gather their tools, I dig my cell out of my purse and call my son.

"Yeah," he says, his voice ragged and husky.

"That's quite the greeting," I say. "Are you sick?"

"No," Evan says. "Sleeping."

"Sleeping? It's early afternoon. Don't you have class?"

"Not today, Mom. I had a big paper due and a test this morning." He yawns. "And I've got midterms coming up soon. I needed a nap."

"I didn't know college students napped," I say. "I didn't know fraternity boys napped."

"We call it instant midnight," he says.

"What?" I ask.

"Instant midnight," Evan replies. "It's a phrase some of the older guys made up. A lot of afternoons, if the guys are tired from studying or hungover, they come back to their rooms, lock their doors, close their blinds and pull the curtains. It goes from daylight to midnight. Instant midnight. Get it?"

"Now I do," I say with a small laugh. "But a nap in the middle of the day sounds so frivolous."

"What was that book Grandma loved?" Evan asks. Goose bumps again cover my body. It's as though he is reading my mind, as if he knew I was just talking about books and his grandparents.

"She liked a lot of books," I say, looking at the countless novels lining her side of the bookshelves. "As did your grampa."

"The kindergarten one by that reverend guy," he says. The way he says that is so typical Evan that I can't help but laugh.

"You mean, *All I Really Need to Know I Learned in Kindergarten*?"

"That's it," Evan says. "It had all those rules, sort of like the ones we had in the cottage. What were they?" He stops. "Things like play fair and don't take things that aren't yours."

I smile. My mom and her rules. She believed life was so simple, and yet we all made it so hard. I look at Sonny and think of the past few years of my life.

"She's right," I say to the dog.

"What?" Evan asks.

"Hold on," I say, walking toward the bookshelves as Frank had just moments ago. I slide the Churchill bio back into its empty spot and walk over to my mom's side. I scan the books and, finally, see the one Evan is referring to. "I found it on your grandma's bookshelves," I say.

"Cool," Evan replies.

I flip through it, and a page is earmarked. I scan it and bust out laughing.

"What is it?" Evan asks.

"Listen to this," I say, before reading an underlined passage. "'Think what a better world it would be if…the whole world had cookies and milk about three o'clock every afternoon and then lay down with our blankies for a nap.'"

Evan laughs. "I've got life already figured out," he says. I can hear him stifle a yawn. "Speaking of which…"

"Okay, okay," I say. "Sorry to wake you up."

"You should try it, Mom," Evan says.

"A nap? Now? I can't. There's too much to do. It's…irresponsible."

"You're all responsibility, Mom," he says. "Your whole life has revolved around being responsible for someone."

I look back at Sonny, and my heart jumps. I'm unsure if Evan would be happy or not about my snap decision to take on the responsibility of a dog, so I decide to keep Sonny a secret for now.

"Rule #3 of the cottage, Mom," Evan says. "Nap often." He stops. "What was it you and Grandma used to tell me when I didn't want to leave the beach or stop playing? 'You can't recharge a battery if it's running all the time.'" He stops again. "And you can't be courageous or responsible when you're tired. It's okay. Take care of yourself, Mom. Then everything will take care of itself. Play by your own rules for once. Nap in the afternoon. Like me." He stops. "What's going on, Mom? Why did you call? Is everything okay?"

Those are loaded questions, I think. *Why did I call?*

"I just wanted to hear your voice," I say, not explaining the real reason: something told me to call my son right now.

"Well, you heard it," he says, yawning. "Say good-night, Gracie."

Goose bumps. Again. "I can't believe you remember watching those old shows with your grampa," I say. "I can't believe you remember all of the things he used to say."

There is silence for a moment before Evan says, "Isn't it better to remember the good things than the bad? Say good-night, Gracie."

"Good night, Gracie."

I put the cell back in my pocket, put my mom's book back on the shelf and walk over to retrieve the pills the vet gave me for Sonny from my coat pocket. I make him an early dinner, hiding his pills in his food, take him back out for another potty and then head upstairs, where I take a long, hot shower. I pull on some comfy pj's and pull out the diffuser I still have stashed in a recyclable grocery bag on the floor. I fill it with water, plop in a few drops of lavender and clary sage for relaxation and peaceful sleep, and then choose a soothing blue color, a small ring of light that encircles the diffuser and radiates color like an orb.

Though the day is gray, the white of the snow makes it bright, so I close the curtains tightly. The room is dark but glows in glacial blue.

Instant midnight, I think. *My way.*

I turn on the electric blanket I found, pull the covers back and crawl into bed, Sonny following. For a moment, I feel incredible guilt.

I haven't done this since I was a girl. I remember my life before: rushing to meetings, rushing to get Evan to practice, rushing to the store.

Do entrepreneurs take naps? I wonder.

There is so much to do, but I suddenly feel as though I can't keep my eyes open. Sonny is making a nest at the end of the mattress, circling round and round, digging this way and that, nudging the blankets into a little pile. He finally finishes and looks up at me, happily panting, having worked himself into an excited lather, and thumps his tail.

"Say good-night, Sonny," I say.

He lifts his head and gives a little bark.

I blink hard, once, twice, and then I fall asleep where I dream I am on a wonderful vacation in Michigan taking a nap in the middle of the day.

PART FOUR

Rule #4:
Wake Up Smiling

ELEVEN

March

I am singing "Girls Just Want to Have Fun" at the top of my lungs and dancing around a bedroom on the second floor of the cottage just like I did when I was a girl. I immediately think back to my Chicago school days when I used to watch the older girls dance in the gym at school dances. There was an art to '80s dancing—a mix of pop and punk, lots of arm movement and leg twisting—which I picked up from watching those girls and, of course, MTV.

As I spin, I catch a glimpse of myself in the mirror on top of the bedroom dresser.

I stop. "Hi," I say to my reflection. "I know you."

Although it's been over three decades since I've danced to this song, and everything has changed—my face, my body, my life, not to mention cell phones, laptops, FaceTime, Alexa—I can still see that young girl reflected back.

"Hi, Adie Lou," I say. "Good to see you again."

It's then I realize I am smiling. Even though my hair and face are covered in beachy blue paint, my back aches and I just wrote a $50,000-plus check for work I've yet to see completed, I am smiling from ear to ear.

Since I took a nap days ago, I've slept better than I have in ages. I'm still anxious and exhausted, but—for once—I feel a sliver of peace. And that is something I haven't experienced in years.

"I Wanna Dance with Somebody" comes on, and I whoop.

"I used to love Whitney!" I yell at Sonny, who is watching while I paint. "And Madonna and Cyndi!"

Sonny cocks his head, and his one eye continues to follow me as I dance around the room. "I know you're probably more of a Bruno Mars guy," I call to Sonny over the music.

"Actually, I'm more of a Shania guy."

Standing in the door is Frank. I laugh. "Now, that surprises me," I say as I turn down the music. "I'd guess more old-school for you. Like Johnny Cash. But not as old-school as the Dragoon Lady. She probably listens to opera. Something like *Don Giovanni*." I laugh. "No, no, I got it! Dirges! She listens to dirges!"

As I'm saying this, Frank's eyes grow wider, and he gives me a slicing motion across his throat. That's when Iris Dragoon comes into frame.

"Crap," I mutter, as if I just got busted by my parents for playing the music too loud.

"Good morning, Miss..." She stops, and a grinchy grin slinks across her face. "What are we calling ourselves today?"

I hate when people use the collective noun "we" to be dismissive. It's a pet peeve ever since my copywriting days.

"*We,*" I emphasize, "typically call someone before showing up at their home."

She nods, as if to say "well played," and then produces a document from her handbag. I already know it's bad because Frank is backing away. *I tried to warn you,* he mouths, before disappearing.

"The Preservation Committee has discovered that the fish house behind this cottage is a historic structure," she says, her voice deep and purring in that way cats sound before they pounce. "It was actually built before the cottage, sometime in the very late 1800s. It was an icehouse and storage unit for fish being shipped from Chicago, and for local produce that was being sent to the city. Ships used to come right up to your beach. And our area—as it still does today—produced fresh peaches, apples, asparagus and cherries, much of which were stored right here." She hands me the papers. "Which means you can't touch it."

"I can't what?" I say disbelievingly.

Sonny stands and begins to bark. Iris Dragoon shoots him a look and he whimpers, then backs into a corner of the bedroom.

"It means we—the Preservation Committee and the city—have final approval over what you can and can't do with the structure." She grins as broadly as I had been moments ago. "Have a nice day."

I stare at the papers she handed to me.

"But this is mine," I yell after her. "This is *my* property."

I can hear the front door slam.

I turn, and my reflection is staring back at me as it was earlier. I am wide-eyed, in shock, covered in paint. I am, quite literally, blue. And needless to say, I am no longer smiling.

TWELVE

"I have good news and bad news," Frank says.

He is beginning to sound like a broken record. I take a sip of my coffee to warm my body, but still shiver. It is a bitterly cold Michigan winter morning. The outdoor thermometer my parents bought long ago is stuck on the wrong side of zero, and it is encased in ice that looks eerily blue, the color that is still flecked in my hair, dotted on my skin and under my nails. The temperature is in the single digits, the windchill in the negative numbers and the world looks frozen in place, encased in a thin layer of ice, unable to move.

"I can relate," I murmur.

"What?" Frank asks.

"Oh," I say, trying to cover for the fact that all I've done since coming back to Saugatuck was talk to myself, drink too much, make bad decisions and go broke, "nothing. It's just that my mom always used to say days like this were 'too cold to snow.'"

"She was right," Frank says. "Your mom was smart." He stops. "So are you, Adie Lou."

His words surprise me, and I look at him and nod appreciatively. "I needed to hear that," I say.

"So, let's start with the bad news first," he says.

"Way to good cop–bad cop me, Frank," I laugh. "Go ahead. Rip off the Band-Aid."

"Well, I met with the city," Frank says, "and your fish house *is* a historic property." He stops and looks at me. "*A* historic or *an* historic? You're a writer. That one always gets me."

My mind flashes back to college, and I recite the words of a beloved professor. "With words like *historic* and *hotel*, we now pronounce them with an audible *h*, so using *a* is commonplace today."

"Told you," Frank says. "You are smart. As I was saying— correctly—the fish house *is* a historic property that predates the construction of the cottage. The cottage is historic, too, but since it's been altered over the years before these bylaws were put in place, the committee can't do much about your plans. And, since the fish house is located out here on the lakeshore, it falls outside of the city's historic district, which has much stricter laws on what can and can't be done with historic structures."

"My head is spinning," I say. I look at the thermometer on the patio outside the kitchen, see the windchill and suddenly think of my dad's long-winded stories. He could tell stories that contained no periods and went on for a half hour—swerving this way and that with no clear direction—no ending in sight. My mom would suddenly yell, "Land the plane, Jon!"

"Land the plane, Frank," I say.

He laughs. "Sorry. The bad news is we do have to run everything by the city and the Preservation Committee, but we are only required to retain one of the structure's original walls, and we have to keep what they term as 'the integrity' of the structure's exterior."

I sigh. "Sounds more reasonable," I say. "But isn't retrofitting exterior windows and redoing the wood exterior going to be way more expensive?"

Frank nods. "It is," he says. "But, here's the good news."

"Warren Buffett is waiting to propose to me outside?"

"You like older men?" Frank asks, his bushy face twitching, a mischievous smile now appearing under his beard. "I never would have guessed. Good news is the state offers a tax credit up to 25 percent of qualified rehabilitation expenditures against state income tax or single business tax liability. Unlike the 20 percent federal tax credit, which specifically targets income-producing properties, Michigan's state tax credit is eligible for owner-occupied properties."

"Sounds like a nightmare," I say. "And like I'll have to spend time filling out paperwork."

"You can get a quarter of your investment back, Adie Lou, and then it will begin producing income," Frank says. "It's worth the time and effort."

"Any more good news?" I ask.

"Fresh out," he says. "But maybe some fresh air will do you good. Want to go take a look at the fish house and talk about your plans?"

I start to shake my head no, but instead refill my coffee, grab a coat and follow Frank outside. The cold instantly sobers me, and my eyes water. We walk across the big patio—which will soon be jackhammered up for the new gas line to the kitchen— and head to the left. Frank opens the decaying wood door to the fish house and shuts it immediately to retain what little warmth is inside.

As soon as the door shuts, I feel as if I've gone back in time, personally and historically. The fish house is really no more than a shanty: two rooms, no more than a couple of hundred square feet total, with a pitched roof. Two windows are on each side, but the back wall—which faces the lake—has a huge window. Rough-hewn planks line the outside and inside, and they are weathered gray, almost bone-white. Gaps are present in the planks, and near the foundation, I can see through the walls to the snow outside. Wind whistles through the gaps, and the ancient, single-pane windows are frosted over, intricate, lacy ice patterns visible on each frame like powdered sugar on beautiful Christmas cookies. The floor is concrete, but my dad had scattered hook rugs here and there. On one side is where my dad says they cleaned the fish, and in the other room is where they used to ice the fish and produce.

"I can't believe this place is still standing, to be honest," Frank says. "Your father refused to touch it. Maybe he knew something."

This place was my dad's man cave before there was such thing as a man cave. He didn't use it to run away from my mom, but she had her gardens and he had his fish house. And he did refuse to touch it: the only thing he'd added was electricity and plumbing, including a tiny bathroom in a back corner, barely big enough to turn around in.

I take a seat on my father's beloved daybed.

"Be careful," Frank says. "Mice."

I yelp and stand quickly. Frank walks over and whacks the mattress a few times with his hands. "No takers," Frank says, "not that I would blame them. It's nearly as cold inside as it is out."

The daybed has seen better days. Make that decades. The scrolling wrought-iron frame is badly rusted, and the mattress feels as if it's made of bricks. But, oh, how my dad loved to take naps out here.

Are you sleeping, Jon? my mom would yell from her gardens when we'd all returned from the beach, and the sun and fun would make us feel as if we could barely stay awake.

No, my dad would respond. *Just resting my eyes.*

This fish house was my dad's sanctuary and workshop, boat

storage and smokehouse. He listened to Cubs games on the radio while he tinkered on his first boat before the *Adie Lou,* he'd fire up his smoker—to smoke whitefish and salmon, turkey and ribs—and sit in the door all day and watch it as closely as if he were watching a newborn, adding hickory chips and his own special concoction of "juice" to keep it all moist and tender. He cleaned his fish right outside the fish house, and at night raccoons would swarm the yard looking for remnants. I'd sit on my dad's lap, and he'd pull out a flashlight and shoot it into the dark, the light paralyzing the raccoons in the midst of their midnight raids.

"There's nothing to fear in nature, Adie Lou," my dad would whisper to me. "Fear those who try to control it."

The walls in the fish house are still dotted with my father's favorite things: his prized catches from the lakes—big bass, menacing muskie, supersize salmon—vintage Helmscenes, lighted pictures of lakes and mountains from the 1950s, as well as my drawings, progressing from crayons to watercolors.

I learned a lot from my father in this tiny space, mostly that he was a good, simple man who loved me more than anything and believed I could be anything in the world.

"You haven't touched this place since your parents passed," Frank says, knocking me from my memories.

I shake my head but can't bring myself to vocalize why I couldn't change anything. How much it all meant to me. That I had to protect some sacred space as a way to protect myself from a world that was collapsing around me. Instead, I walk over to one of my father's beloved Helmscenes, a pretty picture of a pristine lake surrounded by pines, a tiny canoe in the middle of the water holding a father and daughter who are fishing. I click the knob on the side of the picture. For a moment nothing happens, but then I can hear it click and zap, coming to life, and it flickers for a moment before illuminating.

"Still works," Frank says. "Now, that's amazing. So, speaking of bright ideas, what are you thinking out here? Honeymoon suite, for sure?"

"Yep," I say. "Open concept, master bath, maybe a small kitchen if people want to make a meal and stay in... Keep the view out the back, maybe add a small porch on one side away from the patio."

"I think it will be fairly easy to retain the integrity of the place," Frank says, "but a bit costly to ensure it looks like it did back in the day. I can do some research and double-check what's allowed and isn't with the city, then double back with you on a final bid." He hesitates. "But, as you know, this place is going to need a lot of work."

"Any guesstimate?" I ask.

"I'm hoping twenty to thirty," he says, "since it already has plumbing and electricity."

"Dollars?" I ask, dizzy.

"Sure," Frank laughs. "New windows, a porch and keeping the exterior 'historically significant' will cost a pretty penny..."

"Again with the pretty pennies," I say. "Big bills are pretty, Frank. Pennies, not so much."

He laughs. "But remember you're going to get some money back, and this is going to be your high income producer. What do you expect to rent it for a night during high season?"

I think of my business plan. "Four hundred twenty-five dollars a night."

"That's 3k a week," Frank says, his bearded face now scrunched, doing quick math. "And 12k a month... With the tax rebate, you could be in the black by end of the summer."

"Really?" I ask, perking up.

"Depending on how stringent the Preservation Committee is with your renovation, especially the exterior," he adds. "They could be sticklers with the type of wood, windows, even nails that we use."

Suddenly, the Dragoon Lady's face fills my head, and I see red.

I rush out the door, around the cottage and to Frank's truck. I return with a sledgehammer.

"I didn't mean to make you mad," Frank says, his face very serious, his hands over his head. "What are you up to, Adie Lou?"

"I'm sick and tired of playing by everyone else's rules," I say, my voice rising. I think of Sonny. "I'm sick and tired of being everyone's lapdog."

I drag the sledgehammer over to the wall that separates the two rooms.

"Adie Lou," Frank says, his tone a warning. "That's one of the only walls in here. We have to keep that intact."

"Do we?" I ask.

Frank's face is a mix of amusement and astonishment, as if he's just seen a unicorn cross the road.

"I've watched enough HGTV to know what I'm doing," I say. "This is like demo day on *Fixer Upper*." I stop and look at Frank.

He shakes his head.

I pick up the sledgehammer, and the weight of it nearly topples me backward. I picture the Dragoon Lady's face on the wall—as if it were a bull's-eye—and summon all of my power, like a strongman who can pull a locomotive or a stranger who can lift a truck off someone after an accident.

The hammer hits the wall with a resounding thud, reverberating through my body, and knocks me to the concrete floor on my rear.

There is hardly a dent in the wall.

"Give it to me," Frank says with great reluctance. "We're probably going to regret this."

I sit up. "Smash the damn wall!"

Frank whacks it once, twice, three times, until there is a gaping hole in it. I jump in excitement. "Yeah, baby!"

Frank laughs at my enthusiasm. I stand and head to the wall, and begin tearing at the old lath and plaster, pulling off hunks and pieces of old wood—plaster literally crumbling around me—until I can see into the next room.

"Oops," I say to Frank, who laughs.

Frank sets down the hammer, pulls his cell from his pocket and begins to shine the light into the wall. "Wow, this is old," he says, turning to look at me, the light directly on my face.

"Watch it, Frank," I say.

He turns the light toward the wall again.

"Hey," I say. "What is that?"

"Where?"

"Down at the base of the wall."

Frank shines his light down. "I don't know," he says. "But let's find out. It's too late anyway."

He hammers repeatedly at the bottom of the wall, tearing pieces of wood away until there is a big, round hole near the floor. He shines his light back into it and says, "Here goes nothing," before sticking his hand into the wall.

"What in the world?" Frank asks.

In his hands is an old tin, about the size of a small shoebox. He walks over and sets it on the daybed.

"Want to do the honors?" he asks.

The tin is warped and rusted, no visible marks or words apparent. It takes a bit of effort to pry off the lid, but when it pops free, Frank and I both gasp. The tin is filled with a delicate stack of papers, folded and tied with a ribbon. As gently as possible, I untie the ribbon, dust particles rising into the air, the ribbon disintegrating. I gingerly open the papers.

"It's a letter," I say, staring at the beautiful cursive, the ink faded but still legible. "From a girl."

I look inside the tin, and then at Frank, my eyes wide.

"It's a time capsule," I say. "We found a time capsule."

THIRTEEN

I am sitting in the middle of my bed, while Sonny sniffs the tin. His nose covers every inch of the rusting box before moving to the items I have scattered on the comforter: a yellowed, tattered newspaper with sections missing, as if they had just disintegrated; an illustration of four women at the beach, titled *Gibson Girl*, their entire bodies covered as if they were going to church; a drawing of a girl with dreamy eyes sporting a bejeweled hat, with *Art Nouveau by Sadie* written at the bottom; and a swatch of satiny fabric.

And, of course, the letter I am holding, which I now realize is trembling in my hands. I begin to read the letter out loud to Sonny, who stops sniffing, lies down, tilts his head and lifts an ear as if he's intently listening to every word:

"May 1892

"Dear Sir or Madam:
"I embrace this opportunity to communicate a few senti-

ments to you. Papa would propose that I am being hysterical, but Mama and I would propose that female hysteria is a myth proffered by society.

"The leaves are just budding out here in Michigan, tender Sprigs underfoot, and I expect this to be my final summer at Cottage.

"My name is Sadie Collins. I am seventeen and to be married this fall, and I want to weep not from Joy but Despair. I endeavor to study at University but Papa protests. He concludes I will not be Lost to the 'Naughty Nineties' but shall be a Wife. I find myself to be in a pickle.

"I also find myself, dear Sir or Madam, to be astonished by the World. It is in change just like the trees and the lake I spy coming to Life outside the Turret. But I feel as Frozen as the fish and the peaches Papa keeps on Ice here to keep our Family prosperous.

"I conclude I am Bless'd and that too many are poor as church mice, but should I not want to be a New Woman as Henry James writes? But, at night, when I gaze beyond the Turret, I know my Stars are cross-grain'd.

"Should you find this, dear Sir or Madam, remember me fondly as the Girl in the drawing and not as the one in Leg O' Mutton sleeves. I humbly implore and petition you to care for this Cottage as if I still retired here every evening. Papa built this Cottage to be my Castle. It is now my Prison. Still, please, do not weep for me. That is not worth a button. Instead, I propose you paint your Cheeks with rouge, I Pray that you may seek your own Stars, and I endeavor that a Smile is forever upon your face.

"Yours very humbly,
Sadie"

"You wanted to look at life for yourself—but you were not al-

lowed; you were punished for your wish. You were ground in the very mill of the conventional."

—*Henry James, The Portrait of a Lady*

I am weeping uncontrollably. One fat tear plops onto the bottom of the letter, immediately crumbling the paper and the tall, stiff cursive upon it.

"No!" I wail, which startles Sonny, who stands and begins to lick my tears.

I look at the remnants of a young woman's life that was not entirely her own.

What became of her? I wonder. Did she find happiness? Was it possible to find happiness?

"I am not a victim," I say out loud to Sonny. "We are no longer victims."

Sonny barks.

I slide off the bed and gently lay the letter on the dresser in the newly painted bedroom. I glance up and see my reflection in the mirror.

"You are not conventional," I say to my face. "This cottage is your castle. Seek your own stars."

I stop and pinch my cheeks like my mom used to do before someone would take a photo, so it looked as if her face were flushed and full of life.

"Paint your cheeks with rouge," I suddenly laugh, my face as bright as the sunshine filtering into the bedroom. "And endeavor that a smile is forever upon your face."

I awake that night with a start. I have been dreaming of Sadie.

In my dream, she is trapped in the turret of the cottage, standing at the window, her breath steaming the glass. I am standing on the front lawn, staring up at her, my arm stretched out toward her. She holds her hand to the window and then, suddenly, pushes it open. I gasp. She is just a girl, her skin dewy and pale, raven hair falling from beneath a bejeweled hat. Sadie stares at me: her eyes are dreamy, hopeful, just like the one of herself in the drawing.

It is nighttime, and stars fill the sky and illuminate the earth in soft light. But in my dream, the world is split in two, like two halves of a film. My half of the world is in full color—modern-day CinemaScope—while Sadie's is in black-and-white.

Sadie steps up onto the bench seat and smiles at me. I know she is going to jump. I know I must catch her. I hold out my arms. Just as she is about to leap, a man's hand reaches for hers from behind. Sadie stops, turns, nods and steps down. As she does, her outfit changes: her hat disappears, and her body is draped in a formal dress with leg o' mutton sleeves.

I take off running toward the lake and don't stop when I reach the water. I swim far out in the lake and when I turn back toward the shore, I can see Sadie waving to me from the turret before the lights in the cottage go dim. As it does, my world changes to black-and-white, and I am swimming in the lake in the dress Sadie was just wearing. I try to swim, but the fabric is heavy. When I extend my arms, the leg o' mutton sleeves weigh me down, and I begin to sink into the lake. I scream, and that's when I wake with a start.

I wiggle my way out of bed, trying not to wake Sonny, and pad downstairs to make myself a cup of tea to calm my nerves. As the kettle heats, I walk into the living room, the cottage creaking with my every step. I stare at Darryl, half expecting him to yawn, and my eyes drift to my parents' bookshelves.

No, I think. *They wouldn't, would they?*

My heart begins to race, and I click on the light. I begin to scan the shelves, but I'm too tired and too excited, and my eyes won't focus. The spines of the books are just blurs.

"Slow down, Adie Lou," I whisper to myself.

I start again, beginning with my mother's books. My heart begins to deflate as I finish scanning the first four rows. The kettle whistles. I ignore it, but Sonny doesn't, and I can hear him jump off the bed, scamper around the bedroom upstairs, and then the click-click-click of his nails as he runs downstairs in search of me.

"Hi, buddy," I say. "Didn't mean to leave you all alone."

I give him a big kiss on the head and then pull over an old ottoman. I step onto it and begin to scan the higher rows of the bookshelves. I am about to give up when I see it.

"No way!" I say. "I can't believe it."

Henry James's *The Portrait of a Lady* stares back at me. I yank it from the shelf, make my tea and sink onto the couch, pulling a blanket over myself and Sonny, who is now settled atop my feet.

I begin to read of Isabel Archer, a young, free-spirited American woman confronting her destiny and getting "ground in the very mill of the conventional."

I wake on the couch the next morning, having again dreamed of Sadie, and I don't move until I have finished the book, stunned at the parallels in the lives of myself, Sadie and Isabel, and of the consequences unconventional women must too often face for trying to be true to themselves in a conventional world.

PART FIVE

Rule #5:
Build a Bonfire

FOURTEEN

I am walking bedroom to bedroom on the second floor analyzing the bathroom framing the contractors have completed.
The cottage's cozy bedrooms have become even more intimate
as precious square footage has been taken to add a private bath
in each room. I add up the cost in my head, and my stomach
lurches.

"What if we added a hall bath?" I ask Sonny, who's peering at
me between open slats. "Or Jack-and-Jills between four rooms?"

No, Adie Lou, I think. *This is high-end, not hostel. No one wants
to share a bathroom with a stranger. Stop second-guessing yourself.*

In some of the bedrooms, closets have disappeared to accommodate tiny, new baths, and I am holding a tape measure and
calculator trying to determine how much room—and money—I
will have left to add a wardrobe, a bed, nightstands, a TV and,
of course, two people.

"Hello?"

The Dragoon Lady! I think, my heart racing. *She's like winter. She just won't leave.*

"Hello? Hello?"

I rush down the stairs in my paint-spattered sweats, seeing red.

"If you came here to gloat—" I start, before I can see her face.

"I didn't, but I can. I'm good at it."

"Trish!" I exclaim as her face comes into view. "What are you doing here?"

"Thought I'd surprise you," she says. "Maybe even help you out a bit. And I needed a break. I'm a month ahead on billable hours. I think the whole city of Chicago is getting divorced." She looks at me. "No offense."

I laugh and then—just as quickly—start to cry, half blubbering and half laughing on her shoulder. She hugs me tightly. "Evan would make so much fun of me for doing this," I say.

"Never be ashamed to cry," Trish says. "Men think they're stronger than women because they don't. But their inability to confront and deal with their emotions is why they're ultimately, consistently weaker than we are."

I think of Nate. "You're right," I mumble into her neck.

I hold Trish at arm's length. Though it is only midmorning on a Friday, and I know she left Chicago at dawn to get here, Trish still looks dewy, fresh, hip and pretty in her skinny jeans and cute sweater.

"Is this what normal looks like?" I ask, staring at her.

"I'd say human," she says, giving me a once-over from head to foot.

"Then this is what inhuman looks like," I say.

"Poor thing," she says. "How's it going?"

Before I have a chance to respond, Sonny comes flying down the stairs and hits the wood floor with such velocity that he slides across it and directly into Trish's legs. "Who do we have here?" she asks.

After I tell her all about Sonny, she says, "Like you need two

major projects to focus on. Oh, Adie Lou. You'll never change."
Trish crouches on the floor with Sonny, who licks her face all
over. "He is a cutie." She laughs. "So, get me a cup of coffee
already."

When I start to grab her bag, Trish says, "I have another one
just like it in my car."

"Excuse me," I say, "but the inn has yet to open for business.
For now, guests carry their own bags."

"What if the owner's clothes are in the guest's bag?" Trish
asks.

"What?" I ask, my eyes growing wide. "You didn't?"

"I did," she says, "because I'm a giver." She stops and gives
Sonny another kiss. "And because you asked. I brought you an
assortment of nicer clothes from your closet, and I maybe even
bought you a few new things."

I release a *whoop!* of joy, which causes Sonny to run around
and bark, and extend my hand to help Trish off the floor.

"Not that you will ever have a use for them," she says, eyeing my current wardrobe. I lift her off the floor.

"Thank you," I say, hugging her again.

"You're welcome," she says.

"For some reason, I packed like I was just going away for a
few days," I say. "I guess I thought I'd be able to run back and
forth to Chicago anytime I wanted." I stop and gesture at myself. "I've been a bit overwhelmed, to say the least."

"Well, at least you can go out in public now," she says.

"Oh, I've been going out in public," I say. "Like this."

Trish laughs. "Now, I want to take a look around. But first,
coffee. The quad-shot Starbucks just didn't cut it this morning."

I usher Trish into the kitchen and pour her a cup of coffee.
The kitchen is a wreck: pizza boxes, ladders and tools stacked
everywhere, dishes in the sink, dog food scattered along the base-
boards, cardboard covering the floor and outlined with workers' grimy, muddy footprints.

"Place is really comin' along, Adie Lou," Trish says with a definitive nod.

I laugh. "It's a construction zone," I say.

"It's also a meat locker," she says. "It's colder than a well-digger's butt."

I laugh again. "Where did you learn that?" I ask.

"Your father," she says. "It's a big Chicago saying." Trish stops. "Do you have any heat on?"

I duck my head, my hair falling into my face. "It's set at fifty-five," I say. "I'm trying to save money."

"You won't save any money if you have to go to the ER with pneumonia." Trish lasers her eyes on me, unblinking, but then softens. "I get it. But at least get a fire going so you can keep the cottage warm. The pipes could freeze, Adie Lou. And the heat will rise, so you can just crank up your electric blanket at night." She glances at my renderings, still scattered across the kitchen counters. "I want to take a look at all your plans and all the work, but I'd like to stop my body from going into hypothermia first."

Trish grabs her coffee and heads into the living room. "Hi, Darryl," she says to the moose. "You haven't changed. Me either? Why, thank you." She kneels and looks into the giant fireplace. "Do you have any dry kindling and firewood stacked in the garage?"

"Yes," I say. "But can you believe I haven't even lit a fire here yet? It didn't even occur to me. I've been living in a deep freeze and obsessing about the cost of heating this place. I'm here…" I stop. "And yet not here."

Trish stands and walks over to me. "First thing you need to remember is to be present," she says. "Isn't that what they say in that yoga class you used to take me to? The one you dreamed of teaching one day. Be present and mindful." Trish puts a hand on my shoulder. "Be in the moment."

"Okay." I nod. "Thank you."

Trish nabs the old log carrier my parents always kept by the fire and heads toward the garage attached to the kitchen. I grab an armload of twigs, and Trish fills the carrier with firewood.

"You need to clean the garage out," Trish yells over. "Actually use it for your car rather than storage."

"Haven't had time," I call back. "And I plan on using some of that stuff in the rooms."

Trish returns carrying the logs, her body tilted dramatically to one side like an off-kilter pendulum. "How are those sticks coming along?"

I arrange the sticks in an artful pile in the monstrous fireplace grate and then show Trish my hair, locating a piece of blue paint and pulling it free.

"You look like a Smurf in Witness Protection," Trish says.

"I feel like a Smurf in Witness Protection."

I grab some newspapers from the kitchen, roll some pages into little balls and place them under the grate. I pull a fireplace lighter from a drawer in the built-in—my father always kept a reserve of lighters on the ready for fires, sparklers, rules readings—and give it a few clicks until it comes to life. I light the papers, and Trish and I wait for the sticks to catch fire.

The flames lick the sticks, sputter and go out. I try again to the same result.

"Screw this," Trish suddenly says, opening every cabinet below the bookshelves. "Aha! I knew it. Voilà!" I move closer and see a box of Duraflame logs.

Trish pulls one from the box, nestles it atop the twigs until it is sitting flat and then puts the lighter to it. The Duraflame lights immediately.

"Easy peasy," Trish says, setting two small logs atop the Duraflame.

The logs catch quickly and, within moments, the fireplace is aglow. Trish grabs her coffee and a camp blanket draped over the couch, slumps into a high-back chair and sighs. She sips her coffee, stares into the fire and says, "I know you've been going through a lot, Adie Lou, but I wanted to tell you I was wrong. My life is good, but it's in neutral. What I'm doing now will be no different than what I'm doing in ten years." She looks at me. "I admire you. You're taking risks. You're doing what you dreamed." Trish begins to sing, "That girl is on fire."

I laugh. "Thank you, Alicia Off-Keys."

"Fire," she says again.

"I got it the first time," I say. But when I look at Trish this time, her eyes are wide. She leaps out of her chair, the blanket flying. "No! Really! You're on fire!"

"What?" I ask, before turning to follow her gaze.

Smoke, thick and heavy, is billowing out of the fireplace and into the cottage. I take a step back, grab a book off the shelf and begin waving it back and forth to clear the air. "Open a window!" I yell at Trish.

The smoke dissipates enough for me to catch a glimpse of the entire fireplace opening. Fire is shooting up the chimney.

"The flue's on fire!" I yell, grabbing Sonny. "Call 911"

Frank rushes through the patio door and into the kitchen. "What's going on?" he asks. He sees the fire. "We need to suffocate it," he says, immediately shutting the flue. "Do you have baking soda?"

"In my toothpaste," I say unhelpfully.

Frank rolls his eyes, grabs the log carrier and runs out the door. He is back a few seconds later, huffing and puffing, the carrier filled with sand. He tosses it on the fire, and it goes out, just as I hear the sirens of firetrucks.

I run outside with Trish just as two men run up my yard. I expect to see the cottage engulfed in flames, but there is no fire shooting from the top of the chimney.

"We got the flue shut and fire out," Frank calls to the men.

The two men hurriedly put up a ladder as another truck arrives, and men surround the house.

"Why aren't they using a hose?" I ask Frank.

"They're going to use a chimney kit," Frank says. "It's a dry chemical extinguishing powder."

"Adie Lou, are you okay?"

I turn. "Scooter?" I ask. "What are you doing here?"

"Small town," he says. "I'm a volunteer fireman. What happened?"

"Chimney fire, out of nowhere."

"When was the last time you had the flue inspected?" he asks. "You probably have an insane buildup of creosote."

"I don't know," I say. "No clue."

"I know a great flue guy," Scooter says. "I'll have him stop by."

"Sounds romantic," I say. Scooter laughs as a fireman gives a thumbs-up and yells, "All okay!"

I will myself not to cry by petting Sonny. Trish stands behind Scooter and catches my eye. *Who's this?* she mouths. *So cute!*

Scooter turns as if he can hear her. "Hi," he says. "Scott Stevens. Although Adie Lou calls me Scooter."

"Hi, I'm Trish, Adie Lou's dearest friend who's never mentioned you to me her entire life," she says. "It's nice to meet you."

Scooter nods. "It's nice to meet you, too," he says, turning back to me. "If you need any extra help here, Adie Lou, let me know. I'd be happy to lend a hand."

"Thank you," I say. "I'm doing okay right now."

"Really?" Trish asks loudly, motioning to the chaos around her with both arms.

"Well, I'm around," Scooter says. "And I'll let you know after I take a look at your boat."

"Thanks," I say, "for everything."

"Bye, Adie Lou," Scooter says. "Bye, Trish."

After the fire department is gone and Frank returns to the fish house, Trish and I grab the remaining luggage and then clean up the fireplace. We look up at each other and burst into laughter. "You look just like Mary Poppins!" we say at the same time. Trish takes a seat on the floor, already looking exhausted, light-years away from the way she appeared just a couple of hours ago. I know she now understands all I've been going through.

"Aren't you glad you came?" I ask.

Trish says, "Yes," while shaking her head no.

"Is it too early for lunch?" I ask.

"Yes, but it's not too early for a drink," Trish replies. "Is there a place around here?"

"It may be winter, but it's still a resort town," I say, "which means there's *always* an open bar somewhere."

We wash our faces, put on some makeup and change. I wear a pretty turtleneck, jeans and a pink leather jacket Trish bought for me. I put an exhausted Sonny in his crate in the bedroom, and he falls immediately asleep after a morning of unexpected excitement.

Trish stops to grab her coat on the way out the door and notices the Cottage Rules sign.

"I forgot about this," she says. "Your parents used to make everyone say it before they could come in the cottage, right? They lit those sparklers. It was so cute."

I smile.

Trish points her finger at Rule #5—*Build a Bonfire*—and cocks her head at me. "I think you already checked this one off the list for the day."

FIFTEEN

"You ladies want another round?"

"Yes," Trish and I respond at the same time, before bursting into laughter.

We are sitting at a small table at Bobber's, a dive bar that sits at the end of the dock overlooking the harbor. In the summer, the scene is majestic: the sun on the water, the town in the near distance, boats zipping by. Bands play on the dock, boats tie up and order drinks, people dance and jump into the lake and, at sunset, howl at the moon.

In the winter, people sit in the dark and drink. The lake resembles a frozen pond, and the wind rattles the tiny bar as if it were made of papier-mâché.

It is early afternoon, clouds are rolling in over the lake, and it is nearly pitch-black.

A waitress I know only as Doris, who has been working at Bobber's since I was a teenager, brings us two more glasses of white wine. Along with her not-so-customery customer service,

Doris is known for her eyebrows, which resemble caterpillars, and the shocking color of her hair.

"Her hair is dyed steakhouse hostess black," my dad used to say.

"Want me to add a little ketchup to your white wine so you can call it rosé?" Doris asks with a twinkle in her eye, refusing to give up her incredulity after we'd initially ordered our afternoon pink drink of choice. She'd laughed so hard at us at first that she lapsed into a coughing jag that could only be fixed by heading outside into the cold to smoke a cigarette. When she returned, Doris was none too happy when we opted for white wine rather than vodka or whiskey.

"We're good," Trish says.

"Don't get too carried away," Doris says, rolling her eyes.

"She's a treat," Trish says as Doris walks away. "Real warm and fuzzy."

Saugatuck memorabilia fills Bobber's, every square inch of wall space covered. Pennants and fishing gear dangle from the old wooden rafters, and vintage bar signs fill the space. A sign over Trish's head reads, "There's One in Every Bar," and features a jackass ordering a drink. A plaque over my head states, "If You Sprinkle When You Tinkle, Be a Sweetie and Wipe the Seatie."

"Cheers," I say, lifting my glass. "Thank you for coming."

"Back atcha," Trish says. She takes a sip of her wine and makes a face—it's not the expensive bottles she's used to drinking. In fact, it's not even as good as the green beer we drank in college. She looks at me closely. "I feel the same way you did when you refused to sign the papers at RL."

I cock my head at her and take a sip of wine. "What do you mean?"

"Guilty," she says. "Not truly understanding or sympathetic with all you're going through. This is a lot of change in your life, Adie Lou. This is a lot of stress." She stops. "I don't think I could handle everything you're dealing with. I'm too used to my life the way it is."

"Thank you," I say, "but I don't feel like I'm handling things very well."

"You are," Trish says, her voice filled with pride. "You're going to pull this off, you know. Your inn is going to be a huge success. I can feel it. Do you know what you're going to name it yet? Or are you going to be like those new age parents who need to see their baby born first before they can put a name to its being."

I pull out my phone. "Hold on," I say, as I watch the site on my phone fail to load. "One bar." I take a sip of wine as the page finally loads. "Voilà!"

I hold out my cell, which features a template of what will eventually be the home page for my inn.

"'The Summer Cottage,'" Trish reads. "'Where the Only Rule Is to Leave Your Troubles at the Door.'" She looks at me, a huge smile on her face. "This is beautiful. It's so...*you.*"

"Every room is going to be themed around one of my family's summer cottage rules," I say excitedly, my voice rising, before launching into my ideas about women's empowerment weekends.

"I think you're onto something, Adie Lou," Trish says, her voice matching my excitement. "I mean, I know your inn will be gorgeous, and you'll make it warm and inviting, but I meet so many women who have given their whole lives—their entire hearts and souls—to others, from husbands and jobs to raising children and caring for aging parents. And too many end up at our age without ever really knowing who we are or what makes us happy. Society too often treats mature women as though we have an expiration date. I see so many of my clients end up in therapy to try and deal with an end result they often didn't create, and they seek help because they feel as if they're wrong." Trish takes a sip of wine, her eyes darting around the bar. "But what they really need is empowerment. What they need is a sense of self. What they need is nurturing. What they need is hope."

My heart races with her words of encouragement.

"What if I were to recommend clients who might need a

week of empowerment? And asked some of my attorney friends to do the same?" Trish asks in a rush.

"Isn't that a conflict of interest?"

"No," Trish says. "To be honest, once the papers are signed, I usually stay in touch with my clients because they are often lost. You could be onto a bigger idea than you think."

For a moment, I forget about the chimney fire, the insane amount of work I have left to do, the Dragoon Lady, my diminishing savings account and let myself feel unabashedly excited.

"You ladies need another round?"

I hear a gravelly voice and think it's Doris again, but when I look up a man in full-on *Duck Dynasty* camouflage who looks as if he's been drinking for days is standing at our table.

"No, thank you," Trish says, lifting her glass. "Still good."

Trish and I resume our conversation, trying to ignore the man, whose beard is nearly touching the table.

"What are you drinking?"

"White wine," I say. Trish kicks me under the table.

"White wine!" the man bellows toward the bar, before suddenly taking a seat next to me, his legs now pressing against mine. "Name's Jerry. Friends call me Buck, 'cause I get one ever' time I hunt. See my buddy over there at the bar? We got two bucks this mornin'. Celebratin' 'cause we'll be eatin' some good venison."

"That's great, Jerry," Trish starts.

"Buck," he interrupts.

"Buck," Trish continues with a faux smile. "But my friend and I haven't seen each other in a while, and we'd like to catch up." She smiles even bigger. "Thank you for understanding."

"I would think two women sitting alone together drinking in a bar on a weekday afternoon want some companionship," Buck continues, nudging me over in the booth with his behind. "Rude not to accept a drink." He motions with his hand for his friend to join. When he just sits down by Trish, she takes her wine and dumps it in his lap.

"Oh, my gosh," Trish says, a shocked look on her face. "I didn't see you there. You're camouflaged."

I bust out in laughter, spewing wine across the table.

Buck stands, nearly knocking over the table. "You ladies got a problem?" he says.

Trish stands. "I do," she says. "When I say we don't want to be bothered, I mean it."

"That's why you two are alone," Buck says, slamming his fist on the table. "You're as cold and icy as the weather. You don't like men."

"No," I say. "You don't like women." I stop and turn to him until his beard is brushing my body. "And I do like men. I just prefer them with teeth and a respect for women."

Buck mutters an expletive under his breath at me, and I follow Trish's lead: I toss my wine into his lap.

Both men turn and stomp out of Bobber's.

Trish and I look at each other, a stunned look on our faces, the reality of what just transpired settling in. Before we can utter a word, Doris totters over and says, "You ladies okay?"

We nod.

"Sorry about all that, but you handled those rednecks better than anyone else ever has," she says. "Drinks on me!" She quickly returns with two shots of whiskey. "But if I'm payin', you're drinkin' somethin' I pick. Strong liquor for strong women. Cheers!"

Trish and I clink our tumblers and down our shots, before wandering over to the jukebox.

"Got a quarter?" I ask Trish. She fumbles in her pocket and hands me one.

"G-24," I say, as the quarter jostles around and the music starts. "'This One's for the Girls' by Martina McBride," I whoop, the whiskey warming my blood and making the lights in the bar even brighter.

Trish grabs me, and we dance across the bar floor, acting as if we're wearing boots and cowboy hats, acting as if we're as young as the day and don't have a care in the world.

SIXTEEN

"We love you!"

Trish is blowing kisses at the driver of the Saugatuck Shuttle, a service that transports the elderly and the drunk around town for a dollar. Neither of us had two dollars combined—after inserting our dollars and spare change into the jukebox—so the young woman driving the shuttle let us ride for free thinking, I'm sure, from the way we're acting and dressed that we're resorters just blowing off steam on a week off from work. When she stops on Lakeshore Drive in front of the cottage, however, she does a double take.

"Thank you!" Trish yells.

"Sssshhhh!" I say, pulling out my cell and clicking on the flashlight. "It's only 6 p.m." I can see the Dragoon Lady fielding calls from unhappy neighbors, smiling, licking her lips and drinking sherry like a cartoonish Batman villain.

"Sorry," Trish yells, her finger over her lips, thinking she's being quiet.

We stumble up the steep steps, holding on to one another. "I haven't been this drunk this early since college," I say.

"I haven't been drunk this early since my firm's holiday party," Trish say. "It's like the Walk of the Dead. But way less fun."

We laugh, our voices booming in the cold, quiet, winter's night. I head directly upstairs to take Sonny outside, while Trish rushes to the bathroom.

"We have the same idea!" she yells to Sonny.

When I return, Trish is opening another bottle of wine.

"You think that's a good idea?" I ask.

Trish looks around the demolished kitchen. "Think this is a good idea?" she asks.

"Open it," I say, filling Sonny's bowl. "I need to have fun!"

"I need to have some food," Trish says. "The bowl of peanuts didn't really soak up the two bottles of wine. What do you want to do for dinner?"

"Hold on," I say, picking up my phone and nodding to the pizza boxes on the floor. "I have them on speed dial."

"Want a fire?" Trish says, her voice filled with sarcasm. She heads into the living room, slumps into a chair and takes a healthy sip of wine. "What a day."

"I've had a lot of crazy days since I've been here," I say. Although I told her about my arrival experience, the Dragoon Lady, the skyrocketing renovation budget, the backbreaking work, and all the uncertainty at the bar, I suddenly rush upstairs yelling, "I can't believe I forgot to show you this."

I return with Sadie's letter from the time capsule.

Trish reads the letter, her eyes softening as she does. "This is so beautiful and heartbreaking," she says. "We feel as if we've come so far as women, but so many things have remained the same in society."

Trish stares into the empty fireplace for a second, then suddenly stands and walks over to the Cottage Rules sign. She points at Rule #5. "Fire!" she says, her voice booming off the beams and vibrating throughout the cottage. "Build a bonfire!"

"What are you talking about?" I ask.

"We need to build a bonfire, a ceremonial one," Trish says, her eyes fixed and unblinking, gesturing confidently as if she's in court trying to convince a judge. "This place needs to be smudged."

"I already tried that," I say, taking a sip of wine, Sonny curled up on a blanket by my feet. "Didn't work."

"What happened?"

"Wind blew it out on the front porch," I say. "I think that's telling."

"See!" Trish cries, causing Sonny to sit up and tilt his head. "Bad juju!"

"This cottage doesn't have bad juju," I say. "It's always been filled with love."

Trish walks over and pats my head like I'm Sonny. "It has been," she says, "but not the past few years. Your divorce, the loss of your parents, the renovations, the Preservation Committee, the budget..." She stops and looks around. "It's filled with ghosts. And we need to show them the door. Now, where's your smudge stick? I know my new age girl has one somewhere."

I stand and return a few seconds later with my smudge stick of sage, an abalone shell and a feather.

"Atta girl," Trish says. "Now, where are your essential oils?"

I dash upstairs and return with my kit.

"I think we need to add some of those to the sage," Trish says, "to really do the trick."

"When did you get into all of this?" I ask, setting my kit down on an end table. "I thought you were too logical for oils and smudging."

"You taught me well," Trish says. "I can't sleep without lavender in my diffuser, and I haven't been sick in a year since I started dabbing tea tree on my nostrils every day." She stops and looks at my case. "That said, my collection of oils isn't as big as yours. You win."

"Nate used to call all of this BS," I say, opening my kit filled with small bottles of oils. "He thought it was nonsense."

"And that's why you're onto something here," Trish says. "Women are sick and tired of being told by men what's appropriate or logical. I mean, they've had control of everything for a long time, and how's that worked out?"

I laugh and look through my oils.

"Okay," I start, pulling out my alphabetized oils to read their labels. "How about a little allspice to strengthen our will and determination in gaining our objectives? A touch of amber to protect us from ill will and bad luck. Some balsam fir to break up negative conditions. A little bergamot for success and money, and some camphor for harmony." I continue my search. "Chamomile attracts good luck and money, and—Oh!—champa will bring balance and clarity and help create a calming and sacred atmosphere." I laugh. "How about some cinnamon orange to enhance success, love and lust."

"That never hurts," Trish says.

"Geranium rose will break all hexes and is perfect for blessing new businesses," I continue. "Lavender—your favorite, Trish—brings tranquility and peace at home, and I'll also add a little violet for peace and calm and to protect against evil. It changes luck!"

"I think the sage is too wet to catch fire now," Trish laughs. "Okay, what do we do now?"

I grab a lighter and hold it to the sage. After a few tries, it begins to smoke. I use the feather to waft smoke over our bodies. "I'm shocked we didn't burst into flames considering all the liquor in us."

Trish coughs dramatically as smoke wafts around her face, making her resemble an apparition. "I think a bad spirit already escaped from my body," she says. "I think I need a drink." She grabs her wine and begins to walk.

"No," I say. "We have to walk around the cottage counter-clockwise. And chant."

I begin to walk toward the living room, and Trish puts a hand on my shoulder.

"Air, fire, water, earth," I chant. "Cleanse, dismiss, dispel."

After a few times, Trish catches on and chants with me in between sips of wine. We make our way around the first floor—Sonny in tow—before moving to the second, then the renovations in the attic and, finally, the turret.

"What about the fish house?" Trish asks. "Where you found the time capsule."

We head outside and into the fish house. When I enter, the sage bursts into flame.

"I'm freaking out," Trish says. "Why did it do that?"

"It's working," I say. "A lot of history—good and bad—in here."

As we walk, the sage calms and begins to smolder.

Take that, Dragoon Lady, I think.

We head back into the kitchen, and I extinguish the sage.

"We're not done yet," Trish says. "It's time for my part."

I cock my head like Sonny does.

"I told you that you need to purge," she says. "We're having a bonfire."

"It's too cold," I say. "Ground is too wet."

"No, it isn't," she says. "Your dad still has that firepit just off the patio. Let's use it one last time before you cover it in concrete. And we have lots of Duraflame logs. I'll clean the snow out of it and grab some sticks. You pull things from the cottage with bad energy that need to be burned, or items you need to purge."

I look at Trish, but she just stares at me, unblinking. I crack immediately. "Okay," I say.

"Good," she says, taking a slug of wine before grabbing her coat.

I jog upstairs—every light is on after our smudging ceremony—and head directly to the bedroom that Nate and I used to share. I haven't been able to sleep in here since I returned. I look around the room, memories flooding my mind.

I can't sleep, Nate used to say. *It's too quiet.* He would plug in a white noise machine that would mimic the sounds of crickets or lapping waves.

Open a window, I would say. *You can hear the same thing for real.*

I walk over to Nate's side of the bed, always farthest away from the door, a preferred placement that always irked me. I open the nightstand and inside is the little white noise machine he loved. I tuck it in the crook of my arm and move to the closet.

A few of his clothes remain. I don't know why he left them. Perhaps, they contained bad memories for him, too.

There are some old jeans, a few flannel shirts, some sweaters stacked on the shelf above the rack. I begin to rifle through the hanging clothes, and my heart stops: Nate's beloved YALE sweatshirt.

The ironic thing is, Nate didn't attend Yale. He received his bachelor's, master's and PhD from two other top private colleges and universities. But I can still remember the Saturday morning that he walked into our kitchen in Chicago wearing this sweatshirt. I thought he was playing a joke on me, or was giving it to a colleague, but he wore it to coffee and began to wear it regularly on weekends when we'd head out for coffee, brunch or an afternoon glass of wine. My dad ribbed Nate when he wore it to Saugatuck the first time, but that didn't deter Nate: he wore it to the local coffeehouse, and I realized he loved the attention he received by wearing it, the stolen glances and admiring whispers, the silent adoration from total strangers.

I yank the sweatshirt off the hanger, which spins in a circle, jangling loudly.

I walk out of the bedroom and into the room I've been using. There, on the dresser, is the letter from the Dragoon Lady. I grab it and begin to head outside but stop and head to another bedroom. I stick my head inside the room and see a piece of the old wood floor from the closet that is being turned into a bathroom. Next to it is a wallpaper sample I am considering, one of Michigan lighthouses.

Something old, something new, I think. I grab both and finally head downstairs.

When I step onto the patio, I see a huge fire. Trish hasn't just started a bonfire, she's started an inferno.

"I don't want the fire department back again today," I say.

"Settle down, Adie Lou. I've got it under control. This is a ceremonial cleansing bonfire, so it has to be rip-roaring."

Trish's face is red, and the fire makes her look almost tribal.

"What did you gather?" she asks, finishing her glass of wine. Her words are now a bit slurry, and it sounds as if she just said, *Whadjougrabber?*

I show her, and she tells me to take a seat in one of the two iron chairs she's pulled in front of the fire.

"Just speak from the heart and tell me what these represent and why you need to let them go," Trish says. "When you are ready, say 'I release you. I am done.'"

I start with the noise machine, which simply melts in the flames. I move to the wallpaper and wood, which burn easily. I hold up the sweatshirt in front of the fire, and I can see Nate's face clearly.

"When I asked you about why you bought this and why you wore it, you told me, 'It's comfortable.' I stared at you, waiting for you to laugh, to tell me the truth. But you didn't. And that's when I realized I was married not only to a shallow man who sought attention but also a liar. You will never know who you are because you do not know your true authentic self. You will never know true love because you only see the surface and don't love yourself.

"I release you," I say, "I am done." I toss in the sweatshirt, and the fire happily consumes it.

Finally, I hold the Dragoon Lady's letter near the fire. "You do not control my destiny or the destiny of my summer cottage," I say. "I acknowledge the importance you see in your work and actions, and I hope you will acknowledge the importance you see in my work and actions. Like the Phoenix, this cottage will be regenerated and born again. Like the Phoenix, this cottage will obtain new life by rising from the ashes of its predecessor.

"I release you," I say, tossing the letter into the fire. "I am done."

The fire leaps higher.

For a moment, Trish and I sit in silence, the fire crackling, warming our bodies on this frigid night.

"Dang, girl," Trish suddenly yells. "That was some powerful stuff!"

Trish stands, grabs my hands, and we begin to dance around the bonfire, howling at the moon.

We stop when we see a young pizza deliveryman standing on the patio, the box trembling in his hands, his face etched in fright and confusion.

"No one answered the door," he says. The fire illuminates the peach-fuzz on his baby face, the too-big hat on his head, the bangs in his eyes.

He takes a big step back, a horrified look on his face, and Trish runs inside to grab her purse. As she signs the receipt, she says, "There's a big tip in there for keeping your mouth shut. Can you do that?"

The young man nods his head furiously and then takes off running. We can hear his tires squeal on Lakeshore Drive.

"I'm starving," Trish says. "And I need another glass of wine. Smudging and purging is exhausting."

SEVENTEEN

"My head," Trish groans, wandering into a bedroom I am painting.

I shoot her a sad look and shake my head, a trick I learned from my father when I'd oversleep.

"Thank you, Dr. Guilt," Trish says. "I need some water, coffee, aspirin and a greasy breakfast. Stat."

I put my paintbrush in an oversize baggy and zip it shut to keep it from drying out—leaving Sonny asleep on the tarp—before grabbing Trish's hand and leading her down the stairs, where I gather water, coffee and aspirin for her. "I only play a doctor on TV," I say, pulling a carton of eggs and a pack of bacon from the refrigerator.

Trish laughs and rubs her head. "That'll do," she says, downing her aspirin and a glass of water, before taking a big gulp of coffee. A huge smile lights up her face. "What a night. We had fun, didn't we?"

I match her smile. "We did. I did." I walk over and hug her from behind. "Thank you."

"Why aren't you hungover?" she asks with a slight groan.

I pull a mug from a cabinet and fill it with coffee. "I am, albeit not as much as you. You pretty much had that last bottle of wine yourself."

"Oops," she laughs.

"You know, despite my hangover, I actually feel…better," I say. "More centered. More focused. More in tune."

"Smudging, cleansing, two bottles of wine and a few shots of whiskey will do that," Trish says. She pulls up a stool and watches me fry the bacon and eggs. I put some bread in the toaster, and grab some butter and jam from the refrigerator.

"You've always taken such good care of people," Trish says, her voice suddenly emotional. "It's nice to see you take care of yourself for once."

"Thank you," I say, preparing her plate. "You mean, like now?"

Trish laughs. "I'm serious," she says. "Few would have the courage to do what you're doing."

Trish grabs a piece of toast and a fork and then completely devours her breakfast before I have even taken three bites. As she grabs another cup of coffee, she notices my renderings for the cottage. "Finally," she says. "I can see what you have planned from top to bottom."

I walk over and stand beside her, pointing this way and that, explaining what Frank and I have changed since I did these. Trish listens intently while inhaling a second piece of toast, this time smothered in homemade blueberry jam from a local orchard.

"I have some ideas," Trish says. "Promise you won't get mad, okay?"

I narrow my eyes.

"Hear me out," she says. "I've been in more luxury homes

and mini-mansions than you can shake a stick at. I've held meetings at the finest hotels, restaurants and country clubs. I've seen a lot, Adie Lou, especially how people that spend money expect to be treated." Trish stops. "First impressions are critical. Word of mouth can make or break a new business. If people love a place, they'll not only return but they'll talk it up to everyone they know. I'm just worried that you can't see the forest for the trees right now. You're in survival mode."

Trish grabs her coffee. "So, you're planning to make breakfast in here, right?"

I nod and show her my kitchen plan that not only includes commercial-grade appliances but also expands the current island into a huge L-shape that extends into and replaces the little breakfast table my parents used.

"I like this," she says. "And food will be served in the dining room?"

I nod again.

"What about when the weather's nice?"

"I haven't thought about that."

Trish walks to the patio door. "What if you extended this patio, really tricked it out? This could be your outdoor yoga patio!" she says, her voice escalating. She hurriedly pulls on her rubber boots sitting by the door and walks outside, excitedly kicking snow off the patio with her feet. "You could surround it with shrubs—make an area private from the kitchen and the fish house—maybe put a fountain on the wall and a large Buddha on one side. It would be perfect."

I look at the space as it is now and has been recently —the concrete cracked from the constantly shifting ground and extreme temperature shifts, moss covering it in the spring and fall, the DIY outdoor kitchen my father tried to build.

"Didn't you say that you have to take all this out anyway to run a gas line?" Trish asks. "Why not just make it fabulous?"

I once attended a celebratory party in East Hampton given by the CEO of one of my firm's previous clients after we'd won a Clio award, and the inn where I stayed had the most stunning yoga space in its garden.

"You know, I always wanted to teach yoga. I dreamed of having my own studio," I say, as much to myself as to her. "That's why I crammed in 200 hours over busy weekends while everyone else was still sleeping to get certified. Nate thought it was silly, but it was important to me."

"You can envision it," Trish says, breaking my thoughts. "That's good." She hesitates. "Because I have more ideas." She comes back inside, knocking the snow off of her boots on the rug, grabs my renderings along with my hand and drags me outside. We head toward the back of the cottage, away from the kitchen, trudging through ice-packed snow. "So, the downstairs is essentially broken into two primary areas. You have the entryway, living room and kitchen on one side separated by a long hallway dividing the dining room and laundry room from a first-floor bedroom and bath your parents planned to use when they got much older." Trish stops and looks at me. "I'm so sorry about your parents, Adie Lou. I know you thought they'd live forever."

I nod, and I can still see them here. This was *their* sacred ground before cancer and heartbreak.

"They're still here," Trish says, and I believe her because I can feel them beside me, every day. She squeezes my hand, then squats and lays out a rendering on the ground. "This is going to serve as your owner's suite, right?"

I continue to nod.

"That makes perfect sense," she says. "You're separated from guests so you can have your privacy. You're on the first floor so you can start breakfast service early without disrupting anyone. But…" Trish stands. "You forgot about guests. Where will Evan stay when he visits in the summer? You don't want to sacrifice a room rental, do you?"

VIOLA SHIPMAN

My eyes widen. "Oh, my God," I say. "I never even considered that."

"My suggestion is to enlarge the space back here—blow out the back of the cottage—add another bedroom for Evan...and me!" Trish laughs and turns toward the woods—dense with pines and sugar maples—and says, "I'd add a sunroom back here that is purely your space, a retreat that allows you to regroup, maybe doubles as an office."

"Cha-ching!" I say, acting as if I'm operating a cash register. "Do I look like a Kardashian?"

"Better," Trish says. "Your face moves."

I laugh. "Seriously, how much will all of this cost?"

"A lot," she says. "But, Adie Lou, I'd rather see you spend the money and get it right than have to retrofit everything later on. How expensive would that be, if you had to shut down your inn for a few months to renovate yet again?"

Her words hit me hard. "I never considered that either," I say. "I'll ask Frank. I like your ideas."

"Good!" she says, picking the rendering off the ground and again grabbing my hand. "I've got more!"

She nearly skips as she pulls me around to the front of the cottage, the wind off the lake growing stronger. "Cold air is sobering me up and clearing my head," she says. "Bad news for you!"

She continues, "Okay, the dining room can remain as it is, but..." She stops and gestures to the wide, front porch. "Look at that porch! It's perfect for summer and fall breakfasts. Add a few café tables, leave that swing...it couldn't get any cuter." She turns and scans the lawn and the lake. "I'd put up a few cute, little signs that say BEACH! with arrows to direct guests. Oh, and I'd add a couple of picnic tables on the front lawn. People can order a pizza and picnic right here." She stops. "This is a ten-million-dollar view, Adie Lou. People want to come here and sigh. What was the first rule of the cottage?"

"Leave your troubles at the door," I say, a smile overtaking my face.

"Your parents knew something very important," she says. "They knew the secret to life. That's rare." Trish turns to me. "You do, too. It just took you a while." She hugs me, and when she lets go, the wind nearly rips the renderings from her hands.

"Let's go inside," I suggest.

Sonny greets us at the door. Trish and I kick off our shoes and continue the tour, going from room to room on the second floor and attic, discussing design and how much to charge based on views and size of the rooms.

"You're also going to have to invest in some pampering and marketing products," Trish suggests. "Cushy robes and slippers in every room, nice bath products like L'Occitane, coffee mugs with the inn's logo on them, guest books with restaurant names and numbers, things to do and places to go."

My heart begins to race.

"And I'd add small laundries on each floor to ease turnover of the rooms as well as ease for housekeepers."

My eyes widen, and my heartbeat quickens even further.

"You have considered that, right?"

I shake my head, and the unfinished attic space begins to spin. "I didn't even budget for help, much less the other stuff," I say. "What was I thinking?"

"Sweetie," Trish says, her voice soft, like when I talk to Sonny. "You're going to need some part-time help to clean rooms and bathrooms, do the laundry, help in the kitchen. You weren't expecting to do it all yourself, were you?"

This time, I nod. That's exactly what I'd thought.

"You were on an adrenaline rush," Trish says, "and that's okay...for a while. Now, it's time to slow down and be very calculated."

"Any pointers on hiring?" I ask, my mind racing. "I've been

on lots of hiring committees, but this time I'm calling the shots on my own."

"Go with your gut," Trish says.

"Gee, thanks."

"Seriously," she says. "I've hired people who are perfect on paper, or who have told the most compelling stories, even though my gut has told me otherwise." Trish stops. "You're smart, Adie Lou. You've met lots of people and been through a lot in your life. You can tell who's full of—well, let's just say beans—and who's not."

She continues. "You're in a different situation here. You'll be hiring part-time workers, so many will be coming and going. And you can't afford to offer health or retirement at this time to anyone."

"You think?" I ask with more than a hint of sarcasm.

"But let that be a long-term goal perhaps," Trish says. "You might find an older woman, who is divorced like you, and wants a new start. Or you might find someone who has never gotten a break his or her whole life, and this is the place that provides it. If you find that person, hold on to her. I've found workplace loyalty and longevity is key to corporate success and is just as beautiful as lifelong friendships like ours."

"Thank you," I say.

"Do you mind if I take a look at your business plan?" Trish asks. "I know a lot about them."

We head downstairs and into the kitchen, where I pull up Excel on my laptop. Trish pulls up a barstool and hunches over the computer.

"Uh-huh... Okay... I see," Trish mutters to herself.

"What?" I ask. "What do you see?"

Trish looks at me, her face pained. "You're not going to break even this year," she says. "Too much money going out, uncertainty over filling rooms, total budget still in question."

I groan, as she pulls up the calculator on my laptop. She taps furiously for nearly a minute, jotting notes on a pad of paper I have sitting on the counter.

"But," Trish continues, "what if I went back to Nate and pushed him on the sale of the Lake Forest home."

"No," I say, my voice rising. "I can't do that. We had an agreement. It's not fair."

"Nothing's fair in love and war," Trish says. "And divorce is both."

"He probably did me a favor anyway," I say. "He just made the inevitable happen a bit more quickly."

"He cheated on you, Adie Lou," Trish says, her voice fiery. "That's not doing someone a favor. That's being a selfish jerk. They haven't gotten the final papers back to me anyway." She looks at me closely, and I begin to interrupt. "Hear me out," Trish says, wagging a finger. "Receiving half of the money from the sale of that home instead of a third will be much better for you overall than receiving monthly alimony until Evan graduates. You will get a lot more money, and you would be able to do all of the work you want on the cottage without taking out a loan. You'd also have some cash on hand to get through this first year. I think a judge would look very favorably on this arrangement. In essence, you're walking away with what's legally yours."

My heart is beating a mile a minute. "But what if Nate and his attorney disagree? What if they fight us on this?"

"Oh, they will," Trish says, "but they won't have any legal standing." She stands and puts her hand around my back. "How much will you see Nate after Evan graduates?"

"Rarely," I say.

"Exactly," she says. "Don't let pride get in the way. Let me do what needs to be done, okay?"

"Okay," I say.

Trish hugs me. "And now, let me help you do what needs to be done. Where should I start painting?"

We head to the second floor, Trish grabs a brush, I turn on an '80s station and we begin to paint, stopping on occasion to dance when a Wham! or Madonna song plays.

As the sunlight fades on a winter Saturday, Trish and I—exhausted but happy—order some Chinese food and plop down in front of the TV. I click on the television and scroll through the guide as I slurp a box of lo mein with cheap chopsticks.

"Oh, my God!" I yell, causing Trish to drop the egg roll she's eating. "No! Look what's on!"

Trish looks up and laughs. "It's meant to be," she says.

I turn up the volume, and we watch *Ice Castles*, reciting lines out loud as we slurp noodles, and I—for a brief moment—am just a college girl again watching movies with her best friend in our pajamas.

PART SIX

Rule #6:
Go Rock Hunting

EIGHTEEN

The sun is coming up over the woods, illuminating the natural creek that is formed when the winter snow begins to melt and the spring rains come. I glance at the thermometer—upper thirties and abundant sunshine.

A gift from Mother Nature, I think. *Thank you.*

Winter is not over, I know, though the weather forecasters are predicting a warmer than average March. I suddenly picture the meteorologists on TV.

Why are female meteorologists forced to wear cocktail dresses on air, while men can wear suits? I suddenly think. *Why are women often held to different standards than men although they do the same jobs?*

I think of the time—at a holiday party years ago—when a drunken male coworker, ten years my junior, same job title, fewer accounts, bragged about the holiday bonus he was receiving.

"Yours must be huge," he slurred, "considering you pulled in a Clio this year."

I hadn't received a bonus.

"Do you mind if I ask how much you make?" I asked, knowing he likely wouldn't remember the conversation in the morning. When he happily blurted a figure that was roughly 30 percent higher than mine, I left the party in a rage and arranged a meeting with my boss the first day back in the offices.

"But you have a family. Your husband makes a wonderful living," he told me, as if that were a rational explanation.

When I demanded equal pay, my boss offered a 3 percent increase and said he'd "try" to catch up my pay. He never did. And my coworker was promoted ahead of me, time and time again.

I stare at the ribbon of water sparkling like tumbling diamonds. My mom loved this little stream, the way it appeared out of nowhere and meandered through the woods, down the dune and into the big lake.

"That's the difference you can make in this world," she would always tell me. "The big lake wouldn't be grand without all of the tributaries that feed it. Sometimes, you don't know the difference you make when you're going it alone."

I understood what she meant but regret not asking her more stories about her life. I regret not quitting my job when I was given a small raise, for not going to HR, for not doing *anything* but silently accepting this is the way the world works for women.

Don't live with regret, I can hear my mother saying to me.

Decaying leaves and pieces of white birch bark float quickly down the little stream like boats, and as the sun angles more, I can see directly to the bottom. Sand, rocks and colorful stones compose the creek bed. Sandy soil is the hallmark of west Michigan's ground. When my mom would garden, each shovelful of earth was half soil, half sand. And nearly every shovel turn would unearth a rock or stone that had been deposited at some point over the years from the shoreline.

I smile. Besides gardening, my mom's passion was collecting rocks and stones from Lake Michigan's shoreline. I grab a cup of coffee and pull a coat on over my robe as I head out the front door and onto the screened porch. I set my coffee onto an old log my parents used as an end table and yank down the plastic sheets I still have hanging over the screens. A cold breeze ruffles the screens, and they seem to sigh in happiness at their newfound freedom. I grab my coffee and take a seat on the barn-red glider.

"Hello!" I say into the morning air as the cold of the glider makes its way through my coat, robe and pajamas. "Still March in Michigan."

I take a sip of coffee and exhale, just as the screens had done. My breath stops in front of my face, freeze-framed for just a moment, then—*poof!*—it's gone.

The lakeshore is silent this morning, muffled by the snow that remains. But the cold air makes any noise sound even louder, from the chirp of the cardinals to the squirrels foraging on frozen ground. The lake is already beginning to unfreeze, and a ring of blue-green rims the shoreline, where the melting ice has turned the water the color of the Caribbean. From my vantage point, I can see the arc of the lakeshore as far as the eye can see, beyond South Haven.

"You are so beautiful," I say aloud, my breath hovering in white clouds. I watch it slowly dissipate, and my gaze becomes focused on the immediate: the rocks and stones my mom and I gathered over the decades line the wooden ledges of the screened porch. There are hundreds of rocks, and beyond the dust and cobwebs that have accumulated, I can see each stone's beauty. I can remember the exact moment when and the exact reason why we selected each rock.

We collected the beach glass in 7-Up greens, root beer brown and elusive blue because of its frosty beauty and the hunt itself. It took hours of beachcombing to find a few fragments.

We gathered small, round chunks of granite that we called "bird eggs" because of their shape and beautiful, bright speckled colors.

Leland blues and Petoskey stones—fossilized coral, deposited in Michigan by glaciers, that is the state stone—were collected on our girls' trips to northern Michigan. A rare trip to Lake Superior one summer resulted in endless agates, made up of quartz, reddened by iron and deposited in layers to create concentric circles resembling rings inside a tree in colors straight from a sunset.

My mom and I collected any stone shaped like a heart because of its symbolism.

And we would rush to the beach after every summer thunderstorm hoping to find fulgurite, petrified lightning that is formed when lightning strikes the sand and fuses its grains together.

But my favorites were always lightning stones, brown rocks crisscrossed and embedded with white lines and deposits, as if they had been struck by lightning.

"Septarian stones," my mom would always correct me when I'd use their nickname.

Lightning stones seemed magical to me as a little girl, especially after my mom told me how rare they were. "These stones aren't found often in the world, Adie Lou, only here and in India," my mom told me one day as we slowly walked the shoreline. "That's why many locals believe the area just south of where we live is called Ganges. There's something magical in the water, like the Ganges in India."

That sparked my eventual interest in the healing properties of essential oils, and how nature itself can make you whole and healthy.

I stand—the glider rocking—pick up a lightning stone and blow the dust off it, tiny motes filling the air. I grab my coffee, my head spinning, and head toward the upstairs bedroom I want to name Go Rock Hunting.

"Hey, Frank," I yell from the upstairs window when he and his crew arrive.

"What if—instead of wallpaper—I actually do a wall in here of my family's lake stones?" I ask when he appears. "Wouldn't it be beautiful?"

Frank nods but remains silent.

"And what if we covered the shower floor in smooth pieces of beach glass," I continue, "and do the same to an outdoor shower, so guests can wash the sand off their feet before they come inside?"

"Great ideas, Adie Lou," Frank says gingerly, as if he's trying to talk his daughter out of having another piece of chocolate on Halloween. "But that's more money, you know."

I see dollar signs floating out the door, but then think of Trish. *Just do it right the first time*, I hear her say.

"Let's do it," I say.

Frank nods. "It will be beautiful," he says. "Guests will be lucky to stay here."

When he leaves, I jot down in my notes to add a guide to collecting Lake Michigan rocks and stones to this room, and as I am typing on my cell, a number I don't recognize appears.

"Hello?"

"Adie Lou? It's Scott Stevens." There is a pause. "Scooter."

"Oh, hi," I say. "Up early, like me."

"Entrepreneurs," he says. "Listen, I was able to get your boat over here and take a look at it. Would you have time to stop by today?"

"That sounds ominous," I say.

"Actually, it's good news," he says. "I thought you could use some. But there is something I'd like you to see."

"How about right after lunch? I need to start painting. Rooms, that is. Not artwork."

"There will be time for that one day," he says. "See you after lunch."

I hang up and look at the lightning stone sitting on the floor. It took years to achieve its current state of beauty. It is streaked with history. It is hard on the outside, filled with a lifetime of deposits on the inside.

I pick it up and run my hands over it.

A lot like me, I think.

NINETEEN

"There she is."

Scooter ushers me into the cavernous boat repair workroom of S.S. Boat Works. I gasp.

"Is she dead?" I ask.

"No," Scooter says with a laugh. "She's very much alive and kicking."

Upon first glance, the *Adie Lou* looks as if she's passed away and floating in the air, like a figure in a religious painting. The sun is shining directly into the repair room, and rays of light are splaying around the boat.

"I feel like I should kneel," I say.

"Perhaps," Scooter jokes. "Our work often makes boat owners genuflect."

The *Adie Lou* is on a hoist in the middle of the room, workers underneath. I turn and look at Scooter. "I thought you said you had good news," I say. "This looks like it's going to cost me a lot of money that I don't have."

"That's a fine thank-you," Scooter says, walking toward my Chris-Craft. "Your dad took incredible care of this boat. Probably treated it better than he did his own body."

I nod. "He loved this boat."

"It shows," Scooter says. "The hull needed a little love—got some nicks on it in storage I think—and I'd like to give it a new finish varnish."

"It's pretty shiny as it is," I start to say, running numbers in my head.

"No charge," Scooter says. "On me."

"No," I say. "No."

"I insist."

"I don't like owing people," I say, my voice rising.

I think of Nate and Sadie and of men calling the shots.

Scooter raises his hands as if he's being taken hostage. "Okay, okay," he says. "I was just trying to help. Isn't that what friends do?"

Is it? I think.

My mind races to behind-the-scenes deals by so-called friends at my former company that were made at my expense. I think of all the hours I worked to help pay off my "best friend" Nate's enormous student loan debts. I think of the neighbors in my former tony small town who offered to get me into country clubs, or Evan into the right prep school *if...if...if...*

And then I think of my friend Scooter, who defended the city girl in the small town again and again.

"I'm sorry," I finally say. "Thank you." I search for more words. "Thank you."

"You're welcome," he says. "I just want the *Adie Lou* to be in tip-top shape for your first summer." Scooter stops. "You know, if you're busy and need a captain for sunset cruises, I'm available."

"Thank you," I say yet again. "But I'm trying to be as frugal as I can budget-wise. I'll be doing most of the cooking, cleaning, captaining..."

"I wasn't planning on charging you, Adie Lou," Scooter says. "Thought you'd need a break." He looks around his warehouse. "Running your own business is exhausting. You work nonstop, partly because you love what you do but partly because you have to. Its success is completely on your own shoulders." He stops and looks at me. "I, at least, get a Sunday off. You won't, Adie Lou. Running an inn is 24/7. You will need a break, or you'll break."

The weight of what he says finally hits me, and I suddenly feel exhausted and overwhelmed. My knees buckle, and Scooter grabs me.

"Whoa, there. Are you okay?"

"Yes," I say, shaking my head and taking a deep breath. "Just tired."

"Let's get you to my office so you can rest and get a drink of water," he says. "I have something I want to show you, too."

Scooter gets me seated in his office and hands me a bottle of water. I can feel the color come back to my face.

"Feeling better?" Scooter asks. I nod. "I told you people tend to genuflect around my work."

"Ha ha," I say without a smile. "You're right. I'm too stubborn. I will need a break. Thank you for offering to lend a hand, especially with your hands full here. It means..." My voice breaks, and my cheeks redden. "The world." I look at Scooter. "Sometimes, I feel like this new life I'm trying to build is sitting atop quicksand." I stop, searching for the right words. "It's just so rocky starting over." I stop again. "Quicksand. Rocky. Totally incongruous analogies."

Scooter smiles. "Actually, that's the perfect segue."

"For?"

"For this," he says, opening a desk drawer and pulling out a Tupperware container of rocks. "I found these under one of the front seats." He walks around his desk and hands me the rocks.

"Oh, Scooter," I breathe. "These were from my last boat

trip with my mom and dad." I rifle through the rocks, admiring each one. "My dad anchored near Oval Beach on a beautiful summer day. School had started for both Nate and Evan, but I had so many unused vacation days and saw how gorgeous it was going to be in Saugatuck. I swam around the shoreline all day, while my mom and dad sipped on glasses of rosé, and picked out rocks." I hold one up that is shaped like a heart, and my eyes fill with tears. "I remember screaming when I found this one. I crawled out of the water and handed it to my parents. I said, 'Your love will live forever here.' They toasted, and we sat in the boat watching people walking the beach. It was one of those perfect summer days where, from the boat, the beach looked draped in gauze."

I run my hands over the smooth stone shaped like a heart. "Thank you," I say. "For finding these. For doing all the work. For offering to captain." I stop. "For everything."

"You're welcome," he says in a husky breath. "But I'm not done. I found something else." Scooter returns to his desk and pulls something from it, which he quickly hides behind his back. He walks over to me and says, "Shut your eyes."

"This is getting weird now," I laugh.

"Shut your eyes," he repeats, before adding with a laugh, "and shut up for a second."

I shut my eyes, and I can feel something being placed around my neck. When I open my eyes, a stone necklace is draped over my sweater.

"Remember?" Scooter asks.

I lift the necklace. A series of small adder stones—little gray ones with naturally occurring holes in them—surround a little lightning stone, perfectly smooth and round, crossed with white lines, that has been wired onto a thin leather band.

I look at Scooter, my eyes wide. "You made this for me," I say. "You gave it to me the last day we worked together on the chain ferry. I forgot all about this."

"Obviously," Scooter says. He means to say it jokingly, off-handedly, but it comes across in a more serious tone.

"I must have taken it off before I went swimming one day and just left it on the boat," I say.

"A long time ago," he adds.

I study the necklace and stones. "I never asked, but when—how—did you do this?"

"Every time we finished work and would run down Mt. Baldhead to Lake Michigan to go swimming, you'd go rock hunting," he says. "If there were a stone you put back down, or dropped, or said wasn't big enough, I picked it up." Scooter stops and shuts his eyes as if remembering, a huge smile lighting his face. "I thought you should take a piece of Saugatuck—of us—to college with you."

My heart leaps. I don't remember Scooter being this thoughtful before. Or was I just not paying attention? Was I too young and self-involved to see... I dismiss the thought that is forming.

"It's beautiful," I say. "Can I keep it?"

"Of course. I made it for you."

Scooter looks at me for a beat too long, running his hands through his silver hair, and I can again feel my knees get a bit weak.

"It will ground me," I say. "I need that right now."

"I'm glad," he says. Scooter kicks at his office tile with the toe of his boot and dips his head. "Listen," he starts, his eyes on the ground like a little boy in class. "I was thinking...you know, maybe...we could...you know..."

The confident quarterback—the one who everyone said never got happy feet on the field—is really kinda cute when he's nervous, I think, stifling a smile.

"Well..." he continues, still kicking at the floor. "Maybe we could go for a walk sometime, grab dinner?"

Is he asking me out? As a friend? Or on a date?

"I'd love that," I say, still unsure. "Let me know a time that works."

"Tonight," he says as though he's about to explode. "Does that work?"

He really is nervous, I think.

I think of my afternoon. I think of the fact I have no food in the cottage. I think of how much I don't want pizza again. Maybe ever again in my life.

"Sure," I say.

"I'll drop by your cottage around four," he says.

"Four? Is there an early bird special somewhere?"

He smiles. "I was thinking we could go for a quick walk on the beach before dinner, before it gets dark," Scooter says.

"It's awfully cold," I say.

"Won't get much warmer or clearer than this, I guarantee," he says. "And the snowmelt is a boon for rock hounds. The melting ice and rushing water usually uncovers lots of beautiful stones that get buried under sand during the summer months. And the water is so clear right now. It's sort of a perfect storm."

"Am I a rock hound?" I ask.

"Yes," he says. "You can't be a rock lobster in these parts."

I laugh. "We played a lot of B-52s when we didn't have riders on the chain ferry, didn't we?"

"We thought we were so punk," Scooter says, his voice wistful. "But really, we were just kids." He stops and kicks at the floor again before looking at me, his eyes sad. "We were just kids."

The emotion of his words moves me. I nod in silence.

"See you at four?" he asks.

I nod again and stand, unconsciously touching the stones around my neck.

"The necklace looks beautiful on you, Adie Lou," Scooter says as I leave.

I pass by the *Adie Lou* floating in midair, and I suddenly feel as light as she does.

TWENTY

As if led by divine intervention, I steer my car toward the local library. It feels as if it's on autopilot.

I haven't been to the Saugatuck-Douglas library since I was a girl. The little library sits in the midst of downtown Douglas, Saugatuck's neighboring town, in an adorable white clapboard building that looks like a dollhouse come to life. My mom often volunteered at the library, and I spent countless hours here as a little girl on rainy days.

I park the car on the street and head into the library. I can still feel my mother's hand holding mine.

What was it she used to always say about Erma Bombeck and librarians? I stop and stare at the library. Oh, yes. My mom told me that Erma once said, "As a child, my number one best friend was the librarian in my grade school. I actually believed all those books belonged to her."

"I still do," my mom would laugh.

The library smells just the same as it did when I was a kid.

And it feels the same, too: like a magical place filled with secrets I needed to unearth.

And that's exactly why you're here, Adie Lou, I think.

The library has certainly changed since I was a girl who used to read Nancy Drew and Judy Blume. Public computer areas have replaced the soft chairs in which I used to curl up to read. I take a seat at a computer, log in and enter my search: *Sadie Collins*.

Sadie Robertson from *Duck Dynasty* appears, followed by Phil Collins and then an endless array of selfies of modern-day Sadie Collinses on Facebook and Instagram.

My, how things have changed.

I narrow my search: *Sadie Collins, Saugatuck Michigan. Ancestry.*

A few searches catch my eye: there are a couple of pieces from the local paper over the last few decades about the original cottages on Lakeshore Drive, including mine. But there is no later information on Sadie, and I don't know her married name or what became of her.

There is one common denominator, however: all the articles quote Iris Dragoon, president of the historical society.

"Excuse me," I say to a librarian who is passing by. "I'm searching for a woman whose father built my cottage. Would the library happen to have any information like that? Or do you have any thoughts on the best way to search for that information?"

The librarian pulls on the readers dangling around her neck, peers at the computer over my shoulder and then gives me the most bemused smile. "I'd go speak with Iris Dragoon," she says.

"You would?" I ask. The words just fly out of my mouth unexpectedly.

She places her hands on my shoulders and gives them a squeeze. "Well, *I* wouldn't," she says with a laugh. "But it sounds like you need to."

"I don't want to," I say, unable to hide my emotions, like a kid who is told he has to get a needle.

The librarian laughs. "I don't blame you," she says, leaving me to my research.

TWENTY-ONE

"See?"

I try to follow Scooter's mitten as he gestures into the air, but all I can do is laugh.

"Those look great on you," I say, trying to keep a straight face.

"They do, don't they?" he says.

Scooter is sporting a pair of sock monkey mittens. I was worried his fingers would get frostbitten during our walk, and made him wear the only pair of gloves I could locate: a pair that Nate "won" years ago during the white elephant Christmas gift exchange my parents so loved. They always held it on Christmas Eve, after a few glasses of champagne. Nate, of course, was aghast and refused to wear the mittens. He thought they were childish, just like the white elephant exchange.

Scooter holds up his hands and wiggles his thumbs, making it appear as if the two sock monkeys are boxing. I laugh.

"Totally age appropriate," I say.

"If we could live in a world filled with sock monkeys, Rock

'Em Sock 'Em Robots and Lite-Brites, it would be a better place, wouldn't it?" He stops and looks out over Lake Michigan. "Kids just want to grow up as fast as they can." He turns and looks at me. "We didn't know how good we had it, did we?"

Like earlier in the day, the raw emotion and innocence of his words touch me. In a stocking cap and mittens, his cheeks ruddy from the wind, his eyes bright, Scooter still looks like a young man, a kid at heart. And, in a way, he's right. As adults we're confronted with life's often unending cruelty: loss of dreams, death, divorce, aging, health and money issues. I watch Scooter as he kneels near a creek, his reflection staring back. He waves at himself with his mittens, and a boyish smile appears.

He ran from his demons and returned, I think. *Innocence intact, despite all of life's setbacks.*

"See?" he asks as he had earlier and gestures broadly again. "This is why I wanted you to come down here. You missed a lot of this as a city girl who spent winters in Chicago."

I follow his mittens toward the base of the dune where a large culvert is located. There was a washout on Lakeshore Drive decades ago—the road and dune collapsed in the midst of heavy rains, and historic summer cottages disappeared in front of our eyes like a game of Jenga—and the Army Corps of Engineers had to reinforce the dune, reengineer the water flow and rebuild the road. A creek just a short distance from Cozy Cottage's beach steps has been created, and now flows from the woods, under the dunes, through the culvert and into the lake.

"Snowmelt replenished the creek, and the rushing water uncovered all these stones," he says. "No one has seen these beauties before. You're the first."

I kneel and look into the creek. "It's like a runway show," I say, "but for rocks."

The creek bed is filled with bird eggs, limestone, sandstone and beach pebbles of basalt volcanic rock. Under the ice-cold crystal-clear water and last of the day's sunlight, the creek bed is filled with color and shape, and its beauty is breathtaking.

I look at Scooter. "Thank you for showing me this," I say. "And thank you for the *Adie Lou*. You're making my dream seem more and more like reality every day."

I think of the unintended romantic double entendre hidden in those words but am still glad I said them.

"You're welcome," Scooter says, after considering the words. Then he stands and shows off his coat as if he were a game show model.

"What are you doing?" I ask.

"Showing you all the pockets I have," he says. "Knowing you, I came prepared to be loaded down with about a hundred pounds of extra weight."

"Are you talking about me or the rocks?" I ask.

Scooter laughs. "Load me down."

"Do you want to walk for a few minutes maybe?" I ask. "It's cold, but I have to say it feels refreshing to be out here right now. Maybe head toward Pier Cove and then turn around?"

"That would be nice," he says.

Pier Cove is a tiny section of public beach just south of Saugatuck-Douglas. While Oval Beach is the gem of the area—named one of the most beautiful beaches in the world by *Condé Nast Traveler* and Douglas serves as the pretty public beach to the small town's residents—Pier Cove is but a tiny swath of sand that sits along a curve in the lakeshore featuring another freshwater creek and beautiful homes tucked along the dunes.

Pier Cove was once hailed as "the busiest port between St. Joseph and Muskegon." Before the Civil War, Pier Cove was a bustling community and a major point for lumber distribution between Chicago and Milwaukee. With the exhaustion of the lumber supply in the late 1880s, a huge fire and the coming of the railroad, the sawmill was moved and Pier Cove diminished. But when fruit became a major shipping commodity in the 1880s, Pier Cove's economy again grew to contain a warehouse and two piers that revived the villages. In 1899 a freeze killed much of the local harvest, and shipping at Pier Cove was reduced to passenger traffic, with commercial activity ending less than two decades later.

We walk south in silence, little breeze in our faces, no noise save for the whistle of the wind across the icy lake and the creak of barren aspen trees.

"Look," Scooter finally says, putting his hand on my arm to slow me. "Look at the contrast."

He points to the lake and then to the shoreline. The frozen lake makes it look as if we might be walking in Antarctica while the dunes make it seem as if we might be in the Southwest.

"Have you ever been to New Mexico?" Scooter asks, as if he's reading my mind.

"No," I say. "You?"

He nods. "When I was on my cross-country journey of discovery," he says, before looking at me. "Makes being lost sound very sexy, doesn't it?"

I laugh. "Was it?" I ask. "Not sexy, I mean, but did you find what you were looking for?"

He continues to look at me, thinking, not saying a word, for so long that I begin to feel as if I shouldn't have asked the question.

"I did," he finally says. "I found me."

Scooter's eyes soften, and he looks toward the shoreline, where large chunks of the dunes have collapsed and then refrozen, leaving breathtakingly intricate sand patterns in the steep banks.

"I think New Mexico is one of the most beautiful states in the US alongside Michigan and California," he says. "The quick snowmelt and lake wind created these works of art." Scooter walks toward the shoreline and runs his mitten along the dunes. From my perspective, it appears as if a monkey is scrambling for cover.

"See how these hold their shape due to the freezing temperatures? They remind me of the cliffs in New Mexico," he says. "I toured a lot of the cliff dwellings that Pueblo people built over seven hundred years ago. Seven hundred years," Scooter repeats, shaking his head. "We are just babies, Adie Lou, in terms of our society and history. But we think we know it all, have all the answers." He rubs his hand over the embankment and then suddenly digs into its side, and chunks of sand collapse to the ground. "We really don't know much of anything."

Scooter walks back to me and continues, his gray-green eyes glowing. "And as kids in America we think we know it all. We're told who we should be and what we should do and where we should live before we've figured it out ourselves. And that leads to some very..." He stops and cocks his head. "Let me think of a more delicate way to say it... That leads to some very messed-up adults.

"Being lost for a while is a good thing," he says. "It allowed me to reevaluate my life and where I wanted to be and what I wanted to do."

"And you chose here?"

"So did you," he says.

"So our parents were right?"

"Our parents and grandparents took great risk to find a place of peace here in Saugatuck," he says. "We both felt it wasn't big enough or good enough, didn't we? What we did, though, was play by everyone else's rules. You got married. I played football. You got a corporate job in Chicago. Who were we pleasing? And why? Most people sleepwalk through life playing the game. They're like sheeple."

"Sheeple?"

"Part people, part sheep," he says, "following the herd mentality." Scooter turns around and starts walking back toward the cottage. The north wind slaps our faces. "You're lost right now, and that's actually a good thing. It's good to be scared, excited, alive, isn't it?"

I slow and look at the patterns in the embankments. "I feel like that right now," I say, pointing at them, "as though my entire soul is splayed open, and the world can see every scar, laugh line, pockmark, heartache that's inside me."

Scooter stops. "And that's beautiful," he says. Without warning, Scooter leans in and kisses me, ever so softly and briefly, on the lips.

"I didn't expect that," I say.

"I've always liked you, Adie Lou," Scooter says. "Even when we were kids."

"You were always my friend, Scooter," I say.

"Isn't that the best place to start?" he asks.

My eyes widen at his wisdom. I put my hands on his cheeks, rise up on my toes and kiss him again.

What am I doing, I think suddenly as my lips are on his. I'm in my forties. I can't date again. I can't go through the endless questions and the unearthing of our embarrassing quirks. Oh, God. I can't endure the unveiling of my body and the awkward first sex.

I push Scooter away.

"I have to take this slowly," I say, my mind suddenly filled with images of Sadie Collins and Isabel Archer, and the marriages that seemed to doom us all.

"Oh, she of mixed messages," Scooter says. He looks at me. "But I understand. Me, too."

"I'm a little overwhelmed right now," I say. "I already have a man in my life... Sonny."

Scooter laughs. "Slow down," he says. "Let's just take it one day at a time. That's all we can do in life. Adie Lou, I want you to find yourself first. Get your inn up and running. Empower women who have been lost, just like us. I want you to know

I'd never want to get in the way of your dreams. I want to help fulfill them."

Scooter grabs my hand, and we walk in silence toward the cottage, my heart beating so loudly in my ears I wonder if he can hear it.

When we reach the little creek near my cottage, we both kneel onto the shoreline, ice pebbles scattered across frozen sandy ripples, a winter Zen garden surrounding us.

I take off my mittens, hike up my coat sleeve and dip my hand into the water.

"Yow!" I exclaim at its iciness, before plucking a lightning stone. As I do, the necklace Scooter had made for me years ago pops free. I plop on my rear on the cold shore and compare the two. "You know, these stones have special properties." I stop suddenly. "Sorry. Nate said all of this was nonsense and psychobabble."

Scooter looks at me. "I'm not Nate."

Our gaze is unbroken for a long time before I nod and continue. "I think it's why I was always drawn to them," I say. "The minerals in the stone provide peace and harmony so that you can face daily challenges with confidence and grace. And it's supposed to make us understand things about our lives that we didn't understand before." I stop and hold up the stones in front of my face. "And, they're also quite effective when you need to make something new out of something old, be it a home, a job…" I hesitate and smile. "Or a relationship."

"Let's gather all the stones we can, then!" Scooter laughs.

Together, we pull pretty stones from the icy creek, Scooter filling his pockets until he resembles a kangaroo. As we're about to leave, Scooter points into the creek. "Look," he says.

"I can't believe it," I say, reaching in to pull out a smooth bluish-gray rock in the shape of a heart. "Just like I used to collect with my parents." I stand and hold the stone in front of my own heart. "Thank you. I think I needed to find this today."

"Your heart?" Scooter asks, his voice filled with irony.

I nod.

"Look," he says again. I at first think he's talking about another rock, but the sun is setting behind Lake Michigan, slinking slowly into the horizon.

After its glorious departure, Scooter and I head for the steps. We immediately slow on the first one, shocked by how much weight we've added to our bodies. "I don't think I can make it," Scooter laughs. "I think you added two hundred pounds on me."

"No," I say. "These are special rocks. We can't throw any away." I get behind him and push, and we take it one step at a time, stopping on each landing to catch our breaths.

"I feel like a pack mule," Scooter says, slowly trudging up the steps to the cottage.

"Better than a jackass," I laugh.

"Oh, I can be that, too, sometimes."

When we reach the top, we're both panting. I'm drenched in sweat, despite the temperature, and my hair is sticking to my neck and face.

"I think we need to go somewhere very dark to eat," I say.

"Lots of dark dives in Saugatuck," he says. "I'm starving."

"Me, too," I say, walking onto the screened porch. I head directly to the ledge containing all of the heart rocks my family has collected over the years, adding the newest one to the collection and feeling as if—despite my fears—perhaps, just perhaps, it might have been the one I've been searching for all of these years.

PART SEVEN

Rule #7:
Dinner Is a Family Activity

TWENTY-TWO

"**M**om! I'm here!"

I hear loud honking on Lakeshore Drive, followed by Evan's voice bellowing out of the car. I can't help but smile: it's the same thing I used to do when I arrived here to see my mom and dad.

I rush onto the screened porch. "Stay here," I tell Sonny, sternly wagging a finger to keep him from barking. "And no bark, okay, buddy? At least give me time to explain."

Despite the snow, Evan rushes up the steps—taking them two at a time—his body skidding to a stop at the very top.

I shut the door just in time.

"What took you so long?" I ask. "I was starting to get worried. It's almost five."

"We had a little party to celebrate the start of spring break last night," he says.

"A party to celebrate the fact everyone is going to party?" I ask. "Oh, that's right. It's college."

He laughs, and I feel a pang of guilt. "I'm sorry you're missing Florida with all your friends," I say.

"I'm not," Evan says. "This is where I want to be." He stops and smiles. "Especially since I got to sleep until noon, and the guys had to get up at 5:00 a.m. to drive."

I laugh and open my arms. Evan hugs me tightly and then releases one long arm from around my back to check the unraveling Nantucket basket on the front door. His face droops.

"No sparklers," he says, sounding just like a little boy again.

"Sorry, but I've been a little busy," I say, nodding at the front yard, which looks like a construction zone.

"I know," he says. "Habit."

Before I can stop him, Evan opens the door, and Sonny is standing there to greet him. Sonny barks, stands on his back legs and then stretches as if he's trying to give Evan a hug.

"And who's this?" Evan says.

"Didn't I mention Sonny?" I ask innocently. "I found him. Someone abandoned him on Lakeshore Drive."

"Mom," Evan starts, sounding a lot like me when I disapprove of something. "You don't need to take on any more responsibility."

Evan suddenly takes a seat on the round rug by the front door, and Sonny crawls onto his lap and starts licking his face. Evan laughs and then holds the dog's face in his hands. "What happened, little guy?" he asks, before looking up at me. "What happened, Mom?"

"Don't know exactly," I say. "We think he was either born this way and a breeder dumped him, or he was abused."

Sonny rolls over in Evan's lap, and he pets the dog's stomach. Sonny sighs.

"I would've done the same thing," Evan says. He plays with Sonny for a few moments and then says, "It's nice to have a dog. Finally. Grandma and Grampa always did. Why didn't dad ever want us to have one?"

"Too messy," I say.

Just like life, I don't say. His father never liked to deal with un-tidiness. He preferred to sweep things under the rug.

Evan rolls Sonny onto the floor and stands. "I can't wait to look around," he says. "I want to see what you've done."

We start on the main floor, and I show him the plans for the kitchen, the fish house and my eventual owner's suite. When we head to the second floor, Evan says, "Why did you take my room, Mom?"

I begin to explain, but he looks at me—his face changing, as if he seems to understand—and says, "I can crash in another room. No biggie. I'm used to sleeping anywhere."

I smile, relieved, and then laugh when I comprehend his words. "Oh, you are, are you?"

"Figure of speech, Mom," he says, rolling his eyes.

"Oh, it is, is it?"

"Let's keep moving," Evan says, heading toward the attic.

He looks at all the construction and then at the renderings I'm holding. "I love that every room will be themed around a cottage rule," he says. "I think people will love that." He stops. "I do."

Finally, we climb to the turret, where we take a seat and look out over the lake. Evan sits in silence, watching Lake Michigan. Though it is overcast, there is enough of the day's last light to highlight half my son's face, to divide it into parts, shadow and light, man and boy.

"We grew up here," he finally says, unconsciously petting Sonny, who has curled up beside him on the bench seat. "This summer cottage is our connector, Mom, the piece that con-nects generations of our family. It means a lot that you saved it."

"Thanks, Evan," I say. "That means the world to me. It wasn't easy."

"You're actually starting to think like a millennial."

I bust out laughing. "Watch your words," I warn jokingly, reaching over and jostling his shoulder.

My mind instantly fills with memories of the countless interviews I conducted with recent college graduates. Millennial applicants for job openings—entry-level copywriters and designers, assistant media planners, researchers and account executives—acted as if traditional workplace rules didn't apply to them.

Can I work from home?

Have you considered eliminating print advertising completely?

Does this company treat its employees like family?

"It's an entry-level job!" I wanted to tell them. "You don't get to make up the rules! You should be grateful for the opportunity."

It took a lot of control—and jabbing of pens into my leg—for me not to walk out or roll my eyes.

"It's not a bad thing, Mom," Evan says, breaking me out of my thoughts. "Every generation is different." He stops and then gestures around the turret. "But there are things that unite every generation, too. Emotions, places, people. You were just as good of friends with your parents as I am with you."

I nod. "True."

Evan continues. "Starting this B and B is a very millennial thing you're doing, Mom, whether you like to admit it or not. You're taking a risk, you're putting passion first, you're realigning your entire work-life dynamic, you're thinking in terms of missions, you're being spontaneous, you're willing to relocate." He looks at me. "Those are all admirable things. Millennials get a bad rap by you older folks, but I think maybe we've just been raised to have the opportunity and blessing to focus on what matters most to us." He stops. "I realize Grandma and Grampa and so many others before me couldn't do that. But it's not a bad thing."

I smile at my son, his face still divided by light.

"Yes, you're right," I say. "Millennials—including you, my dear son—have always challenged my way of thinking, but I see that you all may be onto something bigger than simply playing by the old rules. And I'm all for that."

Evan nods, his blond bangs falling into his eyes. He puffs out his lower lip and—with one big exhale—blows his hair back.

"I'm starving," he says. "What do you have here to eat for dinner? I don't think I can do another pizza."

"Me either," I laugh. "I've been living off of pizza."

I duck my head. "But I don't have much here," I say. "I haven't been too much of a grocery shopper of late."

"I get it," he says. "So what do you want for dinner?"

"You know all the places," I say. "What sounds good?"

"Mom," Evan says in a parental tone. "What's Rule #7?"

"Dinner is a family activity," I say.

"That means we eat together," Evan says, continuing to sound like a parent. "And we always made our first meal together whenever we arrived, remember? You'd do the salad, Grampa would barbecue, Grandma would make her famous potato salad, baked beans and cucumbers and onions, Dad and I would take turns cranking the ice cream maker."

I smile.

"What can we make out of air?" I ask.

Evan laughs. "Let's run to the store and get a few things. Whip up a nice dinner."

"You can cook?" I ask, eyes wide.

"Surprise," Evan says, waving his hands in the air.

"Who are you?" I ask.

"A millennial," he laughs. "Who are you?"

I look out over the lake for a second before turning to Evan.

"A millenni-mom," I say.

Evan stands and holds out his hand to help me up.

"I've missed you," I say, my voice filled with emotion.

"Back atcha, Mom," Evan says, his stomach rumbling. He turns to Sonny. "Ready to go shopping?" Evan pets Sonny on the head and laughs. "For Halloween, we totally need to put a patch over his eye and make him a pirate."

I laugh. "Remember when you were a pirate for Halloween?"

Evan laughs even harder. "I remember," he says. "You were so busy with work that year. You made me a patch out of duct tape and thought about giving me a steak knife to carry around."

"It made a good sword," I say.

"I was eight, Mom," Evan says, again laughing.

"I would have put duct tape over it," I say. "I'm sorry. I was an overwhelmed mom. I guess I wasn't mother of the year."

Evan pulls me into him. "You've always been mother of the year, Mom." I shut my eyes, and I feel happier than I have in a long time. "Now, let's shop."

TWENTY-THREE

I watch in astonishment as Evan smashes garlic, dices onion, chops peppers and carefully removes seeds from jalapeños. He drizzles some olive oil into a large stockpot and adds the vegetables, turning them with a wooden spoon. When they're tender, he adds an assortment of beans to the pot along with some chicken stock. Evan plops in some tomatoes and green chili sauce, and then runs out to the grill to check the chicken breasts.

"Glad you kept this going in the winter," Evan calls, the cold air rushing through the door. "True Michigander. Grilling in the snow."

"The old grill won't be around much longer," I say. "New gas line. No tanks."

"Smart, Mom," Evan says. "New appliances will be gas then, too?"

"Yes," I say, as Evan races back inside and over to the spice cabinet. He carefully considers the spices—blowing the bangs from his eyes as he picks each one up to read—before choosing cumin, chili powder and a bay leaf. He adds a dash of this and a pinch of that, tasting as he goes, before shaking in some more salt and cranking a bit more pepper, tossing the bay leaf on top.

"I feel like I'm watching *Stranger Things*, and a mysterious force has taken over my son's body," I say with a laugh, taking a sip of a lovely Malbec he also suggested at the store after scanning bottles of wine with his Vivino app.

"We all take turns cooking Sunday dinner before our weekly fraternity meeting. It's our way of re-creating a sense of family." Evan says this matter-of-factly. My eyes grow even wider, and he catches me. "I watch *Rachael Ray, Pioneer Woman*, the *Barefoot Contessa*," Evan continues, tossing a dish towel over his shoulder. "When we're not watching sports, we watch the Cooking Channel or HGTV."

Evan grabs a large plate from the cupboard, heads to the grill, pulls the chicken from the flames and returns. "Once those cool a bit, I'll dice them up, add them to the stoup, and we'll be ready to chow down."

"Stoup?"

"Rachael Ray," he says with a laugh. "It's her term for stew meets soup." Evan opens the refrigerator, pulls out the sour cream, hot sauce, cheese and cilantro.

"Some of the most successful entrepreneurs today are chefs," he says. "They've learned how to brand themselves so well." He stops and looks at me, continuing to pull cilantro leaves from their stems. "And they're women. You should be aware of what they're doing and how."

I take a sip of wine as Evan dices the chicken and adds it to the stoup. He gives it a big stir, picks up a soup bowl off the counter and ladles in the stoup. Evan turns and—ever so delicately—adds a dash of hot sauce, a handful of cheese, a spoonful of sour cream and a scattering of cilantro.

"Bam!" he says, imitating Emeril Lagasse's Cajun accent. "Dinner is served."

I wait for Evan to sit at the counter—the only clean space left to eat in the kitchen—before taking a bite. My taste buds leap, and a smile crosses my face. "Evan, this is really, really good. I mean, really good."

"Thanks, Mom," he says, blowing the steam off his spoonful of stoup before taking a bite. I swear I can see his cheeks flush with pride.

"Cheers!" I say.

He lifts his water glass.

The stoup is so good, and we're both so hungry that we eat in silence for a few moments. Finally, I stop, take another sip of wine and admire my son. "I should hire you," I say with a laugh.

Evan polishes off his stoup, rises to fill his bowl again, and when he returns, he looks at me and says, "Why haven't you asked for my help with any of this, Mom?"

The tone of his voice—almost wounded—takes me by surprise.

"You're in school," I say. "You're so busy and I've been overwhelmed. The divorce, leaving my job, selling Lake Forest, moving here." Evan's eyes are on his soup bowl. "I didn't mean to upset you. It was never my intention. I just never imagined asking you to help."

Evan sets down his spoon and takes a big drink of water. "I'm a business major, Mom," he says. "I know I'm just a college kid, but I've taken accounting, marketing, management, entrepreneurial finance…" He stops. "I mean, I kind of want to be like you when I grow up. I want to run my own business, do my own thing." He looks at me, and his voice warbles a bit. "You're kind of kick-ass…you know, for a milleni-mom."

I can feel my eyes water. "Oh, Evan," I say. "That means the world. Honestly, it never crossed my mind to bother you with all that's going on in my life now. But, I'd love to go over my plans with you…my website, the renovation, my budget forecast. Trish was just here, and she helped me see things I never considered." I stop. "It's hard not to see you as my little boy."

Evan smiles. "I'll always be your little boy, Mom," he says.

"Okay, then," I say as I stand. I put my bowl in the dishwasher, refresh my wine and turn to Evan. "Where do you want to start?"

"Everywhere," he says. "Your entire business plan, including financials and forecasts. And I'd love to hear your marketing strategy, since that's what you did for a living—where and when you'll be advertising, and how much that will cost, especially since you don't have an existing customer base."

I take a deep breath and fill my wineglass even more.

Evan laughs. "I have some tough professors," he says. "They always say, 'There's nothing to be scared of if you're prepared for everything.'" Evan stands and looks at me. "So, let's prepare for everything."

I take a sip of wine. "Then let me start with the Dragoon Lady," I say.

"She's still alive?" Evan asks, a look of shock overtaking his face.

"And kicking," I say. "Mostly me. In the butt."

Evan laughs. "Grandma never liked her, did she?"

"Now I know why," I say, opening my laptop and filling Evan in on the historic restrictions on the fish house.

His eyes grow wide as I tell him about my run-ins, and they grow even wider when I show him the renovation costs and summer forecasts as well as my ideas for women's empowerment weekends.

"I can tell you that you're already not charging enough for the rooms, Mom, based on our lakeshore location and how nice they're going to be," he says. "And you haven't factored in any revenue for your weekends. You can offer packages as well as each option individually, like yoga, essential oils…" He stops and smiles. "Cooking with your kids," he adds. "We could do classes together."

"I love that," I say.

"What if this were my summer internship?" he asks, before holding up his hands. "No pay, of course. Just room and board. I can crash on a pullout in your suite."

My heart quickens. "I love that, too, but wouldn't that mess up your plans for working at the bank in Chicago? And wouldn't that make for awfully tight quarters? Trish suggested adding an extra room for you actually."

"That's smart," he says.

"Which really means a room for her, too," I add with a laugh.

"You'd have your own bedroom, and I'd have my own space then," he says. "I live in a twelve-by-fourteen room with another guy and sleep on a top bunk. I can do it. Can you?"

I nod vigorously, set down my wine and hug my son.

His words ring in my ears, and I feel alive and empowered.

I can do it, I think. *Especially now with my son's help.*

TWENTY-FOUR

"What are you doing?"

"I want to Facebook Live this, Mom," Evan says. He is holding his cell phone about a foot away from my face, which is bare of makeup and flecked with paint.

"Why?"

Evan lowers the phone and exhales, a look of exasperation overtaking his face. "You should know this, former ad exec," Evan says sarcastically.

"I was really part of the old-school side," I say. "Print, radio and TV. People more, um, your age did the online advertising."

"The techies?" Evan asks with a laugh. "The millennials?"

I set down my paintbrush. "It's ironic, really, because my generation was among the first to embrace technology on the fly. I actually took a typewriting class in school, before working on gigantic PCs and then moving to Macs. I learned everything from email to design by the seat of my pants. I do know technology, but it's moving at the speed of light these days."

"Then let me show you," Evan says.

I take a seat on the floor, and Evan walks me through Facebook Live and various other apps on his cell, like Instagram and Snapchat.

"I didn't know my phone could do all of this. I just learned how to increase the font size on my text messages," I say with a laugh.

"Consumers want a more personalized experience these days," Evan says. "We can use before-and-after footage on your website and Facebook page, videos of you doing a lot of the work yourself. People love that. It's why shows like *Fixer Upper* are so popular," Evan continues. "And we can add historical photos of the cottage—and even pictures of us and Grandma and Grampa—on Instagram. That way people feel a deeper connection, and, thus, are readily willing to spend their money for that experience." He stops. "And all of this might even generate some local or national media attention for you."

Evan leans over with his cell again. "Look," he says, tapping furiously on his screen. "We can hashtag the heck out of this on Instagram to get you not only new—but the right—followers, and isn't word of mouth still about the best advertising?"

I nod. "You've learned a lot in college," I say. "Besides how to drink."

"Hey, I had water last night with dinner," he says.

"That's because you were hungover from the night before," I say.

"Well played, Mom," Evan says. "Now, I want you to give this all a shot for a little while."

"What?"

"I want you to create accounts for this inn on social media," he says. "I'll walk you through each app, but I want you to do it and get each started, so you'll know how to do it when I'm not here."

I stare at him.

"C'mon," he says. "If you learned how to go from typewriters to Macs and did it all on your own, this should be a snap." He stops before adding, "chat." He smiles when I don't. "Just a little tech humor. Get it? Snapchat."

For the next hour, I am the student, and my son is the professor, and my heart quickens and my creativity is sparked with each new thing I learn.

"Now let me teach you a thing or two about design," I say, picking up my paintbrush. "My app is a bit more old-fashioned."

I stand up and start to paint the walls of a guest room that will be themed around the cottage rule Everyone Must Be Present for Sunset. With each brushstroke, the wall brightens, a beautiful Creamsicle orange making the room glow like a sunset.

"That's a bold color, Mom," Evan says.

"I know," I say, stopping briefly and taking a step back to study the wall. "But I'm doing a beautiful wallpaper behind the bed that will really ground this color, and the bathroom will feature framed sunset photos we've taken over the years." I stop. "I want guests to feel as if they're part of our family." I begin to paint again, before I realize Evan is surreptitiously holding his cell. "Evan," I say, sounding a threat and brandishing my paintbrush. "Don't. I look too Grey Gardens to be taped."

"Too late," Evan says. "And besides, what you just said is perfect. It will make great footage for social media." He taps his screen and looks at me. "Would you mind doing something a little more dramatic now?" Evan asks.

"Besides quitting my job and starting a B and B?"

"For me to tape," he continues. "I was thinking of *Fixer Upper* again. Chip loves demo day, and viewers do, too."

"I'm paying someone to do that," I say before I suddenly remember my own demo day at the fish house with Frank.

What an adrenaline rush, I think. *And what a discovery.*

I quickly relay this to Evan. "I totally forgot about it in my excitement to see you," I say.

"What if we found something else?" he says. "Live."

The word *live* reverberates in my head, and my mind ricochets back in time to the spring of 1986 when my parents and I were riveted to the television to watch Geraldo Rivera open Al Capone's secret vault. It seemed like the entire country was captivated by the spectacle of what he might discover.

"Okay," I say quickly. "Can you ask Frank if we can use his sledgehammer?"

"Okay," Evan says, before rushing toward the door, a big smile crossing his face.

"Meet me in the attic!" I call.

Evan returns in a flash, huffing and puffing, sledgehammer in tow. He hands it to me.

About three-quarters of the attic has already been demoed, and new rooms have been roughed in by Frank and his team, but there is an original wall near the stairs that has yet to be touched. I was unsure initially about what to do with this awkward space. But Trish has convinced me a laundry room here would save me not only time but also my back.

"Let's do this!" Evan says, lifting up his cell.

I pick up the sledgehammer, the weight of it making me take a big step backward. I can hear Evan stifle a laugh. I turn toward the cell phone and say, "An original wall in Cozy Cottage. Here goes nothing!"

I whack the wall, and the impact reverberates through my entire body.

"You look like a human Slinky," Evan says with a big laugh.

I look, and there is a round indentation in the wall. It's not a hole really but more of a dimple. I pick up the sledgehammer and swing again, and again, again, until I'm out of breath and my shoulders and back are aching.

"Ha!" I say when I see I've finally knocked a few holes as big as baseballs in the wall. I walk over and pick up a crowbar and begin to remove some of the wall. I make some headway before turning to Evan.

"Your turn," I say with a big smile, reaching for the cell phone. "Show me what you got."

Evan hands me his cell and picks up the sledgehammer. "Okay, let me show you how it's done," he says, blowing his bangs out of his face. Evan slams the wall over and over, and when he stops to look, he's made about as much damage as I had. A look of frustration covers his face, and he goes to work again, whacking the wall until he drops the sledgehammer from exhaustion. Big, gaping holes dot the wall under the staircase. I return Evan's phone to him and go to work on the wall with the crowbar again, revealing old lath and plaster underneath. I work my way down the wall until I've created a hole big enough for my body to wiggle through. I grab my own cell from my pocket and turn on its flashlight. I shine it around the dusty space.

"Here goes nothing again," I say, hunkering my body and stepping inside the wall.

I scan the flashlight around the space, expecting to see a mouse or two, but it is quiet. I squat and again look around the space, this time more slowly.

"What's that?" I ask, my voice echoing in the cramped quarters.

Evan approaches and turns on his flashlight, too.

There is a small wooden box—almost like a built-in chest—directly under the staircase.

"Can you reach it?" he asks.

I nod and crab walk toward the stairs, finally taking a seat on the floor when I reach it. I try to open the box, but it won't budge. "Hand me the crowbar."

Evan extends his body as far as he can and passes the tool to me. I position it under the lid and put my weight on it. There is a loud crack, and the wooden top splits in half. I pull off part of the top, get on my knees and point my flashlight inside.

I scream.

"Mom!" Evan yells. "What is it? Are you okay?"

I look more closely into the box and, against my better judgment, stick my hand into it as if I'm on the old game show *Fear Factor*. I turn to Evan, holding up the item that made me yell.

"What in the hell is that?" Evan asks. "Gross, Mom."

The look on Evan's face freaks me out, and I suddenly toss it toward him as if I've lost all control of my body.

Evan's scream matches my own.

"Sorry, Facebookers," Evan says, moving toward the mysterious item with his cell aimed directly at it. He kneels and says, "I think it's a cow's foot." Evan turns his cell back toward me.

"What else is in there?" he asks.

"More of the same," I say, reaching into the box and pulling out another one that looks exactly like the first.

"What do you think it is?" Evan says, his voice now panicky.

"I don't know," I say. "I just know I want to get the hell out of here."

TWENTY-FIVE

Evan and I are seated on the leather couch in the living room, legs crossed, facing one another, camp blankets draped over our laps. We are on our cells furiously Googling what we have discovered, which are scattered across the coffee table in front of the fireplace.

I look up and laugh.

"What's so funny?" Evan asks.

"Darryl," I say, nodding at the moose. "He's looking at those things on the table like Whoopi Goldberg looked at Demi Moore in *Ghost* when she said, 'You in danger, girl!'"

Evan laughs. "You and your movie references. What's that old-timey one you and Trish love so much?"

"*Ice Castles,*" I say, putting my hand over my heart as if he's just said the most hurtful thing in the world.

"Didn't mean to offend you," he laughs.

"It's not that you forgot the name of the movie, it's that you

actually said 'old-timey.' It's not like I grew up churning butter and wearing pioneer dresses like *Little House on the Prairie.*"

Evan stares at me. "When was *Ice Castles* released?"

I scan my brain and then quickly double-check on my cell.
"Nineteen seventy-eight."

"That was more than forty years ago, Mom," Evan says. "I
think it qualifies as old-timey."

My heart flutters for a second as I think how quickly forty
years have flown. I remember my mother telling me to savor
every moment and to not regret a thing because, in the blink
of an eye, life would pass and I would be her age. I thought she
was crazy and that it would never happen.

I scan the cottage, thinking of its life, my family's life and
how much history lives within these walls.

"I've got the answer!" Evan says, the excitement in his voice
making me jump. "I've been sending photos and a little bit
about our cottage, including all the Capone stuff, to an American history professor whose class I'm in at college. He just sent
me some background and a few links." Evan grows quiet for a
minute, reading.

"Don't leave me in suspense," I say.

Evan laughs. "Sorry. These aren't cow's feet, they just look
like them. According to Dr. Samuels, they were part of the bag
of sneaky tricks that bootleggers used during Prohibition. He
says bootleggers used all sorts of ingenious methods to evade
Prohibition agents, from hollowing out Bibles to camouflaging
trucks with a faux brick facade, so they could transport liquor."

"So, what are these things?" I ask.

"Dr. Samuels believes they are what was called a 'cow shoe.'"

"A what?"

"A cow shoe," Evan says, picking one up off the table. "He
says it's a wooden block carved to resemble the hoof a cow,
which was attached to a strip of metal that could then be strapped
to the shoe of a bootlegger or moonshiner." Evan stops and stud-

ies it before handing it to me. I take the cow shoe reluctantly, but begin to admire the craftsmanship and ingenuity of it the more Evan explains.

"So Dr. Samuels says these were used specifically by bootleggers to cover their footprints, especially in the snowy or muddy woods," Evan continues. "The hoofprints deterred agents who were tracking them. Essentially, bootleggers could crisscross remote fields or even wander behind restaurants, and agents would just think cattle was roaming. And get this—Dr. Samuels thinks the inventor behind this got the idea from a Sherlock Holmes story in which the villain made his horse's prints resemble a cow's."

"So does he think Capone and his gang used these?"

Evan nods excitedly, his bangs bouncing. "He does. He thinks they probably ran a small operation from this cottage and supplied many west Michigan restaurants and speakeasies. Resort areas wanted their booze, it seems. Dr. Samuels says they likely ran the liquor in the winter, and these threw the Prohibition agents off." He stops and looks at me. "Just think of the history under this roof."

It's like he can read my mind, I think.

I watch Evan's face grow serious. He scans the cottage as if he sees it for the first time. "Capone, Sadie's letter, your grandparents, my grandparents...*you*." He stops again. "This is more than just a cottage. It's alive."

The emotion in my son's voice touches me, and I reach out and pat his leg. "It is."

Evan grabs his phone again. "Mom, you should see all the comments we've already received about finding this stuff in the cottage."

"Really?" I ask.

Evan nods. "Yeah. We had a few hundred people watching on Facebook Live."

"Is that good?"

"It's really good," Evan says, "especially considering very few were my friends. And we got a ton of comments." Evan begins scrolling, and his smile grows bigger as his eyes scan. "A lot of folks already want to book when you open. So, we have to get your website and online reservation app now. And, oh, my gosh, Mom, listen to this. A local TV station out of Grand Rapids heard about our discovery, and they want to interview you about the cottage's history and renovation. It's exactly what you need to launch the inn and get the word out."

"Oh, Evan," I say, my heart racing. "I don't know how to thank you."

I reach over to grab his hand, but instead grab the fake cow's foot he's still holding. I take it from him and hold it up to my ear as if it were a telephone. "Hello? I'm trying to reach Evan."

He rolls his eyes. I continue, since he refuses to play along. "Okay, then. U-Haul? I need a truck. I'm moooo-ving. Last name, Patty. First name, Cow."

This time, Evan groans, and then another serious look overtakes his face, and he reaches over and grabs the cow's foot from my hand. "I have an idea," he says, his eyes growing wide. "Pardon yet another cow pun here, but I think we've found your bargaining chip, Mom."

"What do you mean?"

As Evan explains, a grinchesque smile—much like one I've seen before—slowly covers my face.

"Keep your friends close and your enemies closer," Evan says. "Isn't that exactly what Capone would do?"

PART EIGHT

Rule #8:
Ice Cream Is Required

TWENTY-SIX

April

Sunlight is tumbling into my nearly completed master suite, and the space is filled with light. I can picture where my bed will be placed and my reading chair will be angled. The bedroom is warm, the reading nook in my little sunroom even warmer, and I do a spontaneous pirouette as I walk into my en suite bathroom. The tile is complete, and I run my hands over the walls and counters before taking a seat directly in the middle of my oversize shower.

Budget be damned, I think, looking up at my rain showerhead before feeling my tile again.

"Carrara marble, you sure are pretty," I say out loud to my bathroom. "Okay, faux Carrara marble, you sure are pretty."

I listened to Trish, Frank and Evan, who all encouraged me to splurge on my master suite, telling me I would need a spa-like refuge and retreat at the end of every day. Even the faux marble was more than I wanted to spend, but...

A smile crosses my face.

...I have a plan.

I cross my legs and position myself like a Buddha in the middle of my huge shower. I quiet my brain, align my mind and body and outline my plan of action. After a few seconds, I feel something in my lap, and I open my eyes to find Sonny—now much bigger than he was weeks ago—trying to lie down.

"You're squashing my organs, big guy," I say. "And I need those."

I give him a kiss on the head, push him off my lap, stand and walk back into my bedroom. I slide open the newly installed French doors to test them. As I do, I brace myself for the shock of cold air, but instead a warm breeze greets me.

I sigh and inhale.

There is something about the first warm day of the year in Michigan. It arrives unexpectedly, like a message in a bottle that just suddenly washes up to shore.

I call Sonny, and we walk out onto the small wooden porch that Frank has built, just big enough for two chairs. It is hidden from the rest of the cottage—set behind the wall of the new bathroom—but is bathed in sunlight. Sonny immediately lies down on the patio, his body soaking up the sun. I kneel to pet his fur, already warm, when I see a cluster of snowdrops blooming just behind the patio. I smile.

The first warm day is just like these delicate white flowers, I think. *It comes as a pretty surprise. Yes, there will be more cold, but this offers promise.*

I stand and look around. *Just like the progress on the cottage.*

I tilt my face toward the sky, shut my eyes and let the sun warm me, calm me, lull me.

"I can almost taste summer," I say to myself.

Suddenly, an image of Saugatuck's local ice cream shop fills my mind.

Lick Effect Ice Cream—possibly the corniest but most appropriate name for an ice cream shop ever—has been a mainstay in town ever since my mom was a little girl. The shop is tucked just off the main drag—Water Street—and down a narrow alley in a tiny space. The shop makes its own ice cream and waffle cones, and the only sign that the shop has opened for the season is when a mannequin—outfitted in a wig and sequined bikini—is positioned in a window over the storefront, its legs—which have been made over to resemble waffle cones—jutting into the alley. When its waffle cone legs are uncrossed, Lick Effect is open for business. When they are crossed, it is closed.

Like spring in Michigan, Lick Effect has no definitive opening date. The first warmish early spring day, the mannequin will appear and the shop will suddenly open. The first frigid fall day, the mannequin will disappear and the shop will be closed for winter.

"Do you think?" I ask Sonny, who has now rolled onto his back so the sun can warm his tummy.

The hopeful lilt in my question causes Sonny to roll onto his feet, amble over to me, jump into my arms as if he were giving me a bear hug and emit one loud bark.

"Okay," I say. "Let's go."

Sonny and I drive into town, windows down, and we both inhale the scents of and listen to the sounds of Michigan coming back to life after winter: the warming of the ground, the scent of fresh pine and lake humidity in the air, the birds chirping, chain saws buzzing. Saugatuck, too, is coming back to life: though it's too early for the shops to plant their window boxes, cheery flags now flap in the breeze, storefront doors are open, tourists walk the streets and I can smell fudge being cooked in big copper urns in the local candy shop.

My heart quickens as I park on Water Street and grab Sonny's leash. We walk down the street and turn into the alley. I keep my eyes on the ground, the anticipation almost too much to take.

"Is she there?" I ask Sonny, who cocks his head at me.

I look up and let out a little squeal of delight. There sits the mannequin—dressed in its summer bikini—its waffle cone legs jutting into the alley.

"Sonny! I knew I could taste summer!"

There is a little hitching post for dogs in the alley, underneath a sign that reads Pet Parking. I secure Sonny's leash and say, "Wait! Back in a jiffy!"

Bells on the front door announce my arrival, and an older woman I recognize as the owner greets me.

"I knew it!" I tell her. "I had a feeling today would be the day."

The woman laughs, her cheeks quivering. Her hair is white and pulled up under a pointy cap that features the store's logo—a lake effect storm of white over the lake, the snow swirling into a perfectly formed ice cream cone over Michigan. She is very tan, almost the color of the saddle-brown leather seats in my car.

"Am I the first customer of the season?" I ask.

She laughs again. "Oh, no," she says, her white apron already flecked with a rainbow of colors. "I think the locals secretly microchipped me years ago. First sunny day over fifty-five degrees, and there's a line forming before noon." She stops. "Actually, I open and close the shop based as much on the weather in Florida as Michigan. If it's gonna turn nasty here earlier in the fall, I head to Florida. But if it's going to be a glorious October, I stick around. On the other hand, if it turns rainy in Florida, I like to head back to Michigan to watch everything come back to life. Like today." She smiles and looks around, even though we're the only two in the store. Then she lowers her voice and leans over the glass counter, whispering to me conspiratorially. "Wanna know the real truth? When my six months are up in

Florida, I have to head back. It's really not a mystery. IRS is the one who really has me microchipped."

I roar, my laughter echoing off the walls of the little shop.

"You look familiar," the owner says. She removes the plastic glove she's wearing and extends her hand over the counter. "I'm Teresa."

"Adie Lou Kruger," I say, finally getting my name right. "I've been coming here since I was a little girl with my mom and dad. Bet you hear that all the time, right?"

"Oh, my goodness," Teresa says. "You're Jon and Jo's daughter, right? I sure do miss them. They were characters."

Characters. I smile.

"They sure were," I say. "And I miss them, too." I hesitate. "Actually, I'm starting a new business in town. Turning my family's summer cottage into a B and B."

"You say that as if you're on trial," Teresa says. "I heard about your endeavor already. Word gets around town fast."

I nod.

Teresa continues. "You know what they say about resort towns, don't you? 'The nice part about living in one is that when you don't know what you're doing, someone else does.'"

I nod again. "So true," I say. "Actually, do you mind if I pick your brain for a second? I know you're busy, but…"

"Don't apologize," Teresa says. "Of course. I may not have all the answers, but I'll sure act like I will." She winks. "Hit me."

"What's your secret to a successful small business?" I ask.

"Staying sober during business hours," she says in a deadpan.

I laugh. "It's just that you've been around forever," I say. "And I've never heard a bad word about you or your business."

"That just means you haven't been listening," she says. "Seriously? I just focus on the important things—a great product and great customer service. What sets us apart from all the other ice cream shops around the region? We make the best ice cream in small batches. Our waffle cones are handmade in front of customers. These are recipes passed from my parents and grandparents, ones I found in an old recipe box. I believe in consistency and honesty. I work long hours, but this little business has helped put my kids through college and allowed me to work only six months a year. I think that's a pretty good trade-off."

I listen intently. "Thank you," I say. "I think I just need a little encouragement. It's been a long few months of renovation and work." I stop. "And spending money." I hesitate and continue, my voice suddenly quaking with emotion. "I just want to do right by my parents. I just want to do right by our cottage."

Teresa reaches her hand across the counter. I take it, and she squeezes my hand. "Are you following your heart?" I nod. "Are you doing what you love?" I nod. "Then you'll never work a day in your life. You will be successful."

I can feel a lump in my throat. "I needed to hear that. Thank you again."

"What else is going on?" Teresa asks out of the blue. "I can tell something else is on your mind."

Without hesitation, I spill my guts about Iris Dragoon.

"The Dragoon Lady?" Teresa asks. "You have my sympathies."

"You call her that, too?" I ask, my eyes wide.

"She's been a thorn in my side for years," she says. "First year in business, Iris and her brood brought me a 'welcome basket.'"

"I think I got the same one this year!" I say with a laugh.

"I bet your 'welcome' was under false pretenses, too," Teresa says, nodding, her hat seeming to make an emphatic exclamation point. "Iris claimed my mannequin, its bikini and its waffle cone legs were, quote unquote, 'too racy' for a family-friendly resort town. When I refused to take it down, she forced me to appear in front of the city council, alleging that the mannequin and its legs were dangerous to pedestrians, that it might fall and injure someone."

"What did you do?"

"I fought her," she says. "I spent a lot of money I didn't have my first year in business hiring an attorney to respond to her claims and then on an engineer to ensure the mannequin was 'secure.' What's she hammering you about?"

I fill her in about the history of and renovation to the fish house as well as the plan that Evan has hatched, although my heart pings at the realization I didn't have the courage to follow up with her about Sadie Collins.

A smile grows on Teresa's face. "I love it," she says. "You know, she's really just a modern-day Gladys Kravitz. She's bored and lonely, so she takes her frustrations out on other people. She thinks it's for the good of the town, but the town would never change if she had her way. Change is inevitable. And change is usually a good thing." She stops. "And this is Saugatuck. We may be family friendly during the day, but Iris needs to step out at night. It's like Peyton Place after dark. And that's really why people come to a resort town." She looks at me and then reaches for a new plastic glove. "Honestly, look at what a good businesswoman I am. I haven't even asked what I can get you."

I look through the shiny glass at the endless options. My mouth waters as my eyes scan cappuccino chocolate chunk, cotton candy confetti, Mackinac Island Fudge, county blackberry, Milky Way, snickerdoodle and Superman. But my eyes lock on the container filled with Smurf-blue ice cream. "Double in a waffle," I say.

"You're a true Michigander," Teresa says with a laugh.

"But I'm from Illinois," I say.

"Not if you order this," she says with a wink.

There is a phenomenon in the Great Lakes known as Blue Moon ice cream. The ice cream is iridescent blue, marshmallowy sweet and has an elusive taste that many describe as a combination of lemon and fruit. I think it tastes like the leftover milk from a bowl of Froot Loops. It's addictive, and the recipe is largely kept secret by the different dairies, ice cream makers and shops in Michigan and Wisconsin. Blue Moon ice cream turns your tongue blue, and it is a favorite of children.

And mine, I think.

Teresa turns on the waffle machine, which sits on a table between the long rows of ice cream. When it is hot, she opens it and pours in some homemade batter and shuts the lid. After a few seconds, she pops the lid open and removes a razor thin waffle with tongs, immediately and expertly twisting it into a tight, rolled cone. She plops in two huge scoops of ice cream, which begin melting and trickling down the side. Teresa slips it into a wrapper and hands it to me along with a fistful of napkins.

I take a bite and shut my eyes. I am immediately transported back in time. I can feel myself standing in this shop between my parents, all of us licking giant cones. When I open my eyes, Teresa is smiling at me.

"It's nice to feel like a kid again, isn't it?" she asks. "Even if it's only for a second."

I nod and reach for my purse. "On the house," she says.

"Oh, no," I say, pulling my wallet free. "I insist."

"No," she says. "Consider it an inn-warming gift. I wish you only success and happiness, Adie Lou." She reaches into a container by the cash register and removes a doggy biscuit. "And we can't forget your friend out there."

"Thank you," I say, taking the biscuit and my ice cream and heading for the door. "Truly."

"You need something sweet before the sour," she says with a wink.

I head out the door, bells jingling, feeling as light and happy as they sound. I hand Sonny his treat, and we stroll to the long boardwalk that winds along the channel leading to Lake Michigan. It's still too early for the big boats to have returned to the marinas that dot the boardwalk, but a few hardy fishermen in johnboats are working the banks.

The sun is shining, the water is sparkling and Saugatuck resembles a fairy-tale village in a pop-up children's book. Sonny and I take a seat on a bench near the water, and the dog barks when ducks approach looking for handouts.

I hold on tightly to Sonny's leash and my cone as the ducks stand their ground, squawking as loudly as the dog is barking. Sonny stands on the bench, and the ducks flap atop the water. I laugh at the showdown, before the ducks do a swift U-turn, swimming away quickly enough to make waves.

I take a bite of my ice cream, and then hold it up in front of the sky and the water, my eyes filled with shades of blue.

Suddenly, I realize I am smiling. I am in a resort town on a pretty day eating an ice cream cone for lunch. I am living the dream.

Without warning, the ducks return, again squawking for food, which causes Sonny to bark.

Showdown, I think, watching the ducks and Sonny duel. *Making waves.*

My mind turns to my meeting with Iris, and yet, for once, I feel empowered by Evan's plan and my talk with Teresa.

Time to ruffle some feathers, I think, finishing my ice cream.

TWENTY-SEVEN

The Dragoon Lady is alone.

I wasn't expecting this.

I was expecting her to be surrounded by her Red Hat posse. Seeing her all alone unnerves me. I had entered the Saugatuck Country Club like Al Capone, guns blazing, ready to do battle with the Blue Hair Gang. But one-on-one with my nemesis— my personal Eliot Ness—freaks me out.

As I approach Iris, who is sitting as rigid and upright as the floral arrangement on the table, I feel dizzy.

I should have brought Sonny—who I left in the car, his ears blowing in the air-conditioning like Snoopy's were when he was battling the Red Baron—for backup.

"You're late," Iris says as a greeting. She checks her thin gold watch and gives me a tsk-tsk.

I check my cell. "It's 2:01," I say, already exasperated.

"As I said..."

She sips her tea without making a sound. She has yet to look at me.

I take a seat and scan the dining room at the country club. It is octagonal and lined with floor-to-ceiling windows that overlook the first hole of the golf course. It's old-school—parquet floors and white linen tablecloths—and the tables are filled with distinguished silver-haired couples in plaid golf sweaters.

My parents were not country club people. My dad liked a beer on his boat. My mom socialized with women who baked, and cleaned their own houses. New-and old-money locals referred to families like ours as "the ones whose parents bought their cottage when property was cheap."

A waiter approaches as quietly as a whisper.

"What may I offer you, ma'am?"

I glance at Iris, who has yet to look me in the eye. For some reason, I think of when Trish and I dined this winter at RL in Chicago.

"I'll have a manhattan, please. Thank you."

There's my reinforcement, I think. *A stiff drink.*

For the first time, Iris looks at me. The waiter shoots me a bemused smile and disappears.

"It's awfully early for a drink," the Dragoon Lady says.

"It's five o'clock somewhere," I say for some reason, sounding like a total Jimmy Buffett Parrot Head.

The Dragoon Lady checks her watch. "Where?" she asks pointedly.

She makes me feel like a kid who constantly gets busted by a teacher for not having done her homework. Thankfully, the waiter brings me my drink, and I take a healthy slug.

"Why am I here?" the Dragoon Lady asks, staring at me before glancing around the club.

She's embarrassed to be here with me, I think.

I take another gulp of my manhattan. "I have a proposition," I say.

She raises an eyebrow and takes a sip of her tea. I wait for her to say something, but she doesn't utter a word.

"Well, okay, then…" I fumble my words and reach for my bag. I pull out the requirements the Preservation Committee has provided for the fish house, and then the proposal Frank and I have for it. "I'd like to…" I stop and rephrase my request. "I need to renovate the fish house into a honeymoon suite," I say.

"That's not possible," the Dragoon Lady says, cutting me off. "It's historic."

"I realize that, and we plan to keep the structure's original look, but I need the flexibility to turn that space into a guest cottage." I stop and pull out more papers. "As you can see, it's vital to the inn's success. It has the potential to be my biggest moneymaking room."

"I don't care."

"Excuse me?"

"I said, I don't care," she continues. "You should have considered all of this before embarking on this endeavor."

I can again feel the rage build inside me, but I think of Evan, and the plan we have carefully orchestrated.

"I need this," I start, trying to play to her emotions.

"Honestly, I don't care what you need."

I forgot she has no emotions.

"Well, then," I start casually, "I guess you don't care about this."

I pull from my bag the time capsule and letter I discovered in the fish house.

"Or this," I continue, pulling out a cow shoe.

The Dragoon Lady motions for the waiter. "I'm not interested in the trash you picked up at the antique mall to decorate your inn. Check, please. I only had the tea. Thank you."

"You're right," I say as the waiter leaves. "This is trash. This old time capsule and letter I discovered in the fish house from Sadie Collins, the daughter of the man who built my family's cottage." I stop. "Oh, and this. This is just some, old original bootlegging trickery from Al Capone."

Iris turns to me, looking me in the eye for the first time, and scratches her head in thought, her two wigs sliding ever so slightly atop her head.

"I was thinking I could either give them to the state historical society, or sell them via Sotheby's to help retrieve some of the cost I'll need to spend on your renovation and loss of income from the guest suite." I stop and look at her. "Or, I mean, I *guess* I could, well, give them to you and the historical society. What a coup that would be for you and the town, right?"

I take a sip of my manhattan and lean back in my chair. The waiter drops off two checks, and I reach for my wallet.

"Oh, my dear, I'll take care of your bill," the Dragoon Lady says.

"How sweet of you," I say, "but I really must be going."

I begin to stand, but Iris grabs my arm as I start to put the items back in my bag.

"Can't we talk?" she asks.

"Perhaps," I say, trying to match the evil smile she always gives. "Let me know."

I am as ruthless as Al Capone, I think. *I outwitted the Dragoon Lady!*

I turn to leave—my back straight, walking on air—when I hear her say, "By the way, your tongue and mouth are blue. You might want to see a doctor."

I scamper away and head directly to the ladies' room. I lean into the mirror, open my mouth and groan. I look like Smurfette. My lips, mouth and tongue are stained blue from the Blue Moon ice cream.

"You're a real class act, Adie Lou," I say to my reflection. I turn around quickly, remembering the last time Iris Dragoon humiliated me. At least, I am not wearing Evan's sweatpants today. I may not have been Capone, but I still won in my own way.

I stick my tongue out at myself in the mirror and am laughing like a little kid when Iris enters.

"We might have a deal," she says without preamble.

How can she catch me at the most embarrassing moment every time? I think. *It's as if she's microchipped me.*

I turn with as much composure as I can muster. "Okay," I say.

She nods and reaches for the restroom door. I try to stop myself from saying what comes next, but I can't. "But I need your help first," I say.

Iris turns and raises an eyebrow. "You do, do you?" she asks.

"I do," I say.

"All right, then," she says sweetly before adding, "I'd do anything to help you from looking so blue."

She smiles.

I hate you, I think. "Thank you," I say instead.

Looks like I've just made a deal with the devil.

TWENTY-EIGHT

Iris's black boots echo on the floors of the historical society building as she walks around turning on lights. A series of spotlights suddenly pop on overhead, and I am illuminated as if I'm on trial.

I turn to see an exhibit behind me.

U.S. Lifesaving Service and Shipwrecks on Lake Michigan

Hanging in front of a series of panels is a restored 1854 Francis Metallic Surfboat from Saugatuck Harbor, an all-iron lifesaving boat. The panels explain that it is one of America's first official lifeboats. It is surrounded by Lake Michigan shipwreck and lifesaving stories.

I watch Iris navigate her hallowed halls, and I can see why she is so at home in here.

Everything is old and preserved, just like her, I think.

"Do you know much about the historical society?" Iris asks, her clipped tone echoing in step with her boots.

"I'm familiar with it," I say. "But I don't know much about it."

She shakes her head with great sadness. "Like most," she says. "May I show you around?"

I nod, and Iris leads me to the front of the building, which sits directly on the banks of the Kalamazoo River on the opposite side of Saugatuck, whose white buildings gleam in the water's reflection.

"This building is a simple structure in the Prairie-Craftsman style and was originally built as the village of Saugatuck's first water pumping station, completed in 1904. It was designed by John Alvord, better known as the principal engineer of the Chicago Water System."

It sounds as if she's given this tour a million times, I think. *Just like me on the chain ferry.*

"Water drawn from several large wells at the foot of Mt. Baldhead was pumped by large gasoline engines in the pump house up to a one-hundred-thousand-gallon reservoir at the top of Lone Pine Dune north of Mt. Baldhead, from which it flowed by gravity through pipes crossing beneath the river to buildings and street hydrants in the village," Iris says, gesturing at a series of prettily designed panels that show Saugatuck at the turn of the century. "By the 1950s, water pumping and electrical generating functions had been moved to larger locations, and the building fell into disrepair. By 1970, the building's heavy slate roof had pushed out the walls and broken the interior tie-rods. A portion of the west wall had fallen in, exposing the interior to the elements. Windows and doors were in bad shape, and much of the brickwork needed repair."

She stops and looks me directly in the eyes. "My husband and I offered to lease the pump house from the village as a summer cottage in return for restoring the building. We became one of the first permanent lakeshore cottage families and helped save this building from demolition. I started the historical society and museum," she says. "This building has now been designated as a Michigan Historic Site and is listed on the National Register of Historic Places."

Iris's expression is curious now. "I know you don't like me, but I'm not so different from you," she says. "We love this town. We love its history. We want what's best for it."

Does she mean this? I think. *Or is she saying it to get what she wants?*

"An exhibit here averages about $15,000 to construct, and we operate on donations alone," Iris continues. "We want the next generation to understand our town's history and become its next stewards." She stops. "Like your son."

Oh, she's good.

"Now, what is it I can help you with before we discuss a potential deal?" she asks.

"It's Sadie Collins," I say.

"Yes," Iris says. "I would be very interested in her materials. They would be of great value here." She stops. "So, what is it you need to make that happen? I'm guessing you'd like us to ease our restrictions on your fish house."

I look at her. "I do," I start, "but my request is actually of a more personal nature."

Iris lifts an arched eyebrow. "I see."

"I can't get her out of my mind," I admit. "I dream about her. I worry about what happened to her. I've researched her online, but I really can't find out much information. I thought maybe..." I stop. "That you could help."

"You need my help?" Iris asks, raising her other eyebrow.

"I do."

"Okay, then," Iris says with a definitive nod, her two wigs sliding oh so subtly. "Follow me."

Iris leads me to a storeroom lined with shelving cabinets with long, thin drawers. She scans dates on the front of the drawers, opens one and pulls out an old, hand-drawn map.

"This is a plat from the late 1800s," she says. "Let's start here. This shows division of land by family name."

Iris lays the large plat on a desk and turns on a lamp. "Look," she says, pointing with a polished nail to a large square of land on the lakeshore. "Collins. And here. Collins." She continues, her voice rising in excitement. "More here, here and here."

"Wow. They owned hundreds and hundreds of acres. How rich was her father?" I ask.

Iris goes to a bookshelf and pulls down a big, hardbound volume with an old spine. "This is a history of Saugatuck," she says. Iris flips through the book and stops. She points at a series of old black-and-white photos. "Grover Collins owned the orchards here. Peaches, apples, all the fresh fruit that was shipped to Chicago. He also owned fishing boats. They froze fresh whitefish and salmon from Lake Michigan and sold that in Chicago, too. He was a very rich man."

A stern-looking man in a suit and hat is standing in his orchards, arms by his side, unsmiling.

"Any idea what happened to Sadie?" I ask. I stop and pull her letter from my bag. "He forced her to get married." I stop. "She couldn't even make her own decisions."

Iris reads the letter with a hint of a frown. "Like so many young women of her time," Iris says in a voice that's barely audible. "Like so many young women of my time." She looks at me. "Hold on. I think I might know where to look."

Iris leaves, and I can hear her footsteps in the museum. I look at the photos again and then return my attention to the plat on the table.

Collins. Collins. Collins.

Dragoon. Dragoon. Dragoon.

What? I think, my eyes widening.

I lean down and study the plat. The Dragoon name covers a large swath of the map.

"What's so fascinating?"

I jump at the sound of Iris's voice. I lean up so quickly that my head bumps the lamp on the table. "Nothing," I say.

She walks over and lasers her eyes on the map and then me. "I knew you were a bright girl," she says.

"Your family…" I start.

"Not *my* family," Iris says, her voice cold but pointed. "My *husband's* family."

Iris squares her shoulders and looks at me, unblinking. My blood runs cold.

"I am not much of a sharer," Iris starts, her tone softening, catching me off guard. "As you might have noticed."

I giggle uncomfortably.

"Please," she says, gesturing toward two chairs by a desk. "Sit."

I do, and Iris joins me.

"Did you know I was married for over fifty years?" Iris asks me.

"Amazing," I say. "Congratulations."

"Save your congratulations," Iris says, putting the book she is holding in her lap and wagging a nail at me. "Extend your condolences."

I cannot contain my look of total shock, and I stumble over my words. "I…uh, don't know what to say."

"Your Sadie and I are not that different, it turns out," Iris says. "I come from a well-to-do family in Chicago. My father was an attorney, and I wanted to follow in his footsteps. I went to college and law school, but when it came time for me to start work, my father demurred. He felt it was best I marry a man with whom I'd gone to law school, and whose father ran one of the biggest law firms in Chicago. It was an arranged marriage of sorts, you see, by both families so that their firms could merge. My family owned a lot of land in Illinois, and their family had a lot of land in Michigan. It was the ideal marriage on paper."

She stops. "I finished top of my class, and let's just say my husband wouldn't have graduated had it not been for some familial influence." A wry smile crosses her face. "There's a lovely law library named after him." She stops again. "I worked hard. There weren't many women of my era graduating law school, much less top of their class. And I had so many offers. I admire people who work hard and dream big. My husband didn't try at anything. He just expected people to fall at his feet. He knew that I saw through him, and so he spent his whole life trying to put me in my place.

"Do you have any idea what it's like to marry a man who was inferior to you in college, and then have him treat you not only as if you had no dreams of your own but also as an inferior for the rest of your life?" she continues.

"I think I do," I say.

"My husband treated me like he did his associates and our staff," Iris says. "As if we didn't matter. And I put up with that for nearly my entire life. I could have divorced him, of course, but I got used to being comfortable in life. Like so many women of my era, the men controlled all of the money. My husband earned all the income and invested it without consulting me. Due to his influence, I worried I could never land a job if I left him. And my family's wealth was passed along to my older brother to manage. He was just like my husband." She stops, leans toward me and whispers, "I popped a bottle of Veuve when they both died. I felt like such a monster." She leans back and says with a wink, "But that's the wonderful thing about women. We're survivors. We outlive the men."

She takes a deep breath and continues. "I started my own life after that. I ran committees, I fund-raised, I made this community my career. But you've made me realize I have treated people the same way my husband did. People dislike me as much as they did my husband." She smiles wryly at me. "Oh, yes, I know what people say about me, what they call me." I flush. "But you stood up to me. You challenged me. I'm not only a wee bit envious of you, Adie Lou, I'm rather proud of you, too."

"Me?" I blurt.

"Yes," she says. "You left an unhappy marriage. You followed your dreams. I felt like I wasn't even worthy of pursuing my own dreams. You've embarked on a new life and career, which is something Sadie and I weren't able to do. It wasn't an easy path that led you here, it was a treacherous road. And yet you're here. Doing things your way." Iris stops and considers me. "You *are* the unconventional woman, Adie Lou."

Iris's voice begins to betray emotion, and I am so taken aback that I reach over and take her hand. She grips it tightly, nods her head definitively, and then clears her throat and opens the book in her lap.

"My colleagues and I did a lot of research about a decade ago on some of the original lakeshore cottage owners and their histories," she says. "The Collins family, of course, is in here. I'd forgotten if we had included any mention of Grover's children, but we did. Here."

Iris hands me the book and points to a paragraph in the middle of the page. I begin to read and, as I do, tears fill my eyes. They fall—plop, plop, plop—onto the page, wetting the paper. I look up at Iris, my lips quivering. "She took her own life?" I am devastated to discover Sadie's sad fate.

Iris nods. "They ruled it an unknown malady to save face for the parents, but decades later, her family admitted she took her own life in Chicago." She stops. "I'm so sorry."

Iris reaches out and pats my leg. "You're strong, Adie Lou," she says. "Stronger than you even know. Never forget that."

I nod as tears trace their way down my cheeks.

"I guess," I say, stammering, "I wanted a happy ending."

"Then go write your happy ending, my dear," Iris says.

I stand and, without thinking, pull Iris into a hug. She holds me closely for a moment, and then I hand over the time capsule and the Capone cow foot. "This will be perfect for an exhibit here, don't you think?" I ask.

Iris smiles. "I do," she says. "And I think the fish house will make a beautiful honeymoon suite, don't you?"

TWENTY-NINE

"I don't know whether I should admit this or not," I say, "but this is the second time I've been here."

"In your life?" Scooter asks, his eyes wide with shock. "That's hard to believe. How did you not know about this place? It's a Saugatuck institution."

"Today," I say, my voice an embarrassed whisper. "My second time *today*."

Scooter laughs so loudly that the people waiting in the snaking line outside Lick Effect Ice Cream turn to stare. "You should be embarrassed to admit that," he says, before taking my hand in his and giving me a soft kiss on the head. "Actually, you're a woman after my own heart."

"So far, my diet today will have consisted of a manhattan and two ice cream cones," I say, taking a few steps forward in the alley.

"Isn't that the base of the FDA's food pyramid?"

"For either a child or a drunk," I say.

"Or a drunk child," Scooter says, unable to contain a whooping laugh at his own joke.

People in line around us turn to look at him again. "They're wondering who the crazy man is who says 'drunk child' in public," I say, nudging him with my elbow.

"No, they're wondering who the crazy woman is who eats ice cream multiple times a day."

We laugh in unison as the door jingles, and we finally make our way inside. As we stare into the ice cream case, Teresa spots me and waves. "Back again?" she asks. "For more ice cream or advice? Or both?"

"Ice cream only this time," I say with a big smile. "Thank you for your time earlier today."

She gives me a big wink. "No problem," she says. "I'll be around if you need any more, at least until the kids get off school and can start work."

"By the way, I think I put out Iris Dragoon's fire," I whisper. I can't bring myself to call her the Dragoon Lady anymore.

Teresa looks me over. "I don't see any ashes," she says. "Congratulations."

Scooter cocks his head at me. "We'll talk over ice cream," I say, giving him a wink as big as the one Teresa gave me.

Scooter turns his attention to the ice cream, and my heart begins to race.

You can learn a lot about a man by the ice cream he eats, my grandmother always said.

At the Chicago grocery she and my grampa owned, my grandma observed the eating patterns of neighbors and families for decades. She knew Mrs. Hawkins wanted a pot roast every Saturday, and every ingredient Mrs. Trigiani needed for her special Sunday sauce. ("Americans call it spaghetti sauce," my grandma told me, "but Italians call it Sunday sauce.")

But my grandmother firmly believed—after witnessing the

eating habits of men for decades—that the ice cream a man ate showed who he truly was.

Vanilla? Plain but steadfast.

Chocolate meant an all-American type of guy at heart, but one who never yearned for excitement or adventure.

Men who ate strawberry were as sweet as the fruit, but forever little boys.

Scooter leans into the case, his breath fogging the window. His eyes scan the tubs and then the labels on the case. He looks at Teresa, who is waiting patiently, holding her ice cream scoop in the air. I turn again to Scooter. He opens his mouth, and I hold my breath.

"Rocky road," he says. "Two scoops in a waffle cone, please."

He's a keeper, Adie Lou, I can hear my grandma say. *Adventurous, curious. Has led an up-and-down life but is an optimist who wears his heart on his sleeve.*

"Good choice!" I blurt.

Scooter turns, a laugh escaping when he sees my face. "You get excited about ice cream, I can see," he says.

I nod.

"Still a Blue Moon girl?" Teresa asks me. "In a waffle?"

I nod again.

After she makes our cones and scoops in the ice cream, Scooter and I pay and head outside. We stroll toward the river until we find an open bench. It is a surprisingly warm evening for early April, and I take a deep breath.

Spring is coming, I think. *There is still a nip in the air, but for Michiganders, this is downright balmy.*

"This weather makes me want to start planting my window boxes and annuals," I say, watching the town's lights reflect in the water.

"You remember where you live now, right?" Scooter asks. "It can snow in early May. In fact, it usually snows for the Tulip Time Festival." Scooter licks his cone and continues. "You can't start planting until Mother's Day. Right before you open for the season."

My heart jumps. "That's six weeks," I say, my voice high. "Until I open."

"You sound surprised," he says. "Are you ready?"

"That's like asking Marie Antoinette if she were ready for a haircut."

"So, you're not ready?" Scooter asks.

I stare into the water. "Can you ever be ready?" I ask. "Were you ready when you took over for your father?"

Scooter licks his cone as he considers my question. "No," he says. "I don't think you're ever ready." He stops and looks at me. "Being an entrepreneur is a bit like playing football. It requires endless preparation—exercise, drills, knowing the playbook, trusting your teammates and coaches, mental toughness and endless hours watching tape. But, eventually, you just have to strap on your helmet and go play the game."

"I knew I should've watched more football," I say with a chuckle. "But that's good advice." I lick my cone and look over at Scooter. "I'm already fully booked for Memorial Day weekend."

"That's awesome!" he yells. For some reason, his tone and football speech makes me feel as if he's going to high-five me, but he transfers his ice cream cone to his other hand and puts his arm around me. "I'm really proud of you."

"Thanks," I say. "I'm thrilled. And mortified." I lean into Scooter. "Trish talked up the inn to everyone in Chicago, I think, and my former colleagues helped me secure some great advertising and media in some influential magazines, newspapers and blogs. Best of all, the local media went crazy over the Al Capone video that Evan shot." I stop, take a long lick on my cone and continue. "Speaking of which, I met with Iris Dragoon today. That's what Teresa and I were talking about in Lick Effect."

"And you're still alive?" Scooter asks. "Fill me in."

I do, and his smile grows wider as I build the story to its climax.

"You're amazing," he says. "And so is she. Color me shocked."

"Speaking of color," I say, opening my mouth and wagging my tongue. "The whole time I was playing Capone, it looked like I'd drank a bottle of Nyquil and eaten a box of blue crayons."

Scooter laughs. "That is quite a sight," he says. "You know you look like a Smurf."

"Yeah," I say. "That analogy crossed my mind as soon as I saw my reflection."

Scooter squeezes me and draws me close. "A very smart, very savvy, very beautiful Smurf."

I look up and into Scooter's eyes.

"This is me, you know," I say. "A woman in her forties with a blue tongue who likes her ice cream way too much, who is starting over, who has a son, who still may not know who the hell she is or what she's doing."

Scooter considers this for a moment and then kisses me. He tastes like rocky road.

He's a keeper, Adie Lou, I can hear my grandma say again.

I can't help it, and I think again of Sadie and of Iris and wonder, *Do I need to be kept?*

PART NINE

Rule #9:
Be Grateful for Each Day

THIRTY

May

I am standing and smiling much like I have done in every mile-stone photo of my life, from high school and college gradu-ations to my prom and wedding. My spine is rigid while my stomach is sucked in, and I am holding my breath while main-taining the demurest of smiles.

"Uh-huh, uh-huh. I see."

I would guess the age of the county health inspector to be twelve years old. I had expected a grumpy, weathered, elderly man—say a Wilford Brimley—but instead was surprised to be greeted by a scrawny young man named Zach Millwood who bears an uncanny resemblance to Screech, the nerd in the TV series, *Saved by the Bell*, that I loved when I was younger.

"Interesting. Yes. Yes."

The fact I even needed a health inspection came as a bit of a surprise. I mistakenly thought that since my B and B had only eight rooms for rent that I didn't need to pass any inspections. But, in Michigan, owner and family rooms count toward the total number of rooms, and a B and B with over nine rooms must be licensed with the county health department when serving a full breakfast.

"I assumed I didn't need an inspection," I say to Zach, whose entire body is nearly inside my freezer.

He leans out of the freezer, his cheeks red and his lashes icy. "You know what they say about assumptions?" he asks. "Makes an ass out of you and me."

I think of Trish, and when she told me that in college.

Zach throws his head back and laughs as if it's the funniest thing anyone has ever said, and then reinserts much of his upper body—along with his notepad—back into the freezer, where he remains silent for much too long.

"What did you find in there?" I ask. "Bigfoot?"

Shut up, Adie Lou, I tell myself. *Why do you babble when you get nervous or people are quiet?*

Zach doesn't respond.

"Body of my ex-husband?"

This time, Zach reappears, eyeing me suspiciously before writing furiously.

"I was just, you know, joking."

Zach stares at me. "I assumed you weren't funny," he finally says. He waits a beat, and then breaks into uproarious laughter. "Get it? Assumed? I used that word again."

"Good one," I say, nodding. "You're very funny," I continue, attempting to butter him up.

"Thanks," he says. "Everyone says I probably should have gone into stand-up."

"Oh, yes. God, yes," I say, continuing to nod excitedly. "You're like Seinfeld. Maybe Ellen. It's a talent."

Zach returns to scribbling on his notepad.

"So? What's the verdict?"

"Guilty," he says.

My heart leaps into my chest before Zach starts to laugh. "Get it? You asked what the verdict was?"

Suddenly, I feel like pushing Zach into my freezer and closing the door. Instead, I smile and hold my breath.

He looks down at his pad. "A few issues," he says. "You need to move the kitchen cleaning supplies away from the prep and cooking station. And you need new cutting boards, but, overall, everything is brand spanking new—refrigerator, oven, freezer, pots and pans."

"Do I pass?"

"Like a speeding car," Zach says. "Get it?"

Get out, I want to say. Instead, I smile and say, "Good one."

THIRTY-ONE

"I used to think a punch list consisted of booze, juice and fruit," I say.

Frank laughs and looks down at his list. "We might need a drink after this," he says.

Frank's punch list—the document prepared at the end of construction that details every item that needs to be addressed before final occupancy and payment—is three pages long. We start in the kitchen and move from room to room. The amount of work and endless tasks to be completed is overwhelming: hardware in all the bathrooms, missing trim pieces, flaws in the paint, plumbing fixtures that have been installed incorrectly, light fixtures that have yet to be installed.

"And I wanted every threshold between the bedroom and bathroom to be marble," I say, my voice rising in exasperation. "Some are wood, some are marble, some are missing. I have staff coming to train next week, and a soft opening in two weeks in which I'll be doing a dry run of the entire operation, from turndown to breakfast to yoga and activities."

Frank tucks his punch list under his arm and looks at me. "I promise you this will all be done by next week, Adie Lou."

I look at him, my face etched in skepticism.

"I promise you," he says, before repeating it slowly again. "I. Promise. You."

I nod.

"Don't freak out," Frank continues. "Right now, you can't see the forest for the trees. That's natural. Just try and take a step back. Look at all you've accomplished in such a short time."

Sonny barks his agreement, and then leaps at Frank for a hug.

"I don't know what he's going to do when you leave," I say. "He will miss you." I duck my head. "I will miss you. You're like my Eldin."

"Who?" Frank asks.

I smile and think of the house painter on TV's *Murphy Brown* who showed up one day and never left her house.

"A friend," I say, which is the truth. Frank has been my friend.

He leans down and gives Sonny a kiss on the head. "I'll miss both of you," he says. "This project has meant a lot to me, Adie Lou. You're like family. I feel like I'm part of something special here. Something big." He stops, and a huge smile comes over his bearded face. "But with an old cottage like this, I know I won't be gone for long." Frank winks, and I laugh.

He is my Eldin, I think.

"Let me earn some money first," I say.

"I'll be back this afternoon, and we'll get started on the punch list." He turns to leave but stops. "Take a deep breath. Take it all in. You should feel very proud."

The cottage creaks as Frank departs.

I do as he suggests: I take a deep breath, step into the hallway, shut the door and my eyes, and act as if I'm in the B and B for the very first time.

I open my eyes and am greeted by a sign on the door that reads:

Room & Cottage Rule #9
Be Grateful for Each Day!

I smile and imagine that, as a guest, this cheery but direct reminder would immediately clear my mind of life's clutter, just like arriving at the cottage did every summer.

I open the door, and the room's cheery colors—pale blue walls, white trim and crown molding—greet me like a warm hug. The ceiling in every room has been covered in wood slats, painted bright white, and a wooden beadboard bed—crisp white and covered with an expensive blue duvet and loads of pillows with nautical symbols—floats like a cloud in the room. A pair of vintage oars are crisscrossed over the bed, and the walls are adorned with simply framed watercolors that my mother and I painted together over the years. Every painting—the lake glowing at sunrise and sunset, a sandcastle being built by a child's hand, marshmallows on sticks roasting over a bonfire, my dad napping on a hammock strung between two sugar maples, pink roses climbing a trellis and lavender-blue hydrangeas in full bloom—sum up the room's rule.

I look out the new, larger window that not only enhances the view of Lake Michigan but also keeps the cold air from penetrating the cottage. The ice is gone, the water is deep blue and lapping waves lull me into a relaxed state. I walk into the new adjoining bathroom, which is small but welcoming and well-laid-out. I splurged on the bath products and towels—thanks to Trish's advice—and the bathroom is a nice mix of luxury hotel and homey cottage.

I roam from room to room, each one surprising me with its own personality. Soak Up the Sun is happy and yellow, while

Boat Rides Are a Shore Thing is filled with photos of the *Adie Lou* and vintage boat finds given to me by Scooter. Shiplap walls line the Wake Up Smiling room, while an adorable wallpaper dotted with, appropriately enough, tiny ice cream cones greets guests to the Ice Cream Is Required room.

But perhaps my favorite of the cottage's guest rooms is Go Rock Hunting. I took a risk—and spent some cash—to have Frank create a wall behind the bed built out of the rocks and lake stones that I have collected over the decades. The result is a large-scale art piece that resembles the stone walls and fireplaces in the historic cottages of northern Michigan.

"Not bad, Adie Lou," I say to myself. "Not bad at all."

Sonny leads the way up the turret, whose staircase has been re-vamped and widened. Although my heart didn't want to change a thing about my beloved childhood hideaway, Trish had warned the staircase was, in her words, a lawsuit waiting to happen so, at great cost and anxiety, I had Frank blow out the opening and build an easy-to-climb staircase—with a rail—for guests. I found some vintage curtains my grandmother had used long ago in her bedroom—forest green with scenes of deer and rabbit scamper-ing through a forest of sugar maples, their leaves ablaze in fall color—and reupholstered the cushions my father had made for the turret's circular seat. A mix of new and old end tables, along with two ottomans topped with vintage trays, have been placed for guests to set their drinks and food. I added a small wet bar and a microwave—which Frank cleverly notched into a space once eaten up by the old circular staircase—to serve wine and appetizers at sunset.

I take a seat, and the view takes my breath. I briefly think of the hole in the roof that greeted me not so long ago, but the spec-tacular view of the lakeshore again transports me. In the haze, I can see my life as it was flashed before my eyes: as a young girl playing in the waves with my parents, as a teenager lying out with my friends, as a new mom building sandcastles with Evan.

Now, I'm alone, I think.

As if reading my mind, Sonny nestles next to me. Stroking his fur relaxes me, and I think of how strong he was to survive, how strong I am to have survived, and I picture myself as a modern-day Wonder Woman who has somehow overcome the odds.

You are the unconventional woman, I can hear Iris say.

"C'mon, kiddo," I say to Sonny, standing. He jumps off and leads me down the stairs to the kitchen, the new appliances—a restaurant-quality Wolf stove, huge refrigerator, double ovens—gleaming in the sun. I open the patio door and forget how much the space has been transformed, especially now that the construction on the fish house is completed and Frank's crew and equipment have finally disappeared. The new concrete patio has been divided into two distinct spaces, separated by a row of arborvitae. The smaller side features a built-in grill and cooking station. The larger side showcases a built-in water feature, a six-foot-high meditating Buddha sculpture, a Tibetan singing bowl and some beautiful polished planters that I will fill with trailing vine and annuals. The concrete pad merges into what will soon be newly planted sod, a large outdoor space where I will lead—weather permitting—my yoga sessions. The space looks nothing like my parents' largely forgotten patio, and I am awestruck by how gorgeous it is, especially now that the trees are once again leafing out and providing a verdant canopy over the space.

Sonny walks over to me and does a perfect downward dog.

"You're hired," I say with a laugh, bending down to pet him.

I cross the lawn to the fish house, now a pretty guest cottage and honeymoon suite tucked behind a newly planted hedge. "Thank you, Mr. Capone," I say. "Thank you, Sadie." I stop. "Thank you, Iris."

I worked with her to ensure that the guest cottage retained the authentic look and character of the fish house, down to its shingles. And a plaque citing its historical significance was added

to the front. I open the door and smile. But I was able to renovate the space completely, adding new, bigger windows, a small
kitchen as well as a master bath.

Most importantly, I kept many of my father's favorite things
that made the fish house so special. Vintage Cubs pennants have
been made into pillows, some of his prized catches are mounted
on the wall alongside my drawings. But the cottage's center-
pieces are his vintage Helmscenes. I softened the overall look
of the cottage with beautiful fabrics and lush throws and rugs,
but it still feels like a throwback, a getaway cabin, a place where
you want to hide from the rest of the world.

I shut the door and smile again when I remember what I had
named this cottage.

Guest Cottage & Cottage Rule #3
Nap Often!

"In honor of you, Dad," I whisper, running my finger over
the plaque.

I head inside, Sonny on my heels, and stop in the entry. There
are two new additions to the wall where my family framed the
Capone bullet hole. A copy of Sadie's letter now sits framed
above Capone's infamous outburst, while one of the cow shoes
used by Capone's bootleggers is centered in a shadow box below
it.

"This place has quite a history, doesn't it, Sonny?" I run my
hands over the glass that holds Sadie's letter.

*I humbly implore and petition you to care for this Cottage
as if I still retired here every evening.*

"I tried," I say. "I've given it my all, Sadie."

I read the end of the letter out loud, my voice echoing back
to me. "'Papa built this Cottage to be my Castle. It is now my

Prison. Still, please, do not weep for me. That is not worth a button. Instead, I propose you paint your Cheeks with rouge, I Pray that you may seek your own Stars, and I endeavor that a Smile is forever upon your face.'"

As I turn, I see the Cottage Rules sign by the front door, my eyes locking on Rule #9: *Be Grateful for Each Day!*

"I think I finally am," I say.

THIRTY-TWO

"Adie Lou!"

I rush down the stairs, a roll of paper towels in one arm and a bottle of Windex in the other, alarmed by the panic in Frank's voice. Sonny follows on my heels. When I hit the landing, I can see Frank blocking the front door—arms outstretched, hammer drawn like a sword—as if he's a warrior trying to fend off interlopers on *Game of Thrones*.

"What in the world?" I ask before I finally see: Iris and her minions are standing on the porch. I take a step forward, and my eyes widen. Behind Iris is a throng of townsfolk—Dale from the coffee shop, Teresa from the ice cream shop and various other business owners and innkeepers from Saugatuck. In the back stands Scooter, a tool belt around his waist, giving me a sheepish grin and wave. "What in the world?" I ask again.

"We're here to help," Iris says. She looks at Frank. "Excuse me."

Frank doesn't budge.

"It's okay, Frank," I say. He looks doubtful. "Really, it is."

"I take it you haven't told him about our burgeoning friendship," Iris says, brushing by a stunned Frank.

"What are you doing? Why are you here?" I ask in a rush.

"Gladys was at the coffee shop earlier, and your handyman..."

"His name is Frank," I say to Iris, "and he's a contractor."

"*Frank*," she starts again, emphasizing his name, "was waiting for his coffee and telling Dale how much last-minute work needed to be done on your inn. Gladys told me, and I made some calls."

I suddenly think of the game telephone I played as a girl.

"And voilà! Here we are! Word gets around fast in a small town," Iris continues.

Teresa steps forward. "Remember what I told you about resort towns? The nice part about living in one is that when you don't know what you're doing, someone else does."

I laugh.

"The really nice part," Teresa continues, "is that we always have each other's backs." She looks at Iris. "Even when we don't see eye to eye."

Iris nods but doesn't blink.

"We work together, not against one another," Teresa says. "If your business is strong, ours will be stronger as a result."

"So, what can we do?" Dale asks.

I turn to Frank. "Can you use a hand or twelve?"

Frank nods, still a little speechless.

I begin to say thank you but am suddenly overwhelmed by emotion. "I'm so touched," I say. "I know how busy you all are. I don't know what to say."

"Just tell us where to start," Becky, another innkeeper in town, says.

"Come on," Frank says. "Follow me."

"You okay?" Scooter asks.

I nod. "You didn't have to come," I say.

"I didn't?" Scooter whispers in mock relief. "Try telling that to Iris Dragoon." He kisses me. "And I didn't want to look like the only jackass in town who refused to help you. As you now know, word gets around fast in this town." He leans down, glances at Iris, who didn't head upstairs, and whispers, "You now have the mob behind you."

"Good," I say. "It's part of this place's history anyway."

Scooter disappears, and, within a few moments, I can hear hammers, electric drills, vacuums.

I turn to Iris, who I now realize is the only one who has come dressed as she always does: Joan Collins pantsuit, full makeup, wigs fluffed.

"I'm not so handy," she says, giving me a big wink with a false eyelash. "But I'm a great organizer and supervisor."

"You are," I say.

"Do you mind if I take a look around?"

"It didn't stop you before," I say, matching her earlier wink.

"Touché, Adie Lou."

I head back upstairs and return to cleaning, my nervousness and exhaustion fading with the camaraderie of the group. I order pizzas to feed the throng, and we are eating when Iris walks in the front door.

"May I speak with you for a moment?" she asks me.

The group grows quiet—as if I've passed a note in class and gotten busted by the teacher—and I follow Iris down the hall toward my suite.

"I'm sorry," I say. "I got so busy again. Where did you go?"

She pulls a small, beautifully wrapped box from her bag and hands it to me. "For you," she says.

I cock my head and shoot her a questioning look, but she says, "Go on, open it."

I rip off the pretty gift wrap and open the box. I pull back a bed of tissue paper, look at Iris and smile, my eyes instantly misting.

"I pulled a few strings to have it made so quickly," she says. "That's why I wanted to look around your inn first. I wanted this plaque to match the others. I thought you needed one for your own suite." She stops, and I swear I can hear her voice waver just a touch. "I thought the rule breaker needed to add one of her own to her family's."

ADIE LOU'S COTTAGE RULE
ALWAYS BE AN UNCONVENTIONAL WOMAN!

"It's perfect," I say. "Thank you."

"It is," she says with a nod.

Impulsively, I grab Iris and hug her with all my might.

"Are you okay?" she asks loudly.

I release her and turn to see her minions watching us, their mouths open, as if they've come across two unicorns crossing the road.

"She was choking," Iris says. "I saved her life."

The women nod and exhale with relief, my near-death experience more believable than a hug from the Dragoon Lady.

"Come on, ladies, we have a fund-raiser at seven," Iris says, continuing to cover, "and we are not leaving until we've hit our $10,000 goal."

As Iris exits, she turns and gives me another wink.

To unconventional women! she mouths.

THIRTY-THREE

My gratefulness is short-lived.

The first morning of my inn's dry run is in full swing, and I am drenched in sweat and could already use a strong drink. All of the local innkeepers I spoke to urged me to hold a full weekend run-through before officially opening, like when restaurants do a soft opening. I invited dear friends from Chicago and Saugatuck for the weekend, and some of Scooter's workers and clients filled the rest of the inn. I told them to take the weekend seriously, to act as if they don't know me, and—so far—everyone has turned in an Oscar-caliber performance.

I nod at each of my pretend guests who are gathered in the dining room eating breakfast and nod politely before rushing out onto the porch, hiding behind the arborvitae hedge and screaming into a dish towel.

"You have eggs in your hair."

I look up, and Trish is smiling at me, her head and coffee cup cocked at ironic angles.

I manage a small laugh. "These are *my friends*," I say. "What is a cottage filled with paying strangers going to be like?"

"*Lord of the Flies*," Trish says, "but just a touch more civilized." She stops. "Sort of like your marriage."

I smile and sigh. "This is way harder than I imagined," I say. "Do you know the woman I hired to help with breakfast service and cleanup didn't show this morning, or even bother to call? And the person I hired to clean rooms and do laundry texted and said she was going to be two hours late because her car wouldn't start."

"Welcome to the world of entrepreneurship," Trish says, not an ounce of sympathy in her voice. "Every single day is going to be a battle for survival until, one day, it's not."

"Gee, thanks for the pep talk," I say.

Trish sets her cup down on a small table and holds out her arms. I slump into Trish's body, nearly knocking her off her feet.

"It's not all going to be roses. You dreamed of this," Trish whispers into my ear. "Look how far you've come. You should be grateful."

I pull out of her arms. "If you post a picture of a sunset on Instagram, or say 'hashtag blessed' right now, I will never speak to you again."

Hashtag blessed, Trish mouths, before breaking into a laugh. "I didn't say it out loud." She stops and takes a seat in an Adirondack chair whose wooden back has been cut to resemble the iconic shape of the state of Michigan.

The sun is playing hide-and-go-seek with puffy white clouds that resemble cotton balls. The arms of sugar maples are waving in the warmish breeze, and the lapping of Lake Michigan in the distance fills the air.

"Look at what you've created here," Trish says. "It's magical. People dream of a getaway like this. You made that possible. And, you get to live here every day."

"Remember the winter?" I ask. "The chimney fire? My bank account?"

"It's exciting to be alive, isn't it?" Trish asks. "It's exciting to control your own destiny."

"Do you have more coffee?"

I look up, and Herb—one of Scooter's employees—is looking at me. He shrugs his shoulders in his Michigan State sweatshirt and holds out his empty cup.

"And can I get another muffin?" Herb's wife, Linda, asks. "And some woman is still complaining about her pillowcase."

"And her husband is still complaining about the music," Herb says.

"Yes, of course," I say with a smile. "Thank you. Sorry for the delay. I'll be right there."

I look at Trish. "My destiny is calling."

THIRTY-FOUR

After completing breakfast service, cleaning the kitchen and starting the first of a dozen loads of laundry, I turn and scream, thinking a ghost is standing before me.

Tori, the college girl I hired to help clean rooms, yawns.

"You scared me," I say. "How's your car?"

"My car?" she asks. "Oh, yeah. Um, so, it's fine."

My antennae go up. My experience as a mother has already taught me that Tori is lying. Her eyes are bloodshot, her mascara smudged, the back of her hair is ratted, and she would likely make a ghost scream, too.

"What's wrong with your car?" I ask.

"My car?" she asks again, as if I'm Alex Trebek and have stumped her on *Jeopardy*. "Like, the battery."

Tori seems nothing like the sweet, college girl I interviewed multiple times over the course of the last month, the one who was a "hard worker" and "needed the job to pay off college loans."

"But it's fine now?" I ask.

"Yeah," she says.

I am already tired and overwhelmed; Tori is making my blood boil. She has yet to apologize or ask what she needs to do.

Calm down, I tell myself. *You need her today. Think like a millennial.*

"I'm excited for you to start and be part of my team," I say. "As you know, this is the big test run."

Silence.

"So," I continue, "like I showed you in training, I want you to start cleaning the rooms. Strip the beds, remake them, clean the rooms and bathrooms, do the towels and sheets, make sure bath products are restocked. We'll need to set up the turret for happy hour at five. I'll be making some light appetizers, and I'll have chocolate-chip cookies ready at three. Just check the tiered cookie stands in the dining room and refill them when they get low. You should have the checklist on your phone. If you have any questions, just come see me. I'll be leading yoga for guests at 11:00 a.m."

Tori nods as she pulls gloss from her purse and applies it to her lips. She then musses her hair—her look is intentional, I suddenly realize—and retrieves her phone.

She's double-checking the list I've sent her, I realize, relieved. Finally.

But when she doesn't respond, and I watch her type a quick message on her cell, I see red.

Think like a millennial, I tell myself again.

I grab my phone, pull up Facebook and type in Tori's name. A flurry of photos greets me, most of which show Tori doing shots last night, dancing at a club in Grand Rapids and "hooking up" with a guy named Gabe.

Part of me knows I've been in her shoes, and part of me still understands the emotions and thrills of being young. But I've also held jobs since high school, and I have never missed a day of work much less treated an employer with disrespect.

Think like an entrepreneur, I hear my brain whispering.

"You're fired, Tori," I say. She stops texting long enough to finally look up. Her face doesn't register much of anything. "Go sleep it off."

Trish appears in the hallway and watches my first fired employee shuffle away, still texting.

"You have a gift for picking employees," Trish says. "Need some help until you can find another winner?"

I bust out in laughter. "I'm laughing only because it will keep me from crying right now," I say.

Trish holds up a pillowcase that is covered in makeup. "Did she sleep here last night?" Trish asks.

I switch the washer cycle to hot.

"Things will go better with yoga," Trish says, throwing the pillowcase into the washer and giving me a side hug.

They don't.

Along with Trish, I have two former colleagues from work and two wives of Scooter's employees. Only Trish has done yoga before.

"Last time I exercised I wore leg warmers," a woman named Dee cackles. Her hair is dyed red, and she has a big bow on one side of her head. Dee has shown up for yoga wearing mom jeans, while her friend, Sandy, sports a skirt and heels.

This is what I dreamed of? I think.

Trish looks at me and mouths, *Smile!*

"This is not about competition," I begin. "This is not about competing with anyone else. This is about finding your inner strength and inner peace," I say. "I'll go slowly from pose to pose, and I will come around to adjust each of you as needed."

"My husband's the only who does that," Dee says with a cackle.

I take a deep breath. "Still your mind," I say.

"Let's start with mountain pose," I continue, standing straight, planting my feet firmly in the ground and positioning my hands in prayer at my chest level while pulling my shoulder blades back. "Shut your eyes. This pose requires us to be present and aware, to stand rooted and tall."

I open my eyes. Dee and Sandy are standing as if they're about to knock back a beer, legs loose, shoulders slumped. I walk over to position them. "Plant your feet in the ground," I whisper to them. "Gently activate your quads to lift the kneecaps and stabilize your posture. Like this," I say, demonstrating.

Both women seem incapable of standing straight without wavering. They resemble flower stems in a stiff breeze, waving to and fro unsteadily.

"Let's move to child's pose," I say, lowering myself to my knees. "Bring your big toes together, spread your knees wide, sink your hips back over your heels as your chest lowers to the ground. Walk your fingertips to the front of the mat and relax your forehead down, allowing the chest to open and your mind to soften. Like this."

I hear a series of alarming pops and look up to find Dee and Sandy lying flat on their stomachs as if they're tanning on the beach. I walk over to them. "Like this, ladies," I whisper.

"We can't do that," Sandy says. "Bad knees."

"Have you tried?" I ask.

"Isn't this close enough?" Dee asks.

"Let's try downward facing dog, then," I say, returning to my mat and demonstrating the pose.

"Who do you think we are," Sandy says. "Jane Fonda?"

"Jane Fonda is eighty," I say, my yoga demeanor dropping and the tension in my voice escalating. "And she can still do downward dog, I promise you."

Trish looks up at me, her eyes wide. *Smile*, she mouths again.

I take a deep breath. "Remember, it's yoga practice, not yoga perfect," I say. "We must remember we are all on a journey, and every day we can do better, be better, improve our minds, bodies and spirits."

I continue. "How about sukhasana?" I ask, sitting cross-legged on the floor, my back straight. "This is also known as easy seat."

Anyone can do it, I don't say.

Again, there is more popping like someone is going to town on a sheet of Bubble Wrap. I look up and am nearly blinded by the sight of Sandy sitting cross-legged in her skirt. Dee is seated sidesaddle.

Before I can move to correct them, they stand, knees popping. "Yoga's too easy," Sandy says. "We're gonna hit the town and shop. Get in some real exercise. What time's happy hour?"

I open my mouth, but Trish stops me before I can insert my foot.

"Five p.m.," she says, her voice chipper. Trish looks at me and winks. "Though a few of us might start a wee bit earlier."

Twenty-four hours later, my guests check out, and my first weekend as an innkeeper is complete.

When the last person pulls out of the driveway, I look at Trish. "Now, this is my happy hour."

"Your first guests arrive in less than a week," Trish says. "You need to hire two new people before then and work out a lot of kinks."

As I clean up the dishes in the dining room, I pick up a dirty plate and act as if I'm going to Frisbee it at Trish's head.

"Hashtag grateful," she says.

PART TEN

Rule #10:
Go Jump in the Lake!

THIRTY-FIVE

May

"The kickoff to Memorial Day weekend looks to be one of the coldest on record. Could we be talking snow flurries tonight? Stay tuned."

I click off the TV and then throw the remote into the living room, where it slides across the wood floor before stopping on the hook rug by the front door. Sonny jumps up from his pouf in the kitchen and chases the remote. He nudges the remote off the rug and then goes round and round on the circular rug before dropping into a tight little ball.

"I wish I could be as relaxed as you," I say, unconsciously pulling my robe tight over my pajamas as if to ward off the coming cold. "First guests arrive in…" I stop and check the kitchen clock. "Four hours." I look back at Sonny. "And it's like winter outside. I'm doomed."

Sonny looks at me, sighs and closes his eyes.

Memorial Day weekend on the coast of Michigan is iffier than zip-lining with a ball of yarn. Some Memorial Day weekends are cool and rainy, spring refusing to turn over its reins to summer. And some are sunny and in the seventies, a gift, warm enough even for brave souls to...

My eyes drift from Sonny to Rule #10 on my parents' Cottage Rules sign: *Go Jump in the Lake!*

Sonny opens his eyes, thinks I'm looking at him and thumps his tail. I wave at him, and he sighs dramatically. I match his with one of my own.

"And some Memorial Day weekends," I say to myself, "are nightmares."

Somehow, I had forgotten that there were a handful of Memorial Day weekends growing up when it spit snow, we lit a fire every night, stayed inside, read and built fortresses out of sheets and blankets. As a kid, I certainly didn't love a wintry kickoff to summer, but there were ways to pass the time. As an innkeeper, I couldn't imagine anything worse.

I walk into the dining room, where I've hung a chalkboard in an ornate frame. On it, I've written—in beautiful, looping calligraphy that took me hours as well as many glasses of wine and erasers to create—the activity schedule for guests:

Friday
5:00 p.m.—Welcome! Bubbles & Bites (Happy Hour in Our Turret Overlooking Lake Michigan)

Saturday
7:00 a.m.—Coffee
8:30–10:00 a.m.—Farm to Table Breakfast (with coffee and mimosas)
11:00 a.m.—Yoga (on the patio)
2:00 p.m.—Orchard/U-Pick/Winery Tour

6:00 p.m.—Champagne Sunset Boat Ride on the *Adie Lou* (sign-up required)

Sunday
7:00 a.m.—Coffee
8:30–10:00 a.m.—Farm to Table Breakfast (with coffee and mimosas)
11:00 a.m.—Yoga (on the beach)
1:00 p.m.—Sandcastle Competition on the Beach
3:00 p.m.—Rock Hunting on the Lakeshore
6:00 p.m.—Champagne Sunset Boat Ride on the *Adie Lou* (sign-up required)

Monday
7:00 a.m.—Coffee
8:30–10:00 a.m.—Farm to Table Breakfast (with coffee and mimosas)
11:00 a.m.—Restorative Yoga (on the beach)
1:00 p.m.—Checkout & Goodbyes

Nearly everything, I now realize, revolves around good weather, or, at least, decent weather.

"Not snow," I say, my voice rising and echoing in the dining room. "Not windchill. Not this crapfest!"

Sonny opens his eyes and stares at me.

"What do I do now with my guests, Sonny?" I ask. "Build fortresses out of blankets?"

Sonny seems to know this is both a sarcastic and rhetorical question, so he shuts his eyes and refuses to acknowledge it.

I head back into the kitchen and go over the checklist I've printed that details every hour of the weekend: what I'm making and when; staff schedule; turndown service. I've planned every minute. My heart begins to race as my mind flashes back to last week's disastrous run-through at the inn.

I've planned every minute as if things will go according to schedule, I think, correcting myself.

"Don't panic, Adie Lou," I tell myself. "You've got this. Remember what Scooter said—'You can prepare all you want, but sometimes you just gotta play the game.'"

"C'mon, Sonny," I say, heading into the living room and up the stairs. "One final walk-through."

Sonny and I recheck every guest room: personalized guest books, with maps, and my own dining, driving and shopping recommendations, sit on each dresser. The rooms are clean as a whistle, the bathrooms spotless.

"Better go take a shower," I say. "Today is not a day to rush or be off guard, right, boy?"

Sonny barks. And then he lifts his head and barks again.

I cock my head, just like he's doing, and realize that he's not barking in agreement with my question. He's barking because the doorbell is ringing. Over and over again.

I tighten my robe, head downstairs and open the door.

"Can I help you?"

I am greeted by a gray-haired couple who look to be in their sixties. They are surrounded by a mountain of luggage, and the woman is wearing a giant red hat festooned with feathers.

"Hi! We're the Cranstons!"

I blink hard, once, twice.

"We're here!"

I continue to stare.

"Mark and Mildred," the woman says. "Cranston."

"I don't know any Cranstons," I say.

"Isn't this The Summer Cottage Inn? Aren't you Adie Lou Kruger, the innkeeper?" Mark asks.

Oh, no, I think, trying to pull it together while not allowing shock to register on my face. *They're over three hours early.*

Mark pulls a pair of reading glasses from the front pocket of his jacket and takes a step back, closely eyeing the cottage and then me. He then yanks his cell from his jacket pocket and taps on it. "Sure looks like you," he says, holding the phone up to my face.

Mark has pulled up a picture of me from the inn's website. I smile.

"That's me all right," I say with a small laugh. "I'm so sorry, but check-in's not until 3:00 p.m."

"But we're here," Mildred says, waving her arms, the jumble of necklaces and bracelets she's wearing setting off a cacophony of brain-jarring jangles. "You're not just going to throw us out on the streets, are you?"

Mildred's face—which is caked in heavy makeup—sags. "Are you?" she asks again, the red circles on her cheeks drooping, her tone pitiful.

"Of course not," I say quickly. "I'm still doing a lot of last-minute things. Please, come in."

"Good," she says. "Because I need to use your ladies' room."

Mildred enters, the feathers from her hat brushing my face. I sneeze, and Sonny begins to bark.

"Who's this?" Mildred asks.

"Sonny," I say. "The inn's mascot."

Mildred takes a step back. "Oh. I see."

"He's very friendly," I say. "And I'll have him in my suite most of the time."

She takes another step back.

"Are you allergic?" I ask.

"No," Mark says for his wife. "She's just not a pet person."

"Messy," Mildred says. "Like children."

"Well," I say in a cheery voice, "I have both."

"I see," Mildred says, her arms now raised as if she's going to be mugged.

"Let me put him in my office, while I show you to the bathroom."

I lead Mildred to the new guest bathroom Frank encouraged

me to build on the main level, and then trick Sonny into my suite by pretending to have a biscuit in my robe pocket.

"C'mon, Sonny," I say.

"Who doesn't like dogs?" I ask Sonny once my door is closed. I pat the bed, and he jumps on it, wagging his tail for a treat that doesn't exist. "And children? People who cover their furniture in plastic and put down rubber runners on their carpet, that's who." I steam for a second. "And who shows up four hundred hours early?" I take a deep breath, go to the bathroom and dab some lavender onto the back of my neck.

When I return, Mildred and Mark are in the kitchen. Mildred is opening cabinet doors, and Mark's head is in the refrigerator.

"Can I help you?" I ask.

"It's lunchtime," Mark says. "What are you serving?"

I can feel my last nerve—the lone cable that's keeping my personal elevator from collapsing a hundred floors—begin to fray.

Keep it together, Adie Lou, I think.

"This is the inn's opening day, and you're my very first guests," I say in a faux chipper voice, which makes me sound a bit like a demonic pageant contestant. "Could I get a photo of you two to commemorate this historic moment?"

Mildred turns, her face beaming. "How thoughtful of you," she says, a slight Southern lilt in her voice.

My plan of distraction worked, I think, my heart soaring.

"I'm very photogenic," Mildred tells me. "I'm president of my Kentucky town's Red Hat Ladies," she continues, her voice filled with pride. "I'm always in the local paper for our philanthropic and social duties. Always have to look my best. Never know when the paparazzi might jump out and take your picture, am I right?"

I nod.

"Where do you want to take the picture?" Mark asks, as Mildred licks her fingers and slicks down his hair.

"How about the front entry?" I propose, leading them in front of the Cottage Rules sign. "Every room in the inn is themed around one of these rules, which are meant to remind visitors of what's most important in life—the simplest things. My grandparents owned this cottage, and my parents came up with these rules and created this sign."

Mildred analyzes the sign and turns to me. "Kinda dull, don't you think?" she asks. "And the lighting here is terrible." She cocks her head in thought, the feathers on her hat fluttering, as if Mildred is about to take flight. "How about the entrance to our room?" Mildred suggests, a big smile on her face. "First check-in." Mildred looks at me. "What room are we in?"

I don't know off the top of my head, I want to say. *You're THREE HOURS early.*

"I know we've already paid in full," Mark says, his chest puffing.

"Let me check," I say with a smile.

Thankfully—after inspecting other inns—I placed a small stand in the entry, much like the ones restaurants place their hosts and hostesses behind. Scooter built it from reclaimed wood, and it's not only beautiful but fits the decor of the cottage. He added hooks for room keys, space for my laptop, calendar, notepads and maps. I place my laptop on the top of the stand.

"You're in…" I begin, before nearly choking on my words. "Go Jump in the Lake!"

It takes all of my willpower not to bust out laughing.

How appropriate, I think.

"It's a beautiful en suite," I say, "decorated with my family's photos and paintings of Lake Michigan. And, yes, you're paid in full." I stop, squelch a laugh and say with complete sincerity, "I picked this room especially for you."

Mildred beams.

"I can show you to your room," I say, grabbing the key. "It's on the third floor."

Mildred's face sags. "Third floor, Mark," she says with a big sigh.

"We have a ranch," Mark says. "Mildred likes ranch homes."

"This is a historic 1800s cottage," I say. "Lots of nooks and crannies."

"And steps," Mildred sighs.

I move toward the steps when Mildred says, "Our luggage…"

I look at her.

"I can store it for you until 3:00 p.m.," I say. "There are some wonderful lunch spots in Saugatuck. I know you're hungry."

"But our luggage will be in our room when we return, right?" Mildred asks, her voice rising, her head shaking, her feathers—literally—beginning to ruffle.

No, Mildred, I want to say, thinking of the mountain of luggage on the front porch, my back already aching. *You're responsible for that. This is a B and B, not the Four Seasons.*

Instead, I inhale my lavender and say, "Yes, of course."

"Good," Mildred says. "And do you offer a welcome glass of champagne?"

I need one, I think.

"Bubbles and Bites are at five," I say. "Champagne will be served."

"But not now?" Mildred asks. She has yet to move.

"Of course," I say. "Let me show you to your room first."

As I head toward the staircase, the Cottage Rules sign fills my eyes.

"Go Jump in the Lake, Mildred!"

I didn't mean for the words to come out, but they do.

Mildred's eyes widen, and she stares at me.

"Your room," I say, the hidden meaning in my proclamation giving me the strength to move forward. "This way."

"Oh," Mildred says. "Yes."

THIRTY-SIX

I click my cell, and its light illuminates the front porch.
Nine thirteen p.m.

I grit my teeth so hard I can actually hear them grind. I force myself to stop, worrying I might crack one and spend my first weekend as an innkeeper looking like an extra from *Deliverance*.

It is pitch-black, and I am rocking on the glider—Sonny's head in my lap—waiting for my final guests to arrive. Other innkeepers had warned me about the dreaded "late arrivals"—those who showed up hours after check-in—but I didn't anticipate it happening day one.

Right now, I think, remembering the words of Mrs. Dawkins, one of Evan's teachers who became a good friend, *my classroom is 90-10.*

She used to say that every year 90 percent of the children's parents in her classroom—like their kids—were incredible people. But 10 percent were a nightmare, and—in the beginning—she ended up focusing nearly all of her energy and attention on the smallest, most negative percentage.

"I learned I was shortchanging the ones who needed me most," she said.

I think of my first guests—an adorable couple named the Donovans and a sweet woman named Bev and her husband—who have been so kind and gracious.

Don't shortchange them, Adie Lou, I tell myself. *Don't let the marvelous Mark and Mildred and these latecomers take away from the others'—and your—experience.*

All of the inn's guests have gone to dinner, and the cottage, for a blessed moment, is silent. Cozy Cottage is at rest.

The snow flurries have ended, and the skies have cleared, making it abnormally cold, even for May in Michigan. But the stars are spectacularly bright, and I lift my head and search the night skies.

Spring up and fall down, I can hear my father say. *The Big Dipper shines high in the sky on spring evenings but close to the horizon on autumn evenings.*

When it was warm, my dad would let me sleep on the front porch in a sleeping bag, the waves lulling me into a deep slumber. When he'd tuck me in, he'd lie down beside me, and we'd search the skies, my dad pointing out the planets and the stars, naming each one.

I nervously click my phone again. There's an app for stargazing now. Just hold it up to the sky and—Bingo!—it tells you.

As I wait, I study the stars and then the cottage, thinking of my dad.

Where does the wonder go as you age, I muse. *Did I trade in the magic of this place for selfish reasons?*

I am exhausted. So tired, in fact, that my head is buzzing and my shoulders ache. Sonny groans and rolls onto his side, making the glider swing.

I look out over Lake Michigan, and it looks as if it's cloaked in ethereal light. I look up and spot the Big Dipper.

My mind turns to Sadie. When she looked out the turret, she saw the same stars—the same Big Dipper—as I do now. But her stars were "cross-grain'd."

Mine seem to be shimmering with hope and pointing in a definitive direction.

The Big Dipper seems to be telling me—with its bright stars—that life is all interconnected, a connect-the-dot pattern to something bigger if we just take the time to see it, to follow it.

"No," I say to myself, petting Sonny. "There is wonder, and this place is still magical. I'm just sharing it now with the world." I stop. "I am seeking my own stars."

I consider how many times my parents sat in this exact spot—on this same glider—waiting for me to come home. How many times did my grandparents do the same? And now, that continues, just in a completely new way.

My first day has not gone as planned. For some reason, I anticipated all of the guests arriving at the same time, like summer campers descending from a bus. I was planning to hand them sparklers—as my dad had done with my family for so long—and recite the rules of the cottage to them as an introduction to the beauty and spirit of the inn. But Mildred and Mark had thrown me off-kilter, and by the time I'd showered, I returned to the front desk to find more guests who'd arrived early.

Sonny's breathing calms me, and I shut my eyes and listen to the soundtrack of Michigan. Over the rhythmic thump of the waves, the peepers sing and the bullfrogs moan.

Once spring establishes itself in Michigan, nature returns after a winter of hibernation, and a chorus of insects and frogs sing their glorious return to life. My dad, like so many Michiganders, calls a certain frog that lives in these parts "peepers" for their distinctive call—a single, high-pitched peep—which is known as a harbinger to spring and summer. As the heat and humidity increase, their peeps become a deafening chorus. Accompanying them, cicadas serve as altos to their sopranos, and their calls—akin to violins—rise and fall from song to silence as if a conductor were leading them. The baritones are the bullfrogs, whose resonant, resounding moan reverberates like a bass drum over the landscape.

The sound of a car engine shatters the symphony, and I open my eyes. Headlights illuminate Lakeshore Drive and the dunes. I squint my eyes and scan the darkness. The car—a white BMW SUV—slows, and I can now see its illuminated interior: a strip of soft blue rings the doors, and the dashboard navigation shines. It turns, and the gravel drive announces its approach. Sonny wakes and elicits a deep, long growl, a warning woof that echoes across the lakeshore.

"It's okay," I say as much for him as for myself. "Is this finally our last guests?"

I stand and usher Sonny into the cottage, luring him into my suite before turning on all of the outdoor lights for the new arrivals.

"I'm at least going to do things correctly for one set of guests," I say.

I grab three sparklers and a fireplace lighter from the basket on the front door. As the guests make their way up the steps, I can hear what sounds like a man and woman arguing.

"Traffic was a nightmare because it's Memorial Day weekend," the woman is saying.

"I had to work," the man says.

"Until six on a holiday Friday?"

"Yes," he says. "Someone has to work."

My eyes are wide when they approach.

"Welcome to The Summer Cottage Inn," I say, finding a reserve tank of energy and enthusiasm. "You must be Mr. and Mrs. Caldwell. I'm Adie Lou Kruger. How was your drive?"

The two glare at one another, and I nervously shuffle my feet in the awkward silence. Finally, the woman says, "Hi, Adie Lou."

"Hello," I say uncertainly.

"It's Trey and Cissy," she says, her eyes growing as wide as mine just were.

"Hi," I repeat, sounding like a parakeet.

Am I supposed to know these people? I think.

"Trey and Cissy Caldwell," she continues, her voice filling with irritation. "Remember?"

Oh, my God. The Caldwells. *Nate's* Caldwells. The bond trader and his snooty wife. The epicureans who get invited to all the hot Chicago restaurant openings. The couple who don't watch TV. The ones who had a chef and maid and twin girls who modeled for J. Crew.

I realize I'm not speaking.

"Oh, my gosh! Trey and Cissy! I'm so sorry. I didn't put two and two together. It's been a crazy first day," I babble. "How are you? How long has it been?"

"Well," Cissy says.

I hate people that say "well" when you ask them how they are. I'm not specifically inquiring about their health. It's a common phrase. You can say "good."

She continues, "I think the last time we saw each other was when we went to that lecture by the Swedish philosopher at the university, and we all went out after." Cissy smiles like the Cheshire cat, her perfectly capped teeth shining in the darkness. "You fell asleep at the table, remember? Nate got so upset at you for being a bad hostess."

I remember now. I was exhausted from working all day, getting Evan to after-school practices, making him dinner, finding a babysitter and being bored out of my mind. And that was the night Nate thought it was so hilarious to call me *Dr. Adeleine* when he got drunk.

I hold out my arms and give Cissy a hug, before doing the same to Trey, who I inadvertently poke in the back with my sparklers and lighter.

"How are you?" I ask.

"Crazy busy," Trey says. He stands back and looks at me. "How are you?" he asks in a tone that suggests I've recently been institutionalized.

"Lots of changes," I say.

"We heard," Cissy says, her voice etched in false concern. "Nate told us."

I nod. Told them what?

"What brings you here?" I ask, searching for the right words. "It's so nice of you to support me my first week."

"We thought we needed a getaway from work and the kids," Cissy says.

"You came to the right place," I say.

"Yeah, we felt we needed a change of pace," Trey says. "Felt like roughing it for a new experience."

Roughing it?

"Well, I'm sure Nate told you this was my family cottage, and I've turned it into an inn," I say. "I'm so proud of all the changes, and I think you're going to have a magical stay."

"So," Cissy starts, her Botoxed face attempting to show confusion. "You work here?"

"Yes," I say. "I own and run the inn."

Cissy stares at me.

"It's my business," I clarify. "I'm an entrepreneur now."

"Oh," she says. "How interesting."

Interesting?

"Well, I'm sure you're exhausted from the drive, so let's get you checked in so you can relax and unwind," I say. "But first…" I hold out a sparkler for Cissy and Trey. Neither one moves.

"This was something my mom and dad did at the start of our summer holiday," I say. "It's a bit corny, I know, but the purpose is for visitors to leave their troubles at the door, which is the first rule of the cottage."

"So," Cissy says, her face again pinched in confusion. "What exactly are we supposed to do?"

"Here," I say, reaching into my jacket and pulling out a small postcard I had made for guests listing all the cottage rules with the inn's contact information at the bottom. "I light your sparklers, and we recite the rules before they go out."

"Doesn't that seem silly?" Cissy asks. "Childish?"

"Doesn't that pose a legal concern?" Trey asks. "What if someone burned themselves?"

"It's a sparkler," I say. "It's innocent fun."

Cissy and Trey look at each other with a tinge of sadness and amusement, and then give me a patronizing look, just like they used to do the servers at any restaurant we went to if they didn't meet their standards.

"We'll pass," Cissy says. "But cute idea."

"Just make sure you're covered under your insurance's umbrella policy," Trey adds. "People sue for anything these days."

My heart sinks, and I open the front door for them, quietly sliding the sparklers and lighter back into the basket before stepping inside and behind the stand.

"How quaint," Cissy says. "Oh, look, Trey. The Al Capone bullet hole Nate told us to look for."

My head jerks upright like when Sonny hears the word *cookie*. *Nate?*

Cissy looks at Trey, her face registering what I think is guilt. "Nate told us all about this place years ago," Trey says. "He just loved it here."

No, he didn't, I think. *That's a total lie.*

"Well," I say, acting as if nothing is wrong, "you're in the fish house."

"The *what?*" Cissy asks.

I laugh. "I'm sorry. It was once a cold storage outbuilding for fruit and fish that was being shipped to and from Chicago," I explain. "It's on the historic registry. It's been completely renovated and turned into a private guest cottage. I think you'll love it."

I can see Cissy is still unsure. "And," I continue, "it's away from all other guests. You wanted a getaway. This is a getaway." I look at my laptop. "You're paid in full, and here is your key. If you'll follow me."

I grab two of their bags and wheel them through the dining room and kitchen, over the patio and to the guest cottage. Trey tosses a bag over his shoulder and carries two more, while Cissy carries her Kate Spade.

"I hope there's heat," Cissy says, shivering. She pulls her tiny arms around her tiny body. She looks like a pretzel.

I unlock the door and turn on the lights.

"This was my father's favorite place," I say, wheeling their luggage toward the closet, "and it's decorated with some of his favorite things in the world."

Cissy walks toward one of the Helmscenes.

"What is this?" she asks.

"Turn the little knob on its side," I say.

She does, and it flickers to life.

"Wow," she says. "This really is roughing it."

I take a deep breath. Exhaustion—and the attitudes of my first day's guests—is getting the best of me. My head is now pounding so loudly I can barely see. "The bed has luxury linens, the bath features designer products, I've stocked your refrigerator with coffee and orange juice and baked some fresh muffins in case you just want to stay in your room in the morning." I walk over to the large window at the back of the guest cottage and open the curtains. "And you have breathtaking views of Lake Michigan." I try to contain myself, but I can't, so I say as politely as I can, "This guest cottage may have a throwback design and feel, but I'd hesitate to call it *roughing it*."

Cissy looks at Trey, her eyes wide. She's not used to being talked to in this way or challenged.

"Well," Cissy huffs, "it's too quiet out here in the wilderness.

I'm used to all the noise and buzz of the city. Where's my sound therapy machine, Trey?"

I can feel my eyes bulge.

Trey sets his phone down on a table by the door, shuffles through a bag and pulls out a small machine. He sets it on a nightstand next to the bed and plugs it in.

"What sound would you like, my dear?" he asks.

Cissy cocks her head. "How about ocean waves?" she says. "That always lulls me to sleep."

Trey flips on the machine, and the sound of rolling waves fills the room.

"Aaahh," Cissy says. "Now I can sleep."

I turn to the window, unlock it and throw it open. "Why don't you try cracking a window?" I ask. "Listen. It's the real thing."

"It's too cold," Cissy says, again throwing her arms around herself.

I inhale, walk to the wall and show them the thermostat. "You can control your own temperature here," I say. "There are extra blankets in the closet, and—if you get too chilly—you can flip on this little electric fireplace."

I turn and head toward the door. "If you need anything, don't hesitate to ask."

I am about to leave when a hear a phone buzz. I feel for my cell in my pocket, but it is quiet. I look down, and Trey's is buzzing.

Incoming call, it flashes. *Nate Clarke.*

What in the world? I think, looking at Trey and Cissy. Is he just being nosy? But then the penny drops. He sent them here to spy on me.

I smile as if all is right in the world. "Well, get some rest, and I'll see you in the morning. Good night."

"Good night, Adeleine," they say in unison.

Adie Lou, I think. *It's Adie Lou.*

I shut the door and walk casually across the patio. Once inside the cottage, I sprint to the front desk and open my laptop. I search the Caldwells' reservation.

My eyes scan when it was booked and how. Online. In late March.

I rub my eyes. But they seemed to know so little about the place or the cottage they'd booked.

I open the reservation.

A woman named Betty booked the room for Trey Caldwell, I read. I don't recognize the phone number she left with the reservation. I must have assumed it was Trey's assistant. Who did I send the confirmation email to?

I click on the screen again.

Betty.Simmons@fremontuniversity.edu

Oh, my God! Nate's university. That must be his assistant! Why would he book this for them?

My head pounds, and I feel sick to my stomach. I head into my room, rub some lavender on my neck and take Sonny out to tinkle.

I look up at the sky and immediately locate the Big Dipper. It now appears as if it's fallen on its side and is dumping the entire constellation directly on my head.

Before I crawl into bed, I crack the window despite the temperature. The sound of the lake fills the room and instantly calms me.

I pull the sheets around me, set my alarm for 4:30 a.m. and call Sonny to my side.

"How was your first day, Adie Lou?" I ask myself, stroking Sonny's fur. "Oh, just terrific, Sonny. Perfection. Everything I dreamed."

I think of Nate and the Caldwells, my head spinning. The front door opens, and I can hear Mildred's voice echo in the entry. "Mark, go check and see if there are any more chocolate-chip cookies! If so, get four!"

Go Jump in the Lake, Mildred, I think, releasing a little giggle before falling into the deepest sleep of my life.

THIRTY-SEVEN

I lift my head and smile.

The sun is glinting over the edge of the woods that back the cottage, quickly melting the light frost that has coated the grass and casting the earth in an otherworldly glow. The light gleams through the fronds of the newly unfolding ferns, green arms stretching as if they've just woken up. May apples cover the forest floor, and the early light makes the Michigan forest resemble a jungle thicket. The bark on the trunks of the spindly pines—the ones that creak in unison and sympathy with the cottage during a windstorm—glows red, a stand of white birch dots the woods like uniformed sentinels, while the smooth, pale gray bark of the beech shines, for once demanding attention.

Beyond the color, however, the early-morning sun has divided the world into two distinct halves. Half of the world remains cloaked in darkness, while the other half is awash in light.

Perhaps that is how we all tend to see the world, I think. *Either filled with light and hope, or darkness and despair, depending on our own light level.*

I look over at Sonny, who has angled himself into a shaft of light. When he sees me staring at him, he thumps his tail on the wet ground and belly crawls toward me, rolling over on his back. His world, too, is divided in half, filled with both light and darkness. Sonny thumps his tail even harder as I stop to scratch his stomach.

He only chooses to see the light, I think, *in spite of everything that's happened to him.*

I take a seat on my pad, and Sonny puts his head on my lap. For a moment, I stop moving.

I have been awake since 4:30, and yet I feel abuzz with energy. Although my first full day as an innkeeper was trying, to say the least, I woke this morning with a sense of purpose. I woke with a sense of "light."

I zip up my jacket, blow on my hands and stare at my little garden, also awash in light. The ferns on my burgeoning asparagus—which, unfortunately, I cannot pick the first year they're planted—look in the light like spiderwebs floating in the sky. The dew on the grass sparkles, and a misty fog is rising from the forest floor.

I return my attention to the rhubarb I'm picking, moving Sonny off my lap and then moving onto my knees on the cushioned pad. Sonny paws at the damp earth like he's assisting my efforts. I cannot take a full harvest of rhubarb my first season, so I cut only three large, firm stems, enough for my rhubarb sour cream coffee cake.

Like last night, I can hear my father talking to me in the quiet of the morning, like he used to do when we'd rise early and work in his veggie garden.

Remember, you can only harvest rhubarb in months without an r, he would tell me. *May, June, July and August.*

"Thanks, Dad," I say to myself, before turning to Sonny. "Ready?"

He jumps up excitedly and runs in a circle on the patio. I open the door, and he sprints inside. I get him his breakfast and then start on the guests'.

I look at the kitchen clock: 6:30 a.m. Lots more to do, I think. Better pick up the pace.

I start the coffee and fill the big urn in the dining room. On my last trip, I run my hands over The Summer Cottage Inn mugs that I designed, taking and filling one for myself. I shut the door to the kitchen, knowing there will likely be a few early risers who, like me, will want coffee ASAP.

I preheat the oven and then prep the sausage-egg casserole and the vegetarian tortilla casserole, continually referring to the flour-flecked, handwritten recipe cards from my mom and grandma's old recipe box. I had found it hidden in the back of one of the cabinets and spent countless nights thumbing through all the recipes, not realizing they would be the foundation for what I would make at the inn.

In the city, cooking had seemed like such a luxury. We always seemed to be in a rush, and that defined the way we ate. Cereal or English muffin for breakfast, lunch delivered in, takeout many nights for dinner. It was ironic to me that Nate—like the Caldwells—was such a foodie, and yet he didn't like to cook.

Maybe he didn't like my cooking, I think. *Maybe what I made was just too homey and old-school.*

My grandma loved to bake. She sold her own pies and cakes at their grocery in Chicago, and customers begged her for the recipes, but she'd never share them.

"They're like family," she told me.

My mom and dad loved to cook, too. They made what they termed "big, lake breakfasts," which were really brunches centered around my dad's blueberry pancakes or my mom's Belgian waffles and Cap'n Crunch French toast. They made their own jams and jellies—strawberry, blackberry, red raspberry, apricot—so even my PB&Js were downright haute cuisine.

I cover the two casseroles with plastic wrap and slide them into the refrigerator, before washing the rhubarb, drying it in a dish towel and placing it on the cutting board, where I chop it into small pieces. An errant piece falls to the floor, and Sonny hurriedly scoops it up, turns it around in his mouth, before spitting it out directly at my feet and shooting me a dirty look.

"Tastes better in a coffee cake with lots of sugar," I tell him.

I pull out cinnamon, flour, sugar and brown sugar, all while referring to the recipe card for my grandma's rhubarb sour cream coffee cake with cinnamon streusel topping.

"Oleo," I laugh, reading the old-school name for the margarine she once used. "Butter's back, Grandma," I say, pulling it from the refrigerator.

Though the only thing I used to make was reservations, as Trish joked, and despite the fact I'm juggling all new recipes on my very first morning turning out breakfast for guests, I am not nervous. In fact, I am calm. As I mix ingredients, there is a stunning peace to waking at dawn and cooking, a rhythm to the routine, a great satisfaction in what I'm creating.

I make two huge coffee cakes and slide them into the oven. As I slice cantaloupe and strawberries, I hear a coffee cup clinking in the dining room. I dry my hands and stick my head out the kitchen door. A middle-aged man in jeans and a hoodie with Ohio State University emblazoned on it is stirring creamer into his coffee. An iPad is in the crook of his arm.

"Good morning, Mr. Donovan," I whisper.

"Morning, Adie Lou," he says. "And, please, call me Steve."

He turns, takes a big sip of his coffee and continues. "You're up early."

"Breakfast," I explain.

"Already smells amazing," he says.

"You're up early, too," I say. "How'd you sleep?"

"Like a baby," he says. "The sound of the lake is like a sleeping pill. Do you mind if I sit in the living room and do some work while I drink my coffee? Thought the moose might keep me company while my wife sleeps."

I smile. "His name's Darryl," I say. "He's very quiet, but he's great company. And he'll look over your work when you're done. Those eyes catch everything."

Steve laughs. "You have a beautiful inn."

The emotion in his voice catches me off guard. "Thank you," I say, my heart quickening its pace. "I appreciate that."

"Shame you have to work while the rest of the world is on vacation," Steve says.

"What about you?" I ask. "This is supposed to be a respite from the real world."

"Is there ever a respite from the real world?" he asks, his voice tinged with sadness. "This place reminds me of being a kid. My grandparents had a little cabin in Wisconsin. I loved it there. Used to go up for most of the summer. Swam, fished, read books, skipped rocks. Dreamed I'd be an author, writing books there."

"What happened?"

"My dad sold the cabin after his parents died," he says. "Dream kind of died along with it." Steve looks at me. "Real world came calling." He stops. "Is this what you always dreamed of doing?"

"I wanted to be Wonder Woman," I say, "but this is turning out to be pretty darn close."

Steve shakes his head, a big smile on his face. "I admire you, Adie Lou." He nods toward his iPad. "I have a hundred emails to answer. They just keep regenerating. They're like *Gremlins*. Remember that movie?"

I laugh and nod, and then sniff the air.

"Excuse me, I think my coffee cake is about ready. You get some work done. Enjoy the quiet, and let me know if you need anything."

I literally whistle as I work, dancing around as I cook to

the '80s station that Alexa is softly playing. A half hour later, I emerge to check the coffee again, and the entire living room is filled with guests, a mix of men and women of all ages, all of whom are working on their laptops even though it's a holiday weekend. Their faces are etched in exhaustion and stress.

I think I've already forgotten my former life. While I now have a job that also consumes me—I mean, I can't even leave my office—it no longer feels like work. Even the darkest days have been tinged in excitement and light.

"More coffee?" I ask.

"Thank you," they say, barely looking up from their laptops.

I fill their cups and, a little before 8:30, I bring Alexa into the dining room and tell her to play classical music, despite last week's run-through guests who objected, I guess, to the sound of violins.

I begin to line the buffet with chafing dishes and then bring out the food, setting explanatory nameplates before each dish: the two casseroles, the coffee cakes, fresh fruit, a pot of steel cut oatmeal, a variety of cereals, along with bacon and sausage. I place wheat, white and rye bread near a toaster, along with a variety of jams and jellies made by a local orchard and pie pantry.

I retreat back into the kitchen—other innkeepers have instructed me to let guests find their own flow—and place the remaining casseroles in the oven to bake. I crack the kitchen door and watch the guests gather for breakfast.

It's a bit like watching students on the first day of school claim their places in the lunchroom. Some guests—like Mark and Mildred, who is already dressed and in full makeup, feathered red hat atop her head—are the first in line and first to sit at the expansive dining room table.

Other guests hold back, eyeing the crowd and the space. Some continue to sip coffee in the living room, while a few remain asleep upstairs.

"Good morning! What's your name? Where are you from?" Mildred asks every guest who passes.

Everyone responds politely, some joining Mildred and Mark at the table. Others, I notice, are not your typical B and B patrons: they take their food and find a quiet spot elsewhere, while some whisper that they want to eat in the turret.

Many couples do not speak as they eat. Some read the newspaper or a book while their spouse stares at a cell phone. Some couples plan their itinerary for the day, writing down timelines and activities.

What a fascinating social dynamic, I think, spying on my own guests.

I step out of the kitchen to refresh the food.

"Have a seat," a middle-aged woman named Bev says.

"Oh, thank you, but I can't," I say. "Too much to do."

"Have a seat," Steve insists from his chair under Darryl in the living room.

I pull up a chair at the dining room table, and guests bombard me with questions, about Saugatuck, the cottage and its history, what it was like to renovate it. But most of the questions center around buying a second home in Saugatuck.

"Where should we look?"

"What do you think of the market?"

"How expensive is the lakeshore?"

"What's it like to live here?"

"It's..." I stop, searching for just the right word, and my voice wavers with emotion when I finally find it. "Magical."

I tell them the story of my grandparents and of coming here every summer as a girl, and they stare at me—eyes wide—captivated by my every word.

I head back into the kitchen with an armload of dirty dishes, and I fill the sink with soap and turn on the faucet. My legs feel shaky, and I take a seat by the patio door and pet Sonny, who has laid his big head in my lap.

"They want the dream," I say to Sonny, my voice still shaky. "They want a little peace and happiness." I stop. "They want to be a kid again. They want to regain the joy we lose as adults."

I smile. "They want to leave their troubles at the door. They want the rules of this cottage, Sonny."

He stands and licks the tears from my face, when I hear a soft knock on the kitchen door.

"Would it be possible to get some more of the casserole and coffee cake?" Bev asks when I open the door. "My husband loves everything, but he's too embarrassed to ask."

"Of course," I say. "The casserole is warming in the oven. I'll bring both out right now."

I bring out the coffee cake and then place the casseroles in the chafing dishes, shutting the door behind me each time to hide the growing mess in the kitchen.

"Can I ask you how to get to this winery?" Mildred asks.

"Can you tell me where this cottage is located?" another man asks. "My navigation app keeps locating it in the middle of Lake Michigan."

I laugh. "Let me get you both some old-school maps," I say, returning from the entry and taking a seat at the dining room table. I chart out how to get to each place, when Steve walks in to fill up his mug with coffee.

"Um, Adie Lou," he says. "There's water coming from underneath your kitchen door."

I turn, and a lake has formed in the dining room. As I try to run into the kitchen to shut off the faucet, I slip and go down— hard—splashing water everywhere.

Steve sprints into the kitchen, while guests throw their napkins into the water.

Mildred walks up and extends her hand.

"Is it too soon to say, 'Go Jump in the Lake, Adie Lou?'"

I look at Mildred, her red cheeks sagging toward me, the feathers on her hat flying, and I laugh like a kid who just got finished engaging in a food fight.

"No," I say to her, taking her hand. "Not at all."

THIRTY-EIGHT

"**N**o flood!" I announce following Sunday's breakfast.

The guests break out into spontaneous applause.

There is a distinct difference in the guests today: people finally seem more relaxed.

This, in spite of my waterworks and the abnormally chilly and windy weather that has forced the cancellation of nearly all of my planned activities, from yoga to sunset cruises.

And yet fewer people are working on their laptops, more are interacting, and more are, well, just chill.

How long does it take people to unwind and finally relax? I think. *How long did it take me to relax on vacation?*

"We were supposed to have a sandcastle-building competition today," I say. "But I think it might be too cold to spend hours on the lake. But for those who might be interested, I thought we'd just cut directly to the rock hunt and go on a long beach walk. So, maybe around one we'll leave from here. Meet me in the lobby, and bundle up!"

Nearly every guest—including Trey and Cissy, who have yet to join the others for breakfast—is waiting in the entry when I walk out. We head to the beach, me handing out extra scarves, mittens and gloves for those who I see are unprepared.

"This wind is sobering," Bev says, as the group heads toward Pier Cove.

I point out different rocks and stones to the group, sharing stories of how my parents and I collected them, and most guests excitedly begin plucking ones they want to take home.

Even Trey, I notice, is hunkered down over the stream running into the lake, picking stones from the clear, cold water and examining each one closely.

Cissy is staring out over the water—looking like a model in her expensive coat and leather gloves, stunning and serene as if she's filming a perfume commercial.

"So, did Nate send you guys here to spy on me?" I ask, startling her.

She turns, her face falling, my question catching her completely off guard.

For a split second, I can see by her expression that she is thinking of lying to me, but instead she flashes the softest of smiles and says, "How did you know?"

"This doesn't seem like your type of vacation," I say. "Oh, and I saw Nate's name flash on Trey's cell when I was checking you into your room. I then double-checked your reservation, and saw that someone in Nate's office had made it."

"Nice job, Nancy Drew," Cissy says with a small laugh.

She turns to me and puts her hand on my shoulder.

"I'm sorry," she says. "I didn't want any part of this, and I certainly don't want to hurt you."

"What's this all about?"

Cissy turns toward the water, sighs and then turns back to me. "Trey says Nate misses you."

"He *what*?" I ask, my voice suddenly bellowing over the roar of the lake, loud enough to cause guests to look at us. "What about Fuschia?"

"I think they didn't work out," she says, adding with an eye roll, "Shocker. According to Trey, Nate wonders if he made the right decision. Between us? I think he's kicking himself, and he wanted us to gauge if you were truly happy."

I turn toward the lake, and it suddenly begins to spin.

Did I give up on our marriage too soon? *No*, I think. *He gave up on me, though.*

I feel dizzy, and I think of Evan. What does this even mean? Would he be better off with his parents back together?

"Whoooop!"

I turn and see Steve running toward the water, shucking his coat and gloves as he does. He runs directly into the lake, screaming, and dives in, headfirst.

"What's going on?" I yell.

He emerges, his face blue, his lips trembling. "I've always wanted to do that!" he says, shaking his arms. "Polar bear plunge!"

"Are you crazy?" Steve's wife says, bringing him his coat and gloves. "Have you lost your mind?"

"No," he says, laughing and turning to the group. "When did we lose our sense of adventure? When did we stop being kids?"

Steve looks at me and says as his teeth chatter, "What rule of the summer cottage is that, Adie Lou? Go jump in the lake?"

"Number 10," I say.

All of a sudden, my eyes well with tears.

"Are you okay?" Steve asks.

Before I can answer, Mildred kicks off her shoes, rolls up her pants and takes a few clumsy steps into the water. "It's cold!" she yells.

"Mildred," Mark says, approaching the water. "Get out of there. You'll catch your death of cold."

"Nonsense," Mildred says with a yelp, before leaning down

and splashing her husband with water. She wades out of the lake and calls to me, "Time I have a little fun, right?"

I nod, seeing Mildred—like I now do Iris—in a completely different light. And then I think of what Evan's teacher had told me.

I didn't give in to the 10 percent, I think, a smile emerging. *These guests have honed in my joy rather than my negativity and stress.*

I turn to Cissy. "I made the right decision," I say. "I love my new life."

I stop and look at Steve and Mildred, who are giggling like children.

"You can tell Nate to go jump in a lake," I continue. "He never did."

PART ELEVEN

Rule #11:
Build a Sandcastle

THIRTY-NINE

June

"*Fantasma! Fantasma!*"

I am stripping sheets and remaking beds on the second floor when I hear my new employee, Esme, scream. I sprint out of the Go Rock Hunting room, Sonny following and barking his head off, and round the corner into the Boat Rides Are a Shore Thing room, where I see Scooter with a sheet draped over him, his head sticking out, a sheepish look on his face.

"I'm so sorry," he is saying over and over to Esme. "I thought you were Adie Lou."

He turns when he sees me and flails his arms, the sheet flapping, making him look very much like a ghost.

"It was a joke. I wanted to surprise you."

"Surprise or scare?" I ask, narrowing my eyes. "Are you okay, Esme?"

"*Sí*, Adie Lou," she says, before looking at Scooter and wagging a finger. "*Dia de los Muertos* is already over."

"*Lo siento mucho,*" Scooter apologizes, pulling the sheet off his body. "*Lo siento mucho.*"

"I can take over in here, Esme," I say. "If you don't mind changing the laundry and then starting on the bathrooms, I'd appreciate it."

"*Sí,*" she says, giving Scooter a wary look one last time. "*Vámonos,* Sonny." The dog follows his new best friend out the door.

"Sorry," Scooter says again, dragging the word out for emphasis. "I wanted to see if you survived the weekend. I'm sorry you weren't able to take the *Adie Lou* out for a sunset cruise."

I take a seat on the mattress and begin tugging fresh cases onto the pillows.

"Yeah, I survived," I say. "The weather was a total nightmare, I had to cancel nearly all of my planned activities, I considered killing my first two guests, and my final guests arrived six hours late and—oh!—were sent as spies by my ex-husband."

I toss a finished pillow onto the bed and then begin pulling the next case on another one.

"Besides that, Mr. Lincoln, how was the play?" Scooter asks, his eyes wide.

"You know, in spite all of that, I have to say that it was pretty remarkable," I say. "I surprised myself."

"In what ways?"

I pull the case onto the pillow and toss it on the bed before looking at Scooter. "In every way." I stop. "I think...no, strike that... I *know* I made the right decision in spite of everything I've gone through. This is what I was meant to do."

Scooter takes a seat on the bed and puts his arm around me. "I'm proud of you, Adie Lou," he says.

"Thanks."

"So..." he finally says. "What about the spies? Aren't you going to tell me about that?"

"Let's just say I made the right decision about that, too," I say, slapping his thigh.

"Okay," he says. "I won't ask any more questions."

"Thanks, Barbara Walters."

"You're dating yourself," he says.

"I thought I was dating you," I say.

Without warning, Scooter pulls me close and kisses me with such passion I fall back onto the bed, Scooter on top of me. He kisses me again, and I feel as if the world around me is falling away—the mattress, the room, the cottage—and it's just us, holding one another while floating in the air. It feels nice. It feels right.

"You smell like fabric softener," he finally says with a small laugh.

"You're so charming," I say, as he kisses me again.

When I open my eyes, I scream. There is yet another apparition hovering in the door.

"Ghost!" I yell as Scooter sits upright.

"What the hell?" he yells.

"*Fantasma!*" I hear Esme yelling, Sonny barking wildly. "*Fantasma!*"

Esme rushes into the room and tosses the laundry basket she is holding over the ghost's head as if she is corralling a wild horse. She holds on to the basket as the figure struggles to free itself.

"Oww! Stop!" the ghost yells, before struggling to shrug off the basket and then the sheet.

"Evan?" I ask, bolting upright.

"*Tu hijo?*" Esme asks.

"Your son?" Scooter asks.

Sonny barks.

For a moment, we all stare at each other, doing hammy double takes, as if we're in an episode of *I Love Lucy*.

Finally, Evan says, "Actually, I think I'm the one who should be a little bit scared by what I just saw."

"I'm sorry," Scooter says, scooting away from me on the bed, his hands in the air.

"C'mon, Ethel," I say, grabbing Evan's hand. "Let's talk."

FORTY

"This isn't how I pictured you two meeting for the first time," I say, standing in the kitchen making sandwiches.

"That's not how I pictured surprising you," Evan says. "At least I know we both have the same sense of humor."

"That may not be a good thing," I say.

We both burst into laughter at the same time.

"You know, I've been ghosted before, but this takes it to a whole new level," Evan says. "Such a normal family."

"Don't I make you proud?" I ask. "Walking in on your mother making out with a stranger, and then getting a laundry basket thrown over your head?"

"Like a Hallmark movie," Evan says.

"How do you know about Hallmark?"

"All the girls watch them on campus," he says. "I've been forced to watch a few of the holiday movies, too." Evan blows the bangs from his eyes. "They're not so bad." He hands me a tomato, and I can tell he wants to ask me something.

"Yes?"

"When were you going to tell me about your friend?"

"Friend? That sounds so old-fashioned," I say.

"That's what Grandma and Grampa always used to say, wasn't it?" he asks.

"It was," I say, a smile crossing my face as I remember. I take the tomato and begin to slice, avoiding eye contact with my son. "Soon. I just didn't want to seem like I was rushing things." I look up at him. "I didn't want to upset you."

"I know," he says. "I appreciate that. Don't get mad at me for asking, but do you think you might be rushing things? I mean, the divorce, the job, the inn, the renovation, the grand opening...and a boyfriend?"

I finish slicing the tomato, thinking of the right thing to say. Nothing comes.

"Probably," I say, placing slices of tomato on top of the turkey breast. "Believe me, I've questioned and second-guessed myself more than a victim in a Lifetime movie." I stop and look at Evan. "But it feels right. It feels nice to feel good again...to feel young again...to feel happy again."

Evan nods. "I bet," he says. "Good for you. And I want you to know I'm okay with it, really. I just want you to be happy." He grabs his sandwich and shoves it in his mouth, taking a monstrous bite. "I mean, it's way better than seeing your potential new stepmother on campus."

"Now that would be a Lifetime movie," I say with a laugh. I take my sandwich and head toward the patio as Evan polishes his off without a plate. "Grab another one and join me."

We take a seat and Evan looks around. "This is beautiful, Mom," he says. "I still can't believe all that you've done in such a short time." He takes a bite of his second sandwich. "You should be so proud. I'm so proud of you."

"Thanks, honey," I say, my heart in my throat. "It's so good to have you home. I can't believe you're going to be here for the summer. I need the help."

Evan laughs. "Gee, thanks, Mom."

"That's not what I meant," I say, taking a bite of my sandwich. "But it's true. How were finals?"

"Good, I think," he says. "I feel like I did really well. Grades should post in a week or so." Evan finishes his sandwich and downs a bottle of water. "How did your first weekend go?"

I fill him in on more of the details—save for the information about his father—and he leans forward, enraptured by the stories.

"Well, I hope I can take some of the pressure off," he says. "When do the next guests arrive?"

"I have a few midweek guests, but the inn is booked again for this weekend."

"Wow," Evan says, reaching over to pull a piece of crust off my sandwich and feeding it to Sonny. "That's great."

"It's my first women's weekend," I say.

"That sounds ominous," he says with a laugh. "Is it okay for a man to be here?"

"Depends on the man," I say with a smile, before explaining the various weekends and activities I have planned. I get up and begin to deadhead a few flowers around the patio. "I can't tell you what it was like to see a group of strangers come into our cottage and—after a few days—become real people again. They became the people we used to become when we'd come here for the summer." I toss some spent stems onto the patio. "I felt like I finally had found my purpose."

Evan smiles. "That's amazing, Mom," he says. "But I have to ask one more question. Is it weird to have strangers here?"

A cardinal lands in a tree and begins to chirp, deep red on vibrant green. I cock my head, just like the bird, and turn toward Evan. "I feel like the cottage has found its purpose, too," I say.

"So, what do you want me to do around here?" Evan asks. "I have some ideas, but I know you do, too."

"I'm impressed," I say. "I half expected you to spend most of your days hanging out on the beach and meeting girls."

"Oh, that's definitely on my list," Evan says with a big smile. "But in the few minutes I will have free..."

I laugh. "Let me hear your ideas first," I say.

"Hmm," Evan says. "From that misdirection, I have a feeling I might not like your ideas as much as mine."

"You know me too well," I say. "I just think your ideas are going to be, well, a little more fun than mine. Shoot."

"I want to focus on marketing and social media," Evan says, his deep voice growing higher with excitement. "I want to post lots of pictures and video on Facebook, Twitter and other social media to show everything the inn and town have to offer. I want to bring it alive for people. In today's world, they need to experience it to understand it."

He continues. "I want to brainstorm some fun contests and giveaways, so that we get people interacting with us and sharing with their friends. And I want to expand your women's weekends, especially since summer will wind down and your outdoor activities will need to become indoor activities."

I pick up the stems from the patio—pulling one from the mouth of Sonny, who has decided to try to eat one while I wasn't paying attention making it look as if he has a green cigarette dangling from his mouth—and take a seat again. "I kind of forgot about that being so focused on the launch and short-term," I say.

"There are so many ways to expand on what you've started," he says. "Seasonal cooking classes, the fall Gallery Stroll combined with your own painting classes, winter women's pamper weekends..."

"What do you mean?" I ask.

"I think some women will love your empowerment weekends, but I also think some women just want to get away from their kids and lives for a weekend," he says. "You could have in-room massages, wine tastings, maybe a fashion show with a local shop.

"And a lot of people love winter, too, Mom," he continues. "We could theme it Winter at The Summer Cottage and have cross-country ski weekends with hot cider and hot chocolate, holiday shopping and decorating, romantic Valentine's getaways… Don't most of the shop owners in town say you thrive in the summer but off-season is what keeps you alive?"

My mouth drops as I stare at my son.

When did he become so grown up? When did he become so savvy? When did he become a man?

"Evan! I love this!" I say.

And then he blows his bangs from his eyes and ducks his head, and the confident man I just saw becomes the little boy I know.

"Thanks," he says, his cheeks flushing.

"My ideas aren't so exciting. More along the lines of manual labor," I say, giving Evan an "I'm sorry" expression. "I need help with a lot of the outdoor maintenance that I really didn't budget for, like mowing, weeding, trimming trees, keeping the steps and patio clear of moss, wiping down chairs in the morning, hauling beach chairs, towels and picnic baskets down for guests…"

"So, I'm the pack mule," he says.

Esme comes out carrying two huge rugs. She walks into the yard, tosses the rugs onto the grass and then lifts them up one at a time, giving them giant shakes. Dust motes fill the shafts of light, scattering this way and that like pollen.

She turns to us and says, "Just like *mi madre*," before heading back inside with the rugs.

Evan looks at me, his eyes filled with embarrassment. "I didn't mean to imply manual labor was beneath me," he says. "I didn't mean that I was too good for it."

I reach out and take my son's hand in my own. "I know, sweetheart," I say. "I know."

I begin to tie the spent stems I've laid on the patio table into a chain, just like I did when I was a girl.

"I couldn't find one person who wanted to work here *and* was actually capable of doing the job until a woman at a local orchard recommended Esme," I say. "Her husband picks fruit all summer, and then they return to Mexico. Their children are always on the move. And do you know what she told me when I interviewed her? 'I want my children to have a better life than me.'"

Without warning, my eyes well with tears.

"That's all any parent wants," I say. "And people judge her and her family every day, but she never complains. She shows up, works hard and helps make this inn run smoothly."

I stop. "We have a lot that is wrong in our country right now, but I can tell you this woman and her family are not one of them."

Evan squeezes my hand as Esme returns with two more rugs.

Evan stands and walks over to Esme.

"Show me how you and your mother do this," Evan says.

Esme looks over at me, a big smile crossing her face. She picks up a rug and flips it in the air—once, twice, three times—before floating it gently to the ground.

"I think you're stronger than I am," Evan says.

"*Sí,*" Esme says. "*Probablemente.*"

Evan laughs.

"You try," Esme says, nodding at the remaining rug.

Evan picks it up, gives it a flip and promptly smacks himself in the face with the back end of the rug.

Esme laughs and claps as Sonny comes running. The dog grabs the rug out of Evan's hands and starts running through the yard, Evan giving chase. He finally retrieves it from Sonny's mouth at the edge of the woods.

"Sonny is *mas fuerte* than you," Esme says. "He did better job. I think it's clean now."

"Do you mind showing Evan what you do during the day?" I ask as she returns with the rugs.

"Of course," she says.

As the two head inside, Evan asks, "Esme is such a pretty name. What does it mean?"

Esme stops. "Emerald," she says, her eyes sparkling. "*Mi madre* said I had the most beautiful green eyes when I was born."

"You do," Evan says, nodding.

I twist the braided stems in my hand and then slip it behind my ear, wondering how the beauty of childhood and equality of humans too often gets lost in the absurdity of adulthood and inequality of the world.

FORTY-ONE

"Esme and I have the inn under control, Mom," Evan says. "Go do your thing."

"*Sí,*" Esme confirms, before bumping Evan with her elbow. "Especially since every guest will be with her."

The two try to stifle their laughter, which only succeeds in making their bodies shake even more.

I try to move, but my legs won't work. My stomach is filled with butterflies, and I feel a tad faint.

"Are you okay, Mom?" Evan asks.

"I haven't been this nervous in ages," I say. "What if they don't get anything out of this? What if they paid all of this money and walk away empty?" I stop, and when I speak, my voice is as wavy as the lake. "What if they see that I'm a sham?"

Evan puts his arm around my waist. "What if, what if, what if," he says in a soft tone. "What if 'ifs' and 'buts' were candy and nuts? Then every day would be Christmas."

I look at him, eyes wide, a big smile crossing my face. That's the old phrase my dad quoted to me and Evan growing up: we all doubt ourselves, which ultimately paralyzes us from becoming who we want to be.

I inhale, hug Evan and take a step toward the door, my legs stronger. I stop on the rug by the front door and turn. "Bring everyone to the beach at noon," I say. "I want to get everything set up first."

Evan nods, and as I turn to leave, my eyes catch on the Cottage Rules sign by the front door, almost as if my father is standing by it, waving his arms and pointing.

I see it, Dad, I think. *I hear you.*

I turn, feeling emboldened, my gait suddenly filled with confidence, and walk out the front door.

It is a magical June day on the lakeshore, the kind of day that guests cross their fingers to get while on vacation. The sun immediately warms my skin.

A gift, my father used to call days like these. *A gift from God, Adie Lou.*

The wind is light and carries the scent of sunscreen, newly mowed grass and gas from boats on the water. But above those is the unmistakable, perfumed scent of peonies.

My mom's roses are clambering up the trellis and about ready to pop, while the hydrangeas that circle the cottage are already as big as VW Beetles, their electric blue and stunning pink blossoms—which will fill my McCoy vases all summer long—just a few weeks away from bursting.

On the way down to the beach, I stop and admire the tiny cottage gardens I planted, tiered surprises of color to greet guests upon their arrival: a stand of iris—tall and proud—in every color from dark chocolate to deep purple; cheery white daisies with centers as round and golden as the sun; and my favorite flower in the entire world, peonies.

My grandma used to say that heaven must smell like peonies, and I pray this is true. I stop and bend down to pull a flower to my nose. I inhale the sweet scent, and then do it again, before admiring the peony's perfection: a powder puff of fragile pink-white petals as soft as a baby's skin, a blossom of breathtaking beauty so heavy it exhausts the stem that holds it.

An army of ants marches around a burgeoning blossom, and they resemble ballerinas performing *The Nutcracker* on a beautiful stage.

I can't help myself, and I pluck the peony I was just admiring and hold it to my nose as I walk to the beach.

A mix of music fills the air: pop, jazz, classical, rock. I turn toward Lakeshore Drive behind me. Bikers, joggers and walkers fill the narrow beachfront road, their heads turned toward the water as if pulled by a magnet. Resorters have their newly washed and shined convertibles out for a ride, tops down, music blaring.

I crane my neck and scan the old road. The ancient limbs of towering sugar maples and pines have created a canopy over Lakeshore Drive, and it resembles a tunnel of trees, a byway for gnomes, perhaps. This simple view remains one of my summer favorites, as pretty as the beach, the dunes, the lake.

Such a difference from this winter, I think.

I turn and look back at the cottage, the turret winking.

Such a difference from this winter, I think again, winking back.

I walk to the beach steps and stop at the top. Lake Michigan is stretched out before me, flat and sparkling like a blue sequined dress. The sandy shore arcs both directions until it fades into a hazy mist like a mirage. The sky is cloudless, and the lack of humidity has turned it as blue as my hydrangeas. Boats and Jet Skis fly by in the distance, the noise briefly overpowering the sleepy lull of the waves lapping the shore before they fade into the distance.

I head down the steps and kick off my flip-flops when I reach the sand.

"Ow!" I say, not expecting the sand to be so hot. "Ow! Ow!"

I step back into my shoes and trudge toward the lakeshore, my sandals flipping sand up my legs.

The lakeshore is jammed today. People walk the shore, and the screams of swimmers diving into the still chilly water echo over the lake. I laugh at the whoops and hollers of visitors to Lake Michigan, who don't realize the water often doesn't edge above seventy degrees until July Fourth.

My little section of the lakeshore is empty, however. When my grandparents purchased Cozy Cottage, they also purchased over a hundred feet of lakeshore frontage. This sandy stretch is worth as much or perhaps more than the cottage itself, and is one of the secret reasons I wanted to keep this in the family.

"People want to be on the water," my grandfather used to say, referencing not only Saugatuck but also Chicago. "And, one day, there just won't be any more waterfront property to buy. And when it sells, few will be able to afford it."

A recent listing near mine for an empty, half-acre lot with fifty feet of frontage was on the market for one million dollars. I pick up a handful of sand and let it filter through my fingers. It looks like gold.

Fitting, I think.

I search for the perfect spot and find a flat area near the lake, where the receding tide has dampened the sand, but the sun has begun to dry it. *Perfect.*

I set down the only things I've brought with me: a bucket filled with a funnel, a cup, a melon baller, a spatula and a small shovel. I take a seat and begin my work: building a sandcastle.

Like painting, writing, fashion or decorating, there is an art to creating a sandcastle. My dad and grampa took sandcastle building as seriously as if they were building a house.

I pick up my shovel and dig into the sand, stopping when the sand turns darker. I squeeze a ball of sand in my hand for a few seconds and roll it around in my palm.

Always use moist sand, I can hear my dad and grampa tell me.

If it stays together in your hands when you roll it around, it's perfect sand for a castle.

This is perfect sand, I think again, a soft wind off the lake tossing my hair around and carrying a soft mist that moistens my face.

I begin to dig in earnest, like Sonny does on the beach, rear in the air, tossing sand left and right. I start with my shovel, but then quickly switch to a bucket in order to move more quickly. When a big reserve of sand is piled high, I find a flat spot and begin stomping around like a horse to create a strong foundation.

I begin to build, using my hands and the shovel to create an imposing wall. I fill buckets with sand and place them on my foundation, creating towers, and then use my cup to create turrets. I create roofs, walls and windows, before using the melon baller and spatula to scoop out and carve doors and details like steps and stonework on the towers.

I stand and brush the sand off my backside, and begin combing the shoreline near the dunes. I find a few nice pieces of driftwood as well as some feathers, which I add to the tops of my towers. I grab my shovel and begin digging a trench to the shoreline, going deep and far enough that water begins to fill the trough I've dug.

"That's quite a castle," a woman says as she walks the shoreline. "With a moat, no less. Very *Game of Thrones*."

"Thank you," I say.

I stand back and admire my work, when I see Evan leading a group of a dozen women down the beach steps. My heart quickens.

"Welcome!" I say. "Thanks, Evan."

He nods and then gives me a secret wink, before heading up the steps again.

I take a deep breath and scan the group. For some reason, I didn't expect the participants in my first women's empowerment weekend to be so varied. I had the guests introduce themselves at breakfast, and the women span ages from their thirties to their seventies. They are of every race and ethnicity, and from all over the Midwest: Chicago, Detroit, Indianapolis, St. Louis, Milwaukee.

"What has brought you here today?" I ask the group. "Something led you to this place and this moment. What was it?"

The sun is beaming on the women, and I can see them change in front of me, as if the light is illuminating not only their faces but also their souls.

"Divorce."

"Unhappy in my job."

"My mother died, and I feel alone."

"Empty nest."

"My children don't seem to appreciate me."

"I want to leave my job and write."

Some of the women become emotional, and others reach out to grab their hands, wipe their tears, give them hugs.

"You may be wondering why I brought you here and why I built a sandcastle," I say.

The women nod.

"I spent a lot of my childhood right here on this beach building sandcastles," I say. "I grew up blessed in so many ways—this cottage, this beach, a family who loved me deeply. Because of that, I grew up believing in love. I jumped into it headfirst, just like I did this lake as a little girl. I ended up marrying a man who turned out to be much different than the one I fell in love with. He cheated on me. How many times? I don't know. I still beat myself up over it. Did I ignore it? How could I not have known? What I do know is that I was raising a child, working full-time, running a house and barely sleeping. When my parents died in quick succession, I not only experienced such monumental, soul-shattering grief, I also experienced an awakening. How long did I have left? What was the mark I wanted to leave on this world? My son was in college, my job wasn't fulfilling, and my husband fell in love with a college student in his class named Fuschia."

The women laugh nervously.

"Uprooting my life and starting over no longer seemed like a risk, it seemed like a necessity," I continue. "That said, I wouldn't change a thing. I had a beautiful son, who has grown up to be an incredible young man. I have friends who have supported me. I have my own set of rules that now guide me." I stop and look at each of the women. "All I can do is speak from the heart. I believe that I am here *because* of all of that, not *in spite* of all of that. My history, good and bad, has made me who I am."

I take a deep breath and continue. "You may not have the tangible assets I do, like this inn and this beach, to start over, but you do have all of the intangibles necessary to become the person you always dreamed—strength, resilience, confidence, realism, independence, kindness, intelligence and souls that are ready to soar. Most importantly, we have the capacity to love greatly, and that is a great blessing and one we should never lose despite how much we may have been hurt in the past."

I can see some of the women nodding their heads, and that encourages me to keep going.

"Listen, I'm not a life coach, I don't have a psychology degree, and I don't know everything that you've gone through in your own lives that has deterred you from your dreams and led you right here, right now—be it children, mortgages, illness, caring for your parents, divorce or just plain old bad luck—but I do know this. We are united as women and that means we can do anything, especially together."

I look back at the inn and can picture Sadie alone in the turret. "We too often let others take our dreams from us. We let fear overwhelm us. We take the path of least resistance. We stop trying to build our own castle."

I pick up my cup from the beach, walk to the lake and fill it with water.

"We destroy ourselves one small decision and indecision at a time," I say, trickling the water onto one of the turrets, which slowly begin to collapse, one drop of water at a time. "It happens so slowly—from childhood to adulthood—that we don't realize what has happened to our dreams and self-esteem."

I pick up the bucket, walk to the lake and fill it to the top.

"And then one day..." I stop and pour the bucket over the top of the sandcastle, images of Iris and Sadie and my previous life flooding my mind. "It all collapses without warning. We realize our castle—everything that protects us, that we believed would keep us safe—is just a facade that can be washed away in the blink of an eye."

I take the bucket and fill it with sand. I take a seat and begin building towers for a new sandcastle.

"But you can start over, you can build what you dream," I say, "and that begins right now."

Slowly, the women join me—where I tell them all about Scooter—and we build a new sandcastle.

Together.

When it is completed, I place the pink peony I picked on top of the highest tower.

"It's beautiful," one of the women says.

"Because it's ours," another says.

"To unconventional women!" I say.

"To unconventional women!" the group responds in unison.

PART TWELVE

Rule #12:
Boat Rides Are a Shore Thing

FORTY-TWO

The *Adie Lou* putters down the channel, garnering admiring glances and appreciative honks from passing boats and captains.

I run my hand over its beautiful varnished wood and lean over to look out the side. I can see the wake reflected on the wood of my shiny Chris-Craft and my face reflected in the water.

I smile and wave at myself, just like I did when I was a girl and my dad was steering the boat.

"You look happy," Scooter says, one hand on the wheel.

"I am," I say. "Despite the fact I'm in a mountain of debt."

"Not for long," he says, nodding with his head behind him. "Look at what you've already created, the lives you've already impacted." He reaches over and grabs my hand, and I hear a chorus of giggles behind me.

"Aaaahhhh," three ladies from the women's weekend sigh in unison.

After a full day of empowerment, many of the women are now acting like schoolgirls.

"Scooter," one of the one women purrs. "You sound like you should be in a romance novel."

"A boat captain?" another says. "How romantic."

"A full head of hair and a full-time job!" Marge, who is in her seventies, exclaims. "Marry him now!"

The women laugh again.

I feel like I did when Justin Brown asked me to go steady on the school bus and placed a mood ring on my finger, and all the girls clapped.

"This isn't very empowered of you," I say, turning around in the front seat to face the women, who are seated in the small second row, which is just big enough to comfortably hold three.

I realize too late that my tone has a decided tsk–tsk to it and that I sound a lot like Iris Dragoon.

Marge, who admitted earlier to the group that she still hasn't discovered who she truly is and desperately wants to write before it's too late, says, "Everyone should be giddy when they're in love." She looks at me. "Or even when they're in like. That's not stereotypical behavior for women. It's simply human behavior."

The word *love* hangs in the air, and suddenly I want Scooter to gun the boat so the word will fly out of it.

"Hear, hear," the other two women say, knocking me from my thought, holding up their champagne glasses to clink Marge's.

"I think the teacher has just been schooled," I say. "I'm sorry."

I hold up my glass as a sign of a truce, and Marge clinks it and gives me a wink.

"Women are demeaned in American society for our emotions," she says. "In other societies, it's revered. Emotion is a strength, not a weakness. It's ultimately what makes women better survivors than men. We're in touch with how we feel. We don't bury our emotions, so we're able to cope better."

Scooter corkscrews his body in his seat, just enough to turn toward Marge.

"You're the writer Adie Lou was telling me about, right?"

Marge's eyes widen, and she smiles. "You called me a writer?"

"You've always been a writer," I say. "You just need to write."

"You should write that," Scooter says, his hair ruffling in the wind.

"Write what?" Marge asks.

"What you just said," he continues. "I bet you are filled with wisdom and advice, and have endless stories about how you and society have and haven't changed over the time you've been alive." He stops and considers what he wants to say, his eyes glowing in the fading sun. "If you just wrote about your life—essays about love, work, not discovering who you are until now—I think you might be onto something." He stops again, and when he speaks, his voice is filled with emotion. "I loved my father. He built my business and taught me so much. But my mom and grandma taught me to be a good person. And their voices, lives and lessons—just like the voices of so many of our elders—were too often overlooked and undervalued." He turns toward Marge. "That's what you should write."

"I think I might be too old," Marge says.

"What about Frank McCourt?" Scooter asks. "He didn't write *Angela's Ashes* until he retired from teaching, right?"

The boat grows quiet with his question, before Marge shouts, "Dammit, you're right!" She turns, leans over the boat and, without warning, spits off the side of the *Adie Lou*.

Everyone is staring at the septuagenarian, mouths open.

"What?" she asks innocently. "It's good luck."

Scooter laughs. "It is," he says. Scooter leans over and spits off the boat.

Marge lets out a big whoop of a laugh, which echoes across the water. "Cheers!" she says, taking a big sip of her bubbly.

Scooter steers the *Adie Lou* down the channel, which mean-

ders past cottages dotting the forested dunes along the river before emptying into Lake Michigan. I provide a history of the
area as we go along, just like they do on the *Star of Saugatuck*,
a historic, two-story paddlewheel boat, which is churning up
water in front of us and heading to see the sunset just like we are.

I feel my phone trill in my pocket, and I pluck it free.

All good here, Evan texts. Everyone enjoying the music and
picnic. Have fun!

Since the *Adie Lou* can hold only three people in the second
seat, we drew numbers on who would get the sunset cruise.
Marge didn't draw a winning number, but another woman let
her take her place, a surprise that brought tears to my eyes and
made me realize how much our group had already bonded in
the course of a day.

Evan and I planned a picnic on the giant lawn at the end of
the boardwalk alongside the river. We laid blankets and set up
tables under the ancient weeping willow whose long limbs reach
the water, sweeping back and forth as if soothing the river.

A white gazebo sits in the center of the lawn. It is the spot
of weddings and celebrations. Tonight, a jazz band is playing. I
set up a large spread of snacks: artisan chèvre from a local farm,
a selection of jams and fresh fruit from a local orchard, herbed
crackers and seedy salt bread from my favorite bakery, freshly
made whitefish dip from the local farmhouse deli and wines and
hard ciders from our local wineries.

I had thought the other guests might be jealous when we
motored by on the *Adie Lou*, but I was pleased to see they were
having as much fun—if not more—than we were.

The boat nears the end of the channel, and I can see Lake
Michigan open up before us.

"It looks like the ocean," one of the women gasps.

It does, I think, agreeing with the common refrain I hear
from guests.

No matter how many times people see Lake Michigan, they

almost can't believe their eyes. When they think of "lake," they think of an inland lake where you can see across to the other side. But Lake Michigan is as big, beautiful and grand as any ocean.

The water is as flat as glass tonight, and Scooter eases the *Adie Lou* onto the great lake with little wake.

"Hold on!" he yells, gunning the boat across the water.

I turn, and the women are yelping, their hair flying, gripping their glasses.

Scooter motors by Oval Beach—Saugatuck's stunning stretch of golden public beach with towering dunes framing it. This beautiful night people amble down the boardwalk, arms filled with blankets, picnic baskets and pizza boxes, ready to enjoy sunset like we are.

The *Adie Lou* putters around the bend of the lakeshore until it slows. I point up at the inn, which—from the lake—looks as if it has been tucked into the dunes grass like it's going to bed under a goldeny-green blanket for the night.

Scooter shuts off the engine, and the boat bobs on the surface as the women take pictures.

"We need a proper date," Scooter whispers in my ear.

I look at him, an amused expression crossing my face. "Ssshh," I say.

"We do," he says. "Meet me downtown at 1:00 p.m. on the boardwalk off Water Street. Your guests will all be gone then, right?"

I nod. "But I have to clean and…"

"I've learned as an entrepreneur that you must take your own time to replenish your spirit," Scooter says.

The same expression crosses my face again. "I didn't know I was dating Deepak Chopra," I say with a laugh.

"You just admitted you were dating me," Scooter says.

"Ssshh," I say again, glancing back at the women, who are still taking pictures.

Scooter reaches over and puts his hand on my thigh, and my skin tingles with goose bumps.

"Okay," I whisper, trying to catch my breath.

"Look!" Marge yells suddenly, making me jump.

I follow her fire-engine red nail, which is pointing toward the beach.

"There!" she continues. "Our sandcastle!"

I smile. The sandcastle we all built earlier in the day is not only still standing—strong, solid, perfectly intact—but beach-goers have added to it. Now, there is a stone wall protecting its entrance. Three sandy horses are on standby near a tower. In addition, a variety of decor—feathers, flowers, shells—have been placed on tops of turrets and onto the castle's walls and doors. The petals of my pink peony flutter in the wind.

But the pièce de résistance is a Barbie doll that someone has stuck into one of the towers, headfirst, feet sticking out into the air as if she is trying to escape.

"She's on the run!" Marge says, letting forth a big cackle.

Somewhere deep inside, I can feel my soul reverberate, as if my entire body is a sound bath and my heart a quartz bowl that is humming and vibrating.

I hope a young girl heard us today and watched us build that, I think. *I hope she believes in herself forever and never gives in to fear or forgoes her own dreams. I hope she is the queen of her own castle and never a prisoner.*

"Look!" Marge says again.

I swivel to look at Marge, whose body is now pointed the other way.

I turn and catch my breath.

The sky is lavender, the clouds dark purple. Within seconds, the horizon has turned red, then orange, before the sun—an orb of magenta—slowly melts into the lake.

I tilt my head and can hear a calm come over the lake, Michigan sighing as the sun sets, her coast taking a moment of satisfaction in all the wonder she has created in a single summer's day.

"Can every day be so beautiful?" Marge asks, eyes wide and still fixed on the horizon as others continue to snap photos. "Can every day be so perfect?"

I pull a bottle of champagne from an ice bucket on the floorboard and turn to the women seated behind me.

I do not say a word as I fill their glasses. I lift my own glass toward the sunset and then to each of the women, remaining silent while gazing intently into each of their eyes.

It can, I think as I stare at each of the women, who came here seeking something—empowerment, confidence, hope—to make their own lives more fulfilled. *It can.*

They nod, and when I clink glasses with Marge, tears well up in her eyes.

Thank you, she is mouthing at me. She then lifts her glass and her head toward the sky.

I turn back toward Cozy Cottage, my heart in my throat, and take a seat. I lean out over the *Adie Lou* and look at my face reflected in the water. I am smiling, tears splashing into the lake below me like a surprise thunderstorm quickly rolling by.

FORTY-THREE

"This is way too *Fifty Shades of Grey* for me."

I arrived at the end of Water Street for my "official" date with Scooter, who was waiting on a bench by the channel. With a blindfold.

"Are you pushing me in? What are you doing? Where are you taking me? This is way too kinky for me."

Scooter cocks his head at me, sighs and shrugs his shoulders.

"It's a blindfold, but I'm beginning to think I should use it as a gag."

I reach out to slap him on the shoulder.

"I just want it to be a surprise," he says, a crestfallen look crossing his stubbly face. "But if you don't want to play along…"

"No, no, no," I say, throwing my hands in the air. "I'm sorry. I don't mean to be so difficult. Do it."

"Blindfold or gag?" Scooter asks with a laugh.

"Ha ha," I say, as he ties the blindfold over my eyes, helps me up and then puts my hands on his shoulders.

"Follow me," he says. "As if you have any choice."

Scooter walks slowly down the boardwalk, which I can feel eventually transition to a sidewalk and then grass.

Without sight, I am suddenly and acutely aware of everything around me, especially the sounds and the smells.

I can hear the water rushing to my left, along with the passing of boat engines, so I know we are still walking along the channel in Saugatuck.

I can also smell the unmistakable scent of beans roasting at the local coffeehouse and the smell of burgers grilling at the Mermaid, so I know the direction we are traveling.

Finally, we slow and then stop, and Scooter eases me onto a concrete bench.

I hear the rustle of footsteps and whispers, and the sound of water slapping land.

"Why is that lady blindfolded, Mommy?" a child asks.

"I should do that to you!" I hear a man say.

"Ssshh!" their companions all whisper in the same, embarrassed tone.

There is a loud clanging of metal followed by a series of creaks, and I can feel the ground around me shaking.

Suddenly, my blindfold is off. It takes my eyes a second to adjust to the light.

"This is my surprise?" I ask at exactly the same time Scooter yells, "Surprise!"

We are sitting in front of the Saugatuck Chain Ferry, where we used to work. The metal gate to the ferry has been lifted, and visitors are flocking down the sloped wooden plank onto the little boat.

Scooter comes in front of me and hunches down. "We live and work in a resort town, but sometimes we forget to have fun here," he says, a wounded tone in his voice. "I just wanted us to have a day like everyone else who comes here during the summer." He hesitates. "Like we used to enjoy as kids."

I feel a lump in my throat as I watch happy tourists scramble aboard the adorably cute ferry, excited for their journey across the Kalamazoo River. The scene is so throwback, so Pure Michigan that I immediately want to erase what I said and throw this day into reverse by a minute.

"I'm so sorry," I say. "I didn't mean what I said. Can I have a do-over?"

Scooter nods.

"What a surprise!" I say, reaching out to hug Scooter.

He breaks into laughter and scoops me in his arms.

"Better?" I whisper into his ear.

He puts me down, grabs my face and kisses me. "Much," he says.

Memories flood my mind as we board the ferry. I feel as if I'm literally stepping back in time, not only in history but also in my life.

The ferry was built in 1838—a sign over the ferry proclaiming that fact—and was originally used to carry horses, rather than people, across the river. Today, it is the only remaining hand-cranked ferry of its kind still in use in the United States, and people happily pay a dollar a person for a little nostalgia.

The ferry still looks as if it's been brought to life off a vintage Victorian postcard: it is painted crisp white and its posts and top are outlined with intricate gingerbread trim.

Scooter escorts me on board, and we cross the ferry and stand near the front. The ferry is jammed today: tourists with bikes, and families with floaties and beach towels, all of whom wish to avoid either the cost of the day pass to the beach or the hour-long wait to find a parking spot on the beach. Even from across the river, I can see the snaking line of cars plugging Park Street.

Scooter puts his arm around my waist, and I lean into him, the sun warm on my face. Two teenage boys secure the ferry—shutting and locking the gates—and then launch into an intense game of rock, paper, scissors.

"Look," Scooter whispers to me. "They're doing the same thing we used to do."

I laugh. "They are!"

The first thing you learn as a chain ferry operator is that your shoulders collapse more quickly than your ego. Although the ferry travels only a total of about a hundred yards across the river, your shoulders feel as if you've hand-cranked to the moon by the time the day is done.

As teens, Scooter and I—along with our friends—would use two tactics to save our arms. The first was rock, paper, scissors to decide who would crank and who would get the easier job of blowing the air horn and sharing the history of the ferry. The other was to solicit manual labor from unsuspecting tourists, by cajoling or embarrassing them.

"Darn it!" one of the teens says after holding out scissors while his friend produced a rock on their third go-round.

As the ferry begins its journey into the river, the winning teen produces an air horn and blows it—to the surprised looks and shocked screams of many on board—to announce to oncoming boat traffic it is in the midst of crossing. He then launches into the history of the ferry. In the midst of his narrative, his friend locks eyes with Scooter.

"Hold on, Tommy! Hold on!" the kid yells, interrupting the same prepared speech I used to give. "We have a celebrity on board."

The passengers all look around the boat, eyes wide and excitedly murmuring, "Where? Where?"

"Mr. Stevens," the teen continues as he cranks. "Would you wave to the crowd?"

Scooter's face immediately turns as red as the chain ferry sign. He gives an embarrassed wave.

"Mr. Stevens is Saugatuck High School's most famous athlete," the teen shouts, as he continues to crank. "He led our high school to its last state championship and nearly went pro."

The passengers clap.

Scooter ducks his head. "This is revisionist history," he whispers.

"I'm quite enjoying this," I say.

"He now brings vintage wooden boats back to life," the teen says, stopping briefly to point at a boat in the middle of the channel. "Like that one."

Again, the passengers on the ferry applaud.

"Why don't you show us that arm?" the teen says, a big smile coming over his face. He winks at Scooter like a carnival barker might a stooge. His face is covered in sweat, and he is beginning to gasp for air.

"Great idea!" I say, encouraging the crowd. "Let's see the famed QB's famed arm!"

Scooter removes his arm from around me and lifts it part way into the air, a big grimace coming over his face. "Old football injury, unfortunately," he says as the passengers groan. Scooter gives the cranking teen a wink as if to say, "I know how to play your game way better than you do."

"But," Scooter continues, his voice rising in enthusiasm, "we happen to have another celebrity with us today, as well! Adie Lou Kruger not only runs the The Summer Cottage Inn here in town, but she was also the very first woman to work on the chain ferry!"

The passengers break out in applause.

"And her arm is still in perfect cranking shape!" Scooter continues, before chanting, "Adie Lou! Adie Lou!"

"Adie Lou! Adie Lou!" the passengers chant.

"I hate you," I say.

"I'm quite enjoying this," Scooter says, giving me a sarcastic wink.

The teen steps aside, giving me a dramatic bow. I place both hands on the giant handle that juts in front of me, take a deep breath and lean into it. My shoulders emit a loud pop, but I put my back into it and begin cranking as if my life depends on it.

"Adie Lou!" Scooter begins to chant again, which fires up the passengers to follow suit.

I find a rhythm in the cranking, just like I did when I was a kid.

"My dad actually trained me to prepare for this," I tell those on board, refusing to act as if I'm already out of breath, despite the fact my heart is leaping out of my chest. "He used to have me make homemade ice cream on our old hand-crank machine. Remember those?"

The older adults nod and smile.

"I want to let every little girl on here know that you can do anything you set your mind to do," I say. "Whether it's to be the first girl to crank the chain ferry, or be president."

Within seconds, little girls are lining up with their moms and dads, and asking if I can show them how to do it. By the time we make it to the other side, I have posed for about a dozen photos.

"You both have better game than we do," one of the teens says as we exit the ferry on the opposite side of the river.

"Old game is the best game," I say. "Have a great day."

Scooter grabs my hand as we head up the narrow path leading from the ferry. "Are you calling me old?" he asks.

"Old football injury, my behind," I say.

"And were you inspiring the youth of tomorrow or simply using them for their youthful arms?"

I laugh.

"You really are amazing," he says, slowing his pace and looking me in the eyes. Scooter kisses me softly on the lips as we stand beneath the pines, and I can't tell if the amazing scent is the trees or Scooter or both.

He always smells like the outdoors, I think.

"Thank you," I say. "Back atcha."

As we head up the narrow dirt path that leads from the ferry to the road, I ask, "Where are we going exactly?"

"Beach day," he says. "I bet you haven't had a real one yet, where you just do nothing."

I think of my days on the beach since I moved here—throwing my Two Buck Chuck on the ice, crying, worrying, working—and shake my head. "I haven't," I say.

"I figured," he says. "Follow me."

We cross the road and head into a circular unpaved parking lot ringed with cars. I look up and then at Scooter.

"We aren't, are we?" I ask.

"We are," Scooter says.

Mt. Baldhead sits before us, the region's tallest sand dune, rising six hundred feet into the air. Three hundred two steps go straight up the middle of the forested dune, like a wooden zipper.

"It's been years since I've done this," I say.

"I've been doing them nearly every day—even in winter—for years," Scooter says. "Great training for the fall ten-mile Mt. Baldhead run. You run these stairs at the halfway point."

"Of course you do," I say, my voice dripping with sarcasm.

"You should do it with me," he says. "And it would make a great weekend getaway for exercise enthusiasts."

I raise my eyebrows. "Not a bad idea," I say. "The last part, I mean."

Scooter laughs and looks at me. "Ready?"

I shake my head no, and we head up the steep steps, a canopy of trees covering the stairway. Every dozen steps or so there is a landing, and people at every elevation gather on them, some taking photos while others gasp for breath. Scooter is like a squirrel, scampering up the steps, taking two at a time, stopping at the landings to wait for me.

Halfway up the steps I am sweating, and people are passing me.

"On your left!" they call.

"I feel like a broken-down Datsun on an autobahn filled with Beamers," I say to Scooter, who laughs.

He grabs my hand. "Let's do the last half together, okay?"

A step at a time, we make it to the top, my thighs shaky and my quads quivering like jelly when we finally do.

"I think this was worth the effort, don't you?" Scooter asks, his mouth agape, his hands on the railing.

From the top of Mt. Baldhead, there is an unobstructed view of all that makes the area so stunning. The towns of Saugatuck-Douglas are stretched out before me like a beautiful oil painting on canvas, the light gleaming off the river and bay. Everything is adorably miniature, like a doll village, even the boats floating down the river toward the lake.

Beyond the towns, the canvas turns to a quilt, blocks of green and gold, squares filled with linear patterns of orchards and vineyards.

"I forget sometimes," I say, "that I am a part of something bigger."

I think I am saying this to myself until Scooter puts his arm around my back. "Me, too," he says softly, before gesturing with his free hand into the distance. "But look. How many people are coming here to experience this beauty because of you and your inn? How many memories are people making in the boats I've restored? We are all so small in the scale of things, but can be so big in our impact on the world." Scooter stops. "We are more than meets the eye."

My eyes shift to a massive cottonwood tree growing straight out of the dune. I remember hiking with my father, who pointed out these trees.

What you are actually seeing is the very tops of the trees, he explained. *The trunk and roots are buried deep below, and yet the tree has managed somehow to grow through the sand. It's just like us, Adie Lou. We can't see everyone's past—the hardships and sadness people have gone through is often buried deep—but we all have the ability to continue growing until the world is able to witness our growth and beauty.*

"Ready?" Scooter asks.

I nod, and we turn in the opposite direction. Through the trees, Lake Michigan sparkles. There is no staircase heading back down the dune, just a mountain of sand, a narrow trail dotted with footprints. When I was young and we would come during the winter, my parents would bring me here to sled downhill. It was a breathtaking ride.

"I haven't gone down this dune in ages," I say.

"There's only one way to do it," Scooter says. Without warning, he grabs my hand, and we start running down the dune, our feet churning sand.

I scream as we pick up momentum, going faster and faster, until the sand, the trees, the water before me is just a blur. When we reach the bottom, I am out of breath, as much from my screams and laughter as the exertion. We trudge over yet another smaller dune, which leads to the parking lot of Oval Beach, and head directly toward the beach. We stop at the edge of the boardwalk and remove our shoes and socks, dumping what seems like pounds of sand.

The beach is jammed this beautiful afternoon with vacationers as well as with resorters who have delayed their journeys back to the city in order to soak up as much of their Sunday as possible. We head right at the end of the boardwalk, where the large beach grows a bit quieter. Scooter grabs my hand, and we walk along the shoreline. I yelp as the still-cool water laps my legs, zigzagging in and out of the lake to escape the waves. Scooter slows and leads me onto the beach.

I look up, and a thatched tiki umbrella—its skirt shaking in the breeze like that of a hula dancer—is anchored over a giant blanket set with two beach towels, a cooler and a picnic basket.

"At your service," Scooter says, motioning toward the setup.

"Scooter, I don't know what to say. This is amazing."

He smiles and pulls me toward the blanket. We take a seat.

"Evan helped me," Scooter says, opening the picnic basket and the cooler. "We packed some of your favorite things—a little rosé, some artisan bread and goat cheese, some gossip magazines..." He stops, reaches into the basket and turns around. "Even a swimsuit."

"You thought of everything," I say, until I see the suit, a one-piece with mesh panels on the sides. "Leave it to a man to pick out the skimpiest swimsuit I own. Which, by the way, I haven't worn in ages. Nor will I be wearing today."

"What? I'm sure it will still look great on you. You do yoga."

"Let me explain something to you," I say, my sweet smile not matching the tone of my voice. "I've had a child. I've raised a child. I've worked long hours at a job, chauffeured my son around for eighteen years, cared for a family, gotten divorced, started an inn, eaten way too much pizza, drank way too much wine and life hasn't afforded me the luxury time to head to the gym or do yoga whenever I felt like it. So—" I stop and toss the swimsuit back at him "—what you see is what you get. And what you don't see is not what you think it is."

I look at Scooter. I have no idea how he will react to my little speech. If he thinks he's getting involved with Christie Brinkley when she was a *Sports Illustrated* cover model, he has another think coming. In fact, if you'd have bet me a few months ago on whether I'd be dating again, much less ever be having sex with a man again in my life, or if I would be joining a nunnery, I would've put three-to-one odds on the nunnery.

"Adie Lou," Scooter says, taking a seat next to me, "I understand. And I'm not the same guy either. My six-pack has been replaced by a six-pack of beer." He stops. "But I still see you as the girl you once were. To me, the years haven't changed you at all."

I exhale, relieved.

"Flattery will get you everywhere," I say. "And it might be time for an eye test."

He laughs and pulls me close, kissing me, his stubble grazing my lips. He holds my face, and the green of his eyes set against the blue of the sky and the lake takes my breath away. This time, I lean in and kiss him, exploring his mouth. He runs his hands through my hair, over my shoulders, down my back and rests them on my waist. My body explodes in goose bumps.

"Get a room!" someone yells.

We look up, startled, and a man is watching us with binoculars while perched in the driver's seat of a Chris-Craft boat going by close to the shore.

"Derek," he says with a laugh. "He works with me. I asked him to keep an eye on my picnic until we got here since he said he'd have his boat out today."

Scooter stands and waves at Derek and then flips him the bird. Derek honks, his laughter echoing across the water, before he hits the gas and speeds away.

"My turn," Scooter says. He self-consciously pulls off his T-shirt emblazoned with his company logo and then steps out of his shorts. He is wearing longish trunks, and though his body has softened since his younger days—he indeed has a little belly—my heart quickens, and I have difficulty taking my eyes off him.

"You look great," I say.

"Liar," he says.

"I mean it." I reach into the cooler. "Glass of rosé?"

"I think there's a beer in there with my name on it," he says.

"Is your name Stella?" I ask.

"It is today," he says, smacking his stomach. "I need one to add to my six-pack."

I pull off the cap and hold the beer up to him, and—as he takes a long draw—I can't help but remember Scooter's body when he was young.

"Remember when girls would give you their numbers on the chain ferry when you'd take your shirt off?" I ask.

"I miss those days," he says with a laugh. He takes a seat as I pour a glass of wine. "You know," he continues, his voice growing soft, "the only number I wanted was yours."

"What?" I ask, putting the bottle of Whispering Angel back in the cooler and taking a sip. "You never asked. You had so many girlfriends. We were just friends."

"You," he says, "always seemed out of reach."

"Me?" I ask, sitting up straighter.

"Yes, you. You were the city girl with loads of friends, headed to college with her future all planned out. You always seemed destined for big things."

"So did you, Mr. All-State Quarterback with a college scholarship."

Scooter looks at me and then out at the lake, taking a sip from his beer, his cheeks already growing red from the sun. "What if the big thing we were always destined for was each other?"

The warmth in Scooter's voice makes my heart stop for a split second. His words seem to drift on the lake breeze like the seagulls overhead who are interested in our picnic. I look into this man's eyes, the kid I met on Lakeshore Drive, the teenager who became my friend, the man who is now becoming my boyfriend.

What if he's right? I think. *What if this was always meant to be?*

I think of what Frank said regarding my maiden name and how it is German for *innkeeper*.

What if this has all been my destiny? I think. *What if I just finally started paying attention? Do any of us pay attention to the signs in our lives?*

"I think you may be right," I finally say, my voice shaking.

Scooter leans across the blanket and kisses me. His tongue is ice-cold at first from the beer but it quickly turns hot, so hot that it seems to melt my mouth and then my heart.

"Oh!" I suddenly yell, looking down to find my glass of rosé in my lap and Scooter's beer foaming and soaking my shorts. My heart is pounding, and I scan our surroundings, wondering what just happened. Finally, I see a football rolling to a stop next to us.

"Sorry!"

A kid jogs up, a University of Michigan hat on backward.

"My friend can't pass at all," he says.

I look at Scooter. "Show them how it's done," I say. "Show me that arm."

A sheepish look crosses Scooter's face. "Nah," he says, grabbing the football off the blanket.

"You don't have to leave everything in the past," I say, leaning over to whisper in his ear. "It's a part of you. Show 'em. Show *me*."

Scooter beams, hops up and tells the kid, "Go long. Then cut in by the old pier over there."

The kid turns and looks where Scooter has indicated before turning back around. "That's, like, forty yards, mister. Got a cannon on you?"

"I do," says Scooter. "Go long."

The kid starts running, and Scooter sets his body, just like he did in high school. While the kid is still running straight down the beach, and yet to turn around, Scooter pulls his arm back and spirals the ball into the air. The kid cuts in at the pier and—when he turns—the ball is there waiting for him. The kid's eyes grow even wider when the football drops into his arms while he's still in full sprint.

"Holy crap!" the kid yells. "Are you a pro?"

"Scott Stevens!" I yell back. "Look him up."

The kid runs over to his friend and starts pointing.

Without warning, Scooter picks me up into his arms and starts running toward the lake. He sprints in at full speed before we plunge into the chilly water. When I come up, water cascading off my face, Scooter is standing there, looking just like the boy I grew up with: handsome, confident, sweet, mischievous.

He pulls me into his arms and kisses me, our lips and bodies wet.

Music from a distant radio carries across the breeze, and I smile when I recognize the song: "Survivor" by Destiny's Child.

Survivors, I think, as Scooter twirls me in the water, and the blue, blue sky spins overhead. *Destiny, indeed.*

FORTY-FOUR

"Are you sure, Mom?"

Evan is white-knuckling the steering wheel of the *Adie Lou*, while Sonny paces excitedly in the back seat, his tail thumping the leather.

I nod. "You got this."

Sonny barks his support.

Evan turns on the boat, and I untie the forward spring line. I hold the rope and lean over to walk the boat out of its slip. Since the *Adie Lou* is so much smaller than other boats and Evan is just learning—pardon the pun—the ropes, it's easier to push the boat from the dock like a pontoon than risk an accident that could further fray Evan's already frazzled nerves.

I hop into the passenger side at the last minute, tossing the rope onto the dock. Evan looks at me, eyes wide, as if he's just seeing me for the first time.

"Mom! Wow! You're really good at this," he says.

"I've had lots of practice," I say.

The truth is, I've always loved this boat, but I've enjoyed being a passenger and copilot more than being the captain. Perhaps it's because my dad was always *THE* captain—I mean, that's even how it was stated on his skipper's cap. He taught me everything about this boat: I know how to tie every nautical knot, I know how to gas her up without scraping the sides, I know how to use a toothbrush to clean the hull, I know how to operate the boat. I just never really enjoyed driving it.

"I think it's the only time you allow yourself to relax," my dad once said. "Here, on this boat, with me."

You were right, Dad, I think.

"Put her in reverse," I tell Evan, "but don't punch the gas. Just ease it out."

It's late on Sunday, and the marina is empty. Most of the boats are in their slips for the week, waiting for their owners to return next weekend. Evan checks behind him a half dozen times before hitting the gas. I jolt forward.

"Easy," I say.

"Sorry."

I turn to check Sonny, whose eyes are wide and seeming to watch Evan's every move, as if to say, "Keep your hands at ten and two!"

Evan eases the boat forward and then putters out of the marina.

"You can go a little faster," I say. "It's okay."

Evan blows the bangs from his eyes and nods before picking up speed.

It is the perfect end to what has been a perfect weekend: my first women's weekend was a success, my first real date with Scooter was dreamy and now I get to spend an evening on my family boat with my son.

Evan heads down the river leading to the lake. Saugatuck is magical from the water as dusk falls over the town. Lights twinkle in rambling cottages, candles burn on the outdoor patios of restaurants, kids roast marshmallows over firepits while their parents sit on docks drinking wine. On the opposite side, people stroll the narrow road that curves along the river, working off their dinners.

I inhale. There is nothing like the smells of a summer evening on the lake. The scent of pine and firewood mingle with the smell of water. I turn and smile at Sonny, who is also sniffing the air.

Dragonflies flitter across the still water, darting off as the *Adie Lou* approaches.

I look over at Evan, his knuckles still white. He refuses to look anywhere but forward although only a few boats are returning up the river and back to their slips.

"Breathe," I say.

Evan exhales, a mix of a sigh and a laugh. "This is Grampa's boat," he says. "I just don't want to mess it up."

I reach over and rub my son's shoulder. "He would be so proud of you," I say. "You're a good captain." I stop. "You're an even better person."

Evan turns to me and smiles like a little kid. *"Mom,"* he says softly.

"I mean it," I say. "I don't say it enough."

"I feel the same about you," he says.

"Thank you," I say. "That means the world."

I do have a good kid, I think, my heart swelling with pride.

I know it sounds corny, but it's true. I have so many friends whose kids have not only caused them heartaches and headaches, but also don't seem to appreciate their parents. Evan not only works hard to be a success and a good person, but he also acknowledges the sacrifices made by me and Nate as well as his grandparents. That is rare.

"I'm a little nervous about taking this out on the big lake, Mom," Evan says as we head down the channel.

I can see the opening into Lake Michigan. There is a northwest wind, and it has turned the big water choppy.

"Why don't you just park in the party cove?" I ask.

Evan looks relieved, and heads the boat out of the channel and into a big circle of water, which is tucked into the shoreline and protected by the dunes. This is the spot where boats moor every pretty summer day, and people hop from boat to boat and party. Tonight, only a sailboat and pontoon are moored, and the party cove is peaceful.

Evan stops the boat in the middle of the cove, away from the other boats.

"Do we need to anchor?" he asks.

"I don't think so," I say. "It's dead calm here. Let's just sit for a few minutes and have dinner."

I've packed a small basket of sandwiches, chips and fruit for us, and a baggie of dry food for Sonny. I hand Evan a sparkling water and open one for myself, filling a collapsible water bowl for Sonny. We eat in silence and watch the fishermen come back in from a day on the lake.

My dad said you could always figure life out on a boat ride. *A wise man once said, "The goal is not to sail the boat, but rather to help the boat sail herself,"* my dad told me long ago when I was trying to figure things out. He took me out on the *Adie Lou*, and we floated and talked.

Dad, you were a wise man, I think, studying my son's silhouette, the shape of his face, the bridge of his nose, the strong chin.

He looks so much like you, Dad, I think.

Evan has always been a sensitive child, an observer. He assesses the people and situations around him before stepping in. But once he's in, he's all in.

"How are you doing?" I ask. "I know school is fine, but life." I hesitate. "You know. With your father and me?"

Evan takes a chip and flings it into the water. A fish surfaces almost immediately, along with a turtle, and the two nibble on it together.

"It was hard," he says, his voice soft, calm and deep, like the water thumping on the side of the boat. "You know, a kid wants his parents to stay together. It's selfish, I know, but you want to feel safe and protected. When that ends, the world is different than it once was. You grow up. You realize you're not a kid anymore, and that life is going to be hard sometimes."

"I'm so sorry," I say.

"You don't need to be sorry," he says. "And you don't need to apologize all the time."

"I'm sorry," I say.

"Mom," Evan says with a chuckle. He stops, looks out over the boat and continues. "I've also realized that I wasn't happy because you two weren't happy. You're different now, Mom. So is Dad. So am I. Things change, and that's okay. What's the old phrase? The only constant in life is change. That's true."

"I hope I'm allowing you to figure things out on your own," I say. "I hope your father and I aren't pressuring you to be someone or do something you don't want. That's my greatest fear."

Evan smiles. "You and Dad may not have been good together, but you've been great parents," he says. "I'm figuring it out. I'm still young."

"Yes, you are," I say.

"But I'm realizing Saugatuck, this place, this lake, our cottage, this boat..." Evan stops and looks around. "All of this is in my blood. What if I want to be part of this someday, part of what our family started and you've created?"

"I would be so proud," I say, "if that's what would make you happy."

"I just don't want you feeling guilty, Mom," he says. "You've spent a lot of your life feeling that way, and it is time that ends."

I burst into tears. I don't mean to, but my son's words feel as if I've just eaten a million balloons. I'm soaring—with hope, elation, love, admiration for the man my son is becoming—and I can't contain my emotions.

"I love you so much, Evan," I say.

"Me, too, Mom."

I reach over, and my son gives me the tightest hug of his life. And then we float in silence on the *Adie Lou*, drifting back and forth and back and forth, going nowhere but everywhere.

PART THIRTEEN

Rule #13:
Everyone Must Be Present for Sunset!

FORTY-FIVE

"I want everything to be perfect."

I place a bouquet of peonies on a table in the honeymoon cottage. White peonies with pink centers sit prettily in an aqua McCoy vase of my grandma's. I rush around arranging more bouquets—roses in Ball jars and sprays of ferns in baskets—until Evan urges me to stop.

"You don't want it to look like a funeral home, Mom," he says.

His choice of words unnerves me.

"You do know who this is for, don't you?"

Evan shakes his head.

"Bob and Grace DeLancey," I say. "They're celebrating their sixtieth wedding anniversary." I stop. "It's just that..." I stop again and fidget with a falling fern to mask my emotions.

I continue, my voice warbly, as if I just swallowed a hummingbird. "It's just that your grandparents never reached that anniversary. I will never reach such an anniversary. It's a big deal, and I want it to be perfect."

Evan walks over and tucks the frond just-so, before putting his hand on my back. "And it will, Mom."

I stand and survey the room.

"They remember when this used to be a fish house," I say. "Mr. DeLancey's father sold goods to my grampa at his grocery. He even came here once, a long time ago."

"That's so cool," Evan says. "I wonder what he will think of all the changes."

"Me, too," I say, my voice hushed.

"Want to help me make them an anniversary cake?" I ask.

"Isn't that an awfully big undertaking?" Evan asks.

"That's the whole point," I say.

"But we've got a full house this weekend. Did they request it? Was it part of a package you offered?"

"No," I say. "I just wanted to do something special and nice for them."

"Nice doesn't pay the bills," Evan says.

I shoot him a dirty look. "No, but sometimes being nice is worth more than money," I say. "Remember what your grampa used to say? Ethics is…"

"…what you do when no one is looking," Evan says, finishing my thought. "I got it, Mom."

"I think if we are always going above and beyond, people remember that," I say. "What did you tell me? Things go viral?"

Evan nods. "Like wildfire." He looks at me and then the room. "Okay, okay, I get it. Let's go make a cake."

We head outside, and I shoot a wary look at the sky. "It can't rain," I say, even as ominous clouds begin to crowd out the blue sky, and the wind shakes the trees. "It's their anniversary."

"You can't control the weather, Mom," Evan says. "Shocking to realize, isn't it?"

A small smile crosses my face. "It is, actually," I say with a laugh.

We head into the kitchen, where I begin to pull out flour, sugar and butter from the cabinet and refrigerator.

"What kind of cake?" Evan asks.

"I was thinking a traditional white cake with buttercream frosting, and that we'd write on top of it," I say. I stop and grab my phone, pulling up a string of emails. "Here, why don't you take a look at the messages Mr. DeLancey's sent to me."

"I love that he's in his eighties and knows how to email and text," Evan says.

He leans his long body against the island and grows silent, his eyes moving left and right as he reads the messages, his index finger tapping my phone every few seconds. When he looks up, his eyes are soft.

"These give me chills, Mom," he says. "They are so sweet. He really loves his wife."

I nod. "That's why I want to do something special for them," I say. "It's rare. Their family is having a big celebration next weekend, but Bob wanted to surprise his wife, too. We were thinking champagne and cake on the beach at sunset."

"I have an idea after reading his emails to you," Evan says. "Isn't a sixtieth wedding anniversary the diamond anniversary?"

I nod.

"And did you notice he calls his wife 'cupcake'?" Evan asks.

I shake my head. "I guess I didn't."

Evan continues, his deep voice rising in excitement. "What if we made cupcakes and then arranged them in the shape of a diamond? And what if we decorated the cupcakes with little diamonds? I'm sure that bakery downtown has edible decorations. Cupcakes are so trendy right now."

"I love it!" I say. "When did you get to be so smart?"

"Birth," Evan says, walking over to hand me my phone and nudge my side with his bony elbow. "Good genes."

"*My* genes," I say.

"Dad might not be street smart," Evan says, "but he's book smart."

"I'll give him that," I say.

I grab my dog-eared version of *The Silver Palate Cookbook*, written by famed chef Julee Rosso, who, coincidentally, owns and runs Saugatuck's beautiful Wickwood Inn, which has been in business for decades.

"Imitation is the sincerest form of flattery," I mutter to myself, flipping through the cookbook to find a cupcake recipe. "I'll pull these together if you want to run into town and get some champagne and those cake decorations."

"Okay," Evan says, his long legs already striding for the door.

"And get the good champagne, too, like Veuve," I call.

"Not the cheap crap you drink, is that what you're saying?" Evan yells back.

I turn on the blender to cover not only my laughter but also the echo of truth.

FORTY-SIX

Evan and I hold umbrellas over Mr. and Mrs. DeLancey as we usher them to the honeymoon cottage. He has a firm grip on his wife's arm as she maneuvers slowly with a cane.

"I hope you had a nice drive," I say.

"We had a nice driver," Bob laughs.

"Well, we're so honored you've chosen to stay with us."

I open the door and usher them inside.

"Happy anniversary!" I say.

Evan retreats and begins bringing in their luggage.

They are about the cutest couple I've ever seen: they resemble Henry Fonda and Katharine Hepburn from *On Golden Pond*—elegant and refined yet comfortable and not fussy—although Bob is much more affable than Fonda's Norman Thayer.

For the longest time, no one says anything, and I begin to panic, thinking they don't like the accommodations, the renovations, the flowers, even me.

Bob is leading Grace around the cottage, and she is studying each piece of furniture, every floral arrangement.

I can hear my heartbeat in my eardrums. I feel dizzy. I sneak a glance at Evan, who is wet from the rain. He shrugs his shoulders.

Unable to take another second of silence, I finally say, "If there is anything you don't like, or if this doesn't meet your expectations...?"

Grace turns, her head cocked, her eyes following my voice.

"Oh, sweetheart," she says. "The room is just beautiful. I love it." She smiles at me. "I have age-related macular degeneration. I can still see, but it's difficult for me to make everything out. Things can look a bit blurry."

Grace stops and thumps her cane on the floor, and then lifts it to tap Bob on the rear. "I have these two to get me through it, though," she says with a laugh.

"Oh, my gosh," I say. "I didn't know. I'm so sorry."

"Please stop apologizing," she says. "There's absolutely nothing to be sorry about."

Evan shoots me a glance as if to say, "Told ya so, Mom."

"It smells like heaven in here," Grace continues, lifting her nose and sniffing the air. "Peonies. My favorite."

"Always have been, right, cupcake?" Bob asks, before looking at me. "How'd you know?"

I duck my head. "I didn't," I say. "But they're my favorites, too."

Grace takes a seat in a chair, her cane perched in front of her, and shucks off her raincoat. I take it from her and hang it in the closet while Bob continues to walk around the room, lost in thought, studying the artwork on the wall and my father's Helmscenes.

"You kept your father's memories alive in here," Bob says. He raises his hand to the picture's knob. "Do you mind?"

I shake my head with a smile, and he clicks it on, the light flickering before illuminating the picture. He runs a quavering hand over the photo as if he were painting it.

"You kept your grandfather's memories alive in here, too," Bob says, turning to look at me. "This cottage may have been renovated, but it still has all the feel of the old fish house."

Bob walks over and takes a seat on the couch I placed against the wall where I found the time capsule. He sighs as he sits, grabbing a cushion and placing it behind his lower back. "Your grandfather," he starts, looking at me before looking at Evan and pointing at him with a shaking finger, "your *great*-grandfather was quite a character."

My heart swells.

Bob removes his vintage-style horn-rim glasses and rubs his eyes. "He was the grand grocer of old Chicago. If you walked in and wanted something that he didn't have, he'd get it for you," he says. "And that wasn't easy. Italian grandmothers wanted a certain sausage, German grandfathers wanted a different sausage, and he'd get it for them, no extra charge."

Evan's eyes grow wide, and he catches my attention. *Like you, Mom*, he mouths.

"I got to know him because my family delivered dry goods all across Chicago. Boy oh boy, could that man tell a story." Bob laughs. "He invited me up to this cottage to fish. Took me way out on the lake, and we pulled in a haul of fresh salmon. He kept it on ice in this cottage, right next to his boat. You know the water came right up to Lakeshore Drive back then, don't you? We could just pull the boat up here. He smoked the fish where your patio is now, and we drank beer."

Bob stops and looks at Grace. "Just one, cupcake," he says to her with a wink.

"Of course," she says. "Like your martinis, right, sweetheart?" Grace says, matching his wink. "You know what men say about martinis, don't you? One martini is all right. Two are too many, and three are not enough."

Evan and I laugh.

"Can't take credit for it," Grace says. "James Thurber. One of my favorites."

"Okay, we had a few beers, and the fish was the best I ever had."

"My father continued that tradition," I say. "He smoked food right outside the cottage just like his father. He kept this cottage just the way his father had." I hesitate. "Sometimes I feel guilty about changing it all."

"My dear," Grace says, gesturing around the cottage, "the point is you honored their tradition. You *kept* the cottage in the family. Change is inevitable. Forgetting is inexcusable."

Images of my parents and grandparents fill my mind. Her words hit me so deeply that my knees turn to Jell-O, and I find myself gripping a wall for support.

"Your grandfather's grocery store in Chicago is now a Gap," Bob says, more than a hint of disgust in his tone. "An IKEA stands where my family's company used to be. We are becoming a homogenized society. We shop at the same stores, we eat at the same places, we dress the same. We are losing everything that made us unique, everything that made us who we are." He stops, brushes some invisible lint from his pant leg and continues. "So many young people today don't know their family stories of how they came to be who they are."

"How can they know where they're going if they don't know where they come from?" Grace interrupts.

Bob's eyes sparkle. "Well stated, cupcake!"

Grace bows her head and doffs an invisible cap.

"She's right," Bob continues. "Miss Kruger..."

"Adie Lou, please," I say.

"Adie Lou," Bob says. "You respect the history of those who came before you, and you respect their heirlooms. Your love for them shines in every detail." He stops. "The Summer Cottage Inn is an heirloom. There will never be another place like it not just because of how it was built, but because of the memories that have been collected."

As if on cue, a gust of wind sweeps over the inn and guest cottage, and the walls shudder.

"Do you hear that?" Bob asks, cocking his head to listen. "Those aren't just sounds. They're the voices of your family— and of all those who came before them—talking to us." Bob looks at me and then Evan. "All we have to do is listen, and they will tell us what to do. The problem is too few of us do."

My knees weaken even more. "Thank you," I say. "Thank you for saying that. Do you mind if I show you something?"

As if reading my mind, Evan heads for the door, saying, "I'll be right back." Moments later, he returns with the copy of Sadie's letter. Bob reads it aloud for Grace, the cottage creaking in concert with his voice.

When he finishes, Grace says, "You listened. You listened."

Bob and Grace appear in the entry dressed to the nines, and guests ooh and aah over their appearance.

"Very *Ocean's Eleven*," says a man. "You look like Sinatra."

"You're the cutest!" his wife exclaims.

Bob is wearing a dapper vintage tuxedo, while Grace is dressed in elegant black slacks and a beaded jacket.

"Are you ready?" I ask.

They nod. Bob takes Grace's arm, and we slowly make our way to the beach. This was Bob's idea: he and Grace had been married on the beach—just the two of them—and he wanted to replicate that intimate memory before the mega-party his children had planned in the city next weekend. Evan will be driving them to dinner after sunset.

"I was hoping for better weather," I say as we walk. "At least it stopped raining. Hopefully, it will clear up by sunset."

"It hasn't dampened our spirits," Bob says. "Has it, cupcake?"

Grace stops and thumps her cane emphatically on the ground. "Not at all," she says, before taking another step very slowly.

Evan looks at me, shaking his head in wonder at their determination. When we make it to the steep beach steps, Evan takes Grace's left side, while Bob holds her right. When we reach the bottom, Grace kicks off her shoes and stamps her cane in the sand.

"We made it!" she crows.

When Grace finally looks up, she cries, "Bob! What have you done?"

Evan and I have set up a small tent with a table and beach chairs perched just-so on the lakeshore. Dean Martin's voice wafts on the lake breeze.

That's amore...

I rush over and grab the bottle of champagne we put on ice. Grace applauds when the cork pops. I fill two glasses as the couple approaches. They grow quiet when they see the cupcakes in the shape of a diamond sitting on a silver platter.

"What do we have here?" Grace asks. "It's beautiful, Bob."

"I wish I could take credit for this," Bob says. "Adie Lou, what did you do?"

"It was Evan's idea," I say.

"Sixtieth anniversary is the diamond anniversary," he says shyly. "And, well, cupcakes for your cupcake."

Grace looks at Evan, her eyes brimming with tears. She opens her arms, and Evan hugs her tightly.

"Thank you," she says. "You are about the sweetest soul I've ever met." She lets go of Evan and looks at me. "You done good."

"Thank you," I say. "So did you."

I hand them glasses of champagne and ease them into their beach chairs.

"Maybe it will still clear off for sunset," I say, although steel-gray clouds are locked in over the lakeshore, and no one is on the beach. "We'll let you two enjoy your champagne."

Evan and I move toward the dunes. The silhouettes of Bob and Grace are as beautiful, delicate and fragile as the outlines of the dark waves, the dunes grass and the aspen trees.

"It doesn't matter if it's cloudy," Bob says as he looks over the horizon, his voice drifting on the wind. "There's still a sunset happening. You just have to look a little harder."

He reaches over and grabs his wife's hands.

"Isn't that right, cupcake?"

Grace turns to him and nods. He leans over, and the two kiss. She raises her glass of champagne.

"Cheers, my love," Grace says. "To sixty more."

Bob clinks her glass. "I love you, cupcake."

I shut my eyes and pray for a miracle, for the clouds to disappear and for the lake to sparkle. I open my eyes, but it is still cloudy.

I watch as Bob turns to Grace. He looks deeply in his wife's eyes and says, "There it is, there it is. There's my sunset."

FORTY-SEVEN

The call of a lone whippoorwill fills the air, and I open my mouth and return its call, whistling just like my father taught me years ago from this very same glider on the front porch.

Whip-poor-will.

I wait and smile when the bird replies.

Whip-poor-will.

It is Sunday evening, and the inn is still. The sound of suitcase wheels on wood, footsteps on stairs, heartfelt goodbyes and car tires on gravel has ended. Nearly all of my weekend guests have returned to their lives in the city, save for a few couples who understand the secrets of a quiet Sunday by the lake.

Whip-poor-will.

My parents did. On bucolic Sunday afternoons, they often retreated to the beach with towels, a bottle of wine and their favorite paperback. It was all really a formality: they went there for sunset.

It was the most important rule of Cozy Cottage: *everyone must be present for sunset.*

"It's the reason we're here," my mom used to say. "There is a miracle in every single one...because we're here...together... They are mini-celebrations. When you look back on your life, you should remember endless sunsets."

I stand, the rocker bucking as I do, and head inside.

"Evan!" I call.

Silence.

Evan had a friend, Cole, from college visit, and they must have gone into town before Cole heads back to Chicago.

Sonny suddenly comes racing down the stairs, running so fast that he skids as he hits the final landing of the staircase and slides into the wall, bouncing off it like a pinball and taking the final stairs in one jump before leaping into my arms.

"He got locked in one of the rooms," Esme calls, her voice echoing down the stairs.

"Are you okay?" I ask, kneeling to stroke his fur.

He looks at me, smiling, and I can feel such love that I plop onto the floor and let him lick me until I start to giggle.

"Want to go to the beach?" I ask, ruffling his fur.

Sonny barks his agreement.

I change into my suit, and tuck sunscreen and a towel into a beach bag Trish got for me that says, Rosé All Day! On the way out, I nab a chocolate-chip cookie I made for guests and pour some freshly made lemonade into a to-go cup.

"So strange," I say to Sonny, "actually grabbing things as if I'm the guest."

I begin to head out the door but stop, seeing the Cottage Rules sign and thinking again of my parents. As if pulled by a magnet, I rotate toward their bookshelves. I scan the shelves.

Which one? I think.

The names of books and authors my parents loved fill my eyes. I look up and down, left and right, and then I see it: *The*

Shell Seekers by Rosamunde Pilcher, one of my mother's favorite books.

I pluck the paperback from the shelf and slip it into the beach bag.

"C'mon, Sonny," I say, finally heading out the door, calling upstairs, "I'll be at the beach, Esme!"

"Que tengas una tarde maravillosa!" Esme yells.

I catch my breath as Sonny and I head toward the beach. The weather has finally cleared, and it is a stunning day on the lakeshore. The water is flat, the wind calm, the sky that deep blue that makes your heart ache. I take Sonny off his leash, and he bounds down the stairs, races across the sand and runs into the lake, barking at me to hurry up.

I lay my towel down and nestle my beach chair in the sand near the dune. I head to the lake, take a deep breath and dive in, yelping as I go under. When I come up, Sonny is dog-paddling around me, his smile even bigger.

I jog back to my beach chair, Sonny following, and dry off. As soon as I finish, Sonny shakes, covering me in water and sand.

"You're a mess," I say.

I try to dry him off, but he takes off in a happy sprint, running this way and that, in joyous circles, the chilly water having exhilarated his soul. I plop into my beach chair, and Sonny sprints toward me and stops right in front of me. He lowers his head into the sand and begins to dig furiously, tossing sand all over me.

"Sonny!" I yell. "Stop!"

He looks up at me briefly, before continuing. He digs until he finds wet sand, and then he turns and turns before plopping into his hole. Sonny looks at me, his face and fur thick with sand, and yawns. He sighs, lowers his head and falls fast asleep.

I shake my head, stand and brush the sand off my body, and then plop in my chair again. And then, like Sonny, I sigh, too.

It is my favorite time of the day on the beach. My parents called it "the bewitching hour," that time around 5:00 p.m. when the angle of the sunlight bathes the world in an ethereal light, making everything—the water, the sand, the dunes—look as if it has been dipped in gold. This is the time when the beach grows quiet, people gather their things and head for dinner.

I remember how my mom and dad would lie on the beach, my dad perched against a pillow of sand, my mom's head on his chest, both reading. I thought those days would never end.

Maybe, in some way, they haven't, I think, lifting my face to the sun and remembering what Bob and Grace said to me.

I grab some sunscreen and rub it over my face and body. I take a sip of lemonade and pull the paperback from my beach bag. I stare at the pretty, beachy cover of *The Shell Seekers* and then open it up. Sand trickles from the pages.

Oh, Mom! I think. *You're still here.*

I lift the book and shake more sand free. Without warning, a piece of paper falls into my lap.

It is a piece of notebook paper, flattened, deeply creased and yellowed. I unfold it slowly.

Oh, my goodness.

It is a Crayola drawing of a sunset, my childish signature written in purple beneath a sky of orange, red and yellow. Staring into the sunset are three stick figures of a mother, father and daughter.

Everyone must be present for sunset! I'd written at the bottom of the drawing. *There is a miracle in ever one…because we're hear.*

I laugh at my misspellings and run my fingers over the drawing.

You must have used this as your bookmark, Mom, I think. *You must have forgotten it was in here.*

I study the drawing and then the pages between, which it had called home for so many years. My heart quickens as I read the following passage Rosamunde Pilcher wrote so long ago: "The greatest gift a parent can leave a child is that parent's own independence."

This catches me completely off guard, and I lift my head to the sky and say a prayer. The sun warms my face, and I can feel a great calm coming over my body. My eyes struggle to stay open. I fold the drawing and again place it between the same pages where it belongs.

I blink once, twice, three times, my eyes heavy, and before I fall asleep, I remember drawing that sunset so long ago, my parents explaining its importance.

Sunsets are like snowflakes. No one is the same, my mom said. *We miss too many of them rushing around. They are celebrations because every day is an accomplishment, a blessing of epic magnitude that we all take for granted. No matter how difficult a day has been, a sunset proves that there is still hope and good things can happen tomorrow.*

See how slowly they seem to take, and then how quickly they fade? my dad asked. *Sunsets are really metaphors for life, which is why we should slow down to enjoy them. Which is why I always want you to appreciate them.*

I wake with a start, my body chilled. Evan is shaking me.

"Mom?" he says.

I open my eyes, and my son is standing over me.

"Here," he says, handing me a hoodie. "I brought some wine."

"Oh, my gosh," I say, sitting up with a start. "What time is it?"

"Almost time for sunset," he says. "Look."

The sun is melting like a Dreamsicle into the water, a puddle of orange on the horizon. Evan pours two glasses of wine and takes a seat on the beach towel, Sonny curling up beside him.

"What are you doing down here?" I ask.

"What do you mean?" Evan shoots me a confused look. "It's sunset. Most important rule, right?"

I nod.

He remembers, I think. *Our cottage rules, our family, our history, and he will never forget.* I look down at the paperback and think of the passage I'd read earlier.

"You were dreaming," Evan says. "About what?"

I look at my son and then at the magnificent sunset.

"This," I say.

EPILOGUE

Rule #14:
Shake the Sand from Your Feet,
But Never Shake the Memories of Our Summer Cottage.
It Is Family!

July 2019

"You're wearing white?"

Trish laughs. "Just kidding," she says, grabbing my hands. She gives them a tight squeeze and when I look up, her eyes are filled with tears. "You look beautiful."

I can feel my heart rise in my throat. "Thank you," I say. "Don't make me cry. I don't want to look like a raccoon on my wedding day." I release my hands and flutter my fingers over my eyes to dry any potential tears.

"What a difference a year makes," Trish says. "You and Scooter. This inn. A totally new start. The old Adie Lou is back!"

"I know," I say. "Oh! What you just said—old and new—reminds me." I look at Trish. "Ready? Something old…"

"Watch it," Trish starts.

I laugh. "Not *you*," I say. "This. Look."

I lift the bottom of my wedding dress. A tiny swatch of satiny fabric I found from Sadie's time capsule has been sewn inside the hem.

"Perfect," Trish says. "Just perfect. And speaking of which, I have the rest of the equation."

She turns and retrieves a small box from her bag. "Close your eyes and hold out your hand," she says. "Okay, open."

In my palm is a beautiful gold cuff bracelet. Three small stones—a heart-shaped pebble, an adder stone with a hole in it and a piece of pale blue beach glass—are set between three diamonds.

"I had the bracelet made by a jeweler in Chicago," she says. "I 'borrowed' the stones from your front porch while I was here. I thought they were perfect."

"They are," I say, welling up again. "Oh, Trish. I don't know what to say."

"I do," she says. "I love you. And I'm so, so happy and proud to call you my friend."

She hugs me and places the bracelet on my wrist. There is a soft knock on the door, and Evan peeks his head inside. "Mind if I come in?" he asks.

"I'll let you two have a minute," Trish says. "It's time for a drink anyway. Evan, did you bring any of your fraternity brothers?"

Evan laughs, and I pretend to cover my ears.

"I did," he says.

"And they're over twenty-one?" she asks.

"They are," he says. "Should I warn them?"

Trish rolls her eyes. "You should congratulate them," she says with a big laugh. Then she leans in and kisses him on the cheek. "You done good, Adie Lou."

"I know," I say, studying my son as Trish closes the door. "You look handsome," I say.

"Thanks, Mom," he says, ducking his head.

Uncomfortable in his black tux, with his hair slicked back, he resembles a small boy who has been forced to dress up for church. He reaches into his pocket and pulls out a bow tie. "Can you help?" he asks. "I can't tie it right, and neither can any of my friends. We tried to watch a YouTube video, but everything's backward."

I smile. "What are moms for?" I ask. I line up the bow tie and begin to tie it, adjusting it as I go, before making a bow and then tightening it just-so. "There."

"Where'd you learn to do that?" he asks.

"Your father," I say. "The man loves his bow ties."

Evan laughs. "I'm just a little nervous, to be honest." He holds out his hands. "See?" They are trembling.

"Oh, honey," I say. "Are you okay?" I stop. "Is this all okay? I thought…"

"It is, Mom," he says. "I really like Scooter. You and him are a perfect match. It's just that…well… I feel like Grampa should be giving you away. Is it okay that a son walks his mom down the aisle?"

"You don't have to do it if you don't want," I say.

"No, I do," he says. "It just feels like…we're all grown up now, aren't we, Mom?" His cheeks quiver.

"We are, sweetheart," I say, holding out my arms. "But you'll always be my baby, and I'll always be your mom."

"I know," he whispers, hugging me tightly.

Evan turns and stares at his reflection, his hands fluttering over his bow tie. They are still trembling a little.

"Is there such thing as a happy ending?" Evan asks. "Or is that just in books and movies?"

I grasp his hands tightly and give them a little shake. "It's not corny to have happy endings," I say, "and I don't like it when people say they're not possible. Look at me. It's a blessing to have happy endings, Evan. They're really just the result of hard work, being true to yourself and a touch of luck."

I kiss him on the cheek and adjust his bow tie just-so once more.

"Deep breath," I say.

"Okay," he says. "Mom? Next time we really talk, you'll be a married woman."

"I know," I say. "Again."

There is a soft knock on the door. Evan opens it, and Nate is standing there.

"I'm glad you could make it," I say. And I mean it.

"I'm glad you invited me," he says. Nate walks over and hugs me. And then he does the same to Evan.

"Hi, Dad," he says.

Nate holds his son at arm's length and just looks at him for the longest time before turning to me and saying, "Our baby."

The emotion in his voice moves me, and I nod. "He always will be," I say.

"I have something for you, Evan," he says. "I know the whole something old, something new adage is for brides, but I wanted to give you this." He reaches into the pocket of his tux and produces a pocket square. Nate unfolds it to show an embroidered *K* on it.

"Oh, my gosh," I say. "Is that…?"

"It is," Nate says. "Evan, your grandfather gave this to me the day I married your mom. He always called a tux without a pocket square a naked suit. It's only right I pass this on to you."

Nate takes the pocket square and holds it in front of Evan. "Do you want a square fold, a throw or a one-point?" Nate asks.

"I have no idea what any of those are," Evan says with a laugh. "You decide, Dad."

Nate begins to fold the fabric, almost as if he's creating origami, and then tucks a perfect white triangle into Evan's jacket pocket.

"One-point," Nate says. "I'm more of a classic." He turns to look at me. "What a surprise, huh?"

I smile.

Nate grips Evan's shoulders and then turns to look at me. "Scooter seems like a great guy," he says.

"He is," I say.

"Of course you'd pick the Fourth of July to get married. It's always been a special holiday to you, hasn't it?"

I nod.

"I'll see you in a few minutes, Mom," Evan says. "If I fall, just step over me."

"Back atcha," I say, and he gives me a big wink.

"Can I have a second?" Nate asks after Evan leaves.

"Of course," I say.

"I just want to tell you how proud I am of you," he says. "Not only the wonderful job you've done raising Evan and the incredible man he's turned into, but also the wonderful job you've done with the inn." Nate hesitates. "I was wrong. I shouldn't have pressured you into selling the cottage." He hesitates again. "I shouldn't have done a lot of things."

His admission feels as if a weight has finally been lifted from my body, and I feel freer, lighter. I think back to when he sent Trey and Cissy to spy on me. I don't know if they ever told him I busted them, but it no longer matters.

"And I'm happy you found Scooter," he says. "You deserve only love and joy."

Again, his words stop me cold. "Thank you," I say. "I appreciate that."

There is yet another knock on the door, and I open it to see a young Thoroughbred of a woman—all legs and lustrous mane—holding a glass of champagne and looking very impatient. "Is Nate in here?" she asks.

I open the door fully and gesture.

"I missed you," she says in a baby voice.

Fuschia has been replaced by Nate's latest girlfriend—*Britney? Tiffany? Stormy?*—who chugs her champagne.

"Ashley..." Nate starts.

Ashley!

"...this is Adie Lou, the bride and my former wife."

Ashley eyes me up and down. "It's, like, nice to meet you. Your dress is totally vintage."

It is? I think. *It's new.*

"Like, congrats," she continues. "So, yeah."

I look at Nate, eyes wide as if to ask, *Why is a college professor dating a human emoji?*

He smiles.

"Thank you," I say to Ashley, who doesn't look up. She is already furiously tapping on her cell with a purple nail. The color of her polish makes me think of Fuschia, and I have to stifle a laugh.

Suddenly, I see Trish in the hallway. She gives Nate an overly dramatic and sarcastic thumbs-up.

This time, I laugh out loud. "I deserve that," he whispers. "You have a good friend—and attorney—there."

"I do," I say.

Nate gives me a hug and then looks at me for the longest time.

"You figured it out," Nate says, his voice coming out as a fragile whisper. "I hope I do, too, one day, Adie Lou."

Adie Lou, I think. *He finally called me Adie Lou. It's like he finally sees the woman I am, the girl I always was.*

I watch him walk away with Ashley as Trish rushes in with two glasses of champagne.

"Looks like you could use this," she says.

"He was actually..." I search for the right word. "Nice."

Trish clinks my glass. "Ready to get hitched?" she asks.

"I am."

I really am, I think.

We drink our champagne, and then Trish peeks her head out the door. "Coast is clear," she says. "Guests are all on the beach."

She escorts me out of the inn. Evan is waiting for me at the top of the steps leading to the beach.

"You look so beautiful, Mom," Evan says.

"Thanks, honey," I say.

"I'll see you on the other side," Trish says, giving me a big hug. As she starts down the steps, she turns. "And I know a great attorney if this doesn't work out."

"This is it," I say.

"You ready?" Evan asks.

I nod and look down at the ceremony I've orchestrated on the beach.

A boardwalk has been set up from the stairs to the shoreline for the guests to walk. I hired a "shoe valet," so guests can trade in their dress shoes and heels for casual flip-flops that have my and Scooter's names and wedding date printed on them. A small arbor sits by the lake where we will exchange vows. The arbor is encircled by lake stones in the shape of a heart. I built a sandcastle in the shape of the inn nearby, and photos of Scooter and I sit behind it.

Wow, I think. *This turned out prettier than I imagined.*

Thank you for cooperating, Mother Nature, I continue, admiring an afternoon in the upper seventies with a light wind.

I take a deep breath and my son's hand, the music starts, people turn and we descend the stairs.

As I walk down the boardwalk, the train of my simple white dress floats on the lake breeze. When I reach the end, Trish is waiting. She is holding a bouquet of roses and peonies from my garden.

"Ironic choice," Trish whispers with a wink. "Roses."

I can no longer control my tears when Evan gives me a soft kiss on the cheek and Scooter takes my hand. *You look beautiful,* he mouths. *I love you.*

"Welcome, friends and family," the minister from the tiny church on the lakeshore begins. "This is a love story that began right up there." He stops and points toward Lakeshore Drive. Guests turn to look. "A love story that began when Scott and Adie Lou were kids. A love story that began when Adie Lou first called Scott 'Scooter' because of his adolescent transportation."

The crowd titters.

"A love story that started out as a friendship," he continues.

As the minister speaks, I can feel myself leave my body. I am hovering over the crowd, and I can see my life flash before me.

I am ten years old, my head out of the car window, excited to spend the summer at Cozy Cottage with my parents.

I am fifteen years old and working on the chain ferry with Scooter.

I am nineteen and in love with Nate.

I am a young mother in my twenties.

I am in my thirties and in a loveless marriage.

I am in my forties and starting over.

I am here.

Life is fleeting, a series of moments that fly by too quickly.

I look out at the lake. *We get caught in the tide and let it carry us, lull us, and when we wake up, we too often have drifted someplace we never expected or wanted to be, I think. We must be the current, not at the whim of the current.*

As Scooter and I exchange vows, I can feel my family alongside me. I can hear the voices of my parents in the sand and the lake. I can hear the voices of my grandparents in the wind whistling through the aspen trees and the dunes grass.

The guests laugh, and I return to my body. Sonny is running down the boardwalk, a diamond around his neck, my golden ring bearer.

"I do," Scooter says.

"I do," I say.

"You may kiss the bride," the minister says.

After the ceremony, we retreat to the inn. A huge tent sits on the grounds behind the guest cottage, and it glows with candles. After dinner, we dance. My first dance with my new husband feels like I am home, at one in his arms as I am in this cottage. We sway to the music, lost in each other's eyes, just the two of us, united. Forever.

My mother-son dance with Evan is a blur—just like his childhood—and when we are done, the music immediately takes a turn. Eighties dance music blares from the speakers, and I turn to see Trish standing alongside the DJ. She shoots me a big thumbs-up and then screams—jumping up and down like a teen girl—before racing onto the dance floor, kicking off her shoes and taking my hand. I follow her lead—kicking off my heels—and we shimmy.

After Trish and I "Walk Like an Egyptian" and get "Footloose," Esme suddenly joins us on the dance floor, and, together, we "Push It" good, laughing so hard we have to take a break to catch our breaths. A Wham! song starts and then abruptly ends.

"I'd like to make a toast!"

I turn, along with the guests, and Iris Dragoon is standing alongside the DJ holding the mic, a glass of champagne raised.

"'Remember me fondly as the Girl in the drawing and not as the one in Leg O' Mutton sleeves,'" Iris begins, before sharing the story of Sadie, her time capsule and how it brought Iris and me together. "That is how I will always remember Adie Lou. The girl who took chances, believed in herself and lived the life she dared to dream." She stops, and, though it is dim, I swear she is crying. "Like Sadie wrote over a century ago and like Adie Lou models every day, I propose we always paint our cheeks with rouge, I pray that we seek our own stars, and I endeavor that a smile is forever upon our faces." She stops and looks at me, raising her glass even higher. "To unconventional women!"

"To unconventional women!" the crowd responds.

As it grows late, Scooter whispers to me, "Are you about

ready? The guests are waiting to watch us drive away." He winks at me.

"I am," I say. "I love you."

"Me, too."

I grab my shoes and begin to walk with Scooter, when I hear, "Mom?"

I jump at Evan's voice.

"Can I talk to you for a quick second before you leave?"

"Of course," I say, looking at Scooter and then Evan. "Is everything okay? Do you need to know anything about the inn before I leave you in charge?"

"No, I just need to ask you something. In private."

My heart quickens. "Sure," I say.

"I'll see you in a few," Scooter says.

Evan leads me into the inn, through the kitchen and dining room, and across the lobby.

"What's going on?" I ask.

He smiles and opens the front door. I drop my shoes on the hook rug as he guides me onto the front porch. It is pitch-black, but I can hear guests stirring beyond, waiting for me and Scooter to depart.

"Evan, what's going on?" I ask again.

"I want to give you my wedding gift," he says. "Are you ready?"

"Ready for what?"

"Ready to recite the rules!" Evan says, his eyes as wide as they used to get when he was a child and he saw his grandparents. "It's the Fourth of July!"

My heart explodes.

"It's the only time I've seen you pay attention to rules," I say, recalling the words I used to say to him.

Evan reaches into the woven Nantucket basket still hanging from the front door, and then turns as if he is a magician, his hands behind his back.

"Ta-da!" he says, producing two sparklers.

"Oh, Evan," I say. "What in the world?"

He hands one to me, and then pulls a long fireplace lighter from the basket and lights them. I giggle when I see the shimmering sparks, just like Evan did as a child.

"Remember, we have to recite all the rules before our sparklers go out," Evan says, his voice warbling with excitement. "First rule of the summer cottage, go!"

"Leave your troubles…" I start.

As I say the words, a chorus of voices joins me. Suddenly, the front yard is illuminated. People are lighting sparklers, and it looks as if a million fireflies are in the air. The guests are holding the Cottage Rules cards I had printed for guests in front of their faces.

My heart leaps into my throat. "Evan…" I say, tears now racing down my face as people recite the first rule.

"Leave your troubles at the door!" the guests yell.

"The second rule of the summer cottage?" Evan calls.

"Soak up the sun!" everyone yells.

"Rule number three?"

"Nap often!"

"Four?"

"Wake up smiling!"

"Five?"

"Build a bonfire!"

We recite every rule as quickly as we can—go rock hunting, dinner is a family activity, ice cream is required, be grateful for each day, go jump in the lake, build a sandcastle, boat rides are a shore thing, everyone must be present for sunset—until we get to the last one.

"And what's the final rule, Mom?" Evan asks. "I just want you to answer."

I look out at the guests, their sparklers ablaze.

"Shake the sand from your feet, but never shake the memories of our summer cottage. It is family."

As I finish, the sparklers fizz out, and the world goes dark. Guests break into applause, and Evan draws me in for a long hug.

"You did it in time!" he says. Evan stops and looks at me. "I love you more than anything, Mom."

"I love you, too."

Evan heads off the porch and down the stairs.

For a brief moment, I stand alone on the front porch, feeling just as happy as the little girl who knew she'd be spending her summers here at an old, shingled cottage sitting on a bluff overlooking Lake Michigan. It is just me and the cottage again. The cool wind coming off the lake whistles, the leaves rustle in the aspen trees, and the needles of the tall pines surrounding the cottage quiver.

The cottage moans, as if it's happily yawning at the end of a wonderful day, and then I hear Scooter yell, "One more surprise! Adie Lou, where are you?"

I step inside and grab my shoes off the rug. There is sand on it, and I smile. I pull them on, scuttle down the steps and take Scooter's hand.

"There's my bride!" Scooter says. "Follow us!"

The crowd murmurs as we head down the beach stairs, which are illuminated with beautiful paper luminaries. The beach is aglow with candles, and the guests begin to yell, "Look! Look!" when they see the *Adie Lou* bobbing on the lake.

"Adie Lou and I have decided to honeymoon in the same town that so many people come to vacation and where so many friends live," Scooter says. "Saugatuck!"

The crowd applauds. "We're not telling you where we're staying, but it's not here!"

The guests laugh.

"May I?" Scooter asks, taking my hand.

I kick off my shoes, lift the train of my dress into the air, holding my shoes with it, and step into Lake Michigan. We wade out a few feet, and Scooter helps me clamber into my wooden namesake.

"Ready!" Scooter yells.

The guests think we are leaving, but the boat remains still. For a few seconds, the crowd is silent, the only noise the lapping of the waves. And then, BOOM!

Fireworks explode overhead, illuminating the night sky.

The guests crane their heads, mouths open, and watch fireworks on the Fourth of July, my favorite holiday, my wedding day.

I get lost in the simple beauty of fireworks on a summer night, and I feel like a little girl again, one whose dreams are as big and bright as the comets and cones exploding overhead. Scooter puts his arm around my back, and I lean into him. The *Adie Lou* rocks gently as we watch the show.

When the fireworks end, I grab the bouquet sitting in the front seat of the boat, hold it over my head and yell, "Line up on the lakeshore, ladies!"

I turn around and toss the bouquet with all my might. I pivot just in time to see the wind catch it and make it take a sharp left turn at the last moment. The bouquet unexpectedly falls into the arms of Trish, causing her to drop her ever-present glass of champagne. A look of absolute horror covers my friend's face, and—before anyone can react—she tosses the bouquet at Iris, whose reaction is even more shocked than Trish's. Iris tosses the bouquet back into the air, where it lands directly in the hands of Ashley.

I laugh as I watch Nate's mouth fall open, his reaction—literally—taking the cake.

Scooter starts the *Adie Lou*, turns on her lights and begins to motor slowly into the lake. I turn and watch the crowd head back up the steps, Evan still standing at the shore, waving. Scooter slows the boat, and then idles her, as I wave at my son, who finally turns, walks across the beach and up the steps. His body is silhouetted on the stairs, the cottage behind him, the moon overhead.

I take a picture of this in my mind and shut my eyes to store it there forever. As I do, the cottage creaks, adding the perfect soundtrack to my home movie. I can hear my father whisper, "Some people don't get the beauty of a summer cottage, but the magical campers do, don't they, Adie Lou?"

"They do, Dad," I whisper, as Scooter heads the boat into the lake, the summer wind tossing my hair and my dress around. "They do."

★ ★ ★ ★ ★

ACKNOWLEDGMENTS

I have been blessed that my life has been filled with incredible optimists. As an author and person, I am usually the realist, the occasional pessimist, always the debater. And yet I know my shortcomings, which is why I've surrounded myself with those whose eyes are wide, hearts are open and souls always hopeful. Even my grandparents, whose lives were hard, believed that every day was filled with great beauty and opportunity. All of this—despite the many difficulties, challenges and tragedies in my own life—has made me an optimist, as well. And that's really what my new novel, *The Summer Cottage*, is all about: being hopeful despite all odds.

To my two greatest optimists, Gary Edwards and Wendy Sherman: thank you for not only believing in my dreams but also showing me that dreams, indeed, can come true, that life is an ongoing grand adventure and that tomorrow will be even better.

Susan Swinwood, *thank you* from the bottom of my heart for the great opportunity to work with you and your entire team at Graydon House Books *and* for believing in me and my work with such incredible faith and enthusiasm. I'm honored and excited for all that lies ahead.

Jenny Meyer, there is no greater honor than seeing my works translated around the world and no greater joy than receiving notes from readers in a dozen different languages. Your work demonstrates the universal power of literature and—in these turbulent, divisive times—the power a book still has to unite people, no matter the state or country, the politics, ideology or miles that separate us, and reminds us of what's still most important in life: family, friends, love and kindness.

Carol Fitzgerald and your entire team at The Book Report Network, you are not only great at what you do but believers in what I do (and wonderful therapists).

Let's be honest: a man writing women's fiction using his grandmother's name as a pen name sounds like a terrible literary remark of *Victor, Victoria*. How would readers respond to that? Moreover, how would authors respond to that? One of my greatest honors, and surprises, has been not just the warm welcome other authors have given me in joining their genre but the overwhelming support, encouragement, friendship, advice, guidance and, yes, wine. The authors I've long admired, and who inspired me to write the types of books I do, have been great guides and inspirations to me, literary Yodas, if you will. My mom, a lifelong nurse and hospice nurse, always told me, "Work with women! They will lift you up, over and over and over." How right she was! So, huge, heartfelt hugs and thanks to Dottie Frank, who is bigger than life, sweeter than my grandma's cherry-chip cake and more giving than a lucky slot machine; Rita Mae Brown (who calls me Tallulah Bankhead) told me never to give up and to always kick a★★ (or *she'd* come for them); Jane Green, whose early novels inspired me to want to write women's fiction; Adriana Trigiani, the literary tornado of positivity; Nancy Thayer, the queen of the summer read and first to blurb my first novel; Debbie Macomber, who supported me from the start; the gracious Laura Lane McNeal; the generous, sweet Caroline Leavitt, whose writing advice is always top of mind; and, oh, yes, two men! The wonderfully kind and talented Richard Paul Evans and Garth Stein.

One note: the resort communities of Saugatuck-Douglas-Fennville where I live have changed my life and inspired my writing. And all of the organizations that seek to enhance the arts, history, preservation and well-being of the towns I love and call home make our community a better place. Moreover, the towns are filled with wonderful souls—artists, authors, entrepreneurs, neighbors as well as countless volunteers and donors—all of whom give of their time and talent to make this the special place it is. So, let me restate the obvious. *The Summer Cottage* is—and all its characters are—a work of fiction, and what I write about in the book is just that: made up in my mind, save for the beautiful towns I call home. So thank you to all the residents of Saugatuck-Douglas-Fennville, and the state of Michigan, for embracing me so fully.

Finally, thank you to my readers. I would not be able to write the types of books that I do—ones inspired by my grandmothers' and family's heirlooms, lives, love and lessons, books about difficult things that happen to good people—without your support. Over the past two years, I've done nearly one hundred events across the United States. I've visited bookstores, libraries, book clubs, women's groups and churches. I've spoken to a handful of readers and to auditoriums filled with hundreds of people. As an author, I spend much of my time alone (usually drinking coffee in an old, but very soft, robe), my characters my company. When I write, I don't think of the outcome: how the book will do, what readers will think, the places I will visit. I'm in another world, joyously lost for months. And when I'm done, and I set out on the road, I still don't know what you will think of my new work.

I've been beyond thrilled that my novels have resonated so deeply with you. Moreover, I've been happy and humbled that so many of you have not only turned out to greet me at events but also that you've brought pieces of your lives and hearts—your own family heirlooms—to share with me. I've been overwhelmed by the many, many readers who have worn charm bracelets and jangled them while I read. I've been touched by the family Bibles, quilts, photo albums, dishes and vases that readers have taken time to bring to events. And, oh, the family recipes and recipe cards you've shared! I can't wait to see photos of your summer cottages and hear your heartfelt stories of your own family, naps on screened porches and reading books in favorite hammocks, BBQs and ice cream, card games at the table, s'mores at the firepit, sand on the floor and wet swimming suits tossed over the railing. Above all this, however, is the fact that you've shared your family histories, your dreams, hopes, sacrifices and souls. We've laughed together and cried together, and there is no greater joy for an author than when readers share as much of themselves as we do with them. So, thank you from the bottom of my heart!

AUTHOR NOTE

Dear Reader,

I'm so happy and humbled that you've chosen to read my new novel, *The Summer Cottage*.

My grandparents—especially my grandmothers—were all tremendous influences in my life, and I use my maternal grand-mother's name as a pen name as a way to honor the women whose heirlooms, lives, love and lessons inspire my fiction. My grandparents' journeys and sacrifices helped make me the person I am today, which is why I like to say that I didn't choose a pen name, a pen name chose me.

I was born and raised in the Missouri Ozarks, and grew up spending summers at my grandparents' log cabin. The cabin was actually in the middle of nowhere. It sat on a high bluff over-looking a beautiful creek—*crick* as we called it—named Sugar Creek. I would get dropped off by my parents on Memorial Day and stay with my grandparents—my parents visiting on weekend—until school started again. We had nothing at the cabin—no indoor shower, no phone, no TV, no microwave—nothing but an outhouse, fishing poles, inner tubes, books and each other. This is where I got to know my grandparents as real people, and my grandmas as real women, not just my grandmas. There was something magical about that old cabin: its creaks and quirks; the smell of the logs, the creek and the fireplace; the sleeping loft jammed with cots; jumping into the ice-cold water; cooking and baking with my grandmas; fishing with my grampa; floating on inner tubes with my mom and brother as we stared into the hydrangea-blue sky; making homemade ice cream with my dad, our shoulders aching as we took turns cranking the machine; ringing the bell on the back door to call everyone to dinner; reading books on a barn-red glider that sat on the edge of a bluff. The only rule my grandparents had at the cabin was to be happy.

My family sold the cabin when my grandparents died and I went off to college. I was devastated. My summers were never quite the same. And the rules of adult life never seemed to fit with my own set of rules.

And then I discovered Michigan. My aunt bought a cottage in a quaint little town in northern Michigan called Leland (Fishtown, they call it) and years later I ended up on vacation in a magical resort town on the west coast of Michigan called Saugatuck-Douglas. I fell in love. The little artists' town was like something out of a Currier & Ives print, and it was nestled in the midst of towering dunes and golden beaches alongside Lake Michigan. I returned a few weeks later and, without thinking, went looking for homes with a real estate agent. I spent two full days of vacation daydreaming. And then the Realtor said, "There's a cottage that just came on the market. I think it may be what you've been dreaming of."

As we drove just outside of town, she pulled down a long gravel drive that sat under a canopy of pines and sugar maples, and I saw a little cottage hunkered in the woods. When I walked inside, I gasped. It was a knotty-pine cottage filled with shiplap and soaring ceilings, old fireplaces, a farm sink like we had in the old cabin, a screened porch with views of enchanting woods, the sounds of Lake Michigan—just a half mile away—filling the porch. It had nearly as much quirk, character and history as my grandparents' log cabin.

"I want it!" I said, though I couldn't afford it.

That turned out to be the dumbest-smartest decision of my life. That cottage, now deemed "Turkey Run" for all the wild turkeys that amble through the yard and call back at the thunder, changed my life. It filled me with so much hope and happiness that I ended up quitting my job, moving to Michigan and becoming a writer. Adie Lou, the main character in *The Summer Cottage*, goes through a similar transformation. And she does it in Saugatuck-Douglas!

The Summer Cottage is inspired by all of this—down to Darryl, the moose head, which was a fixture in my old cabin—which is why I'm so, so proud of this novel. It truly is meant as a tribute to family, love and kindness, things we need more than ever in today's world. It is also a tribute to our shared histories and connections, things we need to rediscover these days. It was written in hopes that readers will take even the briefest of moments to think about and connect with those you love, as well as to pursue your dreams and passion, before it's too late. Mostly, I'm proud that readers will say my grandma's name for centuries to come. I truly hope you love *The Summer Cottage* and that you tell all your friends and family about it…word of mouth is the greatest compliment to an author.

Happy reading and happy summer, no matter where it is you call home!

xoxo,
Viola
www.ViolaShipman.com

DISCUSSION QUESTIONS

1. *The Summer Cottage* was inspired by the author's family's beloved family cabin, where he spent childhood summers with his grandparents. Do you have a summer cottage? What memories does it hold, and what does it mean to you? How long has it been in your family? Do you intend to pass it along? What are your favorite quirks or items in your cottage?

2. *The Summer Cottage* is also inspired by and set in the author's beloved, real hometown of Saugatuck-Douglas, Michigan. Do you live in a resort town, or vacation in a favorite place every summer? What memories do you have there? What emotions does it evoke when you arrive?

3. In *The Summer Cottage*, each chapter is centered around a "cottage rule." Do you have rules—funny or real—for your home? What are the importance of rules in our life? How

do they help us? How do they hinder us? Do you think we have too many rules in society, or too few?

4. Do you still spend time with your family? What does that mean to you and them? Are we losing that connection?

5. Adie Lou, the main character in the novel, wants to recapture not only the dreams she had growing up but also the person she was. Do you have dreams that never materialized? What were they? What stood in the way of those coming true (children, mortgages, illness, caring for your parents, money, divorce or just plain old bad luck)?

6. A main theme in the novel is the importance of home and history. As Adie Lou renovates her summer cottage, she uncovers a fascinating history about Sadie, a young woman who lived in the cottage in the late 1800s. Does your summer cottage or home have a fascinating history? Share.

7. Sadie's history is fraught with sadness and tragedy, as her young life has already been predetermined for her by men. Adie Lou's life and career has also been influenced by men. Has your life or decisions ever been influenced by men in a negative way? How so (divorce, equal pay at work)? How have women and women's rights changed over the last century? How have they not?

8. Another theme in the novel is friendship and how hard women can often be on one another. Adie Lou has a best friend in Trish and a rival in Iris. Who is your best friend? Share some stories. Who is or has been your rival? Why were they your rival? Did you ever make amends or come to an understanding?

9. Paralleling the author's own life, Adie Lou quits her secure full-time job to become an entrepreneur. The author quit

a secure job with benefits to become an author. Are you an entrepreneur? What do you do? How did you do it? If not, have you ever considered becoming an entrepreneur? What would you do? What is driving you toward that goal, or what is hindering you from making it happen?

10. *The Summer Cottage* is about believing in yourself and giving yourself second chances in life, be it in love, at work or at home. Do you believe in yourself? Why or why not? Have you given yourself a second chance at something in life? Are you thinking of "restarting" your life or your dreams? How and why?

11. Running themes in the author's novels are respecting and sharing our family histories, honoring our elders, holding on to our heirlooms and cherishing our past, pain and all. Are we losing those connections today? Why or why not? What are ways you share your family history, honor your elders, utilize heirlooms or cherish your past? Discuss.

12. What are your favorite beach reads? Which authors seem to capture summer for you?

Turn the page for a special preview of
Viola Shipman's upcoming novel

The Heirloom Garden

Coming soon from Graydon House

IRIS

Late Summer 1944

We are an army, too.

I stop, lean against my hoe and watch the other women working the earth. We are all dressed in the same outfits—overalls and hats—all in uniforms just like our husbands and sons overseas.

Fighting for the same cause, just in different ways.

A soft summer breeze wafts down Lake Avenue in Grand Haven, gently rustling rows of tomatoes, carrots, lettuce, beets and peas. I analyze my tiny plot of earth at the end of my boots in our neighborhood's little victory garden, admiring the simple beauty of the red arteries running through the Swiss chard's bright green leaves and the kale-like leaves sprouting from the bulbs of kohlrabi. I nod my head at their bounty and my own ingenuity. I had suggested our little victory garden utilize these vegetables, since they are easy-to-grow staples.

"Easier to grow without the weeds."

I look up, and Betty Wiggins is standing before me.

If you put a gray wig on Winston Churchill, you'd have Betty Wiggins, the undesignated commander of our victory garden.

"Just thinking," I say.

"You can do that at home," she says with a frown.

I pick up my hoe and dig at a weed. "Yes, Betty," I say.

She stares at me, before eyeing my overalls. "Nice rose," Betty says, her face drooping even further. "Do we think we're Vivien Leigh today?"

"No, ma'am," I say. "Just wanted to lift my spirits."

"Lift them at home," she says, a glower on her face.

As she walks away, I hear stifled laughter. I look over to see my friend Shirley mimicking Betty's ample behind and lumbering gait. The women around her titter.

"'Do *we* think we're Vivien Leigh today?'" Shirley mimics in Betty's baritone. "She wishes."

"Stop it," I say.

"It's true, Iris," Shirley continues in a Shakespearean whisper. "The back ends of the horses in *Gone with the Wind* are prettier than Betty."

"She's right," I say. "I'm not paying enough attention today."

I suddenly grab the rose I had plucked from my garden this morning and tucked into the front pocket of my overalls, and I toss it into the air. Shirley leaps, stomping a tomato plant in front of her, and grabs the rose midair.

"Stop it," she says. "Don't you listen to her."

She sniffs the rose before tucking the peach-colored petals into my pocket again.

"Nice catch," I say.

"Remember?" Shirley asks with a wink.

The sunlight glints through leaves and limbs of the thick oaks and pretty sugar maples that line the small plot that once served as our cottage association's baseball diamond in our beachfront park. I am standing roughly where third base used to be, the place I first locked eyes with John. He had caught a towering pop fly right in front of the makeshift bleachers and tossed it to me after making the catch.

"Wasn't the sunlight that blinded me," he had said with a wink. "It was your beauty."

I'd thought he was full of beans, but Shirley gave him my number. I was home from college at Michigan State, he was still in high school and the last thing I needed was a boyfriend, much less one younger than me. But I can still remember his face in the sunlight, perfect skin and light fuzz on his cheeks that resembled a summer peach.

In the light, soft white floaties dance in the air like miniature clouds. I follow their flight. My daughter, Mary, is holding a handful of dandelions and blowing their seeds into the air.

For one brief moment, my mind is as clear as the sky. There is no war, only summer, and a little girl playing.

"You know more about plants than anybody here," Shirley continues, knocking me from my thoughts. "You should be in charge here, not Betty. You're the one who had us grow all these strange plants."

"Flowers," I say. "Not plants. My specialty is really flowers."

"Oh, don't be such a fuddy-duddy, Iris," Shirley says. "You're the only woman I know who went to college. You should be using that flower degree."

"It's botany. Actually, plant biology with a specialty in botanical gardens and nurseries," I say. I stop, feeling guilty. "I need to be at home," I say, changing course. "I need to be here."

Shirley stops hoeing and looks at me, her eyes blazing. She looks around to ensure the coast is clear and then whispers, "Snap your cap, Iris. I know you think that's what you should be saying and doing, but we all know better." She stares at me for a long time. "War will be over soon. These war gardens will go away, too. What are you going to do with the rest of your life? Use your brain. That's why God gave it to you." She laughs. "I mean, your own garden looks like a lab experiment." She stops and laughs even harder. "You're not only wearing one of your own flowers, you're even named after one! It's in your genes."

I smile. Shirley is right. I have been obsessed with flowers for as long as I can remember. My grandma Myrtle was a gifted gardener as was my mom, Violet. I had wanted to name my own daughter after a flower to keep that legacy, but that seemed downright wild to most folks. But my garden was now filled with their legacy. Nearly every perennial I now grew originally began in my mom's and grandma's gardens. My grandma taught me to garden on her little piece of heaven in Highland Park overlooking Lake Michigan. And much of my childhood was spent with my mom and grandma in their cottage gardens, the daylilies and bee balm towering over my head. When it got too hot, I would lie on the cool ground in the middle of my grandma's woodland hydrangeas, my back pressed against her old black mutt, Midnight, and we'd listen to the bees and hummingbirds buzzing overhead. My grandma would grab my leg when I was fast asleep and pretend that I was a weed she was plucking. "That's why you have to weed," she'd say with a laugh, tugging on my ankle as I giggled. "They'll pop up anywhere."

My mom and I would walk her gardens, and she'd always say the same thing as she watered and weeded, deadheaded and cut flowers for arrangements. "The world is filled with too much ugliness—death, war, poverty, people just being plain mean to one another. But these flowers remind us there's beauty all around us, if we just slow down to nurture and appreciate it."

Grandma Myrtle would take her pruners and point around her gardens. "Just look around, Iris. The daisies remind you to be happy. The hydrangeas inspire you to be colorful. The lilacs urge us to breathe deeply. The pansies reflect our own images back at us. The hollyhocks remind us to stand tall in this world. And the roses—oh, the roses! They remind us that beauty is always present even among the thorns."

The perfumed scent of the rose lingers in front of my nose, and I pluck it free and raise it to my eyes.

My beautiful Jonathan Rose.

I'd been unable to sleep the last year or so, and—to keep my mind occupied—I'd been hybridizing roses and daylilies, cross-pollinating different varieties, experimenting to get new colors or lusher foliage. I had read about a peace rose that was to be introduced in America—a rose to celebrate the Nazis leaving France, which was just occurring—and I sought to re-create my own version to celebrate my husband's return home. It was a beautiful mix of white, pink, yellow and red roses, which had resulted in a perfect peach.

I remember John again, as a young man, before war, and I again focus my mind on my garden, willing myself not to cry.

My garden is marked by stakes of my experiments, flags denoting what flowers I have mixed with others. And Shirley says my dining room looks like the hosiery aisle at Woolworths. Because of the war, no one throws anything away, so I use my old nylons to capture my flower's seeds. I tie them around my daylily stalks and after they bloom, I break off the stem and capture and count the seeds, which I plant in my little greenhouse. I track how many grow. If I'm pleased with a result, I continue. If I'm not, I give them away to my neighbors.

I fill my Big Chief tablets like a banker fills his ledger:

1943—Yellow Crosses
Little Bo Beep = June Bug x Beautiful Morning
(12 seeds/5 planted)
Purple Plum = Magnifique x Moon over Zanadu
(8 seeds/4 planted)

I shut my eyes and can see my daylilies and roses in bloom. Shirley once asked me how I had the patience to wait three years to discover how many of my lilies actually bloomed. I looked at her and said, "Hope."

And it's true: we have no idea how things are going to turn out. All we can do is hope that something beautiful will spring to life at any time.

I open my eyes and look at Shirley. She is right about the war. She is right about my life. But that life seems like a world away, just like my husband.

"Mommy! Mommy!"

Mary races up holding a handful of dandelions with white tops.

"What do you have?" I ask.

"Just a bunch of weeds."

I stop, lean against my hoe and look at my daughter. In the summer sunlight, her eyes are the same violet color as Elizabeth Taylor's in *National Velvet*.

"Those aren't weeds," I say.

"Yes, they are!" Mary says. She puts her hands on her hips. With her father gone, she has become a different person. She is openly defiant and much too independent for a girl of six. "Teacher said so."

I lean down until I'm in front of her face. "Technically, yes, but we can't just label something that easily." I take a dandelion from her hand. "What color are these when they bloom?"

"Yellow," she says.

"And what do you do with them?" I ask.

"I make chains out of them, I put them in my hair, I tuck them behind my ears..." she says, her excitement making her sound out of breath.

"Exactly," I say. "And what do we do with them now, after they've bloomed?"

"Make wishes," she says. Mary holds up her bouquet of dandelions and blows as hard as she can, sending white floaties into the air.

"What did you wish for?" I ask.

"That Daddy would come home today," she says.

"Good wish," I say. "Want to help me garden?"

"I don't want to get my hands dirty!"

"But you were just on the ground playing with your friends," I say. "Ring-around-the-rosy."

Mary puts her hands on her hips.

"Mrs. Roosevelt has a victory garden," I say.

She looks at me and stands even taller, hooking her thumbs behind the straps of her overalls, which are just like mine.

"I don't want to get dirty," she says again.

"Don't you want to do it for your father?" I ask. "He's at war, keeping us safe. This victory garden is helping to feed our neighbors."

Mary leans toward me, her eyes blazing. "War is *dumb.*" She stops. "Gardens are dumb." She stops. I know she wants to say something she will regret, but she is considering her options. Then she glares at me and yells, "Fat head!"

Before I can react, Mary takes off, sprinting across the lot, jumping over plants as if she's a hurdler. "Mary!" I yell. "Come back here!"

"She's a handful," Shirley clucks. "Reminds me of someone."

"Gee, thanks," I say.

Mary rejoins her friends, jumping back into the circle to play ring-around-the-rosy, turning around to look at me on occasion, her violet eyes already filled with remorse.

Ring around the rosy.
A pocket full of posies.
Ashes! Ashes!
We all fall down.

"I hate that game," I say to Shirley. "It's about the plague."

I return to hoeing, lost in the dirt, moving in sync with my army of gardeners, when I hear, "I'm sorry, Mommy."

I look up, and Mary is before me, her cheeks quivering, lashes wet, fat tears vibrating in the rims of her eyes. "I didn't mean to call you a fat head. I didn't mean to get into a rhubarb with you."

Fat head. Rhubarb. Where is she picking up this language already?

From behind her back, she produces another bouquet of dandelions that have gone to seed.

"I accept your apology," I say. "Thank you."

"Make a wish," she says.

I shut my eyes and blow. As I inhale, the scent of my Jonathan Rose fills my senses. When I open my eyes, I see our minister approaching, a man beside him, both of their faces solemn.

"Iris," our minister says softly.

"Ma'am," the other man says, holding out a Western Union telegram.

The world begins to spin.

Mrs. Maynard,
The Secretary of War desires me to express his deepest regrets that your husband, First Lieutenant Jonathan Maynard, has been killed...

The last thing I see before I fall to the ground are a million white puffs of dandelion floating in the air, the wind carrying them toward heaven.

ABBY

May 2003

"This is the house I was telling you about."

I twist and look out of the open car window. A smile overtakes my face as soon as I see a rambling bungalow with a wide front porch. A warm summer breeze shakes the porch swing before making the American flag on a corner pillar flap.

Our Realtor, Pam, parks her Audi on the narrow street, barely wide enough for one car to pass at a time, which sits at the top of a very steep hill. The street reminds me of the time I visited San Francisco, only in miniature. Pam rushes around to open our doors.

"Did Daddy put the flag there?"

"Yes," Pam lies to my daughter, Lily. "He's a war hero!"

I can feel my heart split, as if it's been cleaved in two by a butcher.

Pam and I are roughly the same age, early thirties, but Pam

is somehow still filled with the same unbridled enthusiasm as Chance, the Irish setter we had growing up. I am filled only with a dull ache brought on by silent rage due to a confusing war that has stolen the husband I once knew.

Pam salutes Lily, who mimics the patriotic gesture. Pam turns to me and salutes.

"Don't," I say.

"I'm so sorry, Mrs. Peterson," she says, quickly lowering her arm. Her blond bob trembles in the breeze, just like her lips, which are slathered in pink gloss.

"Abby," I say.

"I understand, Mrs.... Abby. It's okay. You must be so nervous about your husband all the time."

I force a smile. "I am," I say. "Didn't mean to be so short."

She turns toward the house, and her Chance-like enthusiasm returns as she reenters agent mode. "This is a Sears kit home," Pam says as my daughter sprints for the front porch and jumps into the swing.

"A what?" I ask.

"A Sears kit home," she continues. "Oh, my goodness, Abby. They're historic now! Sears homes were shipped via boxcar and came with a seventy-five-page instruction manual. Most homes were sent via the railroad, and each kit contained thousands of pieces of the house, which were marked for construction. You can still find lumber that is numbered throughout the house. They did lots of different styles, from bungalows to Colonials."

"This house and the one next door were both Sears homes," she says, before nervously beginning to babble, "but...but... but...the two homes are nothing alike."

I look at Pam, whose face is registering absolute panic, and then turn to look for the first time at the neighboring house.

"That's an understatement," I say. "It looks like a prison."

An imposing wooden fence, which is—no exaggeration—at least ten feet tall surrounds the property. The second story of the home, which looks to be identical to this one, despite what Pam has just said, is all peeling paint. The roof's shingles are buckled, and moss is growing on a shady patch under a towering tree whose first leaves are blush red.

"What's the story?" I ask.

Pam's face turns the color of the tree. She takes a deep breath.

"A very old woman lives next door," Pam says. "Rumors in town are that she lost her husband in World War II and then her young daughter died, too." Pam glances back at the house and then whispers, "Went crazy and has lived alone for years." She stops and resumes speaking in a normal tone and nods at the house for rent. "This is her house, too. Used to be her mom's... or her grandma's... No one really knows anymore. I heard she has to rent it now for money."

"Why would she need more money at her age?" I ask. "These surely have to be paid off by now. Is she sick?"

Pam again whispers. "I don't think so. Who knows? There're lots of rumors about her and that house. They say she has a virtual Garden of Eden behind that fence. She breeds plants, or something like that. She's like a flower scientist. Used to call her the First Lady of Flowers around town. Anyway, I hear she spends all of her money to buy different varieties of flowers. Specimens. In fact, this house used to have a beautiful garden in the backyard. The two gardens were combined at one time. This one has fallen into a bit of disarray, but I think it could be brought back to life with a little love.

"But don't focus on all that," Pam finishes. "Focus on *that*."

Pam sweeps her well-manicured hands in front of her like a model from *The Price Is Right* and a flash of blue catches my eye. For the first time, I realize that we're not on a hill, we're tucked atop a dune overlooking Lake Michigan.

"There's only a peek of the water from the front yard, but the house overlooks the entire lake," she says. "You can even see the pier from your deck if you stand on your tippy toes. This cottage is part of what's known as Highland Park. It's an association of cottages built atop these dunes that dates back to the late 1800s. Isn't it quaint?"

"You buried the lead, Pam," I say. "But I'm sure we can't afford anything on the water. What's the monthly rent?"

She looks at me and tries not to look next door, but her eyes betray her. "I'm sure we can work out a deal if you're interested."

I turn and stare at the imposing fence. *Why would she want someone living here when she's trying so hard to keep everyone out?*

Pam leans toward me. "I can read your mind. Want to know what I think? I think she's just lonely. Wants someone next door in her final years. This association is filled with families. They just pass along the houses from one generation to the next. There's no one left after her." Pam waves her hand at me to come closer, and I lean in even farther. "She has final approval on who rents this house," Pam whispers, even more softly.

"You've met her, then?" I ask. "What's she like?"

"Not exactly," Pam says. "We communicate only via email." She stops. "Sometimes she'll just leave a note in the wreath on the door of her fence. It's written in longhand on a yellow sheet of paper, like they used back in the olden days." Pam stops again. "She's turned down a half dozen other renters. She'll just write 'No!' on a piece of paper after I've shown the listing. I don't how she knows since she never leaves her property. She's like a spy. Personally, I think she's holding out for a young family. I think it's pretty black-and-white."

Her words ring in my ears.

I've always thought it must be a blessing to see life in black or white. It must be easier if things are cut-and-dried. If emotion is removed. Decisions are clear-cut. Me? I've always seen a thousand shades of gray. And that has made for a more difficult existence.

"What brings you to Grand Haven, by the way?" Pam asks. "Did you grow up here? Do you have family here? Are you just wanting to spend a summer with your family near the water?" She stops and looks at me with great concern, before lowering her voice. "I could certainly understand if that were the case."

"No, no, no," I stammer. "I grew up in Detroit."

How do I explain? I think. *Why do I have to explain? I'm too tired to explain anymore.*

A buzzing sound grows in my ears, as if cicadas have nested inside my head. The world tilts like an old *Batman* episode and all its color—the American flag, the brown bungalow, the blue sky, the red tree, Pam's pink lip gloss—turns black-and-white.

"I got a job offer," I continue.

"But," Pam starts, "your husband..."

"Oh," I stammer again. "He...uh... He's back from the war."

"What a blessing!" Pam cries. "I didn't realize. I thought he was—"

She stops short.

Dead? I want to ask. *He is. Just not literally.*

"Goodness," Pam says in a too-chipper tone. "Why didn't you say so?"

Say what? I want to ask. *Say that my husband was returned to me as a shell of his former self? Say that our lives were upended because of a war I never believed in? Say that I'm always worried about my husband because I have no idea where he is or what he's doing half the time when he's not drinking or depressed? Say that I'm an awful person for thinking all of this?*

A thousand shades of gray.

"Yes, it is a blessing," I reply. "It's just hard to talk about."

"I understand," Pam says. She reaches out and touches my arm. "You're doing what you can for your family."

"Yes," I say, forcing a smile.

"Are you a teacher?" she asks. "Or a secretary?"

I bite the inside of my cheek. "I'm a chemical engineer," I say. "Oh!"

"I'm working for a boat and yacht manufacturer here," I continue. "I'm developing a new marine paint to prevent rust and barnacles on ships and docks."

"That's amazing," Pam says. I don't know if she's referring to the job or the fact I'm a chemical engineer. She looks at me closely, as if for the first time, and I can see myself reflected in the slippery gloss coating her lips: my brown shaggy hair, little makeup, big black eyeglass frames. I think of the neighbor's fence. *Perhaps I'm trying to keep the world at bay, too.* "I never think of engineers as being, well, creative."

I nod. "People always say engineers aren't creative, but we are. In fact, my work is a sort of art—scientific painting if you will." I raise my hands and wave them around. "Our world is made of scientific paint mixing. I mean, just look at the air we breathe. It's made up of lots of other things besides oxygen, which is only about twenty-one percent of air. About seventy-eight percent of the air we breathe is made up of nitrogen. There are also tiny amounts of other gases like argon, carbon dioxide and methane." I stop and gesture at the lake. "And what is water made of?"

Pam is staring at me.

"Fascinating," she says as she reapplies her gloss. "Well, this is a perfect place for your family, then. Grand Haven is a water and boating hub. You know this is the Coast Guard City of the US, right? And we hold the annual Coast Guard Festival, which honors and respects the men and women of the US Coast Guard. Your husband should be right at home here. And you, too." She smiles. "Now let me show you the house, okay? And that view!"

Before we can move, Lily races down the stairs and over to the fence separating this yard from the one next door. She clambers atop a large river rock and jumps up to grab a big shepherd's hook jutting off the side of the wooden fence, where it looks like a hanging plant once was located. She tries to climb up the fence like a squirrel, her sneakers raking against the wood.

"Lily!" I yell. "You're going to hurt yourself."

She jumps down.

"Mom," she whines.

"She's a bit of a tomboy," I say to Pam, who cannot hide her disappointment.

Lily presses her face between the tiny slats in the fence. "Whoa!" she says. "You have to see this!"

I walk over to where Lily is standing and position my right eye against a minuscule opening and squint. Beyond the fence is a garden that resembles one of my own chemical experiments. There are dozens of stakes with small flags attached, and they are fluttering in the breeze. Daylily stalks are everywhere, and there is something odd attached to them that I can't quite figure out.

Little is in bloom this early in the season, but I can only imagine what is to come.

I reposition myself and try to peer farther into the yard, but it's too narrow and strains my eye. The one thing I can make out right in front of me, however, is a beautiful arbor with a trellis that looks as if it not only might grow roses but might also have been a pathway between these two houses.

I feel the fence shaking. I look up to see Lily trying to scramble up it again.

"Lily!" I yell.

She hops back to the ground and sprints toward the porch.

"Why don't I show you the house?" Pam asks again. "You just have to see that view."

"Of course," I say.

I turn and walk toward the little flagstone pathway leading to the house. Before I head up the stairs, I look back at the neighboring house.

A curtain moves, nearly imperceptibly, upstairs. I take one step, stop and look again. The window is not open, but the curtain is still swaying slightly.

I take another step, turn on a dime and narrow my eyes behind my glasses.

A shadow flutters and then disappears.